"This is a novel with an emotional core, and that may be what makes it stand out from other thrillers of a similar ilk. A page-turner with the kind of small details that lend unquestionable authenticity." —*Kirkus Reviews*

"[*Without Sanction* is] stunning, with a way of making an insider of the reader. . . . More, please."
—*Booklist* (starred review)

"This is a thinking man's action thriller, kind of what you'd have if you mixed John Le Carre with Brad Thor. *Without Sanction* is cerebral when it wants to be and action-packed when it needs to be. A great combination that Bentley handles in adroit fashion."
—*The Providence Journal*

"You can smell the cordite, hear the explosions, and feel the fight in this one. Action jumps from every page."
—Steve Berry, *New York Times* bestselling author of *The Malta Exchange*

"Destined to be the best debut of the year. Bentley writes with the precision of Lee Child and the wit of Nelson DeMille."
—Brigadier General Anthony J. Tata, U.S. Army (ret.), national bestselling author of *Dark Winter*

WITHOUT SANCTION

DON BENTLEY

BERKLEY
New York

BERKLEY
An imprint of Penguin Random House LLC
penguinrandomhouse.com

Copyright © 2020 by Donald Burton Bentley II
Excerpt from *The Outside Man* copyright © 2021 by Donald Burton Bentley II
Penguin Random House supports copyright. Copyright fuels creativity, encourages
diverse voices, promotes free speech, and creates a vibrant culture. Thank you for buying
an authorized edition of this book and for complying with copyright laws by not
reproducing, scanning, or distributing any part of it in any form without permission.
You are supporting writers and allowing Penguin Random House to continue to
publish books for every reader.

BERKLEY and the BERKLEY & B colophon are registered trademarks of
Penguin Random House LLC.

ISBN: 9781984805126

Berkley hardcover edition / March 2020
Berkley mass-market edition / February 2021

Printed in the United States of America
3   5   7   9   10   8   6   4   2

Cover image by Nik Keevil / Arcangel
Cover design by Tim Green / Faceout Studio
Book design by Kristin del Rosario

To Ang—
my beautiful believer

Surrender is not a Ranger word. I will never leave a fallen comrade to fall into the hands of the enemy and under no circumstances will I ever embarrass my country.

—FIFTH STANZA OF THE U.S. ARMY RANGER CREED

You do not realize that it is better for you that one man die for the people than that the whole nation perish.

—JOHN 11:50, NEW INTERNATIONAL VERSION

PROLOGUE

The front door split from its frame with an ominous *crack* as sunlight flooded the room.

For Fazil Maloof, time seemed to stand still. The afternoon's golden light played across Yana's features, spilling over her thick eyelashes and the dusting of freckles covering her cheeks. In that moment, there were no civil wars, senseless killings, or black-clad jihadis attempting to force their way into Fazil's tiny apartment. In that moment, only his wife and the squirming bundle clutched to her chest truly existed.

And then, that moment was gone.

"Inside," Fazil said, guiding Yana and their daughter into the apartment's safe room with one hand while gripping a pistol with the other. "I'll get the beacon."

"Fazil," Yana said, reaching toward him as her dark eyes filled with tears.

"Quickly, my love," Fazil said, stepping out of reach of her trembling fingers. "Just like we practiced."

Fazil turned on his heel and raced toward the kitchen and salvation. Snatching the coffeepot from the cluttered counter, he found the recessed button beneath the handle and stabbed downward. The plastic broke beneath his fingers as a hidden switch was depressed. A heartbeat later, the carafe vibrated, signifying that the distress signal had been transmitted.

He'd done it. Help was on the way.

Dropping the pot, Fazil sighted down the pistol's stubby barrel as the first jihadi burst through the splintered front door, sweeping the room with his AK-47. Fazil jerked the pistol's trigger just as the jihadi's rifle belched fire. An unseen fist hammered Fazil's shoulder. He stumbled, the pistol slipping. Gritting his teeth, Fazil steadied his grip and fired again.

And again.

And again.

Fazil wasn't a soldier, but he didn't have to be. He'd triggered the beacon. The American would come.

Just like he'd promised.

ONE

The toddler smiled at me from over her mother's shoulder, her eyes sparkling. A pudgy hand snuck past the tumbling curls that framed her face, and her tiny fingers waved.

I didn't wave back.

Not because I didn't know the little girl. I knew her quite well. Her name was Abir, Arabic for *beautiful*, and the raven-haired cutie more than lived up to her name. No, I was ignoring her for a different reason altogether. Like her mother and father, Abir had been dead for almost three months.

But that didn't stop me from seeing her.

I closed my eyes, fighting the urge to return her wave as I had so many times before in the front room of her family's tiny Syrian apartment. Abir's laugh had been almost as intoxicating as her grin. Even now, it took everything within me not to smile on the off chance that the dead toddler, visible only to me, might break her silence and gift me with a giggle in return.

But I didn't smile and I didn't wave, because men who interacted with imaginary children attracted attention. Austin, Texas, might be the self-professed home of the weird, but I had no desire to make the acquaintance of the TSA men and women who worked at this airport. So I tried to ignore Abir, and the shakes started, right on schedule.

The trembling began with a barely noticeable twitch in my left index finger, but left unchecked, the twitching wouldn't stay barely noticeable for long. Taking a deep breath, I curled the offending finger, and two of its brethren, into the opening chord of "Take It Easy" by the Eagles, picturing my hand wrapped around the smooth neck of my knockoff Gibson acoustic.

Don't get me wrong. I liked newer music, too, but Eagles' songs had deceptively simple chord structures that even amateurs could quickly master. As founding members Don Henley and Glenn Frey had proven with hit after hit, sometimes greatness really was masked by simplicity.

"How they looking, sir?"

With a start, I shifted my attention from the phantom toddler to Jeremiah the shoeshine man, and then to my gleaming Ariat cowboy boots. The airport boasted quite a few shoeshine artists, but only one who'd acquired his skills at the polishing school of hard knocks—Marine boot camp.

"Fine job, Jeremiah."

"Thank you, sir," Jeremiah said, adjusting his ball cap over tufts of patchy white hair. "That'll be eight dollars."

Jeremiah's cap was fire-engine red with the words *Vietnam Veteran* emblazoned across the front in yellow stitching. Above the words hung an embroidered image of his Vietnam service ribbon. That was it. No unit designations, Special Forces tabs, or pins denoting previous ranks or medals. Just a faded red hat announcing that, unlike so many of his wayward generation, Jeremiah had answered his country's call to service. Though we'd shared numerous shines, Jeremiah had never once spoken about his time in Vietnam, but I knew that he'd been there. One, because he refused to talk about his service, and two, because he had *the look*.

With Jeremiah, *the look* manifested as an occasional stare into nothingness—a physical reaction to a mental trauma. In other words, Jeremiah's eyes had seen things that his mind wished he could somehow unsee.

I knew the feeling.

I took a ten and a five from my wallet and pressed the bills into Jeremiah's gnarled brown fingers.

"That's too much, Mr. Drake," Jeremiah said with a frown, the expression highlighting the web of wrinkles furrowing his ebony face.

"For the thousandth time," I said, "call me Matt. And the extra money isn't charity. It's to rent your chair for a spell."

Jeremiah shined my boots twice a week—every Monday and Friday at nine a.m.—and had done so for the past six weeks. Even so, we still had a variant of this conversation every time I sat down in one of the four high-backed chairs he called an office.

In a way, the normality associated with our routine was comforting. Some people had service dogs, a shrink on retainer, or a medicine cabinet stocked with pills. I had a seventy-year-old African American shoeshine artist and a secondhand guitar. I guess I was doing pretty well, all things considered.

"Them shakes ain't good, Mr. Drake," Jeremiah said, pointing a shoe-polish-stained finger at my trembling hand.

Or not.

The spasms had crept past my fingers, and now the muscles in my forearms were dancing. I mentally switched songs, from "Take It Easy" to "Ants Marching," trading the simple G-D-C progression for the series of vexing bar chords that Dave Matthews floated across so effortlessly.

No luck.

If I didn't stop the cycle soon, the tremors would evolve into something mirroring a full-fledged seizure, and that couldn't happen. Not now. Because the arrivals-and-departures monitor hanging over Jeremiah's right shoulder showed that the direct flight from San Diego had just arrived at gate five. In less than ten short minutes, my reason for sitting at this airport every Monday and Friday would cross the busy passenger thoroughfare in front of me, heading to gate nine and her connecting flight to Reagan. A ticket for that same flight rested in my right front pocket. Maybe today would be the day I finally used it.

"Mr. Drake?"

"It's Matt, Jeremiah—Matt."

"Mr. Drake, I think the Lord has a word for you."

I looked from the monitor to Jeremiah. This was un-explored territory. In the forty or so days we'd known each other, our conversations had never progressed past the safety of the superficial. Despite my nonregulation-length hair and scruffy beard, Jeremiah had seemed to intuit that he and I shared something of a history. Maybe it was because my broad shoulders and scarred knuckles seemed at odds with my carefully cultivated ragamuffin appearance.

Or maybe the look on my face mirrored his.

Either way, Jeremiah knew that he and I belonged to the same fraternity. Though I was probably at least forty years Jeremiah's junior, and his war had not been mine, we'd still enjoyed the quiet camaraderie of those who had seen the elephant and lived to tell the tale. But based on Jeremiah's earnest expression, this unacknowledged dé-tente was about to end.

"If you've got a message from the Almighty," I said, wearing a smile I didn't quite feel, "I'm all ears."

I risked a look to my right, toward the food court full of tables neatly arranged around a small raised stage. A kid in a retro T-shirt and faded jeans was strumming his way through a fairly respectable version of "Amy's Back in Austin." The space next to the breakfast taco stand, where I'd seen Abir waving from over her mother's shoulder, was now empty, but my shakes continued all the same.

"The Lord wants you to know," Jeremiah said, gripping my trembling forearm with surprisingly strong fingers, "that you can't go back."

At his touch, the tremors ceased. I started to ask the obvious question when two things happened in quick succession. One, the cell phone in my pocket began to vibrate. Two, a man slid into the chair next to mine.

A man with a gun.

TWO

For most people, the buzzing of a cell phone is not a day-altering event. I am not most people. In the six weeks since I'd purchased the phone wedged into my right front pocket, it had never rung.

Not once.

This was because the number of people who knew it was in my possession totaled exactly one. Me.

Unlike the NSA Suite B–encrypted, government-issued smartphone that had been its predecessor, this cell was a simple burner I'd picked up at Costco with a pay-as-you-go plan. I'd left my old phone when I'd left my old life, but in my world, former lives had a way of intruding into new ones.

In the seat next to me, the man with a gun picked up one of the newspapers Jeremiah had arranged in neat piles for his customers. The above-the-fold headline read: *Presidential Race Comes Down to the Wire.*

That might have been the understatement of the century.

"Shine, sir?" Jeremiah asked.

The man with a gun nodded.

To be fair, my new friend was doing his best to pretend he wasn't armed. He had a stylish haircut, and he was wearing a sport coat, slacks, a button-down shirt, and lace-up dress shoes. I might not have even noticed the pistol holstered at his waist except that his sport coat was a bit too tight in the shoulders, forcing the fabric to gather in a familiar clump as he'd climbed into Jeremiah's chair.

Although he'd approached from my left, the man with a gun had ignored the first available empty chair in favor of the one to my right. A cynical person might have believed that he was trying to put as much space between me and the pistol on his right hip as possible.

Interesting.

I fished the vibrating phone from my pocket, looked at the number displayed on its screen, and sighed.

My former boss was a lot of things, but subtle he was not. Most calls originating from Defense Intelligence Agency Headquarters, located on Joint Base Anacostia-Bolling in Washington, D.C., registered on caller ID as a string of random numbers.

But not when Branch Chief James Glass wanted your attention.

James had somehow rigged his phone so that the digits *911* repeating in sequence showed as the callback number. When James demanded your attention, he wanted there to be no doubt who was summoning you.

Still, contrary to what James might have believed, I was no longer in the DIA's employ. Now was as good a time as any to reinforce that message.

Flipping the still-pulsing phone on its side, I popped open the case, removed the SIM card, and snapped it in two. I considered saving the phone, but decided that safe was better than sorry. Turning, I pitched the components into the trash can next to my chair.

In theory, a new SIM card would have rendered the burner phone safe, but theories tended to pale when confronted with the technological might of the National Security Agency. Many a cocksure terrorist had been reduced to a Hellfire missile–induced cloud of organic vapor after the NSA cracked his supposedly impenetrable cell phone. Technically speaking, bringing the NSA's strength to bear against a U.S. citizen was illegal.

Then again, James didn't much stand for technicalities.

A multitone electronic chime, akin more to the warning klaxon of a nuclear reactor about to go critical than to a cell's ringtone, emanated from the armed man's jacket. With his nonshooting hand, my companion reached into his coat's interior pocket and came out with a BlackBerry that he put to his ear.

Jeremiah, who had glanced up when the phone first rang, wore a look of annoyance that quickly turned to something else when the armed man's sport coat briefly opened. The shoeshine artist's brown eyes found mine, and I slowly shook my head.

I didn't know what was going on and didn't much care so long as it concluded in the next two minutes and thirty seconds. Based on experience, that was when she would appear. Then, and only then, would I find out if this day would be any different from the slew of Mondays and Fridays that had preceded it.

"What?" the armed man said into his phone.

I ignored him in favor of searching the now-crowded thoroughfare for her familiar face.

A family of hipsters pushing a designer stroller jostled for space with a young girl in cutoff shorts carrying a guitar case over her shoulder. A businessman, talking into his cell, shuffled to his right, making way for a pair of cowboys in skintight Wrangler jeans and dusty boots.

This was Austin at her eccentric finest, but I had yet to see the purpose of my visit.

I had yet to see her.

"I've got him," the armed man said.

Any minute now. *Unless* . . .

I didn't follow the thought through to fruition. Couldn't. Not now. I needed to believe that today, things would be different. Instead of my transferring my unused ticket to a future flight yet again, things would return to normal. Today, I would board the flight to D.C.

"My name is Special Agent Rawlings," the armed man said, turning to me as he rested his phone on his leg. "I need you to come with me."

"No."

A space in the crowd opened. My heart beat faster.

"This isn't a request. Get out of the chair. Now."

The thing about federal agents was that they worked for bureaucracies, and bureaucracies had their own idiosyncrasies and tribal languages. Over the course of my five years with the DIA, I'd learned that clear, concise communication was critical when working with federal partners. With that in mind, I replied to Special Agent Rawlings in terms I knew that he'd understand.

"Fuck off."

I didn't know why Agent Rawlings had suddenly entered my life, and I didn't care. We were still in the great state of Texas, which meant that police officers could not just arrest people. Not without probable cause or an arrest warrant, anyway. Since my new friend hadn't used any of those magic words, he was relying on intimidation, rather than the force of law, to ensure my compliance. This was unfortunate for him because I didn't really do intimidation.

Rawlings said something in return, and though I'm sure it was both witty and relevant, I wasn't listening. She had just appeared.

Like the silence that breaks out when the houselights dim and the curtain slowly rises, the crowd's murmur faded as Laila took center stage. She'd once studied at the School of American Ballet and still moved with a dancer's measured grace. My role in this Greek tragedy wasn't yet finished—Agent Rawlings was waving over reinforcements while Jeremiah looked from me to the hulking federal agent, trying to pick a side—but I had eyes only for Laila.

To be fair, Laila was an exquisitely beautiful woman. Her Pakistani father and Afghan mother had provided her with a melting pot of genes from one of the most ethnically diverse territories on earth. The areas that were now Afghanistan and Pakistan had hosted countless foreign conquerors, from Alexander the Great to the Mongol Horde, and the region's collective influence was reflected in Laila's appearance. Her dark complexion, and the waves of midnight hair that tumbled to her shoulders, made her unexpectedly green eyes all the more striking.

Seeing her across a crowded room still caused my heart to stutter.

A second federal agent answered Rawlings's summons from the food court. He was clearly the muscle in the relationship and looked the part, with his shaved head, Harley-Davidson T-shirt, jeans, and scuffed work boots. He was built like a fire hydrant, and the practiced ease with which his meaty hands found my left shoulder and arm suggested that this wasn't his first rodeo.

Behind them, Laila followed the flow of passengers toward gate nine, another workweek over. She was heading home and dressed for the unseasonably warm late-October weather in a white tank top and a maxi skirt that hinted and hid in equal proportions. The tank top set off the almond hue of her toned arms, while the skirt's sheer fabric accentuated her hips' subtle curves.

But as much as my wife's body stole my breath, it was her face I so desperately craved. As she passed even with my chair, fifty yards away but oblivious to my presence, it happened. In the space of a heartbeat, Laila's familiar features morphed into something else.

Someone else.

Though I was too far away to see the morbid detail, I knew what to expect: waxy complexion, vacant eyes, lips pulled into a silent scream, and a 9mm hole bored into the center of her smooth forehead.

For the last six weeks, every Monday and Friday, I'd sat in this same chair, waiting for a glimpse of Laila. Each day, I'd hoped to see my wife, but each time someone else's face stared back at me.

Abir's dead mother.

Mr. Muscles jerked me from the chair, handling my one-hundred-eighty-pound frame with ease. To my right, Laila disappeared into the crowd, another chance at reconciliation gone. In that moment, the simmering rage that had been building each time I'd been forced to watch Laila walk out of my life broke through. It wanted a target.

It found one in Mr. Muscles.

My fingers curled into a fist, and I fired a jab into Mr. Muscles's solar plexus, my knuckles sinking deep into his chest. He doubled over, his breath hissing out in a ragged gasp. Grabbing him by the elbow, I pivoted, then locked the hapless agent in an arm bar and slammed him into Rawlings. The two Feds went ass over teakettle, tumbling to the floor as the high-backed chairs tipped.

After I'd endured months of forced passivity, the violence felt good. Maybe too good. But I didn't have long to savor the feeling. Before the surprise had even faded from Rawlings's face, someone tackled me from behind. I went down hard, head bouncing against the scuffed linoleum.

Federal agents were a bit like cockroaches—for every one you saw, ten more lurked in the darkness.

My attacker fired a couple of well-placed rabbit punches into my kidneys. That was a mistake. The blows hurt like a son of a bitch, but he should have forgone the opportunity for payback in favor of securing my hands.

I turned on my side and rocketed an elbow toward where I pictured his nose to be. My elbow crunched against something solid, and the satisfying impact ran the length of my arm.

Goddamn but this was fun. Maybe I should have skipped all those sessions with the Agency shrink in favor of a good old-fashioned bar brawl.

A fist smashed into my cheekbone, sending tiny pin-pricks of light dancing across my vision. A large knee drilled into the center of my back.

Mr. Muscles had rejoined the party.

Callused fingers grabbed the webbing between my thumb and index finger, wrenching upward as handcuffs bit into my wrists.

Mr. Muscles had definitely done this a time or two. Still, he didn't know about the ceramic handcuff key I had sewn into each of my long-sleeved shirts. My retirement might have cost me my Glock and secure cell phone, but I hadn't parted with all my tricks.

"Hold his fucking head still."

The command was spoken in Agent Rawlings's

no-nonsense tone. A meaty hand slammed my cheek flat against the unforgiving linoleum. I prepared myself for another blow, but felt a cell phone's cool plastic pressed against my cheek instead.

"Matthew, cut the shit. It's time to come home. Einstein is active."

The call ended without further instructions, but I wasn't expecting any. Despite my best efforts, James Glass had found me and issued a summons. I'd spent the past six weeks wandering through Austin's wilderness, but my sojourn was now at an end. Like Moses standing in front of the burning bush, I'd been called back from exile and had no choice but to obey.

The Almighty didn't take no for an answer.

THREE

Not for the first time, Peter Redman found himself fantasizing about what it would feel like to slide his fingers around Beverly Castle's aristocratic neck and just squeeze. Though he knew that the President's Chief of Staff shouldn't be entertaining such thoughts, some days Peter couldn't help but wonder what Beverly's soft, smooth skin would feel like beneath his fingertips.

Most of the time Peter just disliked his White House rival.

Today, he hated her.

Taking a deep breath, Peter ignored the urge to physically accost the woman sitting across from him. Instead, he let the sense of this special place center him. Here, in the office housing the most powerful human being on the planet, the weight of history was almost palpable.

If he closed his eyes, Peter could imagine the echo of raised voices as Lincoln's famous council of rivals debated how best to keep the fraying Union intact. Or perhaps it was the sound of two young brothers, one the President, one his Attorney General, quietly whispering as they attempted to call the Soviet bluff in Cuba without igniting the world's first nuclear war in the process.

Though a veteran of almost four years of rough-and-tumble Presidential politics, Peter had yet to lose the feeling of wonder the West Wing engendered. Against all odds, his sense of gratitude for the giants who had walked these halls before him was still coupled with a humility that many of his contemporaries lacked. Peter understood all too well that, although he might be on top of the world today, in the not-too-distant future, his efforts might merit nothing more than a historical footnote. No, Peter's humility was still intact.

His patience, however, was another matter.

"I'm going to make this simple, Beverly," Peter said, doing his best to keep his homicidal thoughts from coloring his voice. "What the fuck happened?"

Beverly jerked at Peter's use of profanity, as if such an uncouth word had never before assaulted her cultured ears. Though well into her fifties, Beverly looked a decade younger—a testament more to the prowess of the legion of plastic surgeons who called San Francisco home than to her genetics.

Still, Peter had to admit that Beverly, artificial or not, had aged well. With her shoulder-length blond hair, blue eyes, and angular, almost Nordic features, Beverly still garnered glances from men half her age. She could have easily been a political analyst for a cable news station.

Instead, she was the Director of the Central Intelligence Agency and a royal pain in the ass.

If Beverly's difficult personality had been her worst shortcoming, Peter could have borne their relationship without thinking about murder every time he saw her sculpted cheekbones or heard her carefully cultivated voice. In his mid-forties, Peter had spent his entire adult life in politics. Assholes he could handle. It was incompetence that drove him batshit crazy.

"I suggest you check yourself," Beverly said, dime-sized spots of red coloring her porcelain features. "I'm a member of the cabinet—"

"Who serves at the President's discretion, a point you still don't seem to grasp. We have an election in four days, Beverly. Four days, and the polls are still within the margin of error. For the next ninety-six hours, nothing happens without my consent. Nothing. Are we clear?"

"You arrogant little shit," Beverly said, her eyes flashing like ice crystals as her lips drew back, exposing perfect teeth. "I don't work for you."

"For the next ninety-six hours, you sure as shit do. How do you think your Presidential aspirations will fare if I fire your ass four days before the election?"

"You wouldn't dare," Beverly said. "The President wouldn't be in office without my fund-raising network."

"Don't flatter yourself. We kicked your ass in the primary four years ago, and you hitched yourself to our wagon. We might have needed you then. We don't now. So, I'm going to pour some coffee, and you're going to tell me what the fuck happened."

Peter reached for the silver carafe in the center of the table and poured portions into two white ceramic mugs emblazoned with the blue Presidential seal. The rich, nutty scent of Texas pecan coffee filled the air.

Peter added cream to his mug and slid the second to Beverly.

"You were saying . . ." Peter said.

Beverly stared at Peter, not bothering to mask the hatred lurking in her eyes.

That was fine. Peter's job wasn't to be liked, admired, or even feared. His only task was to get President Jorge Gonzales, the first Hispanic ever to hold the land's highest office, successfully elected to a second term. Anything else, including the scorn of a party scion and probable future President, was noise.

Beverly held his gaze for a second longer before retreating into herself like a cat sheathing its claws. She reached for the mug of black coffee, lifted it to her lips, took a swallow, and set it down. Then Beverly opened the courier bag at her feet, selected a folder, and placed it on the table.

"Would you like to read the after-action review?" Beverly asked.

"No, thank you," Peter said, eyeing the folder's orange cover and *TOP SECRET* markings emblazoned across the top and bottom in capital block letters. "Please just give me the summary."

This was classic Beverly—all piss and vinegar until she was put in her place. Then she magically transformed into a model civil servant, right up until the moment her finely tuned political instincts sensed weakness.

God but he was tired of her shit. Sometimes Peter thought he had a better relationship with the Republican minority whip than he did with his own fellow cabinet members. His opponents on the other side of the aisle were supposed to be disagreeable; that was part of the game. Beverly, on the other hand, took disagreeableness to a whole new level.

"Certainly," Beverly said.

Her voice now contained the crisp, precise tones that had no doubt served her well when she'd still been an unknown history professor at UC–Berkeley. That was before a speech she'd delivered to a group of students protesting income inequality had gone viral, propelling her into the national spotlight.

Beverly Castle was a lovely woman, but people who dismissed her intellectual prowess because of her looks did so at their own risk.

"At approximately 0200 Syrian time, a CIA paramilitary team raided a suspected chemical weapons laboratory belonging to an ISIS splinter cell. Our intelligence at the time indicated that the laboratory would be lightly defended, if not empty. The intelligence was incorrect, and the paramilitary team was ambushed. In the ensuing firefight, a Black Hawk helicopter was destroyed and four men were killed."

"Jesus Christ," Peter said, almost choking on his coffee. "You decided to kick over the Syrian anthill the weekend before the election? Are you out of your goddamn mind?"

"I'm sorry. Am I late?"

So great was Peter's agitation that it took him a full second to place the familiar voice. In fact, he might have sat at the table, dumbfounded, for another moment or two were it not for the radiant look on Beverly's face and the feeling of dread it engendered in him.

"Not at all, Mr. President," Beverly said, getting to her feet. "You're right on time."

Once again, Peter eyed Beverly's long, smooth neck and promised himself that one day he'd slide his fingers around it and squeeze until his anger just faded away.

FOUR

How are you this morning, Peter?" the President said, waving Peter and Beverly back to their seats.

"The polls are tight, sir," Peter said, pouring the President a cup of coffee as he took an open seat at the table, "but I think we're going to pull it off."

"Come on," the President said, his voice chiding. "I wasn't asking how my campaign was doing. I was asking how you were doing."

"As well as can be expected, sir," Peter said, adding cream and sugar to the President's mug. In spite of his anger with Beverly, Peter felt his lips tug into a smile.

That was the effect Jorge Gonzales had on people.

The son of Mexican immigrants, the President did not have an impressive political pedigree that was tied to generations of family wealth. But what he did have was charisma, a work ethic second to none, and a generally sunny disposition—a rare quality among professional politicians.

Jorge was also a lifelong Texas resident, and he shared his fellow Texans' propensity for putting aside differences and getting to work. Early in his term, with his combination of seemingly endless optimism tempered with a willingness to cross the aisle in order to break through Congress's perpetual morass, Jorge had frequently been compared to Reagan.

Now, four years later, with an anemic economy, unsettled conflicts in Afghanistan and Iraq, and a civil war spiraling out of control in Syria, no one was making those comparisons any longer.

Still, if the world was falling down around him, Jorge didn't appear to notice. After taking a long sip of coffee, the President flashed his trademark grin. "It's not often I get to start my morning with two of my favorite people. Beverly, I believe you called this meeting. What can I do for you?"

Inwardly, Peter winced at the question's naivete. While he had no doubt that Jorge, the man he'd labored beside ever since he'd helped guide the President's mayoral reelection campaign in Houston, meant the question sincerely, Peter also knew that Beverly would take the words at face value.

Though Jorge had handily beaten her for the party's nomination, in Beverly's mind, her time had come and Jorge was nothing but an interloper. The plum post of CIA Director, rarely given to a political rival, had been meant to salve old wounds in an effort to unify the party after a bitter primary.

Instead, the assignment had played into Beverly's sense of entitlement. In her mind, the President and the party owed her nothing less than the nomination once Jorge completed his second term. Anything that didn't help with her perceived rendezvous with destiny was a distraction, including Jorge's current electoral difficulties.

"It's about Syria, Mr. President," Beverly said, shifting in her chair so that she was facing Jorge.

The change in Beverly's position was almost imperceptible, but Peter sensed it just the same. A moment ago, she had been singularly focused on him, but now, like a spotlight moving across a darkened stage from one actor to another, Beverly's magnetism was directed at the President, leaving Peter in the cold shadows.

On more than one occasion over the last four years, Peter had found himself wondering what his relationship with Beverly might have been like had they not been political adversaries. But those thoughts never lasted long. He and Beverly were two sides of the same coin—both committed to their political causes with a true believer's zeal. This soul-encompassing dedication left little room for anything else, least of all romantic relationships.

"What about Syria?" the President said.

"One of my paramilitary teams took down what they thought was a chemical weapons lab," Beverly said. "What they discovered instead was a new chemical weapon. A weapon that didn't register on the team's detection equipment."

"My goodness," the President said, leaning back in his chair, "that is a startling development. But first things first—Peter, I didn't know we'd authorized a covert operation in Syria."

"We haven't," Peter said, savoring the pink spots that again bloomed on Beverly's cheeks.

Fiercely Catholic, the President neither used foul language nor tolerated it from his staff. This quality, coupled with his famously upbeat demeanor, tended to give the uninformed the impression that Jorge Gonzales was nothing more than a Hispanic Mister Rogers.

In this assumption, the uninformed observer couldn't have been more wrong.

Though Jorge's mild manner wasn't an act, his pleasantness masked a mind of startling agility. Peter had seen the President reduce more than one arrogant Republican lawmaker to tatters as he tore apart their arguments with a series of verbal ripostes, all the while maintaining his angelic smile.

Peter had a feeling this might just be one of those moments.

"Can you say that again?" the President said, looking from Beverly to Peter. "I must have misheard you. It sounded like you just said that the CIA launched a covert operation in Syria without my consent or knowledge."

"That's correct, sir," Peter said. "Four men and a Black Hawk helicopter were lost."

Peter delivered his answer with a straight face, but inside he was cheering.

The President didn't abide vendettas between his staff, and anyone caught reveling in another's misfortune received a stern talking-to. But Jorge Gonzales was also not naive enough to think that these high-pressure jobs, and the monstrous egos that accompanied them, didn't generate friction. As such, he alone reserved the right to conduct course corrections in his devastatingly effective manner.

"Beverly," the President said, fixing his CIA Director with his warm brown eyes, "is this true?"

"Like much of what Peter says, it's partially true."

Peter's hands clenched, but he didn't take the bait. Unlike Beverly, Peter understood how Jorge operated, and, for now, he was content to let the President guide the meeting.

For now.

"Please explain," the President said.

"Certainly," Beverly said, again opening the folder she'd offered Peter. She turned past the first few pages, selected a document bearing the Presidential seal, and slid the paper across the table.

"Sir," Beverly said, "I assume you remember this? It's the Presidential finding you authorized six months ago. The document states that your administration will not accept the development of a chemical weapon by any of the jihadi organizations currently operating in Syria."

"I remember," Jorge said, his forehead wrinkling as he read the document.

President Gonzales had been a youthful fifty-five when he was elected. He'd looked energetic in front of the camera, but still conveyed a seasoned politician's steady hand. His quiet, even-keeled personality promised no soaring oratories that led to nothing more than shattered hopes and broken dreams. He'd also promised the nation that there would be no more ill-advised foreign adventures that morphed into never-ending wars.

Instead, he'd pledged to provide calm, competent leadership to a nation that had so desperately craved it.

But that wasn't to say that the last four years had been without cost. The President's thick black hair was now thinning and gray, while the fine lines that had once creased his forehead had deepened into furrows.

His congeniality aside, the President had spent a significant portion of his term in this exact position—poring over documents with a worried expression. In Peter's opinion, much of that worry centered around the slipshod manner in which Beverly Castle ran the nation's premier intelligence organization.

This snafu was just the latest example.

"Good," Beverly said, her diction precise and clipped, that of a doctoral candidate defending her thesis. "Because the final paragraph of this finding directs my agency to make discovering and assessing rogue chemical weapon laboratories our top priority. With this in mind, I leveraged all of my assets, including agency paramilitary teams, to ascertain the state of WMD programs within Syria. According to the intelligence we received, a terrorist splinter cell, operating within Assad-controlled territory, was developing a chemical weapon. A weapon they intended to use in a spectacular attack, possibly against a Western target. The intelligence was passed to us by the Israelis."

Beverly shot the President a look as she delivered the last statement, and Peter knew why. Unlike some of the Oval Office's past occupants, the President had a healthy respect for Israel. Jorge Gonzales likened the Israelis to the region's scrappy kid, unafraid to go toe-to-toe with the schoolyard bully. The President was even a fan of the Daniel Silva novels that featured a Mossad protagonist. If the Israelis really had provided Beverly's intelligence, the President was bound to be more forgiving.

But that was a big *if.*

"In my opinion," Beverly said, apparently taking the President's silence as an invitation to continue, "conducting a covert raid on a suspected weapons lab was part of the mandate granted to my agency by your finding."

"Your opinion?" Peter said, doing his best not to come across the table at the smug woman. "Did you happen to share this opinion with anyone else?"

"Of course not," Beverly said, attempting to wave away the question with her slender fingers. "I am the Director of the Central Intelligence Agency. The scope and responsibilities of this organization are not insignificant. I will not, nor should I be expected to, trouble the President with every operational detail."

On its surface, her answer was plausible. The President went out of his way to recruit capable people, and he believed in giving them the latitude to do their jobs.

Even so, Beverly's actions stretched this philosophy to the breaking point.

While Peter knew that Beverly was interested in the threat posed by the chemical weapons laboratory, her reason for authorizing the operation without Presidential say-so had not been to answer a critical national question or provide the West Wing with deniability.

Beverly wanted an operational feather in her cap.

Her prearranged term as Director was ending shortly after the President's reelection, at which time she would undoubtedly devote herself to laying the groundwork for her own Presidential campaign. If the operation had been successful, she would have been able to claim credit through a series of unattributed leaks to a friendly reporter at the *Washington Post* or *New York Times*.

If it hadn't, the operational details would have been locked away in the iron vault of national security, never to see the light of day. Beverly was a politician through and through, and this botched mission was nothing but an exercise in the sort of backroom maneuvering President Gonzales had pledged to end.

Even worse, the operation hadn't been successful. American servicemen were dead, and with early voting already in full swing and a national media intent on making the race's conclusion as captivating as possible, it would fall to Peter to quietly clean up Beverly's mess.

Just like always.

"Your incompetence is stunning," Peter said, clenching his hands into fists as he leaned across the table. "I have half a mind to—"

"Peter—stop."

Peter flinched at the unexpected interruption, and turned to look in disbelief at the President. Though he hadn't yelled, President Gonzales's words still cracked with a whip's intensity. The steel behind his tone was unmistakable.

"Sir?" Peter said.

"As much as I dislike Ms. Castle's chosen course of action, we will not denigrate each other. Not while I'm still President. Besides, official sanction or not, I believe that, in this case, Beverly acted correctly."

"Mr. President," Peter said, still not trusting that his brain was accurately rendering his old friend's words, "with all due respect, what are you talking about? The polls are essentially tied. What Beverly did—"

"Was what had to be done," the President interrupted.

"The election—" Peter said.

"If voters wake up Tuesday to news that terrorists released a chemical weapon in Times Square, my election will be relegated to an afterthought and rightly so."

The President handed the finding back to Beverly before turning to Peter, his kindly eyes reflecting a rarely seen hardness.

"In normal times, I would agree with you about Ms. Castle's convenient disregard for the chain of command," Jorge said. "But these aren't normal times. However, I do expect to be informed before further covert operations are initiated. If that isn't clear enough for you, Ms. Castle, let me know now, and we will announce your resignation within the hour."

The triumphant smile that had stretched across Beverly's face vanished. Unfortunately, Peter didn't have time to relish his adversary's dressing down, because the President had once again turned in his direction.

"Peter, I know that you have my best interests at heart, but we can't afford to play it safe. Not now. I'm going to authorize a new finding this morning."

"Stating what?" Peter said.

"Stating that all members of the intelligence community are hereby directed to make ascertaining the nature of this new chemical weapon their number one priority. I expect to see plans of action from the Director of each applicable agency on my desk by close of business. That includes you, Director Castle."

"Certainly, sir," Beverly said, her tone respectful, but her lips twitching into a smile as she stole a glance at Peter. "My best are already on it."

"I'm sure they are," the President said, allowing a hint of sarcasm to color his words. "Plans only, Ms. Castle. If another operation is launched without my approval, it will be your last."

"Sir," Peter said, desperate to stop the train the President had set into motion, "I need to bring you up to speed on the initiative I've been working on with Senator Kime. If you'd just give me a minute—"

"Peter, I know without a shadow of a doubt I wouldn't be here without you. You promised that if I listened to you, I'd end up in the Oval Office, and you were right, but this is not the time for politics. One way or another, I will be leaving the Presidency—hopefully in four years, but perhaps in four days. Either way, I intend to ensure there's still a nation to return to once it's my time to become a private citizen again. Beverly, do what you need to do. Peter will handle the consequences. Now, if you'll excuse me, I have a press conference to give."

Without waiting for a reply, President Gonzales got to his feet and exited the room as abruptly as he'd entered. For once, Peter didn't stand as his friend of twenty years strode through the door.

Perhaps because he wasn't certain his legs would support him.

FIVE

A little over four hours later, I stood in front of a slate gray building that perfectly epitomized the Defense Intelligence Agency. Even though the afternoon sun shone brightly from an October sky blue enough to star in a Disney movie, the multistory headquarters building had all the charm of a German bunker overlooking the Normandy coast.

While our CIA cousins had an iconic structure surrounded by acres of prime Langley property, the DIA had a pillbox next to a fishpond.

Everything you needed to know about the perpetual rivalry between the nation's foremost intelligence organizations could be gleaned from an examination of their respective real estate. The tree-lined CIA headquarters in stately old Virginia was like the sophisticated, easily recognizable older sibling, while the DIA's footprint on the

Potomac River's eastern side was the often-ignored kid brother, forever trying to win parental approval.

My former boss might have been able to strong-arm a couple of FBI Agents into tossing me onto the private plane he'd had waiting, but even the venerable James Glass fell short when it came to this steel-and-glass monstrosity.

Still, if the innocent-sounding message James had passed to me via Agent Rawlings's phone meant what I thought it did, he might now have the leverage to raze this place to the ground and try again.

Einstein is active.

Those three words held within them unfathomable potential.

Einstein was the code name we'd given to a Pakistani weapons scientist who'd been selling his services to the highest bidder for the past five years. Analogous to the infamous Khan labs, where Pakistan's state-sponsored nuclear program was born and then exported to customers around the globe, Einstein got his start in his nation's fledgling chemical weapons program. When that ill-advised initiative was shelved, due to substantial U.S. pressure, Einstein took his show on the road.

About eighteen months ago, he'd popped up on our radar after a DIA asset within the Pakistani government reported that Einstein was looking to shop his expertise to someone in the ongoing Syrian crisis. Though a Sunni Muslim by birth, Einstein was more capitalist than religious ideologue. He was willing to lend his technical acumen to whichever party paid his substantial retainer, whether that was the Shias running Assad's government, the Sunni rebels fighting against them, or even the Wahhabi-inspired ISIS caliphate.

I'd voted for killing him outright, before he opened Pandora's box in a civil war that had already consumed an estimated half million lives. James had backed my recommendation, but General Hartwright, the DIA Director, had had other ideas. In Hartwright's estimation, Einstein represented a once-in-a-lifetime recruitment opportunity. Turning him into an asset would provide the DIA a window into a number of the world's most virulent terrorist organizations and repressive regimes.

Rather than kill him, we would recruit him, and I was slotted to be the pitchman.

On its surface, the Director's reasoning made sense, but the cynical side of me wondered if there was more to his decision than met the eye. The CIA and the DIA perpetually battled for funding. A recruit of Einstein's stature would be a huge feather in General Hartwright's cap when he went to war with Congress for next year's budget.

Not to mention Hartwright's murky personal motivations. His tenure as Director was timed to end with this Presidential election. Though he was an Army general officer who'd earned three stars, Hartwright was already on the prowl for his next gig. Needless to say, the successful recruitment of a notorious weapons scientist would look pretty damn good on Hartwright's post-military resume.

Whatever the Director's logic, the end result was the same—I was to make a pass at Einstein. I'd saluted the flag and followed orders, but for the first time in my five-year career as a DIA case officer, a recruitment target had turned me down flat. But now, if I was interpreting James's message correctly, Einstein had experienced a change of heart. He'd established contact. This meant that as his potential handler, I needed to come in from the cold and run my newest asset.

Or did it?

A stream of government employees passed through the set of turnstiles in front of me, heading for the parking lot to my left. At a little after five on a Friday, their shift spent keeping the world safe for democracy was over. Now it was time to brave the D.C. traffic.

Those young enough to be willing to live in a shoebox with three roommates probably had a thirty-minute commute to a flat in the District. The more senior employees with families who favored the roomier, and more affordable, suburbs of northern Virginia or southern Maryland had a good hour-to-hour-and-a-half angst-filled slog.

Laila and I had fallen somewhere in between. Housing in Old Town, Alexandria, was prohibitively expensive to own, but affordable to rent. With the combined salaries of a government employee and a forensic accountant on the path to partnership, we'd been able to find a town house on the water.

The commute wasn't bad. Twenty minutes to DIA headquarters for me and less than ten to Laila's de facto office—Ronald Reagan Washington National Airport. In fact, by now, Laila should have been back at our condo, curled up with a glass of wine, paging through the latest John Dixon novel.

I hadn't been home for six weeks. Not since the night I'd stumbled from our bedroom in a cold sweat, convinced my Syria demons had finally come to claim me. Up until then, the tremors had been a mere annoyance—a random twitch here or there that I'd explained away as a muscle spasm. I was, after all, recovering from a gunshot wound to the leg. But that night, things had been different.

After a particularly bad dream, I'd woken to see a figure standing next to the nightstand.

Abir.

I'd sat up and turned to Laila, but it wasn't my wife lying next to me. Instead, I was sharing my bed with Abir's mother.

In that moment, the tremors began in earnest, rippling from my fingers to my arms. I'd stumbled from our bedroom and down the steps to the living room. My heart felt like it was thundering out of my chest, and my eyes burned from the sweat dripping from my forehead. Desperate to escape numbing panic, I noticed the battered Gibson knockoff propped against the wall.

The guitar had been a college whim, and I couldn't remember the last time I'd seen it, let alone played it. But for some reason, I grabbed the worn neck, settled the cracked wood across my lap, and began to strum. Over the course of a song or two, the tremors, and the accompanying madness, began to fade. For the first time since

I'd hobbled off the medevac flight from Syria, I could think about something other than my horrible failure—the mistake that had cost three people their lives and crippled my best friend.

But the unexpected peace hadn't come without cost. There, in the darkness lit only by the occasional pair of headlights playing across the wall, I saw where this would all lead. Tonight, the tremors had progressed far beyond a simple muscle twitch. Tonight, I'd seen a dead little girl and mistaken my wife for her mother.

What would I see tomorrow?

Or do?

Those were the questions that put things into perspective. Between my military and case officer experience, I'd been on the pointy end of the spear for more than a decade. I'd seen some terrible shit, and the number of friends I'd lost in this never-ending war on terrorism was edging ever closer to double digits.

But this was different.

Before, I'd been able to control my reactions, but tonight was uncharted territory. What if it hadn't been Abir's mother? What if, instead, I'd seen the man who'd killed them?

What would have happened then?

I had no idea, and that was unacceptable. The love of my life was no longer safe in her own home.

Because of me.

I'd married Laila nine months after meeting her. Six years later, I loved her in ways I hadn't known were possible. My wife was amazing, but she wasn't perfect. She had a stubborn streak that made a pit bull look compliant. She'd never give up on me, no matter what I said or did. Her parents had lived the typical immigrant struggle. They'd come to this country with nothing, and she had inherited their endless determination.

No, Laila would never abandon me, even if it meant the destruction of us both. And that was a scenario I simply couldn't stomach.

So I'd protected her in the only way I'd known how. Not trusting myself to go back into our bedroom, I'd left a note explaining that I'd been activated for a fictitious operation, grabbed the old guitar, and walked away.

Like Laila, I hadn't grown up with much. While not immigrants, my parents had eked out a life on a desolate stretch of Utah land they'd optimistically called a ranch. There hadn't been much money, which meant that visits to the vet were reserved for problems that Dad couldn't fix with a home remedy. Potential exposure to rabies was a perfect example. If Dad suspected that an animal had been infected, he put it in quarantine and waited. If, after thirty days, it hadn't developed symptoms, he breathed a sigh of relief and welcomed it back to the fold. But if the animal began to manifest the telltale rabies-induced madness, he put it down.

Period.

This had been my thinking when I'd left. Maybe what I had was curable. Maybe I needed to be put down. The only way to be sure without risking Laila in the process was to institute my own form of quarantine.

I'd gone to school at the University of Texas on an

Army ROTC scholarship and fallen in love with Austin. So with nowhere else to go, and a need to remain anonymous, I'd e-mailed James my resignation letter, FedExed him my secure phone and Agency credentials, and headed back to my college home.

To keep busy, I took guitar lessons and tended bar. A month and a half ago, I'd purchased a one-way ticket to D.C., hoping to surprise Laila as she connected through Austin. But instead of seeing my wife's beautiful face, I'd been confronted with a dead Syrian woman. Shaken but determined, I'd converted the unused ticket and tried again. And again. And again. But the results were always the same. My wife was lost to me.

Now, perhaps, it was time to admit that my quarantine had been a failure. Abir's manifestations were growing more frequent and the tremors more severe. At this very moment, Laila was only a twenty-minute Uber ride away. Maybe it was time to leave the DIA for good and gamble everything on Laila's single-minded tenacity.

But the thought had no sooner entered my head than I discarded it. Perhaps I could turn my back on James, Einstein, and my work. If my time in the Army had taught me anything, it was that no one was truly irreplaceable. James might scream and yell, but surely the DIA had another case officer capable of running Einstein. Even so, there still remained one person on whom I could never turn my back.

As if my thoughts had summoned him, the building's glass doors parted, revealing my best friend's broken form. As he hobbled toward me, I couldn't help but think that perhaps Abir had been the lucky one. Though the toddler had died a horrible death, her suffering was over.

Frodo's had just begun.

SIX

As of late, my life seemed to be divided into two distinct parts—*before* and *after*. *Before* was the man I'd been, and the life I'd lived, prior to Syria. *After* was everything else. For the most part, only I could see this distinction. To Laila, James, and everyone else, I looked like the same man. I probably even acted like him most of the time.

But I knew that I was different.

When I'd first come home, I'd wished that the distinction had been more evident. That there had been something more prominent than the bullet wound in my leg to alert my friends and family to my unseen changes. Then I'd seen Frodo for the first time in the *after* and realized what a selfish thing I'd wished for. Frodo's change was all too evident, even to people who'd never known him in the *before*. And that was a tragedy, because prior to Syria, Frodo had been one of the most dangerous human beings on the planet.

At first blush, Frodo wasn't particularly imposing or, for that matter, memorable. He was a soft-spoken black man with the build of a bantamweight boxer. I'd been thoroughly unimpressed five years previous when we'd first been introduced in a dusty FOB on the outskirts of Mosul. I was on my initial tour as a DIA case officer, and Frodo, a sniper on loan from the organization known simply as the Unit to those who were members, and as Delta Force to everyone else, was assigned as my bodyguard.

I'd never actually learned how he'd earned the call sign Frodo. His real name was Frederick Cates. Frodo bore no resemblance whatsoever to a hobbit, but the practice of giving operators call signs was common in the Unit, so I didn't press. He and I were both veterans of the special operations community. That was all I needed to know.

Even so, we were hardly birds of a feather: a white, six-foot, one-hundred-eighty-pound former ranch hand from Utah and his black shadow who hailed from outside Philly. That Frodo's head even reached my shoulders was due more to the impressive height of his hair, courtesy of the relaxed grooming standards for deployed special operators, than to his stature. Physical prowess aside, I'd scoffed at the notion that, as a former member of the vaunted Ranger Regiment, I even needed a bodyguard.

I maintained that line of thinking for exactly twenty-four hours. Then my first meet went bad.

I never saw the sniper until it was much too late. One moment, I'd been sitting at an outdoor café, enjoying a cup of chai with a would-be asset. The next, a body tumbled to the street from an adjacent rooftop. A body with a 7.62mm hole drilled dead center in his forehead, the strap of his Austrian-made Steyr H550 sniper rifle still wrapped around his dead fingers.

After that, Frodo and I had been inseparable.

But I still had more to learn about my friend. Like many Unit members, Frodo eschewed the bodybuilder persona often embraced by Navy SEALs for a slighter physique skewed more toward endurance than strength. Frodo's ropy muscles and prominent tendons seemed to be crafted from steel cables and iron ingots rather than flesh and blood.

In a different combat zone, in the midst of yet another operation gone south, Frodo had fireman-carried a wounded comrade up two thousand feet of treacherous Afghan mountain to reach the helicopter landing zone. He'd accomplished this feat without so much as passing off his rucksack or body armor.

Frodo's unique combination of sheer athleticism and unmatched tactical competence, along with his astounding ability to put a round from his trusty Heckler & Koch HK417 rifle into any target his eye could discern, made him hands down the best special operator I'd ever encountered. But now the man who'd watched my back in hot spots the world over could barely cross the flat stretch of concrete separating us.

Without thought, I broke into a run at the sight of his hunched, shuffling form.

Frodo's once broad shoulders now sloped forward as

he struggled to manipulate the cane that wound around his still-muscled right forearm in a lattice of webbing and rubber. After seeing his ruined left foot, the military surgeons had wanted to take his leg. Frodo refused to let them. The jihadis had already reduced one arm to a stump, and he wasn't about to give the bastards another pound of flesh.

"Frodo," I yelled, trying to halt his gruesome shuffle. "I'm here."

My shout brought him to a stop. He leaned back on his good foot and tried to extract his remaining hand from the brace to wave. After fumbling with the cane, he settled for a head nod and then continued his awkward movement.

Heading for the turnstile, I pulled up short, coming to a troubled realization. I didn't have my badge. The gate guard would need to buzz me through. Turning left, I sprinted for the lone vestibule housing an undoubtedly bored guard. Forgoing the buzzer, I pounded on bulletproof glass.

"Yes?" the startled guard said.

"Matt Drake. I don't have an ID, but I'm on the roster. Buzz me in."

"Sorry, sir," the guard said, his smug tone coming through the two-way speaker. "Can't admit anyone without ID."

"Look at the roster. Ask me my date of birth, social, grandmother's maiden name. Whatever. Just open the gate."

"Sorry, sir. No can do."

Frodo's cane hit an uneven chunk of pavement. He wobbled but regained his control.

I lost mine.

"Listen closely, 'cause I'm only going to say this once," I said, making my voice low enough that the guard had to lean forward to hear. "You see that man?"

I pointed at Frodo.

The guard looked over his shoulder and then turned back to me.

"What about him?"

"He lost his arm and ruined his leg saving my ass. Nothing I can do about that. But if he slips and falls because you won't buzz me in, we will have a problem. You picking up what I'm putting down?"

The guard looked at me in silence for a beat. I don't know what he saw, but it must have been enough. He gave his computer monitor a perfunctory glance and buzzed me through.

The sound of the electronic lock brought Frodo up short, and I didn't give him a chance to resume his shuffle. Instead, I crossed the distance separating us at a run, and wrapped him in a bear hug.

"How you doing, brother?" I said, trying to keep my voice from breaking.

"Better than you, I think," Frodo said, his deep baritone ringing with the resonance that made it instantly recognizable on the radio, no matter how scratchy the connection.

"What do you mean?" I said, stalling for time. *Had Laila talked to him?* If my crippled best friend took this moment to ask about my marriage, I might just lose it completely. Still, that would be classic Frodo. Even now, after everything, he was still more concerned with my well-being than with his own.

"James. He's been in a mood ever since he talked to you."

"Pissed?"

"Radioactive."

"Then I guess we'd better go see what the big man wants."

"Don't worry, brother. I got your back."

I nodded, not trusting my voice. *Before*, I'd known I was blessed—amazing wife, friends who were brothers, and a job I believed in.

But that was *before*.

In the *after*, Abir was dead, Frodo couldn't tie his own shoes, and Laila might as well have been a widow. In the *after*, everyone had paid a staggering price for my failure.

Everyone but me.

SEVEN

Matthew! What happened to your pretty face?"

The question came from a woman seated behind the mahogany desk in the small waiting area in front of James's office. Her name was Ann Beaumont, and as her drawl suggested, she hailed from parts well south of the Mason-Dixon Line.

Though I'd known her for more than five years, Ann had yet to age. Her shoulder-length brown hair was still gracefully transitioning to silver, and her forehead's fine lines had yet to deepen into true wrinkles. Though she was a bit on the plump side, Ann's elegant wardrobe was a testament to her Southern breeding.

Only a fool would mistake Ann for just another civil servant. Rather than allow herself to be intimidated by her coworkers, Ann had made herself the den mother of all the rough-and-tumble spies who reported to James. At first, I'd found her overfamiliarity irritating, but over the years I'd grown to understand that Ann Beaumont made for a formidable advocate.

"It's nothing," I said in my best *aw shucks* voice. "Just a bit of a misunderstanding."

"Yeah," Frodo said, shuffling to a stop beside me, "you should've seen the other girl."

Frodo usually had a knack for making Ann laugh, and the silvery sound was well worth the effort. But today, Frodo's jibe didn't do the trick. Instead, Ann's hazel eyes welled up as she struggled to speak.

"Really," I said, feeling more than a little embarrassed. "I'm okay. Promise."

"I know you are, doll," Ann said, her voice husky. "I'm sorry for getting all weepy, but I'm just happy to see my boys together again. You've been gone too long, Matthew."

Her rebuke, though deftly delivered, stung. I'd cut her, Frodo, and Laila from my life with ruthless efficiency. I'd thought that quarantining myself might right what was wrong, but now I wasn't so sure. Perhaps all I'd really done was isolate myself from the very people who could have helped me. Fortunately, a commanding voice more at home on a battlefield than in a spymaster's lair boomed from James's office, bringing my introspection to an end.

"Matt—get your ass in here. And bring Frodo."

I stopped to give Ann's shoulder a squeeze and was caught by surprise when she stood and wrapped her arms around me.

"Go easy on him, Matthew," Ann said, her whispered words tickling my ear. "He missed you, too."

And then the unexpected hug was gone, and Ann was shooing me toward the looming door.

Squaring my shoulders, I stepped from one world to another, ready to meet my fate, with Frodo watching my back, just like always.

You look like shit," James said as I shut the door.

"Good to see you, too, Chief," I said, taking my usual seat at his oblong conference table. "Laila's fine. Thanks for asking."

To say that James Glass was an intimidating figure would be a bit like saying that Bill Clinton liked women. Sometimes words just weren't enough.

"What the fuck happened to your face?" James said.

"This is your handiwork," I said.

"What does that mean?"

"It means that the Feds who rolled me up at the airport were a bit overzealous."

"The FBI did this to you?" James said, his question echoing across the room. "Give me a fucking name. I will rip off his head and shit down his throat."

A former Army Special Forces team sergeant before RPG shrapnel robbed him of his right eye and ended his operational career, James refused to acclimate to the DIA's button-down civilian culture. He spoke with a coarseness that came from spending eighteen years kicking in doors and sending would-be terrorists on one-way trips to paradise.

His attire was no better. Rather than adopt the Brooks

Brothers dress code of Senior Executive Service–level civilians, James wore his shirts open at the collar and rolled at the cuffs, exposing tattooed forearms. He didn't own a tie, and when the occasion mandated a sport coat, the fabric strained to contain his wide back and massive chest. A black eye patch, which contrasted sharply with the gray stubble that remained of his hair, completed his wardrobe.

James Glass, DIA Branch Chief and night terror to Islamic jihadis everywhere, did not tolerate bullshit of any sort. With a Mafia don's warped sense of propriety, James would no doubt go to war with the entire Federal Bureau of Investigation if he felt that my honor, and by extension his own, had been besmirched.

And he would probably win.

"Relax, Chief," I said, pouring a glass of water from the carafe at the center of the table. "You can't blame them. They were just following orders, right?"

I took a coaster without being told. Ann was very particular about rings on the highly polished oak table. The coaster I'd selected was imprinted with a close-up of bin Laden, after SEAL Team Six had finished with him. James liked to keep mementos from operations he'd had a hand in, and since wearing a necklace of ears was no longer in vogue, he'd settled for specially designed coasters.

"You sent the FBI after Matty?" Frodo said.

"He wouldn't answer his fucking phone," James said, taking a white foam cup from the floor and spitting a stream of tobacco juice into it. James also wisely chose a coaster before setting his spit cup on Ann's table: Saddam Hussein—post-hanging.

"That's because I quit," I said.

"Bullshit," James said, his single eye glaring at me from beneath the protection of his thick brow. "Men like us don't quit. We stay until they carry us out in a wooden box. You needed space after the last operation. Fine. I gave it to you. Now it's time to get your shit together and get back in the saddle. There's work to be done."

In the *before*, a speech like this would have had me saluting the flag and grabbing my rifle. But this was the *after*. James was right—men like him didn't leave until someone forced them out. But was I still a man like him?

Did I even want to be?

I pictured Laila paging through her paperback while she waited for me to return from a fictitious operation. I'd lied to my own wife because I couldn't look her in the face without seeing a dead girl's mother, yet somehow I was seriously considering returning to work. What was wrong with me?

"You know what, Chief?" I said, pushing away from the table. "Thanks, but no, thanks. Find someone else. I'm out."

"Are you fucking kidding me?" James said, a flush creeping up his bull neck. "I thought you—"

"Chief." Though he'd spoken softly, Frodo's baritone still rang through the room with the unmistakable essence of command. As if he'd been struck mute, James stopped midsentence.

"Matty," Frodo said, turning toward me, "I need you

to watch something. The clip is less than three minutes long. If you still want out after you see it, I'll walk you to the door myself."

I hesitated before nodding, but the pause was just for show. A heartbeat ago, I'd been certain that my career as an intelligence officer was over. I'd faced down the great James Glass. If the President himself had walked into the room, I would have told him to pound sand. At that moment, I would have said no to anyone.

Anyone but Frodo.

Frodo picked up a remote from the table and activated the television hanging on the far wall. The footage was black-and-white, but the quality was fine. I was looking at the inside of a restaurant. Classy place with linen tablecloths, flickering candles, and actual china. The footage began with a panoramic view of the dining room, but zoomed in to just one table as the video began to play.

"Tech guys already did their magic," James said, watching my expression. "Digital zooming, image smoothing, the works."

I nodded as the silent drama played out. A man and a woman having dinner. The security camera was above and behind the happy couple. I couldn't see much of her, but I had a good shot of him. Lots of smiles, expensive suit, fit-looking guy.

"Watch his hand," James said.

I'd already noticed the tremor, but hadn't yet determined if it was real or a function of the digital zoom. A second later, a shudder ran the length of the man's body. The woman got to her feet, reaching the man just as his tremors became a full-blown seizure. He toppled from the chair before she could catch him. She cradled his head in her lap as he thrashed.

The seizure's intensity increased. The man's heels drummed against the floor. His body shook, his hand catching the woman in the face and snapping her head to the side. His back arched, straining at an impossible angle.

Then he sagged to the floor. Motionless.

The woman turned to yell for someone off-screen, providing a close-up of her features. Her lips were curled into a scream, eyes wet with tears.

The video ended.

"What was that?" I said.

"We're not sure," James said, then spit into his cup. "The woman's fine. So is everyone else. The man's dead. Autopsy is still pending, but the preliminary tox screen came back negative. Medical folks say it's probably some kind of brain embolism. Rare, but not unheard-of."

"But?"

"But the man was a CIA paramilitary officer. Less than twenty-four hours ago, he was part of a team that took down a suspected chemical weapons laboratory in Syria."

"Son of a bitch," I said.

"Exactly," James said. "The team came under attack while they were exploiting the lab. The man in the video was attempting to pipette a sample of the chem weapon when the firefight started. The team had to pull out before he could finish, and he contaminated his gloves in the process. He degloved immediately and did an ad hoc decontamination. He seemed fine, but the Agency put him on a priority flight home just in case. They ran him through a full set of diagnostics at Walter Reed, and everything came back negative. He decided to have dinner with his wife before rotating back. He didn't even make it through the appetizer."

"Where did the intel on the lab come from?" I said.

"Israelis," Frodo said. "A Mossad asset learned that an ISIS splinter cell was planning to launch a chem attack on U.S. soil. Supposedly, the chem weapon didn't register on the CIA team's detection sensors. It's brand-spanking-new."

"How did the terrorists get it?" I said.

"A Pakistani weapons scientist for hire created it for them."

"Einstein."

"Exactly," James said. "As I said, the CIA team wasn't able to fully exploit the lab, but what they did find suggests that the building they hit wasn't where the splinter cell was conducting the bulk of their research. If we knew the lab's location, we'd just drop a JDAM through the roof and call it a day. But we don't. In fact, we still don't know what exactly killed the paramilitary operator."

"So we've got nothing," I said.

"Wrong," James said. "We've got Einstein."

"After the raid," Frodo said, "Einstein made contact. He offered to give up the weapon he'd developed and the lab's location. But he had one condition—you. You have to be the one to bring him in."

"Why?" I said.

"Ask him," James said.

"Here's the deal," Frodo said. "The President has is-sued a finding directing the intelligence community to focus exclusively on determining the nature and location of this chemical weapon. As of now, every other tasking has taken a back seat. The CIA has operational control in Syria, but they have nothing on these jihadis or the weapon. Einstein is the only link, and he will only work with you."

On the TV, the woman's face was frozen midscream.

A CIA paramilitary team had stumbled across an un-detectable chemical agent that passed through state-of-the-art protective equipment like it was Swiss cheese, and the terrorists who had the weapon were going to use it in America.

Unless someone stopped them.

Unless I stopped them.

"What happens now?" I said, looking from Frodo to James.

"Get your ass to Syria and do what you do," James said, not bothering to hide his victory grin. "The President has convened a working group, headed by the CIA, that meets daily to update him on our collective progress. I'm the DIA's liaison. Frodo will serve as your handler from here. Get to Einstein. If he can give us the chemical weapon and the lab's location, bring him in. If he can't, suck him dry and put a bullet in his skull. Your flight leaves from An-drews in three hours. Say good-bye to your wife and pack your shit. It's time to go to work."

And just like that, I was back in the game and everything was peachy. Except it wasn't. My guardian angel couldn't cut his own food, my wife looked like a dead Syrian, and a smiling toddler haunted me.

To make things even more interesting, at some point during James's victory lap, my index finger had begun to twitch.

Just peachy.

EIGHT

The pavement flashed by beneath Peter's feet as his sneakers pounded out a precise staccato. Though the GPS on his wrist beeped an affirming tone, Peter didn't need satellite signals to know that he was exactly on pace.

As a skinny high school kid more interested in books than in football, Peter had been an anomaly in his small *Friday Night Lights*–esque town. Even as a teenager, Peter had possessed a startling amount of self-awareness. He'd known by his second week of school that, if he had any hope of surviving the next four years, he needed an athletic endeavor, and he needed it fast.

Enter running.

Peter had shown up for his first cross-country practice, more out of desperation than out of a desire to run, with only the vaguest idea of what the sport entailed. He was too small for football and not athletic enough for soccer, but as his dad had told him, anyone could run.

And run Peter did.

The first mile was the most painful experience of his life. His side ached, his breath came in labored gasps, and his throat was raw from bile. But as the first mile turned into the second, something magical happened. Peter heard the music—a type of undulating rhythm that beat out the pace to the required seven-minute mile in some sort of living tempo. By the third mile, his body and mind were synced. By the fourth, he'd fallen in love.

Peter's gift had led halfway through his freshman year to a varsity position on the team and later attracted the attention of colleges across the nation, including Harvard. Technically, it was a need-based scholarship that relieved a financial burden his firmly blue-collar family could never have shouldered, but Peter understood the truth: He was admitted to Harvard because he could run.

Quite simply, running had changed his life.

If only Kristen instead of Peter had been born with the gift, everything might have been different.

But she hadn't.

With a grimace, Peter increased his pace like he was resetting a metronome. He rocketed down a bend in the path, feet tattooing a rhythm that only he could hear as he tried to push from his mind the vision of the blond, ponytailed girl with the wide Bambi-like blue eyes. Without a second glance he raced by a pair of male runners twenty years his junior, running as if the devil himself were giving chase.

Everything he'd done since the day he'd heard his mom's voice shatter into a thousand pieces over the telephone had been for Kristen. He'd finished Harvard in three years instead of four and turned down a lucrative position with a K Street lobbying firm to volunteer for a previously unknown Texas politician's mayoral reelection campaign. A Texas politician who'd unintentionally made his national debut by offering calm, effective leadership to his constituents after a pair of back-to-back hurricanes had devastated his city.

Peter had watched Jorge's first spontaneous press conference as the future President spoke off the cuff. Jorge had detailed his plan to rescue stranded flood victims in clear, concise statements even as rain streamed from the brim of his faded Astros ball cap.

In that moment, Peter had instantly known that Jorge was destined for greatness in the same instinctive way he'd known when his mile pace was exactly seven minutes. Ignoring the advice of mentors and friends alike, Peter had followed his intuition and moved to Texas.

And his intuition had been correct.

Now he was four days away from a second Gonzales term with projected majorities in both the House and Senate. Peter had spent the last four years cultivating relationships on both sides of the aisle, laying the groundwork for a progressive legislative agenda that would turn America's focus away from pointless wars and toward forgotten priorities at home. Priorities like repairing the nation's crumbling infrastructure, continuing the march toward single-payer health care, and, most important, providing free college education.

For everyone.

Never again would America's sons and daughters have to choose between crippling student loans and flag-draped coffins just because they couldn't afford college. This was the silent promise Peter had made to his dead sister, Kristen, twenty years earlier, and now his promise was almost a reality.

Assuming, of course, that Beverly Castle's incompetence didn't cost Jorge the election.

The thought of his rival's self-righteous smile at the end of their last meeting almost caused Peter to increase his pace again, but he resisted the urge. He might be able to run from the memory of his kid sister's death, but Beverly Castle was a problem he needed to face head-on.

But that didn't mean he had to face her alone.

Glancing at the wrist-mounted GPS, Peter saw that he was a minute ahead of schedule and adjusted accordingly. The person he was meeting didn't tolerate schedule deviations, and by common agreement both parties had left their cell phones behind.

The restrictions his friend placed on these meetings were onerous, but Peter didn't complain. Operational paranoia was to be expected when your sometime running partner was a career intelligence officer.

Circling down through a strand of trees, Peter saw a pair of strategically placed water bottles resting against the base of a wrought iron bench lining the trail. One bottle was full, the other half-empty. The meet was still on, and Peter hadn't been followed.

Peter thought these safeguards archaic at best. In an era in which nearly unbreakable encryptions came with every cell phone, he didn't understand the need for trade-craft that predated his birth. But the man he was about to meet didn't tell Peter how to run a Presidential campaign, so Peter wasn't judgmental when it came to his contact's area of expertise. After all, much had changed since they'd both been homesick college freshmen.

Up ahead, the familiar path split, the branch to the left continuing along the Potomac's sunny banks, while the branch to the right led deeper into the woods. Peter turned right, and within a dozen steps, he was no longer alone.

As always, his companion seemed to appear out of thin air. One moment, Peter was pounding along the path at a precise eight-minute-thirty-second mile, and the next, his former teammate Charles Sinclair Robinson IV materialized at his side.

"I need your help with Beverly," Peter said, not bothering with a preamble.

Because of their respective positions, and the topics they discussed, face-to-face meetings were both brief and rare. As such, both men had agreed to dispense with pleasantries during their infrequent conversations. After the voters sent President Jorge Gonzales back for his second term, the men would have plenty of time to rekindle their friendship. This conversation, however, like most that had occurred over the last four years, was strictly about business.

The business of getting President Gonzales reelected.

"Really?" Charles said, his breathing not the least bit labored. "From what I hear, you need help with Syria."

"You know about the raid?"

"Four Americans dead and a helicopter destroyed. Everyone knows about the raid. Even I would be hard-pressed to spin that shit show."

As the CIA's liaison to the Directorate of National Intelligence, Charles reviewed and had the ability to shape every intelligence assessment that made its way from the intelligence community's combined coffers to the executive branch and, on select occasions, to the press.

Prior to his current assignment, Charles had been the CIA's Chief of Base in Syria. Then, three months ago, Assad had used chemical weapons against his own countrymen without warning, catching Charles completely unaware. In the ensuing political storm, only Peter's quiet maneuvering had kept Charles from being cashiered altogether.

Charles had repaid Peter's patronage by tailoring the intelligence community's assessment of the ongoing Syrian conflict to reflect more favorably the administration's preelection narrative. This effort had proven crucial to defusing the constant barrage of attacks leveled against the administration by Senator Kelsey Price, the Republican Presidential nominee.

But while Charles's efforts had helped negate much of Price's criticism, without someone on the ground he could trust, Peter had no one to supervise Beverly's meddling.

The disastrous raid had been a perfect case in point.

"Can you fix it?" Peter said.

"It depends," Charles said, as always his voice betraying no emotion. "What happened?"

Not for the first time, Peter was glad that he'd renewed his acquaintance with his old classmate. Four years ago, Charles had contacted Peter with an offer the future Presidential adviser couldn't refuse—inside information on the dismal status of the ongoing Iraq War. Peter had taken the tidbits Charles had provided and crafted them into talking points that then–Presidential candidate Jorge Gonzales had used to wallop the Republican incumbent. In exchange, Charles had asked for help with his flagging Agency career.

Peter had been only too happy to oblige.

Despite the chaos that had occurred on Charles's watch three months ago, Peter still viewed the deal he'd negotiated with his old friend in a favorable light. If it was possible to mitigate Beverly's current disaster, Charles would know how.

"Beverly blindsided me this morning," Peter said as the two men barreled across a wooden footbridge. "A helicopter shot down and four men dead days before the election are bad enough. Worse still, the President's supporting Beverly's recommendation. He issued a finding instructing the entire intelligence community to focus on this terrorist splinter cell and the chemical weapon they've developed. The President is seriously considering widening our Syrian footprint days before the election."

"Why?"

Peter shook his head. "I'm not sure he even knows. This undetectable chemical weapon has him terrified. He ceded control of the entire Syrian theater of operations to Beverly."

"Perfect."

Peter tripped and would have fallen if Charles hadn't grabbed his arm. Shaking off the offered hand, he turned on his friend. "Perfect? Have you listened to a thing I've said?"

"You want me to take care of this? Send me back to Syria. I'll find the lab. You can hit it with a cruise missile without risking a single American life."

"How?"

"My network of assets is still in place. If there's a terrorist splinter cell developing a chemical weapon in Syria, my people will know."

Peter shook his head. "Things didn't go quite so smoothly three months ago."

"That's because of that DIA hothead Drake. Without him, my operation would have succeeded. Pulling my team out after the chem attack was a mistake. Our work was just starting to bear dividends."

Peter wiped the sweat from his forehead, considering Charles's proposition.

As the Syrian Chief of Base, Charles had been tasked with coordinating all American intelligence operations in the country. In reality, Peter had given his friend a far more pressing task—finding a way to end the conflict without additional U.S. troops. A war-weary American public had little patience for a third Middle East adventure, especially at the hands of a President who'd run on a platform of ending America's involvement in Iraq. The Republican-controlled Congress had been thundering against the President's ill-defined Syrian strategy, and the politicians' arguments had started to resonate. Peter had seen peace in Syria as a way to defuse those criticisms, and he had given Charles the directive to bring it about.

Charles's solution had been Operation Shogun, a clandestine effort aimed at secretly recruiting and arming a network of Syrian rebels dedicated to just one thing—instituting regime change by killing Bashar al-Assad, the homicidal Syrian dictator.

To support the operation, Peter had ensured that the small contingent of rebels be equipped with what, before, had been forbidden resources: Javelin fire-and-forget anti-tank missiles, Remington Modular Sniper Rifles, next-generation night-vision goggles, secure communications, and priority tasking from the Agency pilots who controlled the assortment of armed Reaper and Predator drones prowling Syria's skies.

In short, everything an indigenous Syrian strike force would need to decapitate Assad's regime.

Along the way, Charles's network had provided a stunning array of intelligence, much of which had found its way into the President's Daily Brief. But before the operation against Assad could be executed, the dictator had launched a chemical weapons attack against the civilian population of Aleppo.

The attack, executed right under the Agency's nose, had been a black eye for both Charles and his network. Beverly, who had resented the fact that the West Wing had pushed Charles on her to begin with, had reacted with predictable fury. She'd recalled Charles and his contingent of Agency personnel to D.C. and disbanded Shogun.

To make matters worse, Matt Drake, the DIA case officer operating in Syria, had turned in a damning assessment of Charles's performance during the chem attack. According to the DIA's official after-action review, Charles had denied Drake the use of the Agency's Quick Reaction Force, or QRF, helicopters after Drake had received an emergency evacuation request from a highly placed asset.

Even now Peter wasn't sure what had actually transpired. What he did know was that Assad's chem attack had caught Charles completely unaware and that Drake and his bodyguard had tried to evacuate their asset by ground without Agency help.

They'd failed.

Instead, the two men had been ambushed and nearly killed. By the time the operational dust had cleared, two Americans had been seriously wounded, an asset and his family murdered, and Charles's credibility destroyed.

Not a success by any measure.

Even so, in the last three months, the Syrian situation had grown steadily worse. The Russians, along with Iran and Hezbollah, were actively helping Assad, while the Saudis secretly funneled money to a variety of Sunni resistance groups. As the territory formerly occupied by the onetime Islamic Caliphate known as ISIS shrank, multiple terrorist splinter cells rushed to fill the void.

At this point, Peter considered Syria to be nothing so much as a distraction, a thorn in his side preventing the Gonzales administration from shifting the nation's attention to a legislative agenda focused on American, rather than foreign, priorities. Every time Peter attempted to publicly sell the idea that Congress could make a down payment on free college tuition by siphoning funds from the military's ever-expanding budget instead of raising taxes, Assad would commit another atrocity. Right on cue, the Republican hawks would point to the Syrian madman and his store of chemical weapons as proof that a robust military was needed now more than ever.

And their damn strategy worked.

Even the vulnerable Republicans who represented states Jorge had carried in the last election were reluctant to cross their party hard-liners when it came to the sacred cow of military spending. But if the current projections were correct, this stalemate would change in four days' time. Polling showed the Democrats picking up enough seats in both the House and the Senate to hold majorities for the first time in four years. So while he still hadn't solved the Syria problem, Peter would now have the votes he needed to move on his domestic agenda with or without Republican help.

But only if someone kept Beverly's new Syrian charter in hand.

Someone like Charles.

If Charles's rebel network found the elusive chem weapon, the President could take the credit, and if they failed, at least no American lives would be lost chasing that white whale. Either way, Peter believed that any problem was solvable as long as Jorge Gonzales was reelected.

But as the morning's polling numbers had demonstrated, that scenario was not a foregone conclusion.

"You sure you can handle this?" Peter said. "The President's future depends on it."

"So does mine."

"What do you mean?" Peter said.

"If I take care of this, I want an office on the seventh floor. Beverly's office."

"Are you kidding? I can't guarantee you the Director's job."

"Of course you can. Agency scuttlebutt is that Beverly's out after Gonzales gets reelected anyway. As much as you may wish it, the world's problems aren't going to vanish after the polls close Tuesday night. You'll need the Agency, but more than that, you'll need a friend running the Agency. Me. Give me your word that I'm the next Director, and I'll take care of Syria."

Peter looked at his friend for a moment, making a show of weighing Charles's offer, but his decision had been made the moment Charles had voiced the bargain. At this point, Peter would have promised almost anything to anyone in exchange for a second Gonzales term. Peter couldn't bring Kristen back, but he could make sure her death hadn't been in vain.

"Okay," Peter said, "you're in. Try and find the chemical weapon or not—I don't care. All I want is ninety-six hours. If Syria stays out of the news, you'll be the next Director of the Central Intelligence Agency. But you're on your own with Beverly. The President made it clear she's riding herd. To get back in-country, you'll have to go through her."

Charles smiled as he clapped Peter on the shoulder.

"I'll be on a plane with my team in two hours. You'll have what you need to handle Beverly before I'm airborne."

Without waiting for a reply, Charles started up the path leading out of the woods, his long legs pumping.

Peter watched his friend and, for the first time since Beverly's ambush this morning, felt a stirring of hope. Beverly might be a colossal pain in the ass, but if Charles did his job, in four short days she'd be nothing but a memory.

NINE

The structure was modest by Old Town, Alexandria, standards—an unassuming two-story town house situated on a quiet side street. Our rental shared a common courtyard with four other units, and the landscaping and raised flower beds bordering the walkway leading to the front door showed Laila's touch. Though the flowers had long since withered, their exotic perfume lingered, reminding me of Laila's dark, fragrant hair.

The clock on the rental's dashboard said that I had three and a half hours until wheels up. More than enough time to say good-bye to Laila, but rather than get out of the car, I sat in the dark, watching as the minutes slowly ticked away.

The front porch light glowed warm and inviting, just as it always did when I was away. Fiercely patriotic, like the children of most immigrants, Laila had wanted to mount a flag holder to the redbrick exterior so that she could fly Old Glory each time I was operational.

I'd talked her out of it.

I loved my country, but the presence of flags in this part of town was rare, and I hadn't wanted to draw unnecessary attention. Such was the life of a spy.

I sucked in a breath, rehearsing what I'd say even as I thought about what I'd do if Abir's mother was waiting for me inside. This unnerving possibility, more than anything else, explained why I was still sitting in the car, listening to the downtown traffic through the rental's open windows.

It had been six weeks since I'd left, but Laila was accustomed to my frequent job-related absences and the lack of communication that went with them. She understood that my job was unique. Oftentimes, I operated under NOC, or Nonofficial Cover, guidelines. This meant that I had to live my "legend" twenty-four hours a day, sometimes under a foreign intelligence service's watchful eyes. During operational periods, I couldn't communicate with her at all.

Laila didn't like the draconian restriction, but after I'd explained its purpose, she'd understood. Still, no amount of explaining would help my wife understand why a dead woman shared her face.

My newly issued cell phone buzzed. I answered, more grateful for the interruption than I cared to admit.

"Drake."

"Matty, it's me," Frodo said, his voice tinged with urgency. "You need to get to Andrews. Now. We're moving up the timetable."

"Einstein?"

"No. Head for Andrews and look for a Gulfstream. Your kit's already on board. I'll fill you in once you're wheels up."

"Roger that," I said, and ended the call.

Secure phone or not, I knew Frodo had communicated as much as he intended to over an open line. My friend was as even-keeled as they came. His abrupt call could mean only one thing—something had changed.

Something significant.

I tossed the phone onto the passenger seat and started the car's engine. I should have been feeling sadness, desperation, or even anger as I drove away, but I felt something else instead.

Relief.

TEN

All right, friends, shall we begin?"

The question was purely rhetorical, but even after almost four years in the Oval Office, and a life of public service prior to that, President Jorge Gonzales was still uncomfortable calling a meeting to order.

Usually, Peter found the President's timid nature charming. But today, he wished that the President would reveal the iron core beneath his sunny demeanor. Jorge had been leading Senator Price by only three points *before* Beverly's Syria fiasco hit the airwaves. Now the President's tenuous lead was likely history.

"Certainly, Mr. President. Beverly, please begin."

The words came from Jeremy Thompson, the Director of National Intelligence, or DNI. Much like his constructed political position, Jeremy was generally a worthless human being.

The role of DNI had been created as a response to the

September eleventh attacks. In theory, the political appointee had been given charge over the sum of the nation's multiple intelligence apparatuses to ensure that the pre-9/11 information stovepiping would never happen again. In practice, the position was a figurehead at best, or a platform for political grandstanding at worst.

The first post-9/11 CIA Director, George Tenet, had quickly demonstrated that he had no intention of ceding his direct access to the President to a politically appointed speed bump, and subsequent Directors had followed suit. Jeremy's very presence at this meeting was sure to lead to friction, and Peter had no doubt that Beverly would be its source.

"Of course," Beverly said, not bothering to look at Jeremy as she spoke.

Although she was seated several places away from the President at the circular conference table Jorge Gonzales preferred for staff meetings, Beverly didn't pay lip service to the Joint Chiefs, the principals, or even the fellow agency directors. Her political fate rested with just one man, and Beverly behaved accordingly.

In his more guarded moments, Peter had to admit that he admired her dogged determination. She'd made no secret of her intention to succeed Jorge as President, and she conducted herself as such.

But Peter's admiration never lasted for long. Time and time again, Beverly had demonstrated that she would trample anyone who stood in the way of her goal, even if that person happened to be the President of the United States.

"Mr. President," Beverly said, fixing Jorge with her glimmering blue eyes, "I'd like to start by relaying an additional piece of bad news."

Peter resisted the urge to interrupt, even as he clenched his fingers into fists beneath the table. This was neither the time nor the place to surprise the President with anything, least of all additional bad news. Bad news should have been relayed ahead of this meeting in a one-on-one with the President or, at the very least, Peter.

This was the time to project unity. It was an opportunity for the President to model the type of reserved, but competent, leadership he expected from his cabinet. Had she been a team player, Beverly would have understood this unspoken tenet and acted as such.

Beverly Castle had been accused of many things over the course of her political career, but acting as a team player had never quite made the list.

"Please continue," President Gonzales said, his steady voice the model of self-control even as the wrinkles lining his forehead grew more pronounced.

Though Jorge would never admit it to his staff, Peter knew that Jorge regretted providing Beverly with the Director's billet. Healing the party was all well and good, but it wasn't worth sacrificing the President's chance at reelection. If Beverly had just been bad at her job, that would have been surmountable. But the combination of her malfeasance and unbridled ambition had come perilously close to sinking Jorge's administration on more than one occasion.

But maybe that was part of her plan. Perhaps the coterie of sycophants surrounding her had determined that Beverly stood a better chance of running on the heels of a disastrous Republican administration than following a successful Democratic one.

Maybe she didn't want the President to win reelection at all.

The thought felt like a punch to Peter's already clenched gut. Could that be true? Could Beverly be working to sabotage their campaign? On any other day, Peter would have dismissed such a ludicrous idea outright. But today, the notion didn't seem quite so far-fetched.

"Thank you, Mr. President," Beverly said, her voice the model of subservience. "As we briefed you this morning, last night a CIA paramilitary team raided a presumed chemical weapons laboratory at great personal cost."

Beverly paused for a moment as if overcome by the thought of losing four operators Peter was certain she couldn't name, let alone pick out of a crowd. Still, her Shakespearean-quality acting got sympathetic nods from the Joint Chiefs seated to her left.

"In any case," Beverly said, "their sacrifice was not in vain. After securing the objective, the team determined that the structure was not a chemical-production facility as we'd originally thought. It was an execution chamber."

Beverly's pronouncement sent a chorus of murmurs rippling down the table. Even these battle-hardened men and women blanched at some of the more graphic depictions of ISIS's brutality. During a particularly heart-wrenching video in which boys as young as eight or nine were made to execute prisoners by shooting them in the face, more than one of the military representatives had turned away from the television screen.

But not Peter. He'd watched every excruciating frame.

Unlike many of his contemporaries, Peter fully embraced the idea that evil existed, and he had no problem applying this label to the terrorists who called Syria home. The fanatics could not be negotiated with or somehow brought back into the proverbial fold.

Where Peter differed with the Republican members of the House and Senate was on the solution to the Syria problem. He had no issue raining down Hellfire missiles on the fanatics. In fact, with Peter's encouragement, the number of targeted drone killings had risen almost tenfold since the previous administration, but he drew the line at committing U.S. troops to the mission.

Peter believed that only Syrians could solve Syria's problems. The U.S. should provide assistance in the form of training, weapons, and even intelligence, but no American lives should be lost to yet another futile attempt to export democracy to a country unable to sustain it.

Yet if Beverly were allowed to have her way, this was exactly what would happen.

"How did you determine that the structure was an execution chamber?" the DNI asked.

As was often the case when the man spoke, Peter had to make a supreme effort to clamp down on the biting reply lurking just behind his lips. Jeremy Thompson's questions frequently put Peter in mind of a poorly written sitcom. The kind of show in which the token new character always asked a series of clarifying questions because the writers believed the audience was too dumb to understand the plot's complexities.

Except that, in the DNI's case, the writers would have been spot-on. The man was as dumb as a box of rocks and twice as worthless.

"The dead bodies were our first clue," Beverly said, responding deadpan.

Despite his irritation with the CIA Director, Peter had to hide a smile at her answer. His adversary had a gift. She could deliver the most caustic of replies without a hint of malice, ensuring that she remained above reproach while still managing to demean and belittle her intended target. More than once, Peter wondered if this was perhaps a block of instruction offered to would-be college professors somewhere between defending their dissertations and obtaining tenure.

A less experienced political hand would have paused for a second at the laugh line, but here, as in most things political, Beverly was too much of a veteran to make a mistake. Instead of celebrating her dig against Thompson, she continued with her explanation as if the man hadn't spoken, further diminishing him in the process.

Good didn't even begin to describe Beverly Castle's political instincts.

"It was the bodies that caught our attention," Beverly said. As she spoke, the wall-length TV screen at the far side of the room came to life, cycling through a series of images. A dim hallway flanked by sealed doors followed by a view of several chambers. Bodies were clustered around what looked like a showerhead sprouting from the exposed piping on the ceiling.

The similarities to a Nazi-era concentration camp were striking.

The images changed, now showing close-ups of the corpses. Here again, Peter forced himself to absorb every revolting detail as faces paraded past the screen in no apparent order—men, women, even children. For a second, he thought that Beverly was using the images solely for their shock value.

Then, in a moment of clarity, he realized what the bodies symbolized.

"What are we seeing?" Jeremy Thompson said, apparently not sharing Peter's enlightenment.

"A sample group," Peter said, the image of a pudgy toddler dragging the words from his lips.

"Correct," Beverly said. "This is part of the reason for my urgency. The victims in each chamber do not appear to have been chosen at random. Each group was composed of eight individuals: two women, two men, and four children. The ages vary from group to group, but the demographic makeup remains the same. As Peter guessed, our analysts believe the victims were sorted into test groups."

"They're lab rats," the President said, the horror in his voice unmistakable.

"That's right, Mr. President," Beverly said. "The terrorists used these people to test the effectiveness of their new chemical weapon. While this is a horrific revelation, it is not the piece of bad news I mentioned at the beginning of this meeting."

"What else?" the President said.

Beverly paused and Peter felt his ulcer rage to life. This was why she'd insisted on sharing the meeting with the Joint Chiefs. The big reveal was about to happen. She was going to guarantee action by releasing the news in front of a larger audience. Amazing.

For an instant, Peter caught a flash of what might have been. With her formidable intellect and uncanny political skills, Beverly could have been a Director that history remembered. If she'd only been content to lay aside her political ambition for the duration of her single four-year term, what she could have accomplished with Peter's help would have been incalculable.

But that was not to be. In the same manner in which the terrorists currently butchering innocents in Syria would never be able to see the error of their ways, Beverly would never be able to rise above her baser nature. She was a politician to her core, and at the end of the day, politicians cared about one thing and one thing above all else—themselves.

"In my update this morning," Beverly said, "I briefed that four members of my paramilitary assault team had been killed. This was erroneous. We've now learned that one of the reported casualties is very much alive."

"Well, that's cause for celebration, then, isn't it?" Jeremy Thompson said.

"No," Beverly said. "He's alive, but he's been captured by the same splinter cell that manufactured the chemical weapon."

"Are you certain?" the President said, his question almost a whisper.

"Yes. His captors have begun posting videos to various jihadi websites. Videos of his torture."

A series of indrawn breaths greeted Beverly's announcement, but the President continued.

"Were you able to confirm the video's authenticity?"

"Yes, sir," Beverly said. "We used facial recognition and several other sophisticated analytical methods to identify the captured paramilitary officer, John Shaw. But the terrorists apparently didn't want to leave anything to chance. In addition to the video, they provided us with forensic evidence."

"What?" Jorge said. "Fingerprints? DNA?"

The President's question was innocent enough, but something about the way Beverly had guided him into asking it raised Peter's hackles. He had the sneaking suspicion that, somehow, the game was about to change once again. And when it did, Peter would be one move behind the CIA Director.

"Not DNA, Mr. President," Beverly said, her voice catching. "They sent us something more definitive. They sent us Shaw's right ear."

ELEVEN

Ladies and gentlemen?" Peter said, his voice cutting through the numerous sidebar conversations. "Ladies and gentlemen?"

Peter slapped the table. "Ladies and gentlemen!"

The background chatter ceased as nine pairs of eyes found his.

This wasn't his style. One of the reasons Peter had never seriously entertained the idea of running for office was because he knew that he was better behind the scenes. Still, this was too much. Left to their own devices, the well-meaning people in this room, Peter had no doubt, would spin up battle plans to rescue Beverly's hapless operator. Battle plans that would undoubtedly result in the loss of more American lives, and the President, as he always did when bum-rushed by his generals, would go along for the ride.

Peter could not allow this to happen. Not when the days before the election numbered in single digits.

"Ladies and gentlemen," Peter said again, his voice less forceful, but his tone leaving no doubt who was in charge. "The content of this meeting has just been classified at the code-word level. Mr. President, might I suggest that you and I take a moment to meet privately with Director Castle?"

"I hardly think this is the time for political posturing," Jeremy Thompson said, wrathful indignation coloring his voice. "Those barbarians have one of our boys. I don't think we should be sitting around discussing poll numbers until they mail us another body part."

New whispers started from the Joint Chiefs at the opposite end of the table. Whispers that Peter knew would lead to an outright mutiny if he didn't act quickly.

"Mr. Thompson," Peter said, resting his forearms on the table, "did you know about Beverly's captured operator prior to this meeting?"

"No, but—"

"Did you authorize the CIA raid?"

"No, I—"

"Were you even briefed that this operation was a potential course of action?"

"No."

The DNI's face grew redder with each admission as even he could now see where the line of questioning was going.

"Forgive me, Mr. Thompson, but you are in fact the Director of National Intelligence, correct?"

"Yes, I am."

Jeremy Thompson almost spit back the answer, shooting a sidelong glance at Beverly as he spoke. For once, Peter knew that he was not the only one thinking murderous thoughts about the CIA Director. But now that he'd shown Jeremy the stick, it was time for a little carrot.

"So, as the Director of National Intelligence, you were not aware that the CIA had launched an operation in Syria. Is that correct?"

From the corner of his eye, Peter could see Beverly shift in her chair. She was smart enough to know that this line of questioning didn't exactly leave her in the best of light. On the other hand, one of the fundamental rules of politics was never to step into the line of fire when your opponent was the target. In Beverly's case, everyone was her opponent.

"That's correct," Jeremy said, his face now a mass of mottled red. Here was the moment when he expected to be handed his walking papers. To be asked to resign in a fit of disgrace in front of the very people he was nominally charged with leading.

Except that the DNI's resignation was the furthest thing from Peter's mind.

"And the reason this is correct," Peter said, his voice softer, almost consoling, "is because Beverly was acting on the President's expressed wishes. The operation was deemed too sensitive to be included in a cabinet-wide update."

"This is highly irregular."

The comment came from General Johnny Etzel, the

first Army aviator to rise to the level of Chairman of the Joint Chiefs of Staff.

"I couldn't agree more, General," Peter said, "which is why I'm asking everyone to leave. The President, Director Castle, and I need a few moments to huddle, after which we will continue this briefing. Until then, please give us the room."

To his credit, the DNI was the first one out of his chair. A political savant the man might not be, but the Director of National Intelligence could recognize a lifeline when he saw one. Pushing his considerable bulk to his feet, Jeremy stood and adjusted his suit. "I'll be outside." He gave Peter a brief nod before lumbering out of the room.

Peter kept his face impassive, but he felt an ember of hope flare to life. A successful political operative was often likened to a mobster's bookie. A large part of Peter's job encompassed keeping track of political debts, and the DNI now owed him a staggering one.

Like the good military men and women they were, the Joint Chiefs followed suit, hustling for the door in a flash of creased uniforms and polished shoes. They might not like what had just happened, but they knew an order when they heard one.

The Secretaries of Defense and State followed. Neither man looked happy, but both shared enough history with Peter to know what would happen should they attempt to assert their independence at this pivotal moment. Also like a mobster, Peter understood the necessity of a good hit job.

All too soon, the conference room door closed with an ominous thud. Then there were three: the President, Beverly, and Peter.

"What was that?" Peter said, eyes boring into Beverly.

"Peter," Jorge began, "is that—"

"Mr. President," Peter said, holding up his hand as his gaze remained locked on Beverly, "how long have we known each other?"

Jorge paused as if Peter's question had thrown him off course. "Almost twenty years."

"And in twenty years, have I ever asked you to sit still and not say a word?"

"Well, no."

"Mr. President, I'm asking now. I need to sort some things out with Ms. Castle. If the conversation makes you uncomfortable, I apologize in advance, but I'd like you to remain silent. After the discussion is over, I'll tender my resignation if you feel that I've crossed the line or represented you poorly. For now, I respectfully ask that you let me speak."

The resulting silence stretched far longer than he would have liked, but Peter realized that he didn't care. History turned on the smallest of events. Things that seemed of little consequence at the time often ended up shaping the world. Case in point, Archduke Franz Ferdinand's driver took a wrong turn and World War I resulted.

Peter was certain that this was one such moment.

"Okay, Peter," the President said, "the floor is yours."

Peter nodded, took a moment to gather his thoughts,

and then turned to face the would-be destroyer of his destiny.

This would have to be done deftly. The President's apparent indulgence aside, Peter knew that, to pull their backsides from the fire, he would have to say things that could never be unsaid. Things that, in all likelihood, would permanently alter his relationship with the President. Peter was willing to shoulder this burden if it resulted in a second Gonzales administration. But that would happen only if he first crushed the head of the serpent that had slithered into their camp.

Taking a breath, Peter locked gazes with Beverly. As always, she looked lovely. Her blond hair fell to her shoulders in perfect waves and her slight makeup accentuated her angular features, making her blue eyes seem that much deeper.

Not for the first time, Peter wondered what had led this woman to a career in public service. Beverly was well-spoken and highly intelligent, and the cameras loved her. With that combination, she could have given Harris Faulkner a run for her money. Why settle for a civil servant's meager wages when there were millions of dollars per year to be made voicing the lone liberal viewpoint on Fox News?

Then, in a moment of clarity, Peter understood. As a talking head, Beverly would have been just another pretty face. Only life as a politician led to true power, and power was what she desired above all else. Accordingly, only the threat of losing that power stood a chance of putting her unbridled ambition in check.

"I'm going to cut through the bullshit," Peter said, "because I no longer have time to spar with you."

He'd deliberately chosen the vulgar word despite Jorge's tenet against profanity. If experience were any guide, this conversation would get worse before it got better, and the President needed to know what lay ahead.

"Please do," Beverly said, her lips curving into a faint smile. "Bullshit doesn't become you."

With a start, Peter realized that she thought that she'd won. That the news of the newly developed chemical weapon, paired with her captured operator, would force the administration down the foreign policy path for which she'd so strenuously advocated. That the President would have to topple the Assad government through military intervention.

Peter had spent many a sleepless night asking himself why Beverly constantly pushed the President toward such a risky confrontation. Today, he knew the answer—her pending resignation.

Beverly's position as CIA Director had been an olive branch. The appointment was more an attempt at reconciliation than recognition of her foreign policy chops, and Peter had treated her as such. Her presence during cabinet meetings had been minimized, and Peter had often relied on Charles to supply him with the Agency's official assessment on a particular issue.

This was Beverly's attempt to turn the tables, to force her way into the President's inner circle. This wasn't meant to ingratiate her with the President; her resignation date had already been set for the week after Jorge's inauguration. Neither was this about revenge—Beverly was too good for that. No, this ploy was all about setting the stage for her final act—ascendance to the Presidency.

"You think you have this figured out," Peter said, putting his thoughts into words, "but you're wrong."

"I'm sorry?" Beverly said.

"No, you're not. What you are is a self-centered, conniving snake."

"I won't be talked to in this manner."

"You will if you ever hope to set foot in this office again. I'm not as smart as you, Beverly. Few people are. But I've finally figured out what you've done. I might be too late to stop you, but I'll be damned if I stand by and do nothing."

"Are you insane?" Beverly said.

"My mistake was in thinking that you wanted us to succeed. That a second Gonzales term would be the best political platform for you to launch your own Presidential bid. But that isn't the case, is it?"

For once, Beverly was silent. Her full lips pressed into thin lines, and her eyes glittered like shards of glass.

"What do you mean?"

The question came from the President. Peter turned slightly to answer, never taking his eyes from Beverly as he spoke. This was the sort of moment when ambitions were exposed and empires rose or fell. Only a fool would turn his back on his opponent now.

"Syria, sir," Peter said, Beverly's twisted logic coming into focus as he spoke. "It's always been about Syria. By pushing you to topple Assad, she was hoping to cement her legacy. Think about it—if we're successful and stop the war, she's seen as prescient and bipartisan. The Joint Chiefs love her, she brings peace to Syria, and a few well-placed leaks to friends at the *Times* or the *Post* frame her as the one who advocated for a more robust U.S. intervention."

"And if we fail?" Jorge said.

"Even better. We know she's about to resign, but the rest of the country doesn't. Picture it—we invade Syria and quagmire ensues. A week later, the CIA Director resigns. Why? She doesn't say, but journalists still put two and two together and arrive at sixty-four. She must have resigned out of protest to our Syria plan. Maybe it even costs us the election, which means that the Price administration now has to fight a war in Syria that they didn't start. This leaves Beverly perfectly positioned to run as the voice of moderation in four years' time. In essence, Syria has become her magical coin—heads, she wins; tails, we lose. The CIA raid was no accident. In fact, I'd wager that her operations folks advised against it. Then again, she had nothing to lose, did she?"

Peter's words battered the President like physical blows. He leaned back in his chair, recoiling from the conversation. For a time, he sat in silence as if what Peter had said was simply too terrible to acknowledge.

But acknowledge it he did. Jorge Gonzales might be known for his sunny disposition and boundless optimism, but he was no fool. Twenty years in politics had given him an up-close-and-personal view of the best and the worst of what humanity had to offer. This wasn't his first betrayal, and it wouldn't be his last.

"Is this true?"

The President directed the question at Beverly. Peter thought he could hear the faintest trace of Jorge's Hispanic heritage beneath the words. His even-tempered friend was rarely upset, but when he became truly angry, he channeled the fiery-tongued Mexican women who'd raised him.

To her credit, Beverly didn't seem upset in the least. She didn't even have the grace to look embarrassed. Instead, she edged away from the conference table and crossed her impossibly long legs as if she were the one granting the President an audience.

"At this point, what difference does it make?" Beverly said. "Over the last four years, you've made it perfectly clear that you haven't been terribly interested in what I've had to say. Why should that change now?"

The President's brown features turned burgundy. "Beverly, I thought you were better than this. Truly. You're going to submit your resignation, and I'm going to make a few calls. By the time I'm done, no one in this town will admit to even knowing you. You might be able to run for city council, but your career in national politics is over."

Peter had seen the President like this only once before. When he reached this level of anger, he took the scorched-earth approach. Last time, Peter had needed the better part of three days to bring his friend in for a landing. The irony this time was that, while the President's anger was more than justified, Peter couldn't let Jorge go thermo-nuclear. As much as he hated to admit it, for the next four days, Peter needed Beverly.

"Mr. President," Peter said, jumping in before Beverly could answer, "I know that you're angry, but let's not be rash. Now that we've outlined our differences, I'm certain that Director Castle will be willing to adopt the administration's Syria policy."

Beverly's answering laugh echoed across the room. "What could possibly make you think that?" Beverly said, her lips curving into something between a smile and a sneer.

"This," Peter said. He opened the black leather folder in front of him, withdrew a single piece of paper, and slid it into Beverly's manicured fingers. The paper was a printout of an e-mail Charles had forwarded him just before the meeting with the Joint Chiefs.

True to his word, Charles had handled Beverly.

"What is it?" Beverly said, reflexively taking the document.

The question was delivered with a haughtiness befitting a queen, but Peter could detect a hint of unease. The thing about breaking the law was that you never knew when your actions might come back to bite you, or how big a chunk of your ass you'd lose when they did.

In Beverly's case, it was a sizable chunk indeed.

"Give it a read," Peter said, relishing the moment.

Beverly's gaze snapped from his face to the President's and back again. Then she dropped her eyes to the single-page document and began to read.

For his part, the President observed the unfolding drama in silence, and Peter exhaled a deep breath. He'd purposely not shown the document to the President beforehand, banking on the probability that he'd be able to trick Beverly into revealing her true colors, and his plan had worked.

Peter watched with rabid fascination as Beverly made her way through the e-mail, and he could tell the moment she arrived at the damning paragraph. She sucked in a breath, and her eyes widened. Then she reread the document as her shaking fingers absently smoothed an imaginary wrinkle from her skirt.

Peter had to give Beverly credit. A lesser politician would have needed the document's significance laid out in painstaking detail, but she had grasped its importance at once. It was a pity the woman couldn't see past her own damnable ambition. She could have been a tremendous asset. Now she was just another liability.

"Do I have your attention?" Peter said.

Though he didn't possess the President's interpersonal skills, Peter understood with every fiber of his being the art of political maneuvering. Early in his career, he'd learned the value of extending grace to a vanquished opponent. Judging by her reaction, Beverly was now vanquished.

The Director of the Central Intelligence Agency swallowed twice and then nodded, apparently not trusting her voice to reply.

"Good," Peter said, "because this is what we're going to do."

TWELVE

So, that's it," Frodo said, his digitally encrypted image staring back at me from the secure VTC mounted on the bulkhead. The Gulfstream's conference room was small but well-appointed. I could get used to traveling on private jets. Sitting back in the leather chair, I tried to process what he'd told me in light of everything that had happened in the last hour.

After hanging up with Frodo, I'd floored the rental the entire way to Andrews Air Force Base. The normally twenty-five-minute trip had taken less than fifteen, and my rush didn't stop at the air base's gate. The airman standing guard had hopped into my car's passenger seat and guided me onto the flight line toward an already idling jet. I'd left my keys with the airman, bounded up the stairs, and dropped onto an overstuffed couch. By the time I'd fastened my seat belt, we were already airborne, the Gulfstream's nose turning east as we shot out over the Atlantic at just under the speed of sound.

We'd still been rocketing toward our cruising altitude when the plainclothes flight attendant had directed me to the aft conference room and secured the walnut-veneer door behind me. Apparently, whatever Frodo had to say was for my ears only.

After hearing the first two sentences, I understood why. Terrorists in possession of a new chemical weapon had been bad enough, but Frodo's update took bad to a whole new level.

"So we're sure the paramilitary officer is still alive?" I said, wishing that the fifteen thousand pounds of thrust generated by the two Rolls-Royce engines could propel me across the ocean even faster. Somewhere, a clock was ticking, and a man's life hung in the balance.

Frodo shook his head. "We're not sure of anything. The Agency team leader swears that Shaw's dead. He checked for a pulse before small-arms fire forced him away from the body. Then again, what would you expect him to say?"

I didn't answer. The scenario was almost too horrible to consider, a nightmare that haunted every member of the special operations community.

The CIA paramilitary team had been ambushed while exiting the execution chamber, and four operators had been killed in the chaos. The remaining team members had recovered three of the bodies, but the fourth, John Shaw's, had been too far inside the kill zone. With mortar rounds detonating all around Shaw, and the Black

Hawk helicopter set to extract them already drawing fire, the team leader had made the heartbreaking decision to leave the fourth operator where he'd fallen. John Shaw was dead. End of story.

Except he wasn't, or at least that was what Einstein claimed. Shaw had been wounded by an exploding mortar. He was severely concussed but still alive.

But not for much longer.

"Any confirmation on Einstein's reporting?" I said.

Frodo shook his head. "Not directly. Video has popped up of the jihadis torturing Shaw, and his ear was given to a Syrian asset, but nothing links Shaw's captors to the terrorists building the chem weapon. Nothing but Einstein."

"You believe him?" I said.

Frodo shrugged. "The jihadi websites are sparking like a live wire, and Internet chatter is off the charts. Something about a big event timed to happen just before the polls open on Tuesday."

"Which somewhat corroborates Einstein's reporting that the terrorists intend to livestream Shaw's execution."

"Correct," Frodo said.

"So, what now?" I said.

"The President's Syria directive still stands. The CIA has theater control over all operations, including any rescue attempts."

"Your old contemporaries must be going batshit."

Frodo nodded. "There's a JSOC theater quick reaction force already established in-country. Notionally, the operators fall under Agency control, but you know as well as I do, JSOC doesn't like to share. In any case, Einstein is our sole piece of intelligence on both the chem weapon and Shaw. So far, he's sticking to his guns. He works with you or no one."

"I really don't like that son of a bitch," I said, thinking about my one and only meeting with the arrogant weapons scientist. "We should have taken him out when we had the chance, DIA Director be damned."

"I hear you, but it is what it is. Why do you think he's holding out for you?"

I'd been asking myself the same question and had yet to arrive at a satisfactory answer. In some ways, Einstein's refusal to work with another handler made sense. He knew me, and in times of trouble, it was human nature to reach toward the familiar. But at the same time, a drowning man will grasp at anything to stay afloat, and this made me wonder whether Einstein was in fact drowning.

"I don't like it, Matty," Frodo said, when I didn't answer. "This whole thing is too convenient by half. What are the odds that our scientist experiences a change of heart just when we need him the most? Not only that, but he's poised to give us exactly what we want—knowledge of the weapons program and Shaw's location. Doesn't seem very likely."

"True, but he's still got us by the balls. If Shaw's still alive, we have to bring him home."

"I agree, but this time, I'm not watching your back. Einstein is a low-life shit bag who sells death to the highest bidder. You might be on the side of the angels, but if he smells a better deal selling you to the jihadis, he'll do it."

"Yep," I said, "so we need to up the stakes."

"How?"

"By making it personal. Here's what I'm thinking."

As usual, it didn't take Frodo long to see where I was headed. Within three or four sentences, he'd grasped my plan. Within five, he was making suggestions. After he signed off ten minutes later, I knew that, while my best friend wasn't heading to Syria with me, he'd still be doing his damnedest to watch my back, even from six thousand miles away. But as I lay back in the recliner and tried to sleep, I couldn't help but wonder whether that would be enough.

During our last op, Frodo had been sitting less than a foot away, and our collective luck had still run out.

That was the day the tremors had begun. I'd been sweating my balls off in the passenger seat of a Range Rover, navigating as Frodo drove. As usual, Frodo realized something was out of sorts before I did.

"You okay?" Frodo said, swinging the SUV left around a slower-moving moped. He clipped the bike's rear tire as we roared past, sending the moped wobbling toward the sidewalk. The driver shook his fist, but Frodo didn't even acknowledge him. In Syria, rubbing was racing.

"What do you mean?" I said, glancing from the map spread across my lap to a device about the size of a deck of cards in the Range Rover's cup holder. A quarter-sized LED, set in the center of the device's hardened plastic shell, pulsed with accusing crimson flashes.

"Your hand's shaking."

"Probably just a spasm," I said, opening and closing my fist as I traced our route across the laminated map with a gloved finger. "We're gonna cross a hardball in about eight hundred meters. After that, turn left at the next major intersection. Eight minutes."

"Roger," Frodo said, now edging to the right around a rusted pickup truck belching noxious smoke.

The Range Rover's knobby tires crested a section of crumbling concrete that passed for a curb before Frodo guided the wheel left, bringing our vehicle back onto the street seconds before he would have clipped a series of roadside stands.

After six months in-country, Frodo drove like a native. Actually, he drove *better* than a native. Unlike the rest of the vehicles in the safe house's extensive motor pool, Frodo's Range Rover didn't have crushed fenders or scraped side panels.

We made a hell of a team—Frodo drove, I navigated, and together, we ran and recruited a string of Syrian agents who provided information on the ongoing civil war. But this time I was terrified that not even Frodo's inspired driving would be enough. The LED had been blinking for the better part of forty minutes, and that was thirty minutes too long.

Like the device itself, the purpose behind the uninspiring hunk of plastic was simple. When I'd first recruited Fazil, he'd been conflicted. Like most Syrians, he'd been horrified by the civil war's endless violence. From the west, Assad and his henchmen were annihilating whole towns under the guise of keeping the peace. From the east, hordes of foreign fighters flying the black ISIS flag were imposing their own interpretation of sharia law and executing all who disagreed with their apocalypse-tinged theology.

Fazil lived in Aleppo, the geopolitical crossroads between the two armies. He'd been only too happy to provide intelligence on ISIS activities, but as much as he wanted to help bring an end to the catastrophic violence, he also worried about his wife and toddler. I sympathized and offered to relocate his family, but his wife had refused. She was determined to remain with her husband.

So we'd compromised. Though a good thirty minutes away from our safe house by vehicle, Fazil's apartment was less than a ten-minute flight. Like that of many Middle Eastern residences, the building's roof was used as a communal gathering place after the blazing sun gave way to the coolness of night. Frodo and I had each conducted an assessment of the roof's structural integrity and arrived at the same conclusion—the flat space was perfect for an ad hoc helicopter landing zone.

With this in mind, I'd presented Fazil with the solution to his problem in the form of a satellite beacon concealed within a coffeepot. If my asset ever feared for his life or family, he need only press a recessed button on the pot and hide in the reinforced safe room we'd constructed out of his toddler's bedroom.

While Fazil and his family stayed safely barricaded away from the threat, his activated beacon would send a coded signal streaking to the sky. There, a geosynchronous satellite would amplify the signal before transmitting it back to earth. When the stream of ones and zeros reached my receiver, the device's onboard microcontroller would activate the LED, telling me that my asset was in trouble.

Simple.

Except when it wasn't.

I'd given Fazil the beacon while sitting in his kitchen drinking chai. His wife had been moving around the kitchen, preparing a snack while holding his precious little girl, Abir, in her arms. The toddler had played peek-aboo with me over her mother's shoulder, flashing me gummy grins just before ducking out of sight.

After handing Fazil the modified coffeepot, I'd given him my word that if he ever had reason to activate the device, I'd be on his roof with the cavalry in ten minutes. But now, when he needed me most, I wasn't living up to my end of the bargain. The ten-minute mark had come and gone, leaving me with an unshakable sense of dread.

"How long you had those tremors?" Frodo asked, accelerating again. The road widened, and Frodo seemed determined to take advantage of the straightaway. In Syria, speed was one of the many weapons we employed against insurgent ambushes, and our vehicles were appropriately modified. But sometimes, even the raw power of the V-8 engine growling beneath the Range Rover's hood wasn't enough to flee the ever-present threat of death. Especially when the desert winds themselves carried microscopic killers.

"I don't know," I said as the spasm progressed from my fist to my forearm. "Never noticed it before. Turn left in four hundred meters. We'll be at Fazil's place in five."

"It's not your fault," Frodo said, taking his eyes from the road and looking at me.

"The hell it isn't," I said. "I gave him my word we'd come. My word."

"You can't predict Assad launching a chemical attack."

"We're in the intelligence business, Frodo. Predicting chemical attacks is what we do."

My eyes tracked the road as my hands found the M4 rifle wedged between my seat and the passenger door. At this point, I wasn't sure who I wanted to shoot first. Assad had struck the civilian population of Aleppo with yet another weapon of mass destruction, but it was Charles Sinclair Robinson IV, the CIA Chief of Base and senior ranking person at the safe house, who I wanted to kill.

Charles had refused to authorize the launch of the two Agency helicopters in response to Fazil's beacon. He'd justified his decision by saying that he didn't want the men flying into a contaminated zone, but I had a feeling his motivation stemmed more from a healthy sense of self-preservation than from concern for the Agency hitters and pilots.

One of the CIA's more harebrained intelligence assessments was that Assad might use chemical weapons in conjunction with a lightning conventional offensive to take Aleppo before the fanatical ISIS jihadis could beat him to the punch. Since our little safe house sat squarely in Assad's projected path, I thought that old Charles wanted to keep the Agency shooters and helicopters close in case his fight-or-flight scenario became a reality.

Hell, Charles might even be right, but at this point, right or wrong didn't matter. What mattered was that I'd promised a man that if he called, I'd come within ten minutes, and I hadn't.

Desperate to focus on anything but the monstrous clock ticking in my head, I stared at a passing grove of trees as the wind gathered the litter lining the side of the road into a trash-filled dust devil. The cyclonic action formed a natural street cleaner, sending the scraps of paper fluttering into the underbrush.

Thirty minutes ago, air currents had carried unspeakable death into countless homes nestled along Aleppo's once peaceful thoroughfares. Maybe even into my asset's home. Now the same breezes cleared refuse from the city's dirty streets.

Wind was a fickle thing.

Just past the grove, on Frodo's side of the truck, a single piece of paper flapped in the errant breeze, fluttering where dirt met the concrete road. But this bit of paper didn't take to the air like the rest of the trash. Instead, it danced on the sidewalk, gyrating in time with the breeze, as if staked to the ground.

"IED!" I screamed. My distracted brain had finally made the connection between the gusting wind and the stationary paper. It was the aiming point for a concealed IED, and this was the moment of truth. Frodo could do one of two things: slam on the brakes, or stomp on the gas. Either choice could be right, and either choice could be wrong. In that split second, the sum of my existence rested on a fifty-fifty chance. Gas or brakes. Heads or tails. Live or die.

Wind was a fickle thing.

Frodo stomped on the gas. The Range Rover surged forward.

Tails.

A blast of heat, blinding light, and a breeze tickling my cheek. Then silence. Pure and absolute silence as my overloaded senses struggled to recalibrate. It was like the violence of the explosion had short-circuited my nervous system. For that blessed amount of time, which seemed like minutes but was only a fraction of a second, I floated outside myself.

Then the world crashed back into place.

I could smell melting plastic, burning fabric, and the tang of superheated steel. And flesh. The unmistakable scent of charred flesh.

I shook my head, trying to clear the afterimages. The cabin seemed much too bright. Then I realized why. The formerly sealed Range Rover was now open to the afternoon sun. The IED had punched a hole straight through the up-armored doors like they'd been made of balsa wood.

I looked left, reaching for Frodo, only to find that the steering wheel was missing, along with a good section of

Frodo's left arm. He liked to drive with one hand on the wheel and one hand on the gearshift. Now his driving arm ended in a blackened stump.

Frodo sat unspeaking, slowly moving his ruined arm back and forth as if his eyes were playing tricks on him. He hadn't started to scream. Not yet. Like mine, his nervous system had been overwhelmed by the tsunami of stimuli, but that neural logjam would clear at any second. Once his brain started taking calls, he'd descend into life-threatening shock in minutes.

Assuming, of course, he lived through the pending violence of the next few seconds.

In the almost decade and a half since the U.S. had embarked on our ill-fated foray into Iraq, several generations of IED bombers had come of age. Technology and tactics had matured far beyond simple command-detonated IEDs. Today's roadside bombs were used to trigger complex ambushes much like my predecessors had used claymore mines to initiate attacks against the Vietcong in the jungles of Vietnam. If these jihadis followed form, the ambush would begin in earnest at any moment.

If it hadn't begun already.

The ringing in my ears eased enough that I could hear what sounded like rain falling on a tin roof. But rain didn't fall from a cloudless sky. The metal-on-metal pinging came from a more sinister source: high-velocity rounds flattening themselves against what remained of the Range Rover's ballistic armor.

Thumbing loose my seat belt, I reached for the vehicle's center console and slapped an innocuous-looking aftermarket button centered next to the hazard light button. A series of pneumatic *thump*s echoed through the cabin as dispensers hidden in the Range Rover's front and rear bumpers lofted smoke canisters into the air.

On the positive side of the ledger, it was hard to hit what you couldn't see. The dense white smoke pouring from the ruptured smoke canisters was specifically modified to defeat even thermal sights.

On the negative, the smoke's presence let our attackers know that we'd survived the initial IED blast. Playing possum was no longer an option. As the smoke settled around us in a noxious gray cloud, the pitter-patter of bullets turned into a full-fledged hailstorm.

"My fucking arm," Frodo said through gritted teeth, fumbling with his seat belt.

"Come on, buddy," I said, releasing his seat belt buckle and grabbing his shirt. "We've gotta find you another ride."

Opening the passenger door, I pushed myself out, butt first, pulling Frodo on top of me as I fell. His stump banged against my chest as we bounced off the pavement, and though he kept from crying out, his black skin turned an alarming shade of gray.

"Stay in the fight," I said, leaning him against the front tire. "Tourniquet your arm."

I could apply the bandage for Frodo, but a good part of combating the devastating effects of shock was mental. The treatment included giving the victim something to focus on, usually by asking a series of questions.

Unfortunately, we didn't have time for a fireside chat, so I gave Frodo a task instead while I retrieved my M4. Peering around the front bumper, I scanned the grove of trees through my red-dot-equipped EOTech sight.

Things were not good. In between shifting clouds of smoke, I counted at least six muzzle flashes. Five had the flashbulb-like signature of small arms, but the sixth was a doozy. The cantaloupe-sized ball of fire had to have come from a crew-served weapon.

Smoke screen or not, a whole bunch of lead was headed in our direction.

As if to emphasize the point, a round pinged off the bumper, peppering my cheek with metal fragments. "How's the tourniquet coming?" I said, jerking back to the meager protection offered by the wheel well.

"Fine."

I looked over my shoulder to check. The tourniquet was on, stopping the spurting arterial blood, and Frodo had given himself a morphine shot. Good. But he was also starting to slur his words.

Not so good.

"Still with me?" I said.

"Who the fuck you talking to? I'm a goddamn Airborne Ranger. Point me in the right direction, and I'll put some motherfucking lead into somebody's head."

Except with one arm, Frodo wasn't going to be leading a bayonet charge anytime soon. I risked a glance over the bumper only to get chased back by a fusillade of bullets.

Sliding onto my belly, I looked under the Range Rover's

undercarriage, panning the EOTech's red dot until I saw several pairs of feet. Easing the M4's selector switch from safe to single shot with my thumb, I centered the crimson dot on the closest pair and squeezed the trigger. The M4 barked, impossibly loud in the close confines, and the feet exploded into a cloud of red mist. The jihadi trying to flank us fell to the ground, and I put two more rounds into his prone form.

No quarter, no surrender. Welcome to big-boy rules, motherfucker.

"Matty, if we're going to do something, we need to do it soon. My arm hurts like a bastard."

"Hang in there, brother," I said, firing another pair of aimed shots at a set of retreating ankles before I joined Frodo behind the wheel well again. "The shit's about to get real."

My suppressive fire sent the jihadis attempting to rush us scampering for cover, but I knew our victory would be short-lived. Once the ambushers got their act together, they'd kill us both without breaking a sweat. All they needed to do was swing their crew-served weapon about thirty meters to their right, pinning us in a classic L-shaped ambush. When that happened, our life expectancy would be measured in heartbeats.

"How we looking, Matty?"

"About how you'd expect."

"That bad?"

Instead of answering, I thumbed the transmit button on the MBITR radio strapped to my chest. "Wolfhound Main, this is Lonestar. Over."

The MBITR was a nifty radio: compact, lightweight, encrypted, and with no analog parts. This meant that, like with most products of the digital age, its performance was binary. It either worked like a champ or had the functionality of driftwood. Normally, the radio chirped when I pressed the transmit button, signifying that its onboard encryption fills were still active. But when I'd just tried to transmit, I'd heard nothing but static. Today was looking like a driftwood kind of day.

I fumbled with my throat mike, checked my Bluetooth-enabled earbuds, and pressed the transmit button again.

"Wolfhound Main, this is Lonestar. Over."

I'd last used the radio minutes before to call in a checkpoint, but now the fifteen-thousand-dollar device might as well have been an Easy-Bake Oven. Awesome.

"Frodo, try your radio."

"Wolfhound Main, this is Lonestar. Over. Wolfhound Main, Lonestar, over. Nothing, Matty."

Fuck me running. That both of our radios had failed at exactly the same time was ominous, but addressing it was not at the top of my priority list. No, that distinct honor belonged to the pair of jihadis moving the crew-served weapon to the other side of the grove.

Shit fire.

Rounds pinged against the Range Rover and the road, sending stone shards into the air.

Frodo and I were in trouble. We couldn't call for air support and couldn't move without getting shot. If we stayed put, the shitheads with the crew-served weapon would stitch us full of 7.62mm slugs from crotch to cranium. Not good at all. Looking over my shoulder, I eyed the series of concrete-and-stucco houses about fifty meters away.

Frodo and I had both spent time in the Ranger Regiment, which meant we were joint heirs to something called the Mogadishu Mile. In 1993, a squad of Rangers had run a mile through Somalia's unforgiving streets during a gunfight after their brothers-in-arms had accidentally left them behind. If Frodo and I somehow survived this shit show, maybe someday someone would christen this the Syrian Sprint.

"Check it out, stud," I said, lightly slapping Frodo on the cheek to get his attention. "We're getting the fuck out of here over to those houses at our six o'clock. I'm going to carry you, and you're going to cover us. Got it?"

"Love to, Matty," Frodo said, the spacing between his words growing as shock and blood loss took their toll. "Where's my weapon?"

"One second," I said before diving back into the Range Rover's cab.

This time the hail-on-a-tin-roof sound of bullets smacking into the Range Rover was accompanied by the angry-fucking-hornet sound of rounds breaking the sound barrier inches from my head. The smoke was starting to clear and the jihadis' aim was improving.

I reached for the electronic display in the middle of the Range Rover's console, pried it loose, and slid out of the car just as a line of fire opened across my shoulder.

"Shit," I said, clattering to the ground next to Frodo. "You hit?"

"Just a graze," I said, eyeing the red patches blossoming through my shirt. "Ready for some payback?"

"You know it."

"All right, here goes nothing."

This was what was referred to as the *moment of truth* in those literary novels my high school writing teacher loved. But since I'm a simple man with simple tastes, I liked to think of it as the *we're about to find out if we live or die* moment. Seems less pretentious that way. In any case, I thumbed the power button to the iPhone-sized electronic display and prayed that the team of contractors who'd retrofitted our low-visibility vehicles had done their jobs. The technicians had assured us that their new system would function without vehicle battery power in the wake of a traumatic event.

Come to think of it, they'd never really defined the whole *traumatic event* part, but if getting T-boned by an explosively formed penetrator didn't qualify, I'm not sure what did.

As the first bit of good news in the last ten minutes, the screen glowed to life. A second later, I heard the whine of activating hydraulics. So far, so good.

"Here," I said, handing the device to Frodo. "You should be able to do this one-handed."

"The screen's glowing red, Matty."

One look at the Range Rover told me why. The device had elevated out of the rear of the vehicle as promised, but the turret seemed to be damaged. One of the struts was bent, preventing the device from articulating.

Fucking defense contractors.

"Looks like you've got a fixed gun," I said. "Come to think of it, that might actually be better. You've only got one hand, but we both know you couldn't shoot for shit even when you had two arms."

"Fuck you."

"Language, please," I said, cinching the M4 across my chest. After making sure the rifle was securely fastened, I reached down, grabbed Frodo, and hoisted him into a fireman's carry.

"All right," I said, trying to ignore my throbbing shoulder, "drop the hammer."

Frodo grunted, and for a heartbeat, there was nothing. Then, with a sound like the world's biggest chain saw belching, the minigun on the roof roared to life.

If you've never seen a Dillon Aero six-barrel minigun let loose a torrent of bullets at a rate of six thousand per minute, then you, my friend, have not really lived. To be fair, since I was on the nonbusiness side of the remote-controlled weapon, I wasn't in the best position to observe its performance.

But the jihadis were.

One moment, incoming rounds were pinging off the Range Rover like a Texas hailstorm. The next, enemy fire ceased as the minigun sent a torrent of tracers hurtling toward our ambushers in a rippling crimson stream.

Unfortunately, I wasn't able to properly appreciate the shock and awe Frodo was laying down, since I was too busy lumbering toward the concrete walls in front of us with the elegance of a drunken hippopotamus. In any case, our respite was temporary. Say what you want about the jihadis, but they hadn't survived three years of constant civil war by being stupid. It didn't take them long to figure out that the minigun, for all its glory, couldn't traverse. So while it made a lot of noise and spewed bullets like a fire hose, as long as you weren't standing directly in front of it, you were relatively safe.

I'd covered half the distance to the stucco wall when miniature dust devils began springing to life at either side of me. At least one jihadi seemed to be ignoring the minigun's fireworks display in favor of taking potshots at the two guys running for their lives.

I'd halved the distance again to less than twelve meters when a burst of automatic weapons fire slapped the wall in front of me, cratering the stucco in a half dozen places.

I shifted course to the right, attempting to put the Range Rover's hulk between the jihadi riflemen and me. My efforts were in vain. At five meters from safety, the bullet I'd been dreading found its way home. One moment I was running, and the next, I was falling forward as a single round tore through my left leg.

The pain was brilliant—white-hot, like the time I'd grabbed ahold of the cow pasture's electric fence as a child. Except this time, there was no one to rescue me from my stupidity. I went down hard, turning my head at the last moment. I didn't break my nose, but I still impacted the grime-crusted street with the dull *thud* of a bag of Quikrete tossed from a pickup truck's bed. Frodo's shoulder made a popping sound as he bounced off the ground. The remote firing device flew from his hands, skidding across the concrete, where it came to rest against the pockmarked wall. Five meters from safety, but it might as well have been five hundred.

We were done.

I pressed my body into a push-up position, then flopped onto my back. Then I pushed against the ground with my good leg until my shoulders bumped into Frodo. Forcing myself into a seated position, I rested my back against his prone form while trying to ignore the waves of agony coming from my leg. If I didn't apply a pressure bandage soon, I'd pass out from blood loss, but that wasn't the priority at the moment. With the minigun silent, the smoke gone, and my left leg no longer functional, living long enough to bleed out was nothing but pure fantasy.

Frodo was strangely quiet, either knocked unconscious or having finally succumbed to shock, but I was still conscious. That meant I had a legacy to uphold. Rangers subscribed to a certain philosophy when it came to dying. Namely, that you faced death with your rifle in your hands, and when your rifle ran dry, you drew your pistol. And then you unsheathed your knife. So, since my M4 still had a full magazine, I was a long way from quitting.

"Matty?"

Frodo's question sounded more like a croak than an intelligible word, but I knew what he was asking. He wanted to know where I was. When it came down to it, no one wanted to pass from this life to the next alone.

"Here, brother," I said, sliding closer as I unslung my

M4. I wedged my back against Frodo's chest, making a T of our bodies. Pulling the rifle into my shoulder, I switched from the EOTech reflex sight to the Trijicon 4x32 optic meant for distance shooting. I panned across the grove, looking for one more target before the inevitable burst of machine-gun fire tore into us.

Faces swam into view, but rather than taking a shot at the first jihadi, I waited until my scope seemed to stop of its own accord. A man with intelligent eyes, a luxurious beard, and graying temples stared back at me. As I watched, he lifted a Motorola radio to his mouth and spoke. Then he traded the radio for a cell phone.

Perfect—a battlefield commander. If I was going down, he was going with me. Evening my breathing, I used the scope's etched markings to estimate distance. Two hundred meters. Usually a walk in the park with an optic like this, but I was shooting from a less-than-stable platform while injured.

Still, as the SEALs liked to say, the only easy day was yesterday.

Centering the man's head in the crosshairs, I took a breath, released it, and squeezed the trigger. The shot broke just as an errant breeze slapped against my cheek.

Wind is a fickle thing.

The man's head snapped back, but didn't disintegrate into a cloud of red mist. Instead, a furrow opened on his cheek from jaw to ear. Dropping the cell phone, the man pressed his hand to his face, blood streaming through his fingers. But rather than duck, he stared in my direction as if he could see my face. And then he did the damnedest thing. Instead of ordering his men to finish us off, or grabbing a rifle, he issued orders with the jerky hand motions of a man who was accustomed to obedience. In response, the jihadis picked up their weapons and melted back into the grove, leaving Frodo and me to die in peace.

Mr. Drake? Sir?"

In an instant, I was transported from the blood and dust of Syria to the Gulfstream's climate-controlled cabin. I lurched upright, my brow slick with sweat. My breathing was as labored as it had been on that day when I'd watched the jihadis mysteriously withdraw minutes before two Black Hawk Direct Action Penetrator gunships graced the horizon. Turned out, the rescue birds had been summoned by our Range Rover's emergency locator beacon. The IED blast had automatically triggered the device, ensuring that our GPS location and status had been transmitted to Wolfhound Main.

Maybe defense contractors weren't so bad after all.

"Are you all right?"

"Fine," I said to the flight attendant standing in the open doorway behind me. "I'm fine."

The flight attendant looked at me for a long moment, his eyes traveling across my battered face. "Okay, then," he said. "We should be landing in Turkey in about six hours. Need anything?"

"Do you have a guitar?"

"A guitar?"

"Yep. Acoustic would be great, but I'll take an electric if that's all you've got."

"My apologies, sir, but we do not have a guitar. Something else, perhaps?"

"Sure. How about a bowl of M&M's? But no brown ones."

"Sir?"

"Not a Van Halen fan, I take it. Never mind. I'm just gonna grab some shut-eye. Wake me an hour out."

"Yes, sir," the attendant said, looking immensely relieved to be leaving the crazy man secluded at the rear of the plane. "Pleasant dreams."

I didn't bother to reply. The Ambien in my pocket guaranteed that I'd sleep, but if recent events were any guide, pleasant dreams were a thing of the past.

THIRTEEN

'm going to start by reiterating that everything said in this room is classified at the Zulu level," Peter said. "Any questions?"

Peter let his gaze travel from face to face as he spoke, making eye contact with each member of the President's inner circle. As he'd intended, announcing a Zulu classification had a sobering effect. The Joint Chiefs gave universal looks of distaste, while the civilian principals showed their nervousness through furtive glances at their counterparts.

New to this administration, a Zulu-level classification had been one of Peter's more successful attempts to stop the multiple leaks that had plagued President Gonzales's first two years. More stringent than even code-word-level classifications, Zulu meant that the revelation of any information was considered treason and thereby punishable by execution.

The penalty had not yet been implemented, thankfully, but the career politicians that inhabited these halls had received the message loud and clear. The occasional call to a reporter might be accepted as part of doing business, but leaking classified material would not be tolerated. Within a week of Zulu's implementation, the damaging leaks had ceased. This aside, Peter had no doubt that Zulu's perceived deterrence was about to be put to the test.

Only after each person sitting at the oval conference table, with the exception of the President, verbally affirmed his or her understanding of the Zulu-level classification did Peter begin to speak.

"Very well. I apologize for the ominous beginning, but as Director Castle alluded to earlier, what we have to discuss could be the gravest threat our nation has faced since the Cuban Missile Crisis."

Peter paused, allowing the weight of his words to register. As agreed, Beverly, seated to his left, reinforced his words with a somber nod of her own. Peter was about to set in motion one of the most elaborate deceptions ever perpetrated. For his lies to have any chance of passing the combined intellect of the men and women surrounding him, he needed Beverly on board, lock, stock, and barrel. Fortunately, thanks to the single page of tightly spaced text he'd passed to her thirty minutes prior, she belonged to him, mind, heart, and soul.

Assuming, of course, that Beverly Castle had a soul.

"As I said before," Peter said, "Director Castle has been pursuing a highly sensitive operation on the President's behalf. Unfortunately, that operation, code-named

Even Flow, was only partially successful. Director Castle, please continue your summary."

The hair on the back of Peter's neck stood up as he surrendered the meeting to Beverly, but he knew that the men and women assembled at this table needed to hear the next lie directly from Beverly's lips. Things had already gone awry with Beverly's ill-timed reveal only moments before. To ensure that the President's inner circle embraced this next deception as truth, Beverly needed to be the one spinning the tale, not Peter.

Besides, with every false word that left her lips, Beverly was binding herself ever tighter to the President. If the worst came to fruition, and Peter's desperate plan exploded in their faces, the career politicians in this room would remember that it had been Beverly, and not President Gonzales or Peter, who had voiced the most damning aspects.

"Ladies and gentlemen," Beverly said, her words clipped and even, "as you now know, a CIA paramilitary team operating in Syria raided a suspected chemical weapons laboratory. Over the course of the operation, casualties were sustained, and now it appears that one team member who was presumed dead is still alive and has been captured. What I did not tell you is that this suspected laboratory sits within Assad-controlled territory."

Once again, the television affixed to the wall behind Beverly flickered to life. This time, the screen revealed a map of Syria with the shifting boundaries denoting territory claimed by the Assad government, ISIS, and various rebel factions. The lines, while drawn in different colors, more resembled an abstract painting than any coherent military map.

This, in essence, was the problem with Syria. The country was a mishmash of violent elements, all hell-bent on destruction. The only thing predictable about the war-torn territory was its unpredictability. Today's friend was tomorrow's enemy, and the town controlled by Assad loyalists yesterday could morph into a haven for former ISIS members over the span of a single night.

It was to this chaotic maelstrom that Beverly wanted to commit America's sons and daughters. Her wanton disregard for the butcher's bill that would undoubtedly accompany any overt U.S. military action still astounded Peter. Peter wasn't an idealistic pacifist. He understood that there were causes worth dying for, but he also knew that Syria wasn't one of them.

"Excuse me, Madam Director, but are you saying that the splinter cell was under the Assad regime's protection?"

The question came from the Chairman of the Joint Chiefs, General Etzel, and Peter made a mental note to keep an eye on the man. Smart military leaders were all well and good, but the brilliant and charismatic ones tended to cause problems for their political masters. President Truman's tumultuous relationship with General MacArthur was a perfect case in point.

"I'm afraid that's exactly what I'm saying, General," Beverly said. "We've suspected that Assad has been extending his patronage to different elements within ISIS for quite some time. This, unfortunately, is the first direct evidence we've seen linking the two organizations."

"What does this mean for that captured operator?" Etzel said.

Peter scratched the man's name on his legal pad. President Gonzales could ill afford an insubordinate general. Etzel might have to be dealt with sooner rather than later.

"As strange as it seems," Beverly said, "we believe this is actually a fortuitous development."

"Come again?"

"While the video we received leaves no doubt as to who is holding our captured operator," Beverly said, directing her response now to the second questioner, Jeremy Thompson, "we think that applying pressure to the Assad regime will allow us to secure our man's release and repatriation."

"So we won't be mounting a rescue?" General Etzel said.

"Nothing could be further from the truth," Peter said.

As much as he enjoyed watching Beverly draw the brunt of the group's criticism, now was the time to provide a united front. The group of advisers had to believe that this was the President's intent, even as Peter kept Jorge's direct statements to a minimum to ensure plausible deniability. That meant that, because Peter was the President's senior adviser, it was his turn to step into the breach.

"We will spare no effort to bring our serviceman home," Peter said, his words tasting like vinegar. "As Director Castle mentioned, we are even now negotiating with the Assad regime to apply pressure to the splinter cell holding our operator."

"Surely that can't be the sum of our plan? Negotiations with a homicidal dictator?"

Etzel again. Peter had assumed, perhaps naively, that once he had Beverly under control, the meeting with the principals would be smooth sailing. Now Peter was beginning to wonder if his shortsightedness would cost them. Maybe he should have brought another principal on board first. Weren't military officers supposed to follow orders? What was going on?

"Of course not," Peter said, meeting Etzel's attack head-on. "If you'd allow me to finish, I was going to say that—"

"I think it's time for me to weigh in."

The voice, while tired, carried an unmistakable tone of command. President Jorge Gonzales had spoken. And though this hadn't been part of the plan, attempting to talk over the President would have been suicidal. What Peter was proposing would be confrontational enough. But if the principals deemed the course of action contrary to the President's wishes, his plan would be dead on arrival.

"While I appreciate what Beverly and Peter are trying to do," the President said, looking at his advisers one by one as he spoke, "ultimately this decision is mine, and you should hear it from me. Of course we aren't relying solely on the Assad regime to free our captured warrior, but I'm not prepared to start a shooting war with another Middle Eastern dictatorship. Not to mention the possibility that our forces might come into direct confrontation with the Russians, who are even now flying combat sorties in support of Assad's ongoing offensive."

"Then how are we responding, Mr. President?" Etzel said.

"We will continue to work through our intermediaries. We will explain to the Assad regime that we know that this ISIS splinter cell is operating in territory under their protection. If our operator dies, we will hold Assad personally responsible."

"Begging your pardon, sir, but what if that isn't enough?" Etzel said.

"I fully expect that it won't be," the President said, his voice heavy. "This is why I've authorized Director Castle to begin setting the conditions for a rescue attempt."

"Sir, wouldn't that be better suited to fall within the purview of the Joint Chiefs? Even if the raid is conducted by one of Director Castle's paramilitary teams instead of a JSOC tier-one unit, we will need a substantial strike package standing by. At a minimum, the carrier battle group operating out of the Mediterranean should be retasked. I would think we'd also want—"

"General Etzel, you misunderstand me," the President said, holding up his hand. "We cannot risk an overt engagement. Putin has invested considerable capital, both political and military, in Syria. He will want to reassure Assad that Russia will defend the sovereignty of the Assad regime. Any escalation on our part, perceived or otherwise, will result in Russia doing the same. But let me be clear. I will honor my solemn oath to bring each and every service member home. With this in mind, Director Castle has been charged with positioning a small, agile package of experienced Syrian operators within striking distance of our captured CIA officer's suspected location. The moment we have actionable intelligence, we will move heaven and earth to bring our man home. Until then, we need to negotiate in good faith with the Assad regime while giving Beverly and the rest of the intelligence community space to work."

"So Director Castle is taking lead on this?"

Jeremy Thompson again. This time, the DNI didn't seem altogether put out by the apparent usurpation of his authority. Probably because, unlike the military members seated around the table, Jeremy was a political animal at heart. While his stock in the administration might currently be falling, there would be other administrations. Especially if this rescue operation turned into another Operation Eagle Claw—the ill-fated attempt by President Jimmy Carter to rescue the American hostages held by radical Iranians forty years previous. When and if that happened, DNI Thompson would be able to stand before Congress with his most sorrowful expression and explain how he had opposed this operation from the start.

Plausible deniability at its finest.

In some ways, Peter envied the man. Much like Beverly in her going-in position, Thompson was now poised to succeed regardless of the outcome. Success, and he could take the credit after wallowing in a bit of false modesty; failure, and he'd have the Joint Chiefs to vouch for his side of the story.

Politics was definitely not for the faint of heart.

"Yes, Beverly has the lead," Peter said, attempting to keep the President from making statements he'd later have to explain. "She will be responsible for coordinating additional assets when and if she decides they're needed. In the meantime, I'd ask that you stand by for additional taskings and contingency operations as the situation progresses. Beverly, am I missing anything?"

Beverly eyed him without expression for a beat before turning to the waiting audience. "Nothing further at this time, ladies and gentlemen. The Deputy Director will institute twice-daily updates. In the meantime, if you have questions, particularly as they pertain to the JSOC units or CSAR assets, have your staff reach out to their counterparts in the Directorate of Operations. Anything further, Mr. President?"

"Nothing operational, Beverly—thank you." The President paused for a moment, staring down at his folded hands. When he looked up again, his eyes were flinty with determination. "I will not leave this man. I swear it to you. The second we have operational intelligence, I will put the full might and power of the United States behind my words. I will not fail him or you."

The speech was a good one, even more so considering that the President meant every word. If the President were left to his own devices, Peter had no doubt that

Jorge Gonzales would gamble everything—his legacy, his political capital, even the election itself—on the faint hope of rescuing a man who was, for all intents and purposes, already dead. This was why Peter knew without a shadow of a doubt that actionable intelligence would never arrive.

Charles Robinson IV would see to that.

The sacrifice of Beverly's operator was tragic, and his unnecessary death rested squarely at the CIA Director's feet. But that was for later. Like the President, Peter had his own solemn oath, and he intended to honor it. If managed correctly, Shaw's tragic death would ensure that others would live.

Sometimes, that was all a soldier could hope for.

FOURTEEN

Director Castle? Director Castle, a word, please."

At the second, louder mention of her name, Beverly turned as if just hearing Peter for the first time. Peter was under no such illusion. Beverly had been making a beeline for her waiting armored limousine. She might have lost this skirmish, but Peter had no doubt that she had yet to concede the war.

Beverly was many things, but a quitter she was not.

"Peter, I'm afraid I'm extremely short on time. Can this wait until I'm back at Langley?"

A few staffers edged by on either side of the narrow hallway, but for the most part, Peter and Beverly were alone. The other principals had left a good five minutes before, while Beverly had remained seated at the conference table. She'd made a series of calls on her secure BlackBerry and then scrolled through her e-mail until the room had emptied.

Peter had his doubts about the entire performance. While he had no reason to believe that there weren't a thousand things demanding the Director's attention, he found the timing suspect. In all likelihood, Beverly hadn't wanted to get buttonholed by one of the civilian principals seeking to increase their standing or a nervous member of the Joint Chiefs ready to offer unsolicited advice on a rescue attempt that would never progress past the planning stage.

This was why Peter had found something to occupy himself with at a temporary desk just down the hall from the conference room. He'd waited until Beverly emerged to make his move. Once she was back across the Potomac in her Langley fortress, Beverly would have the advantage. But here, in the West Wing, she was still on Peter's turf.

"I'm afraid not," Peter said, his voice properly contrite, "but I promise to be brief. If you'd just step in here for a minute?"

Peter gestured toward one of the many closet-sized spaces that had been converted into meeting rooms over the years. The West Wing served as office space for the most powerful man or woman on the planet, but it had all the elbow room of a Silicon Valley start-up. Many of the staffers saw the tight quarters as endearing.

Not Peter.

For him, the lack of space was just damn inconvenient.

Beverly looked from Peter to the empty room and back again. For a moment, he wondered whether he was going to have to physically move her into the meeting space, but after a discreet glance at the broad-shouldered security officer who trailed her, she slipped inside.

Peter followed a step later, closing the door behind him.

As soon as she heard the door latch click, Beverly whirled to face him, all traces of civility gone. "How did you get it?"

The meeting room might have been phone booth sized, but it was soundproof, making Beverly's question seem much sharper without the ambient noises of murmured conversations, clacking keyboards, or buzzing phones.

"Get what?" Peter said.

"The paper. How?"

"Is he the one?" Peter said, inclining his head toward the member of Beverly's security detail they'd left in the hall.

Beverly's eyes narrowed, and she took a step forward, closing the distance between them so that she stood near enough to kiss him.

"Listen to me, you smug son of a bitch." Though she barely spoke above a whisper, the venom-filled intensity of her voice startled Peter, forcing him to fight the urge to physically recoil. "You may think that because of that paper you own me, but I can assure you nothing is further from the truth."

Beverly's porcelain features twisting in anger reminded Peter of the scene from the classic C. S. Lewis novel *The Lion, the Witch and the Wardrobe* in which

Edmund inadvertently unmasks the White Witch's true nature. Here was Beverly unfiltered, in all her terrifying rage. In that moment, Peter knew that his homicidal thoughts about the Director of the Central Intelligence Agency had not been one-sided.

"Beverly," Peter said, with more bravado than he felt, "a girl like you is never owned. She's only rented."

To her credit, he never saw the slap coming. One moment, he was returning her hate-filled gaze. The next, his left ear was ringing, and his jaw was on fire. The impact of flesh on flesh sounded like the crack of a rifle in the room's narrow confines. It took Peter a second to realize what had just happened, but after his brain sorted it out, he couldn't help but smile.

Beverly might have just rung his bell, but she'd also just forfeited the engagement.

"Now that you've got that out of your system," Peter said, resisting the urge to rub his aching jaw, "I want you to listen carefully. As far as I'm concerned, that paper and its contents were nothing more than a warning shot. The President doesn't know what it says, and he doesn't have to, providing you do just one thing."

Beverly stared at him in silence, her chest heaving as she fought to control her breathing. This was the moment she was dreading. The moment when she would find out how much her lapse in judgment was going to cost.

"What?" Beverly said, almost spitting the question.

"Appoint Charles Robinson as your liaison to Syria. He'll function in the same manner as the old Jawbreaker teams during the initial days of Afghanistan. You'll defer all operational decisions to him."

"Charles?" Beverly said. "Again? Are you out of your mind? He was the Chief of Base during the last Syria debacle. I will not agree to this."

"Yes, you will," Peter said, keeping his reply emotionless, "because if you do, you'll be able to leave this administration with the President's blessing. In fact, your first post-exit interview will be done jointly with the President on the network of your choosing. After that, the President will throw his full support behind you as his political heir. This includes persuading Ben that seeking the nomination would not be in his best interest."

Beverly's expression lost some of its anger at the mention of Ben Stevens, the Vice President. An accomplished leader in his own right, the man was popular among the party rank and file. Many of the political pundits were already salivating at the thought of watching the Vice President battle the establishment's queen for the nomination. But a word or two from Jorge would put Ben's aspirations to rest.

Permanently.

"And if I don't?" Beverly said.

"Copies of that paper go to Fox News, the *Wall Street Journal*, and the *New York Times*, as well as the Attorney General. Don't fight me, Beverly. Believe me when I tell you that if we succeed, you succeed."

Beverly dropped her gaze, her shoulders sagging as she took a shuddering breath. When she looked up, her eyes glistened.

"You're a coldhearted son of a bitch."

Peter nodded.

"I'll send Charles," Beverly said, the words coming out in a hiss, "but I won't forget this. Ever."

Without waiting for a reply, she pulled open the door and swept out of the room.

As Peter watched her leave, he realized that for all her political insight, Beverly still didn't understand him. His heart wasn't cold.

It was broken.

FIFTEEN

The fading afternoon sun felt good on my jet-lagged body, but I was still grateful for my Oakley sunglasses. Shouldering my backpack, I picked my way down the flimsy metal steps sprouting from the equally flimsy private jet.

Late autumn in Syria was a lot like late autumn in Austin—temperatures in the sixties during the day, while at night the air cooled down to the forties. But that's where the similarities ended. Syria had a unique smell composed of equal parts car exhaust, stale smoke from countless open fires, and poverty. Its exact nature was hard to put into words, but was unmistakable all the same.

For better or worse, I was back.

The last time I'd arrived in-country, it had been in the cramped confines of a retrofitted Russian Mi-8 transport helicopter with a pair of U.S. Army Night Stalker aviators at the controls. I'd competed for cabin space with an eight-man Special Forces A-team and untold crates of weapons and equipment as we'd hurtled through the absolute darkness of a moonless desert night, barely fifty feet above the ground. This time, I'd flown in the relative comfort of a private jet, in broad daylight, with only one other passenger for company.

Given the choice, I'd take the Russian helicopter and darkness any day of the week.

"I'm gonna throw up."

The statement was made in the matter-of-fact manner I'd come to expect from my traveling companion of the last several hours. Her name was Virginia Kenyon, and she was a PhD chemist on loan to the DIA. In the short time I'd known her, I'd come to the conclusion that, while Virginia didn't talk much, when she did, her words were worth heeding.

After moving the rest of the way down the steps, I offered her a hand, but she ignored it in her rush to solid ground. Without acknowledging me in the least, Virginia ducked behind the skeletal staircase and emptied her stomach with two long retches.

I could empathize. Our pilot, Mehmet, much like his airplane, was more than a bit past his prime.

The DIA Gulfstream I'd boarded at Andrews Air Force Base was not equipped in any sense to fly into Syria. Instead, we'd landed at Incirlik Air Base in Turkey, where I'd linked up with Virginia, who was also waiting on a transport flight into country. Together, Virginia and

I had connected with a pilot the DIA had on retainer to fly personnel discreetly in and out of Syria.

Mehmet and his crew seemed to know the airfield I was targeting, and since some DIA bureaucrat had contracted the pilot's services, I assumed the smiling Turk's aviating skills had been vetted.

This had been a grossly invalid assumption. In the future, I would Uber my way out of Syria before allowing myself to be a passenger in any type of motorized conveyance with Mehmet at the controls.

"Is the lady all right?"

Mehmet asked the question while standing at the top of the stairway, anxiously peering down at Virginia. By the sound of the wet spatter hitting the concrete apron behind me, the DIA chemist was far from all right.

"I think the lady wasn't expecting such a rough ride," I said, since Virginia was clearly indisposed.

"The lady," said Virginia, "would rather be dragged across the desert behind a team of horses than ever get back on an airplane with you."

I couldn't help but smile. Virginia had a bit of a Southern accent—East Tennessee if I were to guess—and it seemed to grow stronger when she was angry. Right now, her drawl was becoming more pronounced by the syllable. But that was okay. The girl had grit, and in my experience, grit overcame a host of shortcomings.

It was obvious that this was Virginia's first operational rodeo. Though her short red hair was tucked under a faded Yankees ball cap, the rest of her outfit screamed government contractor—5.11 pants and tactical boots, a short-sleeve REI shirt, and a Blackhawk backpack. She couldn't have looked more American if she'd been wearing a T-shirt with the Stars and Stripes emblazoned across the front.

Still, I had to hand it to her. When the DIA had called with an opportunity to travel halfway across the world to identify a deadly chemical weapon developed by a rogue terrorist cell, she'd taken them up on their offer. For her gumption alone, Virginia had my respect.

"Sorry," Mehmet said with a shrug. "Radar showed multiple aircraft. Adjusting our flight plan was necessary."

Apparently *adjusting our flight plan* translated into zipping across the border at an altitude only slightly higher than the sporadic power lines. That close to the ground, the heated afternoon air rushed skyward in a series of invisible spiraling vortices, forming hurricane-force updrafts in the process. Flying through them had been the equivalent of windsurfing across a tsunami. I'd ridden broncos that had bucked less, and that was before our pilot had begun evasive maneuvers in the form of gut-wrenching banks that slammed us against our seat belts.

I wasn't an aviator, but I was willing to bet that our relatively safe arrival had had little to do with our pilot's aviation-related prowess. In all likelihood, any Russian fighters patrolling the skies had taken one look at our erratic flight path and concluded that we were destined to crash without their help.

From the feel of our bone-jarring landing, that sentiment hadn't been too far off the mark.

"Now that the lady and the sir have arrived, it is time for us to depart. Yes?"

The worry on Mehmet's face was evident. Maybe the Russian presence had been more aggressive than I was giving him credit for. Or perhaps he'd made a call to a friend or two during the flight and offered to exchange a pair of Americans for a suitcase full of hundred-dollar bills.

Neither possibility was particularly reassuring.

"Take a drink," I said, handing a water bottle to Virginia. "It'll help your stomach."

I stalled for time as I looked across the shimmering asphalt, searching for the vehicle that should have been here already. Instead, all I saw were the crumbling remains of an airport that had fallen victim to the endless Syrian civil war.

The hangar behind me was pockmarked with bullet holes, and its steel sliding door hung slightly askew. The crumpled hulk of a Russian-built transport plane sat at the end of the cratered runway, while the taxiway we'd used as a runway had cracks spider-webbing across its surface. The rest of the airfield looked even worse. The control tower had been reduced to a chunk of concrete sprouting rods of rusted rebar, and the cluster of buildings near the field's access point at the other end of the runway seemed similarly abandoned.

In short, this was the perfect place for a clandestine meet, assuming, of course, my former asset actually showed.

"Where's our ride?" Virginia said after taking a long pull from the water bottle.

And that was the million-dollar question. I searched the crumbling remains of the airport for a vehicle but found nothing. Absolutely nothing.

"My copilot would like me to tell the sir that a car is approaching," Mehmet said.

I glanced up from my phone, on which I'd been scrolling through the chat log on the encrypted Telegram app, reviewing the last text from my in-country contact, which described the car that would be meeting us. I couldn't see anything from my vantage point on the ground, but perhaps the flight crew had a better view.

"What color's the car?" I said.

Moment of truth.

"Gray."

Not good.

"No. No gray. White. White with orange roof."

Thank you, Baby Jesus.

"All right," I said, waving to our pilot, "you're free to go."

Mehmet ducked inside the jet's cabin without answering, the stairs retracting behind him with a speed that belied their decrepit appearance. Slinging my backpack over my shoulder, I grabbed the two kit bags at my feet and yelled to Virginia.

"Follow me. We're out of here."

At the far end of the airfield, a white car with an orange roof nosed through a hole in the cyclone fence and turned past the abandoned guard shack onto the runway.

The vehicle sped toward us even as our jet headed in the opposite direction, howling engines blasting us with exhaust.

The inherent strangeness of the situation wasn't lost on me. Here I was, standing on the tarmac of a bombed-out Syrian airport as my getaway plane lifted into the sky and a mystery vehicle raced toward me with the same reckless abandon. This was one of the many aspects about being a spy that HR tended to gloss over during the recruiting process.

Placing myself between Virginia and the approaching car, I reached under my shirt and slid the Glock 23 out of the Don Hume inside-the-waistband holster tucked against my right hip. I held the pistol along the length of my leg, using my body to shield the weapon from the car's occupants.

"That our ride?" Virginia said.

"I think so."

"Then why the gun?"

"Because thinking so isn't the same as knowing so."

"That's lovely. Just lovely."

East Tennessee was back.

And that was about the time I realized that, although the car hurtling toward us was indeed white with an orange roof, the two following it onto the airfield were definitely not.

Welcome to Syria.

SIXTEEN

"Are we waiting for one car or three?" Virginia said as the convoy raced toward us.

"One," I said, trying to see through the dark tint that shielded from view the front passengers in the first sedan. "What do you have in these kit bags?"

"My portable lab. Instruments, glassware, protective equipment. Nerd stuff."

"No rocket launchers?"

"Surprisingly, they weren't on the DIA-approved packing list. Do we need one?"

"Couldn't hurt."

"Interesting. Are we in trouble?"

"We're in Syria."

The first car, a white Korean sedan of questionable lineage sporting an orange roof like some Syrian version of the *Dukes of Hazzard*'s General Lee, bore down on us like a hound dog on the scent. The sound of its straining engine echoed across the airfield. Behind it, two Toyota SUVs swung back and forth, sometimes on the taxiway, sometimes on the cracked ground baked concrete-hard under the sun's constant assault.

For a moment, I entertained the hopeful notion that all three cars were part of our welcoming party. Maybe the second two were an escort for the first. But that idyllic dream vanished about the time the lead SUV's passenger-side window rolled down, revealing an AK-47.

"That's our signal," I said, grabbing Virginia and pushing her toward the open hangar behind us.

"My gear!"

"We'll buy it back on eBay," I said, scooping my go bag off the concrete with one hand as I kept the Glock trained on the convoy with the other. Out in the open, my pistol was about as useful as a cap gun, but inside the hangar, the close confines might just even the odds.

Assuming, of course, we made it inside alive.

We'd closed half the distance to the hangar when a flash of light streaked from an adjacent building. I had just enough time to register an RPG's telltale smoke trail before the warhead detonated and the first SUV burst into flames.

To his credit, the driver of the second SUV reacted with admirable tactical soundness. He slammed on the brakes and threw the vehicle into reverse.

He didn't get far.

The Toyota's engine had just begun to rev when a second flash of light and corresponding puff of smoke ended in a second explosion. Then there were two burning chassis littering the taxiway.

This turn of events did not seem to bother the driver of the car with the orange roof in the slightest. Instead of fleeing, the driver tooted an emasculated horn twice before making a sharp left turn toward us. The driver's window rolled down, and a friendly hand waved hello. At least I hoped it was hello. It very well could have been *You might as well run before I shoot you to make it more sporting*, but at this point, I was trying to keep a positive attitude.

Or something like that.

"Did the good guys win?" Virginia said.

"I'm choosing to believe yes."

The car rolled to a stop, and the driver hopped out, his trademark cigar dangling unlit from his lips.

"Allah be praised. My American friend has returned. And in the company of a lovely woman, no less."

"Hello, Zain," I said, accepting an enthusiastic hug.

Though Zain's head came barely to my shoulder, the body beneath his unbuttoned shirt was hard, almost desiccated. It was as if the Syrian sun had melted away any superfluous tissue, leaving only sinew and bone.

"Good to see you," I said. "Seems like you had a bit of trouble?"

"Ah," Zain said, dismissing the burning hulks with a half wave of his hand. "This is Syria. Everywhere is trouble."

That was undoubtedly true. Still, I would have preferred an explanation with perhaps a tad bit more detail, so I tried again. "Who were those men?"

Zain replied with an exaggerated shrug. "ISIS? Assad loyalists? Bandits? This is Syria, my friend—one never knows. Much has changed since you left, but much more remains the same. The important thing is that I remember your training—always secure the meeting site beforehand. I knew that lesson. They did not. Now they are dead, and we are not. What else is there to say?"

Volumes as far as I was concerned. Still, that conversation could probably be better had in the safety of Zain's car.

"Okay, my friend," I said, "thank you again for coming. This is Virginia, and we need a ride to the CIA safe house. Do you know it?"

Zain answered with a roll of his eyes. "Everyone knows it. Bags in the trunk, if you please. You'll find body armor and weapons on the seats. Come, come—we must be going. My friends in the hangar will only stay for another hour."

"And then?" Virginia said, dropping one bag in the trunk while I piled the second kit bag and our backpacks on top.

"Then they are off to another client," Zain said, getting behind the wheel as I climbed into the seat beside him.

"Who's the client?" I said.

Another exaggerated shrug. "ISIS? Assad loyalists? Bandits? This is Syria, my friend—one never knows."

How have things been?" I said, watching the scenery pass by in uninspiring vistas. At times, the destruction seemed almost random. Kilometers would pass in which entire villages looked as if the war had passed them by only to be followed by city blocks littered with unrecognizable rubble. The damage might appear to be random, but I knew it wasn't.

Like every conflict, the Syrian war was fought along fault lines, except the fault lines here were familial rather than geographical. Assad's followers were Alawis, adhering to a sect of Shia Islam, while the majority of the population was Sunni. In other words, the country was about as stable as gasoline and matches.

Zain, a Sunni like most of the rebel fighters, glanced at me and then looked back to the road. "Things are bad, my friend. Worse since you left. Rebels are fighting Assad with Saudi help. Assad is fighting back with Russian help. Shia militias and Hezbollah are attacking the Sunnis with Iranian help. The Kurds are fighting Turkey and Assad, and Turkey is fighting the Kurds."

"What about ISIS?" Virginia said from the back seat.

The scientist's question made sense. Even though the operational focus had shifted to rescuing Shaw, we could not lose sight of the mystery chemical weapon. According to Einstein, the jihadis who had it and Shaw were remnants of the now decimated Islamic caliphate.

Zain shrugged as he looked at Virginia in the rearview mirror. "ISIS? ISIS kills everyone."

I let the morbid thought stretch out a beat and then tried to steer the conversation to happier territory. "How's your family?"

"As well as can be expected. When the Americans were still here, people had hope. Now the U.S. is gone, and Russia is here. The players come and go, but our war remains the same."

Zain had been one of my greatest coups from an asset-recruitment standpoint. There were at least three major conflicts engulfing Syria. Two of them were being waged as proxy wars, with Iran supporting Hezbollah through funds and special forces advisers in the form of Quds Force operatives. At the same time, Russia was waging an air campaign on the Assad regime's behalf.

That much killing took an awful lot of matériel, in the form of guns, bullets, and bombs, and that's where Zain and his network came in. A former owner and operator of a fairly successful trucking company before the 2011 uprising against Assad, Zain now paid the bills by transporting weapons across Syria from waypoints established in Iraq and Turkey.

Officially, my driver and his hardscrabble crew were charged with resupplying the myriad rebel groups opposing Assad. Unofficially, I had the sense that more than one truckload of weapons wound up in the hands of whichever militant group could foot Zain's bill. After almost six years of constant killing, the millions of noncombatants had adopted a brand of cynical pragmatism when it came to surviving the bloodshed—do what you needed to do to live through the day. If truth was the first casualty of war, the moral high ground wasn't far behind.

Anyway, as far as I was concerned, the U.S. had lost all moral authority the moment we'd drawn a red line in the sand and then looked the other way as Assad marched straight across it.

"Are you here to stay, my friend?" Zain said.

I shook my head. "An ISIS splinter cell has one of our men. I'm here to get him back."

Zain gave a slow nod, but he didn't say anything for a kilometer or two. When he did break his silence, his comment reflected the same pragmatism I'd felt myself adopting moments after stepping back onto Syrian soil.

"We all do our best," Zain said. He tossed his gnawed cigar out the window before pulling a second from his breast pocket. He unwrapped the cigar one-handed and slid the unlit stogie between his lips. "Will you need help?"

I thought about how to answer as Zain navigated around the hulks of two burned-out vehicles that I assumed in happier days had been a checkpoint.

This was the part of the conversation where I was supposed to provide some sort of God-and-country speech. Something to convince my Arab friend that now that the old U.S. of A. had rediscovered Syria, everything was going to be fine.

But I couldn't. As a seasoned case officer, I'd long since passed the point where lies sprang to my tongue much faster than the truth. But this was different. This was my friend, and it was personal. So I did something unusual. I told my asset the truth.

"Zain," I said, reaching over to squeeze his bony shoulder, "before this is over, I'm gonna need all the help I can get."

SEVENTEEN

I nodded to the bored-looking Ranger standing post in front of the TOC, or Tactical Operations Center. Ten minutes earlier, Zain had driven up to the gate leading into the CIA compound, exchanged pleasantries with the Syrian guard, and pulled his car inside. He'd parked in a makeshift motor pool and told me that he'd wait with the car until Virginia and I sorted things out.

To say the experience had been surreal would have been a bit of an understatement. The location of the CIA's safe house should have been one of the most closely guarded secrets in-country. Instead, Zain had breezed through the front gate like he was delivering pizzas to a frat house.

Unreal.

Then again, perhaps I shouldn't have been surprised. For reasons known only to him, the new CIA Chief of Base had set up shop in the exact same compound we'd occupied three months earlier. Maybe the Agency had a good deal on a long-term lease.

Hefting my backpack, I keyed in the old combination to the cipher pad and was rewarded with an electronic click as the lock disengaged. Without stopping to ponder the absurdity of the situation further, I shouldered my way inside.

The hinges on the reinforced steel door groaned, exactly like they had three months ago. Back then I'd hit the door at a run, Frodo right behind me. We'd been desperate to get the QRF team airborne in response to Fazil's distress signal. Today, I all but slunk through the door, terrified that at any minute my fingers might start to twitch in response to a dead toddler's game of peekaboo.

Amazing what a difference three months could make.

"Where's your badge?"

The question came from an American seated behind a folding table just beyond the door. He was clean-shaven, and his clothes were wrinkle free. He didn't look old enough to buy beer.

He'd glanced up from his laptop as I'd walked in, his pale eyes taking in my travel-worn appearance before adopting a dismissive expression. I wasn't wearing a uniform and wasn't part of his CIA contingent. In other words, I was no one.

"My what?" I said, thinking I'd misheard him.

"Your badge. You can't be in here without a badge."

"Is he serious?"

Though this was her first deployment, Virginia's

bullshit detector seemed to work just fine. In my opinion, she already had the makings of an outstanding field operative.

Deciding to give the boy-man behind the desk the benefit of the doubt, I paused, waiting for the punch line. But he didn't smile. Instead, he stared at me, radiating the self-importance that came only with being a twenty-something kid on his first operational deployment. Unbelievable. I was in an unacknowledged clandestine compound, in the middle of nowhere Syria, and this jack wagon was worried about badges.

"Look," I said, determined not to get off on the wrong foot, "my name is Matt Drake, and this is Virginia Kenyon. We're DIA. I don't have a badge, but I'm sure the Chief of Base is expecting us. Please tell him we're here."

"Sorry," the youngster said, his voice suggesting he was anything but. "All new arrivals go to Building Two for processing. No exceptions. They'll give you a badge at the end of the brief. By then, the Chief should be out of his meeting. Come back later. I'll see if I can fit you in."

And with that, my new friend focused on his laptop, signaling that my audience was over. I took a breath and looked over the man's shoulder, fighting the urge to separate his head from his body.

The inside of the TOC was exactly as I remembered it. Three plasma screens lined the walls. Two showed what I assumed was real-time imagery from orbiting UAVs. The third was tuned to CNN. A series of empty desks was arranged back-to-back in a bull pen configuration, their surfaces littered with secure phones, radios, and laptops. Two doors loomed at the rear of the bull pen. If memory served, the door on the left led to the Chief's office, while the one on the right opened into a small conference room. The cracked wooden door on the right was closed, while the one on the left stood ajar.

It didn't take a genius to figure out where the Chief was holding his meeting.

I slid around the youngster's desk, heading toward the closed door.

"Hey! You can't go back in there."

He was nothing if not persistent.

The conference room door opened. Several Arabs walked out along with a couple of Americans. I was preparing to introduce myself when my eager-beaver friend grabbed me by the shoulder, spinning me toward him. I shrugged his hand away, but the damage was done. Because I was facing away from the conference room door, I didn't see the last two people exit.

Not until it was much too late.

Turning back toward the crowd, I opened my mouth, but the words died on my lips. Seeing Charles Sinclair Robinson IV was a surprise, but something my brain could process. In fact, it was almost as if, on some level, I'd expected him to be here. Chuck was as much a part of the reason why I was back in Syria as Einstein.

The man standing next to Charles, however, was a different story. Finding him in a CIA safe house was a bit more unsettling. Though our one previous meeting had been brief, I recognized him all the same. Then the Syrian wind had kept me from drilling a 5.56mm hole through the center of his forehead. Instead, I'd left him with a puckered scar that stretched from his mouth to the tip of his ear.

Still, wind was a fickle thing. Last time, an unexpected breeze had saved his life.

Today, the air was dead calm.

EIGHTEEN

The man's eyes widened as he saw me. That seemed important, but I didn't have time to consider why, not with his hand already streaking toward the pistol holstered on his leg.

In close combat, action always beat reaction. I'd never win the race to draw my pistol before Scarface, so I didn't try. Vaulting forward, I closed the space between us instead. As I moved, my reptilian mind awoke. Images and sensations flooded my brain in rapid fire.

The man was thick—heavy shoulders, wide chest. Bigger than me.

I slammed into him, driving from the legs. My shoulder crunched against his armpit. I trapped his hand as his fingers wrapped around his pistol.

He stumbled.

I fired three quick jabs into his ribs and might as well have been punching a tree trunk. The first strike landed, but he blocked the second and third, taking the blows on a meaty biceps.

Both big and agile. In other words, trouble.

I smashed him into the wall, hammering my knee into the bundle of nerves along his leg.

Again his agility saved him.

Scarface turned away from me, taking the brunt of my strike on his hamstring instead of his thigh, but the shock to his nervous system worked all the same. For an instant, his gun hand relaxed.

An instant was all I needed.

I grabbed his shirtsleeve and ripped backward like I was pulling the starter cord on a lawn mower. His arm slammed into my chest, fingers opening. The pistol skidded across the floor. I hammered him in the kidney and then spear-handed him in the throat. I was off balance, so the blow didn't collapse his windpipe, but it did get his attention.

He sagged into the wall, ducking behind his fists to protect his face.

I kicked him in the chest, pistoning him backward to create space, and then drew my pistol. I planted the stubby barrel two inches from his forehead, close enough for a contact shot, but not so close that he could depress the gun's muzzle and disable the weapon.

"If you so much as twitch, you're a dead motherfucker."

I was so amped, I wasn't sure whether I'd spoken in Arabic or English, though it probably didn't matter. In my experience, a pistol in the face was pretty universal.

As my brain realized the fight was over, my laserlike focus on Scarface faded, and I could hear shouting in a mixture of languages. Sooner or later, I'd have to start remembering that Frodo wasn't here to watch my back. While I'd been beating the shit out of Scarface, the rest of the room had also been busy. Now everyone seemed to have a gun, and most of those guns were pointed at me.

NINETEEN

"Charles," I said, deciding that now was as good a time as any to reintroduce myself to the CIA Chief of Base, "you need to get this shit show under control."

"Have you lost your goddamn mind?" Charles said. "Put the pistol down, and let him go before someone gets killed."

"This motherfucker is the only someone getting killed. He got away last time but not today. I promise you that."

"What are you talking about?"

"This shithead crippled Frodo. He and I have unfinished business."

"Matt, listen to me," Charles said, moving closer. "This is one of our trusted Syrian commanders. He's my asset, and he's helping to rescue Shaw. You're mistaken."

"No mistake here, Chucky. See this scar?" I shoved the Glock into Scarface's cheekbone, twisting the muzzle. "I gave it to him. If the wind hadn't changed direction, I'd have nailed him in the face. Allah might have been smiling then, but he ain't smiling now."

Scarface let loose a stream of Arabic that my adrenaline-soaked brain had trouble translating, but from the bits I could pick up, I was pretty certain he was telling his men to disembowel me and hang my entrails from the compound's gates. The second part of his speech was directed at Charles, but he stopped his lecture midsentence, mainly because it's hard to enunciate with the muzzle of a Glock stuck between your teeth.

"Goddamn it, Matt!"

"Charlie, I'm starting to get angry, and when I get angry, motherfuckers start dying. So, rather than spill this shithead's brains all over your freshly mopped floor, here's what we're going to do. Yell for the Ranger standing outside to rustle up his brothers and tell them to take Scarface and his men into custody. Then you and I can sort this out like grown men. How's that for reasonable?"

"Put the gun down and let him go. Last chance."

Something about Chuck's tone made me acutely aware that my back was to him. I decided that wouldn't do. Grabbing a handful of Scarface's shirt, I jerked him toward me and hammered the butt of my pistol across the bridge of his nose. I didn't hit him hard enough to break it, but I definitely got his attention.

Scarface cursed. As he grabbed for his bloodied nose, I pulled him off balance and kicked his leg out from under him. He crumpled. I used our combined momentum to force him to his knees, moving to stand behind him with my pistol pressed against the base of his skull.

Now that I could see the rest of the room, what I found wasn't particularly reassuring. Scarface's men had their pistols and AK-47s leveled at me, but that was to be expected. What wasn't expected was the sight of Charles with a Beretta in his hand. His pistol was currently pointing at the ground, but his expression said that it hadn't been pointed in that direction a moment ago.

Interesting.

"Chuck, I'm a bit confused. I just told you that the shithead you put in charge of rescuing Shaw tried to kill me. Aren't you the least bit concerned that maybe your trusted asset shouldn't be quite so trusted?"

My speech had no effect on the three Arab men still aiming rifles at me, but the Americans were a different story. The collection of case officers and paramilitary men exchanged glances, and I saw more than one troubled expression.

Score one for the home team.

"Come on, Charles," I said. "This should be a no-brainer. Let the Rangers secure the jihadis. After that, we can sort this shit out without the wrong someone ending up dead."

Charles started to answer, but a bearded paramilitary officer interrupted. "Chief," the man said, "what he's saying makes sense. We're Shaw's only shot. If we're compromised, we need to know now rather than later."

The way that Charles glared at me, I thought that he

was still going to refuse. But he didn't. Instead, he turned toward the paramilitary officer who'd spoken. "Josh, get the Rangers in here. Have them take these guys into custody. Drake, get the fuck in my office."

"Love to," I said, holstering my pistol as a burly Ranger took charge of Scarface, "but I don't have a badge. Is that a problem?"

TWENTY

What are you doing here?"

"That's a strange question, Chuck," I said, crossing my legs as I eyed the Chief of Base. "Shouldn't we be talking about why your asset tried to kill me?"

Now that I was in his office, the sense of déjà vu was almost overpowering. This was where my life had gone wrong. I'd spent ten critical minutes trying to convince Charles to launch the QRF birds, all to no avail. As usual, Frodo had seen the writing on the wall and he had liberated his Range Rover from the Agency motor pool while Charles and I had still been screaming at each other.

Ten minutes might not seem like a lot, but they could have made the difference. If Frodo and I had left the safe house ten minutes earlier, we might have missed the ambush that ended my friend's career as a commando. With a little luck, we might have even made it to Fazil's apartment in time to stop the slaughter.

Then again, in Syria, luck seemed to be in short supply.

"Goddamn you, Drake. This is my operation. Mine. I won't watch everything go to shit again because of you. My asset heads a network I've spent two years building. Two years. Before you fucked things up three months ago, he was on the verge of ending this war. That all went down the shitter when you and Frodo went rogue. Now, just when I convince him to come back on board, you stick a pistol in his face. You have lost your mind."

Charles's answer brought me up short. Scarface's unexpected presence had provoked a fight-or-flight response. Three months ago, the Syrian had tried to kill me, and he'd seemed intent on finishing the job today. But while my reaction in the TOC had undoubtedly saved my life, I'd been acting, not thinking.

Specifically, I hadn't thought to ask the most obvious of questions—why? Why had Scarface ambushed me, and why was he trying to finish the job now? Perhaps most important, how did Scarface know about me? To answer the first two questions, I needed to start with the third, and the man who could provide the answers was sitting less than three feet away.

Perhaps a change of approach was in order.

"Look, Charles, I know you're the Chief of Base, and I understand you're calling the shots. I'll explain everything. Just talk to me about the Syrian. Who is he, and why is he here?"

"No. That's not how this is going to work. I don't answer to you, but you will answer to me. Either tell me why you're here, or I swear to God I'll have the Rangers throw your ass in a cell. Last chance."

Charles came from old money, and he'd graduated from an Ivy League school. Even here, in the middle of nowhere Syria, he somehow still looked the part of a blue-blood aristocrat—tall and trim with wavy black hair, a square jaw, and perfect teeth. His name-brand wardrobe was certainly not government issued, and a TAG Heuer aviator watch, which cost more than I made in a month, graced his left wrist.

Still, old Chuck didn't look quite so debonair when he was angry. His face flushed in splotches, bringing to mind a toddler in midtantrum. I didn't know much about parenting, but I did know that you couldn't reason with a screaming child. Here's to hoping the semblance went only skin-deep.

"Okay," I said, "fair enough. I have a potential asset in the splinter cell holding Shaw."

"What do you mean by *potential*?"

Charles was still breathing hard, but the red splotches had begun to fade. He was interested. Maybe interested enough to put away the pettiness between us and actually listen.

"I made an approach just before I came to Syria, but the target didn't bite. Now he's resurfaced. He's offered to trade Shaw and info about the splinter cell's chem weapon in exchange for extraction. But he'll only work for me."

"Bullshit."

"It's true. Believe me, I didn't come here just to piss

in your Wheaties. He reached out to us and described Shaw to a tee. He's agreed to provide the chemical composition of the weapon he developed as proof of his bona fides. If he really has access to Shaw, at this point, I'd agree to any demand."

"And if he doesn't?"

I shrugged. "There are no absolutes in this business. You know that. Will he double-cross me? Maybe. But if he can give me Shaw, it's worth the risk."

Charles leaned back in his chair, eyeing me as he rubbed his freshly shaven chin with long, slender fingers. For a moment, I thought that this might be the beginning of something new. That Charles might actually respond to my transparency by laying his own operational cards on the table. Or if he wasn't ready for something quite that radical, I hoped that we could at least set aside the past and start again from scratch.

But in Syria, hope, like luck, seemed to be in short supply.

"What's his name?"

"Who?" I said, thinking that I must have misunderstood his question.

"Your asset. I'm the Chief of Base. Any in-country operation needs my authorization. If you want me to sign off on your plan, then you need to give me your asset's name."

I shook my head. "You know I can't do that. My guy might be a shithead, but he's my shithead. He's Shaw's only hope, and I won't give his identity to you or anyone else. Period. You'd do the same thing in my shoes."

"Here's the thing, though, Drake," Charles said with a smile. "I'm not in your shoes. I'm in mine. Give me his name, and we work this together, or get the fuck out of my country. Your choice."

I looked at Charles as I weighed my options. I'd told him the truth when I'd said that Einstein was a shithead. If the weapons scientist for hire really was the mastermind behind the splinter cell's new chem weapon, then he had blood on his hands and lots of it. In no scenario could he be considered a good guy. I should have ended him when he'd turned down my approach months ago, consequences be damned.

But the issue here wasn't Einstein. It was Shaw. The paramilitary officer had already been tortured and was now slotted for a gruesome death. In response, the world's last remaining superpower had committed every intelligence-gathering asset in its trillion-dollar inventory to the task of locating Shaw. So far, we'd come up bone-dry.

Except for Einstein.

So while my potential asset might be a mass murderer, he was also our only link to Shaw. Einstein had to be protected, especially from the arrogant son of a bitch sitting across from me. Charles was either too stupid or too naive to realize that his trusted Syrian commander was an opportunist every bit as mercenary as Einstein.

And this was the best-case scenario.

At worst, the Syrian might be actively working to undermine our very reason for being here. But I didn't have the time or credibility to convince Charles of this possibility. This meant there was no way I would trust

Einstein's identity, and thereby Shaw's fate, to an operation I viewed as already compromised.

As I looked at Charles, it occurred to me that this was the key difference between us. I knew who Einstein was and planned accordingly. Charles wanted Scarface to be something that he wasn't and was prepared to look the other way in support of misplaced trust. I knew I couldn't change Charles any more than I could magically transform Einstein from the shit bag he was to the hero I wished he could be. But I could protect Shaw's one chance at rescue, and that's what I intended to do.

"Charles," I said, getting to my feet, "someday, you and I are going to have a reckoning, but today's not that day. So please know I mean this with all of my heart—go fuck yourself."

Charles started to speak, but I slammed the door on his reply. The fully evolved part of my brain was telling the rest of me that this wasn't the moment to settle the score with Charles. But my reptilian core wasn't so sure.

I was certain of one thing as I crossed the bull pen with short, angry strides. If I had to endure one more second of Charles's sanctimonious grin, I might just side with my inner alligator.

TWENTY-ONE

Matt! Good to hear your voice, brother."

In spite of everything, I smiled. That was the effect Frodo had on me. Less than five minutes before, I'd been giving serious consideration to wiping the arrogant smirk from Charles's face by knocking out a few teeth. But somehow, just hearing Frodo's baritone crackle over the digitally encrypted line made the situation less bleak. His voice was a lifeline to the sane world that existed beyond the vortex of madness centered on this safe house. I wasn't in this alone, not as long as Frodo was still breathing.

"Likewise, my friend," I said, rubbing the grit from my eyes. "You have no idea how much I wish you were here."

I realized the awkwardness of that statement about a millisecond after the words left my mouth, but Frodo was Frodo. He didn't bother to mention the reason why he wasn't here. Instead, he simply said, "In trouble already?"

"Like you wouldn't believe," I said, eyeing the TOC from my vantage point on the other side of the packed-dirt courtyard.

This had been where Frodo and I had set up shop. We'd spent many an evening discussing how the world might have been different if Jimi Hendrix hadn't died so young. Or at least that was my viewpoint. Frodo was more partial to the Beatles. Either way, I was like a wild animal seeking refuge in a familiar den, and the bit of shade offered by the tin-roof overhang seemed like a natural place to plot my next move.

"Talk to me, Goose."

Frodo was an aficionado of eighties and nineties movies, but *Top Gun* was far and away his favorite, even if the subject had been naval aviators instead of Army commandos. As far as Frodo was concerned, good filmmaking was good filmmaking.

"Couple things, brother," I said. "First off, Charles is the Chief of Base."

"You've got to be shitting me."

"I wish I were, but that's not the half of it. Remember the Syrian who led the ambush?" I didn't have to specify which ambush. As far as Frodo was concerned, there was only one.

"You got a line on him?"

"You might say that. When I walked into the TOC, he and Charles were coming out of the conference room together."

"Say that again."

"You heard me. According to Charles, the Syrian is a local tribal leader. Charles said he's been running him for almost two years."

"Any chance you've got the wrong guy?"

"I think not. He's got a scar stretching from his lip to his ear courtesy of our previous face-to-face. He's our guy."

"Did you take him down?"

I paused, reliving the scene in my mind. Something about seeing the Syrian had pinged my subconscious, but I hadn't known why until Frodo's question had knocked a thought loose.

"I didn't get the chance. As soon as he saw me, he went for his gun. I'd swear he recognized me. What do you think about that?"

"I think you better start from the beginning and tell Uncle Frodo exactly what happened."

So I did. True to form, Frodo didn't offer an opinion, at least not during my telling. When he did interrupt, it was to clarify a statement or ask for additional details. Not for the first time, I thought that if Frodo hadn't become a commando, he would have made a fine therapist.

"Where does this leave you and Charles?" Frodo said after I finished my update.

"Not in a good place. The Rangers have Scarface and his men on lockdown, but I don't know how much longer that'll last. Right now, it's my word against the Syrian's. Charles seems more inclined to believe his asset than me."

"Sure he does. Can you imagine the shit storm if it turns out that Charles's trusted commander ambushed two DIA case officers? He'd spend the rest of his career alphabetizing the CIA's archives. What are you gonna do?"

That was the question that had been bouncing around my head since my meeting with Charles had gone south. Shaw was running out of time. Now that I knew that Charles was relying on Scarface to locate the captured paramilitary officer, Einstein was more important than ever.

But even if Einstein was on the level, I wasn't going to rescue Shaw on my own. That bullshit happened only in the movies. Shaw needed me and, like it or not, I needed Charles. Which meant I needed to find evidence that would bring Charles over to my side—proof of Scarface's involvement that he couldn't conveniently dismiss.

"If I send you biometric data, can you lean on some folks to run it through the authoritative database? Like, today?"

"Son, I'm a freaking commando. I may only have one arm, but I can still convey a sense of urgency to the desk jockeys. What'd you have in mind?"

"I'm thinking I'm gonna make friends with the Rangers guarding Scarface. Then I'm going to ask them to help me enroll the Syrian in the biometric database."

"Hoping for a hit?"

"Yep. Scarface is a bad guy, no two ways about it. Maybe he's splashed his DNA in places he shouldn't have. If our analysts can tie him to a target, or an IED—

hell, even a weapons deal gone bad—Charles won't be able to ignore it."

"I'm on it. But what if his biometrics don't produce a hit?"

"I'll cross that bridge when I come to it. How's Einstein?"

As part of the OPLAN we'd put together during our call on the Gulfstream, Frodo and I had agreed that he would communicate with my asset until I was established in-country. Our reasoning was simple: Because Einstein had turned down my initial pitch, I'd never provided him with covert communications, or cov-com, gear. Cov-com took a number of forms depending on an asset's operational environment, but its purpose was always the same—to facilitate secure communications between a handler and his agent. Since Einstein wasn't a formal asset, he didn't have access to classified gear. But I hadn't let him walk away from our first meeting empty-handed. Instead, I'd pointed him toward a generic instant messaging app. The DIA had developed for the app a software patch that funneled messages through a government server that added NSA Suite B–level encryption.

In the end, I figured this approach offered the best of both worlds. Einstein could contact me securely, but the encryption happened while the data was in transit. This meant that Einstein had nothing in the way of classified-coms gear to turn over to a foreign intelligence service if he were so inclined.

That said, both of us were still at risk. Einstein's chat history made him vulnerable, and if someone rolled me up and compromised my phone, I'd be hung out to dry. To help mitigate this risk, I hadn't installed the chat app on my cell yet. Instead, Frodo handled communication with Einstein via a phone he maintained on his person. Now that I was operational, this needed to change.

"The chem weapon formulation Einstein provided checks out," Frodo said. "Our scientists say it's consistent with what killed the CIA paramilitary operator."

"That shithead has a lot to answer for."

"Focus, Matty, focus. Once we get Shaw back, Einstein can pay for his sins. Until then, he gets a pass. I don't like it either, but it is what it is."

"You're right, you're right. Did he answer your last text?"

"Affirmative," Frodo said, making a rustling sound as he picked up his cell phone. "I'm imaging the app and chat history now. Once you update your phone's software, it'll mirror mine. Einstein came up on the net about ten minutes ago and agreed to a meet. He's texting via Wi-Fi instead of using the cell network, but I've got my favorite NSA analyst trying to localize the phone."

"Is he having any luck?"

"*She's* still working it, you chauvinistic son of a bitch. Her best guess is that Einstein's in Manbij—a city of about a hundred thousand people around one hundred kilometers northeast of Aleppo. She should have a firmer location in an hour or two."

"Wow. Awfully defensive. You wouldn't happen to have a personal relationship with this DIA analyst, would you?"

"Don't take this the wrong way, Matty, but you can't handle the truth."

I smiled. Hearing Frodo quote from his favorite movies brought a sense of normalcy to the operation. This, coupled with the fact that we might actually have Einstein's location, made me think that maybe, just maybe, our collective luck was changing.

"Okay," I said, "anything else?"

"Yep. Einstein has some demands."

"Of course he does. Lay 'em on me."

"U.S. citizenship, a new name, and seed money to start his own laboratory. Oh, and he wants to live in Silicon Valley. Operationally, he said he can provide Shaw's location, but getting proof of life will be too difficult. Also, he's refusing to give anything more until the two of you meet face-to-face."

"I'm not surprised," I said. "He helped develop a weapon that's killed who knows how many Syrians in addition to one of our operators. I'm sure he knows he's not exactly on our good list. He's probably worried that if he gives up Shaw's location now, we'll either throw him to the wolves or drop a Hellfire on him."

"Is he wrong?"

I shrugged. "Probably not. Okay, tell him that the Silicon Valley bullshit is fine. I'll even agree to the face-to-face, if he gives me Shaw's location the second we meet. But without proof of life, there's no deal."

"Making sure he's got some skin in the game?"

"Exactly. Getting close to Shaw won't be easy. He'll probably burn a bridge or two in the process, and that's good. Hopefully, it keeps him from selling me out to his former employers when the going gets tough."

"Damn it, Matty. I should be there watching your back."

"I know, brother. But I don't need another rifle right now. What I need is to know who this Syrian really is and where Einstein is hiding. Until I have that, Einstein has all the leverage. Give me something to make Charles see the light, and then find my wayward scientist."

"I'm on it," Frodo said, and ended the call.

As I placed the phone back in my pocket, I realized that, for the first time in a long time, I wasn't worried about phantom toddlers or unexplainable shakes. Instead, I felt the satisfaction that came only when Frodo and I were operational. Though I'd never told Frodo, I'd always thought he was wrong about the Beatles. In my opinion, John Lennon had been a selfish prick who hadn't appreciated the magic of what he'd had. Then again, maybe I was wrong. Maybe people really did change. Maybe Charles would see the light.

After all, as Don Henley and Glenn Frey had so aptly demonstrated, sometimes hell really did freeze over.

TWENTY-TWO

Peter glared at the men and women next to him, making no effort to hide his displeasure. Nothing raised his temperature like people attending to their personal devices during a meeting, particularly a meeting as important as this one. The first part of Peter's deception plan had been enacted, and he and his staff were now gathered to examine the results.

A heavily sanitized narrative laying out the details behind Beverly's disastrous CIA raid had been leaked to a handful of sympathetic journalists. The raid's true purpose had been stricken from the statement, and the dead operators' affiliation had been altered as well.

Rather than CIA paramilitary officers, Peter had instructed his press secretary to refer to them as Special Forces advisers. He'd further dissembled by stating that the men had been killed assisting the Syrian rebels in their fight against Iranian-backed Shia militias.

While service member deaths in the Middle East were still out of the ordinary, the American public had grown accustomed to the occasional fatality. The U.S. special operators embedded with the Iraqi police fought against an assortment of militants. Their jobs were incredibly dangerous, and their casualty numbers reflected this reality. Peter was betting that the average American wouldn't attach any significance to the fact that the latest round of fatalities had occurred in Syria, rather than in Iraq.

So far, he'd been right.

Even so, the President's challenger, Senator Kelsey Price, was still making political hay of the tragedy. In an interview from the Capitol Building steps, Price had expressed just the right amount of remorse tempered by outrage. According to Price, the current administration's lack of a coherent Middle East strategy was just as much to blame for the American deaths as insurgent bullets.

Unfortunately, Price's attacks seemed to be resonating. In the last four hours, Gonzales's poll numbers had fallen two points, while Price's had risen one.

To add insult to injury, Peter couldn't fault the man's logic. The irony of a Republican attacking a Democrat for irresponsibly employing the military aside, this scenario was exactly why Peter had been determined to resist Syria mission creep at all cost. The American public was tired of their men and women dying in places that most people couldn't even find on a map.

Peter needed to stanch the administration's bleeding, and do so quickly. Otherwise, he risked handing Price a hammer with which he could bludgeon Gonzales all the way until Election Day.

With Gonzales's numbers still trending in the wrong direction, Peter had called a war council. Now he was more than ready to take out his foul mood on whichever staff member had been foolish enough to arrive at the meeting without first silencing his or her electronic device.

Assuming, of course, the perpetrator ever worked up the courage to answer the still-ringing phone.

"Will someone please answer that phone?" Peter said as the electronic ringtone continued.

The four women and two men seated across from him looked at one another in confusion. Finally, Gavin Bledsoe, the pollster, rooted around by his feet, coming up with a leather messenger bag. "I think it's in here."

Peter stared at the satchel as the bottom dropped out of his stomach.

"Sorry, folks," Peter said. "It's mine."

Peter had kept the anxiety from his voice as he spoke, but his heart still thundered. Excusing himself, he grabbed his bag and squeezed out of the narrow conference room, shutting the door behind him.

Once free of the group's prying eyes, Peter set the bag on the floor, digging through first one pocket, then another, until he located the offending device. He shot a look down the hall in either direction, then keyed in the password that allowed him to answer the call, and put the phone to his ear.

"Yes?"

Peter didn't identify himself. He didn't have to. Only one person knew the device's number. Charles had provided him with the secure satellite phone just before he'd left for Syria.

"We've got a problem," Charles said, his voice distorted by the digital encryption protocols. "A big one."

"Give me a minute," Peter said, looking for privacy and finding it in the tiny kitchenette located just off the main hallway. He entered the room only to see a woman sitting over a steaming cup of coffee. Her eyes widened at Peter's sudden appearance, and she grabbed her mug as she stood, splashing coffee across the table.

"I'm sorry," the woman stammered. "I'll clean that up." Reaching for the napkin dispenser in the center of the table, she knocked over a saltshaker, further contributing to the mess instead.

"It's Julie, right?" Peter said, putting his phone on mute.

The woman looked up, midwipe, her eyes showing equal parts surprise and fear. "Yes, sir," she said. "Julie Casillas."

"No need for *sir*, Julie. Peter will do just fine."

The woman nodded in answer, apparently not trusting herself to reply. It was at this moment that Peter realized just how young the woman was, barely twenty if he was any judge. With her olive complexion and dark hair, she didn't look anything like Kristen, but Peter saw his sister all the same.

"You're one of the interns working for Bill down in policy, right?" Peter said.

"Yes, sir. I mean, Peter. I *really* appreciate this opportunity."

Peter nodded and knew that the woman wasn't exaggerating. He'd helped to select the current round of interns and specifically targeted outstanding students who were attempting to pay their own way through college. He'd even managed to change the status of the internship from volunteer to paid and solicited matching grants from each intern's college to help offset their tuition.

No, the half woman, half girl standing in front of him wasn't Kristen, but she might as well have been. Despite her low pay and thankless job, she was here, busting her ass on a Saturday. Women like Julie were the reason he'd entered politics to begin with. Peter would do well to remember that.

"We're lucky to have you, Julie," Peter said, his lips stretching into a genuine smile. "Bill says great things about your work. Don't worry about the mess. I'll finish cleaning up."

"Thank you," Julie said, grabbing the soggy napkins and dumping them in the trash can on the way to the door. "I won't let you down."

She opened the door and slid through before Peter could reply, but her parting comment stuck with him. The twenty-year-old intern was worried about letting him down. In fact, he should have been the one worried about letting her and the countless other struggling young people down.

Taking a moment to center himself, Peter selected a clean mug and filled it halfway full with black coffee.

This time, he smelled the strong hints of Colombian rather than Texas pecan. Taking a confirming swallow, Peter set the mug on the granite counter, thumbed the phone off mute, and tried again.

"Sorry about that," Peter said. "I'm back. You were saying that we had a problem. Is the issue with your Syrian network?"

If Charles was irritated about being put on hold, he didn't let on. Instead, the new Chief of Base got right down to business.

"No," Charles said, "my network is fine. In fact, my trusted commander agreed to dedicate his resources solely to finding and rescuing Shaw."

"Then what's the problem?"

"The problem is that my asset and his men are currently being held at gunpoint by a squad of Rangers."

"What are you talking about?" Peter said as his newfound sense of calm evaporated.

"Matt Drake."

"The DIA case officer?"

"Yep. Ten minutes ago, he walked into my TOC, pulled a gun on my asset, and ordered the Rangers to take him into custody."

"Why?"

"Drake claims my asset tried to kill him during a failed ambush three months ago. The man is delusional. I've worked with my asset for the last eighteen months, and he has been paid handsomely. No way he bites the hand that feeds him."

"Jesus," Peter said, beginning to pace. "Why is Drake even there?"

"I was about to ask you the same question. You didn't know about him?"

"Of course not. Why would I?"

"You're the President's right-hand man. I thought it was your job to know everything."

"You thought wrong," Peter said, his irritation with Charles growing. "My job is to keep us from going to war during the next few days so that the President can get reelected. Your job is to control Syria. Do your fucking job so I can do mine."

"That's funny. From where I'm sitting, I'm doing my fucking job. I gave you the leverage you needed for Beverly, my Syrian network is up and running, and I've got a line on the captured paramilitary officer. In fact, Shaw might have been rescued by now if Drake *hadn't pulled a fucking gun on my asset!*"

Peter wanted to scream back a reply, but took a deep breath instead. His anger wasn't productive. Besides, Charles had a point. He could hardly contain Syria if unwanted guests like Drake started kicking over anthills.

"Okay, look," Peter said, spooning sugar into his mug. "I'll remove Drake from the equation and ensure the principals here understand that Syria is under CIA jurisdiction. No one else comes into, or out of, country without your approval. But you've got to keep your end of the bargain. The President is ready to authorize a rescue attempt for Shaw. He's just waiting for actionable intelligence. You have to make sure that intelligence never materializes. Everything we've worked for is on the line. Everything. If you lose control of Syria, I lose my leverage with Beverly. If that happens, your head will be on the chopping block, right next to mine."

Peter lifted the mug to his lips as he talked. His mind had already transitioned to the next obstacle, so he was completely unprepared for Charles's response.

"Is that a threat?"

Peter slammed the cup onto the counter, sending a black tide sloshing across the granite.

"Are you fucking kidding me?" Peter said. "No, that's not a threat. I just want to make sure you understand what's at stake. You came to me, remember? You said that if I sent you back, you'd take care of this shit. So take care of it. You want to be the next Director of the CIA? Do your fucking job. I'll get Drake out of your hair, but your Syrians best keep the situation under control until the polls close in California Tuesday night. If they don't, the balance of your CIA career will be spent processing HR complaints in some windowless fucking room. Now *that* was a threat. See the difference?"

For a long moment, Peter heard only his own breathing. Then Charles spoke.

"Take care of Drake, and I'll deliver," Charles said, then ended the call.

Peter held the lifeless phone, realizing that his friendship with Charles was over. So be it. Politics was for keeps, and nice guys finished last. Charles might be angry right now, but his bruised ego was nothing the rarefied air of Langley's seventh floor couldn't fix.

Fortunately, the Drake problem would be easy to resolve in the grand scheme of things. Washington was full of ambitious people, and quite a few of them had hitched their careers to a second Gonzales term. Peter might not be able to change the outcome of the Syrian war, but he could bring a wayward DIA case officer to heel.

Shoving the phone into his pocket, Peter left the kitchenette for the sanctity of his office.

The DIA might be an insular organization, but even insular organizations answered the phone when the White House came calling.

TWENTY-THREE

CIA COMPOUND, SYRIA

Imperial, Pasty, or Redneck?" I said to the twenty-something soldier posted outside the door of the confinement area where Scarface and his men were being held.

"Sir," he answered, shifting the M4 strapped to his chest as he spoke.

"Come on, son. I haven't been out of the Ranger Regiment that long. Which are you?"

The soldier looked at me stone-faced for a beat before smiling.

"My skin's too black to be a Pasty, and I'm sure as hell no Redneck."

"My man," I said, extending my hand. "I was a First Battalion Ranger myself."

The Army's Ranger Regiment is a small organization with only three operational battalions. As a rule, Rangers take no shit from anyone who hasn't worn their scroll;

however, competition is fierce within the Regiment, as is the case with most special operations units. Over time, the three Ranger battalions developed their own lore and, with it, informal nicknames. The men in Second Battalion, stationed at Fort Lewis, Washington, near perpetually cloudy Seattle, are known as Pasties due to their notoriously pale skin. Third Battalion Rangers, housed in rural Fort Benning, Georgia, are the Rednecks. First Ranger Battalion, in comparison, hailed from sun-kissed Savannah. Called the First Imperial Ranger Battalion by their members, and the Beach Boys by the envious other Rangers, First Battalion had been my home for three amazing years.

That meant that the Ranger standing guard and I shared a history.

"Is Sergeant Major Hagan still kicking ass and taking names?" I said, starting a round of the *do you know?* game that all Rangers past and present play when meeting fellow commandos.

The grin slid from the man's face as he slowly shook his head. "No, sir. He was killed nine months ago. Training accident. A young private tangled parachutes with him. Sergeant Major Hagan got the boy's chute clear, but his own collapsed in the process."

"Damn," I said, "he was my first sergeant when I commanded Alpha Company. I can't believe I didn't hear about it."

"How long you been out of the Regiment, sir?"

"Long enough for you to quit calling me sir. My name's Matt Drake. What's yours?"

"Staff Sergeant Ray Unruh."

"Staff Sergeants stand guard nowadays, Ray?"

"Ain't much of anything happening as of yet. Figured I'd take a turn and give the boys a break, sir."

"Matt."

Ray paused a moment and then nodded. "Matt."

"You know the prisoners, Ray?"

"Not really, but I recognize the haji with the scar. Before everything went to shit three months ago and this place was shut down, he used to roll into the compound two or three times a week. He always traveled in a big convoy. The rest of his men would stay outside the gate, but the haji and his three lieutenants would come inside the wire for meetings."

"Who'd he talk to?" I said.

"The Chief."

"Every time?"

A nod. "The CIA folks arrived back in-country just a couple of hours ago, and the haji and his men were their first visitors. Supposedly, the Chief is planning a raid to rescue the captured paramilitary officer."

"You don't sound very convinced."

Ray shrugged his massive shoulders. "I wouldn't know. The CIA case officers don't tell us shit."

This did surprise me. "You guys aren't in on the op?"

Ray shook his head. "Nope. The Agency boys have everything under control, I guess. Me and my men thought we'd be part of the action when we got the orders to leave Johnson and secure this place ahead of the CIA contingent's arrival."

"Johnson?"

"It's a makeshift combat operating post where the in-country JSOC folks are hanging out with the remainder of my company. They're holed up about fifty klicks away."

"Then why are you here?"

Another exasperated shrug. "Hell if I know. I guess they needed someone to lock down the compound while the Agency guys ride to glory. Except that from where I'm sitting, ain't shit happening. They jaw-jack with the hajis all day, but nobody's doing mission planning or rehearsals."

"Ray, I need to tell you something, Ranger to Ranger."

"Lay it on me, sir."

"Matt."

"Matt."

"I didn't come here to jaw-jack. I have an asset inside the splinter cell holding Shaw. He's gonna give me Shaw if I agree to bring him out."

"You're going in?"

"Damn straight."

"Need company?"

"All I can get. But first, I need a favor."

"Name it."

"The jihadis you're guarding, they ambushed my partner and me."

"Bad?"

"My partner's missing his arm."

"You talking about Frodo?"

"Know him?"

"He was my squad leader when I first got to Regiment. Finest soldier I ever met. Damn shame what happened. You want me to smoke the jihadis?"

"Not just yet. The Chief of Base thinks I've got the wrong guy. Says the Syrian is his trusted commander, whatever the fuck that means. Anyway, I've got to find a way to prove him wrong. Something he can't ignore. I thought running biometric samples from these guys through the system might be a good start. Awfully hard for the Chief to argue with me if the database comes back with a hit. What do you say?"

"I'd say that Staff Sergeant Unruh is going to follow his orders, and you're coming with me."

The new voice came from over my shoulder. I turned to see standing behind us the same youngster who had asked me for my badge.

"Son," I said, facing the cocksure CIA officer, "I'm normally pretty easygoing, but you seem bound and determined to test my patience."

"After that stunt you pulled, you're lucky you're not the one in handcuffs," the youngster said. "Get your ass to the TOC. The Chief wants to see you."

"Need a little Ranger love?" Ray said, popping the knuckles on his ham-sized fists.

"Not just yet, Sergeant," I said, glad to once again have a fellow Ranger by my side. "But stay frosty. I'll be back."

"Now, Drake," the CIA officer said.

"What's your name, son?" I said.

"What difference does it make?"

"Your name."

"Jason."

"Jason what?"

"Thome."

"Well, Jason Thome, before this is over, you and I are going to have a come-to-Jesus meeting. Now, let's mosey on back to the TOC in silence before I change my mind and decide we should have that meeting sooner rather than later."

Jason's eyes darted from me to Ray and back again. I wasn't sure what he saw, but it must not have been good. Rather than make a snappy comeback, Jason shut his mouth, spun on his heel, and stalked back to the TOC.

True to my word, I followed in silence.

TWENTY-FOUR

My phone started to buzz ten steps from the TOC's door. I glanced at its dusty screen and saw a number I didn't recognize. I considered returning the phone to my pocket unanswered, but didn't. I might not have known the number, but I knew the area code: 202—Washington, D.C. This was probably a call I should take.

"Drake," I said, putting the phone to my ear as I followed young Jason through the TOC's door.

"Chariot. Chariot. Chariot."

The call ended before I could reply, but that didn't matter. The voice on the other end was unmistakable—Frodo. I hesitated in the door's threshold, trying to understand what had just happened. Frodo had just issued a mission-abort code.

Why?

I thought I might be able to slip away without being noticed, but one look in the TOC convinced me otherwise. The televisions that had previously displayed UAV and satellite imagery now showed something else instead. On the screen to the left, a group of men and women in military uniforms was gathered around a conference table. In contrast, the TV to the right showed just one face, and it was glaring at me.

"Matt Drake?"

"Yes, sir," I said, entering the TOC as the door squeaked close behind me.

"You know who I am?"

"Yes, sir," I said again.

I'd never met him face-to-face, but his visage scowled at me each time I passed a particular section of hallway in DIA headquarters. The section that featured portraits of past and present agency directors. General Jonathan Hartwright, former commander of the 82nd Airborne Division and current Director of the Defense Intelligence Agency, was on a VTC conference, and he wanted to talk.

To me.

Not good.

"Glad we've got that settled," Hartwright said, peering over a pair of reading glasses like I was a repugnant insect. "Now, answer me a question if you'd be so kind."

"Certainly, sir."

"What the fuck are you doing?"

"Sir?"

"You pulled a gun on one of our Syrian partners in the middle of the goddamn TOC?"

"Sir, if you'd let me explain—"

"Drake, do you know who I just got off the phone with?"

"No, sir."

"The White House, Drake. The motherfucking White House. Do you think it was a pleasant conversation?"

"Sir, I—"

"It wasn't, Drake. Not by a long shot. I don't want to relive it just yet, so I'll give you the CliffsNotes version. The CIA has operational control over every swinging dick in Syria, and Mr. Robinson is the CIA's Syrian Chief of Base. That means his word is law. Since you can't seem to grasp that concept, I'm pulling you out of country."

"Sir, my agent can give us Shaw."

"Einstein? Bullshit. He's just another sorry sack selling weapons of mass destruction to the highest bidder. Now he's in over his head, and he wants us to bail him out. Mr. Robinson is running this op. If you really think your asset has the goods, turn Einstein over to the Chief of Base."

"No."

"What did you just say?"

"I'm sorry, sir, but I won't do that. Einstein is my asset. I'm the one responsible for his life, no one else."

"Son, I'm not asking. Give Einstein's information to Robinson. Now."

"Can't do that, sir."

"Interesting. Then I'll tell you what you can do. You can get your sorry ass to Turkey and then onto a flight heading west. Once you land back in D.C., you can get yourself to my office so that we can sort out your insubordination face-to-face. But before you do that, you can surrender your cell phone, weapon, and anything else that identifies you as an agent of the United States government. As of this moment, you are persona non grata in Syria. Welcome to civilian life, Mr. Drake."

'll walk him to the gate," Sergeant Ray Unruh said, tapping my minder on the shoulder, though *minder* might have been a bit of an understatement. Not content to allow me to show myself out, Charles had opted instead for a final bit of humiliation. He'd ordered one of the CIA paramilitary guys to escort me off the premises. I'd thought about trying to state my case to the other meat eaters in the room, but in the end, I'd rejected the idea. Though we ran in the same circles, no one else knew me, but they did know Charles.

Besides, General Hartwright's order had been pretty unambiguous. It would be one thing if the trigger pullers could chalk this up to just another turf war between rival agencies, but the Director of the DIA had ordered one of his case officers out of country. That was pretty cut-and-dried. Nobody was willing to step into the breach with me, and I didn't blame them. Well, maybe nobody but Virginia. She'd caught my eye from where she'd been sitting on the other side of the room, but I'd shaken my head. As far as the powers that be were concerned, she was still clean in the sense that she was not associated with me, and I wanted to keep it that way for as long as possible. I wasn't sure where this operation was going, but I had a feeling that I'd be needing the services of a chemist before it was all over. A chemist I could trust.

With this in mind, I'd gathered what was left of my pride and walked out of the TOC, a CIA paramilitary officer dogging my footsteps.

"You sure?" the paramilitary officer said, his distrustful glance flickering between me and Sergeant Unruh.

"Yeah," Ray said. "I got this."

The second operator seemed about to protest, but shook his head instead. "It's your ass," he said before heading back to the TOC.

Ray and I walked in silence toward the compound's entrance until the paramilitary officer was out of earshot. Then the Ranger spoke.

"You really have an asset?"

"I do."

"And he can give you Shaw?"

"Shaw and the chem weapon Shaw's team was searching for."

"How?"

I thought for a moment before answering, considering both my response and its implications. If I gave up Einstein's background, it wouldn't take a genius to deduce his identity. The safer path would be to decline to answer or lie outright. Next to gathering actionable intelligence, a case officer's most important job was to protect his agent. Telling Ray anything about Einstein would put both my asset and, by extension, Shaw at risk. Still, contrary to what I'd said to Frodo, I did need in-country help. To secure that help, I was going to have to trust someone.

Sergeant Unruh was as good a candidate as anyone.

"My asset helped the terrorists build the chem weapon."

Ray looked at me with an incredulous expression.

"Your asset's a weapons scientist?"

I nodded. "And without a doubt a shit bag. But here's the thing I had to learn in this business—the good guys aren't the ones with access to the information we need. Don't get me wrong. In a perfect world, I'd be planning to smoke my asset instead of rescue him, but this isn't a perfect world. To be honest, I don't care if my asset is a good guy or not. I'd do a deal with Hitler if he could help me bring Shaw home. Getting Shaw back alive is all I care about. Everything else is noise."

"'I will never leave a fallen comrade to fall into the hands of the enemy.'"

The words rolled off Ray's tongue without pause, and I nodded. The phrase came from the fifth stanza of the Ranger Creed, and to men like us, the words meant more than just a pretty sentiment. They were a blood oath that united the fellowship of men who willingly put themselves into harm's way on their nation's behalf. This creed, more than anything else, had solidified my decision to return to Syria. The last time I'd been here, a man and his family had depended on me, and I'd failed them. Now it was Shaw's turn. Though I'd never met the paramilitary officer, Shaw was a special operator and therefore part of the select fraternity the Ranger Creed encompassed.

Three months ago, I'd been unable to honor my promise, and a man and his family had been brutally murdered. Now, after my time in purgatory, maybe rescuing Shaw offered me a chance to set things right.

But whether redemption was possible or not, I could no more abandon Shaw than I could have left Frodo inside our burning Range Rover. General Hartwright might have been my commanding officer, but Shaw was my fallen comrade. He and I would leave this hellhole together or we wouldn't leave at all. On this point, the Ranger Creed couldn't have been any clearer.

"What next?" Ray said.

"I'm going to link up with my asset. He's gonna tell me where Shaw is, and I'm going to bring him home."

"By yourself?"

"If I have to. But I'll tell you what I'm not gonna do. I'm not gonna get on a plane just because General Jackass says to. I'm also not gonna sit around and hope that Charles Robinson IV finally gets off his ass before the jihadis livestream Shaw's execution."

"You and the CIA Chief have a history?"

"A long one," I said, meeting Ray's gaze so that he felt the full weight of my words. "Last time I was here, Charles refused to release the QRF when my asset activated his beacon. His entire family died as a result."

"Why?"

A gentle breeze stirred the grit beneath our feet as I thought about how to answer. A section of dusty sky was visible just above the compound's walls. Same dusty sky, same gentle breeze.

Wind is a fickle thing.

"I don't know," I said. "At the time, Charles said he couldn't risk a rescue so soon after a chem attack, but I don't think that was the real reason. The Syrian your men arrested ambushed Frodo and me on the way to save our asset. I don't know if the attack was connected to why my asset wanted to meet, or if it was just part of the fog of war. In the end, it doesn't matter. What matters is that I made a vow and didn't honor it. That won't happen again."

"What about your asset and his family?"

"A recovery team found them two days later. They were all dead, even the toddler. The wife had been raped."

We walked a step or two in silence as Ray digested what I'd said, while I tried to unsee the pictures the forensic team had snapped of Fazil's apartment. I'd demanded to read the classified version of their report while still lying in my hospital bed. Abir had begun to visit me soon after. I didn't need a shrink to understand why.

Even now the thought of Fazil's final moments made my stomach turn. Killing a man was one thing, but killing his wife and baby was a special kind of twisted. The men who'd done it were monsters, and in my experience, there was only one way to deal with monsters—exterminate them.

"What happened next?" Ray said.

"Frodo and I were medevaced to the States. Charles and the rest of the Agency folks were ordered out of theater. The administration thought the whole Syrian endeavor was too dangerous after the chem attack. Here's the thing—I don't know what Charles is after, but I'm positive there's more here than meets the eye. His Syrian asset disappeared just before the QRF birds rescued Frodo and me. I don't know how Charles is connected, but I don't trust him. Neither should you."

Ray held my gaze for a long moment. He had just started to speak when a familiar voice interrupted.

"Need a ride to the airport?"

Jason Thome and the paramilitary officer stood just behind us.

"Don't you have badges to issue?" I said.

"The Chief told me to make sure you were off the compound. You can walk out or my associate can toss you. Your choice."

I thought about taking him up on the offer, but didn't. As much as I wanted to knock his ego down a peg or two, he wasn't important. Shaw was running out of time. That was the only thing that mattered. Instead, I offered Ray my hand. "Wish we could have met under better circumstances, Sergeant, but if you could still do me a solid, I'd appreciate it. There's a chemist who arrived with me. Her name is Virginia. Please look out for her and let her know I'll be in touch."

"Can do," Ray said, taking my hand. And then to my surprise he pulled me into a hug. "Rangers lead the way," he said.

"All the way," I answered.

Without another word, Ray headed back toward the TOC, pushing his way between Jason and his muscle-bound companion. I used the ensuing confusion to slip through the compound gate and slide into Zain's waiting car before the situation with Jason escalated. The Syrian put the car in gear and rolled away from the compound. Only after we'd made the first turn and wound our way onto the main thoroughfare did he look at me.

"Where to, friend?"

"Not sure," I said, unfolding the tiny scrap of paper Ray had palmed me during our hug. "But I think we should start here." I read off the handwritten address, and Zain entered the information into his phone's GPS.

"We will be there in an hour," Zain said. "What will we find?"

"ISIS? Assad loyalists? Bandits? This is Syria, my friend—one never knows."

TWENTY-FIVE

Trouble, my friend?"

I looked up from the cell phone I'd been configuring to see that Zain had turned his attention from the road to me. A cigar rested between his brown teeth. Judging by the fact that the stogie was half-consumed, a good thirty minutes had passed since we'd pulled off the road so that he could pop the trunk on his beat-up car and outfit me with a new kit.

I'd needed quite a bit.

I'd rendered my phone useless by entering the duress password before surrendering the device to Charles, but the joke was still on me. With no weapon, and no way to contact Frodo, my little rebellion against General Hartwright was going to be short-lived.

But that was before I'd taken a look in Zain's trunk.

Where the outside of his sedan was indistinguishable from that of any of the other thousands of battered vehicles roaming Syria, the trunk had been transported from a Michael Bay movie. Body armor, cell phones, and an assortment of pistols and long guns were nestled in custom-made foam cutouts. In short order, I'd outfitted myself with low-visibility body armor, an AK-47 with extra magazines, and a Glock and holster. A combination cell-sat phone completed the load out. While my new kit didn't match the Ranger Regiment's basic issue, it would have made Batman proud.

I then updated the phone's operating system in accordance with Frodo's instructions, keyed in the password he'd provided, and waited for the phone to reimage. In less than fifteen minutes, I had a fully functioning clone of the phone I'd surrendered to Charles, complete with the app Frodo had used to communicate with Einstein, plus their chat history. Included was a private message from Frodo that read, *Try looking for our friend here*, along with a grid coordinate. Frodo's NSA analyst had managed to get a fix on Einstein's phone. Things were looking up.

And that's when I'd hit my first snag.

Keying in Frodo's number from the contact list, I'd dialed and then listened as the call went to voice mail. Next, I dialed the number he'd used to give me the Chariot abort code, and I got the same result. This was not normal. I'd worked with Frodo for the better part of five years. When we were operational, he was available.

Period.

I'd vented my frustration with a sigh, and this was what had prompted Zain's question.

"I'm in trouble," I said, looking at Zain. "This isn't how I thought the operation was going to play out. If you want to reconsider your offer to help, I won't hold it against you."

Zain slammed on the brakes, bringing the sedan to a skidding halt. "Is this joke?" he said, anger swamping his English. "Things become difficult, and I leave? Is this the person you think I am?"

"Of course not," I said, "but right now, I'm a liability. Without my government's help, I'm alone."

"You are not alone. You have me. Tell me what you need. Immediately."

"Okay. We need to get to the address that Sergeant Unruh gave me, but I don't want to go there blind. Can you find out more about it?"

"Of course. I will make calls. We will have answers."

And with that, Zain put the car into gear and began driving with one hand and dialing his phone with the other. I listened as he worked his contacts, directing streams of rapid-fire Arabic at each man who answered. While Zain pulsed his network, I did a little research of my own, starting with Einstein's supposed location.

During a normal operation, my encrypted smartphone would be able to access a password-protected FTP site. The DIA team of analysts assigned to the operation would post up-to-the-minute ISR—or intelligence, security, and reconnaissance data—to the site, much like with a Dropbox account. The prepared data came in the form of a graphic overlay onto which was fused all the intelligence the DIA possessed concerning a particular set of geographical coordinates. The information was derived from a number of diverse sources, including loitering drones, satellite imagery, and the occasional U-2 reconnaissance flight, as well as applicable human intelligence, or HUMINT, reporting.

All in all, it was a pretty good system, and probably completely unavailable to me for this mission. That was my assumption, anyway. General Hartwright's edict had left no room for interpretation. Even if Frodo—or James, for that matter—was still pulling for me back home, an overt act on his part would risk not only his job but his freedom. As of this minute, I was a private citizen operating in a foreign country without the blanket of protection offered by the United States government. While I had every intention of forcing this scenario to change, I knew that this was not yet the time or the place to do so. So, rather than click on the inviting icon that would have led me to the best all-source intelligence the world's remaining superpower could generate, I did the next best thing.

I opened Google Maps.

The app returned imagery, but without context, it was only slightly better than nothing at all. The grid coordinates Frodo had provided were the location of several rambling buildings, connected by a large concrete thoroughfare, all ringed with cyclone fencing. No vehicles, or other signs of life, were present in the dated satellite picture, but that was hardly surprising. This part of Syria encompassed a type of no-man's-land in which territory claimed by the Assad regime, ISIS remnants, and the various rebel groups all overlapped. Anyone who could leave had vacated the city long ago. Those who had been left behind weren't likely to seek shelter so far from the city's center.

"I have bad news, my friend," Zain said, ending his latest cell phone conversation. "You will need to travel to meet your asset, yes?"

I looked up from the Internet search I was running. Bringing Zain into my trusted circle was one thing, but providing him with information about Einstein was something else entirely. I trusted Zain, but I was the only thing standing between my agent and a grisly death. Zain was an asset, but operational security was still operational security.

"Why do you ask?" I said.

"That was Akram. He manages our commerce flowing in and out of Assad-controlled territory. As of this morning, all land routes are closed."

"Why?"

"Assad has mounted a new offensive supported by the Russians. We think they are attempting to capture several key road intersections. In any case, Akram reports that Russian aircraft are strafing any vehicles moving along these roads. For now, we are stuck, my friend."

I swore and then read the Internet search results. Some years ago, the plot of land might or might not have been used for industrial activity—a ball bearing factory, if I was translating correctly—but I could find nothing of relevance now. As I was processing what the route closures meant to my hastily constructed plan, the icon for Einstein's chat app alerted me to an incoming message. A single line of text appeared.

I have what you requested. Time is short.

I thought for a moment, thumbs hovering over the virtual keyboard, and then began to type.

I'm ready. Send meet location.

Just you?

Just me.

The cursor flashed as Einstein replied.

I copied the address he sent and pasted it into Google Maps. The coordinates were for a park about two kilometers south of the ball bearing factory. Score one for Frodo's NSA girlfriend and Einstein's truthfulness. So far, so good.

Confirmed, I typed. *Stand by for instructions.*

Has something changed?

Nothing has changed. Instructions coming.

I hit the Send button and then closed the app before Einstein could engage me in a more protracted conversation.

Nothing has changed. As a case officer, I'd told my share of lies, but that whopper might just take the cake. A more accurate response might have been *Everything has changed. I have no idea how to get to you, much less rescue a half-dead operator from your terrorist friends. Wish me luck.*

"My friend, I have something which needs your attention."

"What?" I said, scrolling through the Google imagery as our car slowed to a stop.

"Them."

I looked up to see four men leaving the safety of a bunker made of corrugated steel. The structure stood in front of a rusted barricade that barred entry to a vehicle-sized gap in a head-high crumbling stone wall. The four men were dressed like locals and carried their AK-47s with the practiced ease of men who knew how to use them.

"What now?" Zain said.

I looked at the men and made a snap decision. Ray had provided me with this address for a reason. Either I trusted him or I didn't. Time to roll the dice.

"Let's drive over and say hello," I said, infusing my voice with a confidence I didn't feel.

Zain glanced at me before putting the car in gear and rolling forward. As we drew closer, I noticed he was mumbling under his breath.

"What are you doing?" I said.

"Praying."

I wanted to give a witty reply, but my mouth had become strangely dry. The men noticed our approach, and while the AK-47s weren't pointed at us, the rifles hung loose and ready. Zain nosed the car up next to the group. Two of the men planted themselves on either side of the hood, ensuring interlocking fields of fire, while a third wandered over to my side of the car.

Ducking his head down to my window, the man spoke a single sentence in heavily accented English.

"Rangers lead the way."

"All the way," I said.

At my reply, a grin replaced the man's somber expression. "Welcome to COP Johnson, Mr. Matt. We've been expecting you."

If only I could say the same.

TWENTY-SIX

The four guards, now more smiles than suspicious glares, directed our car into the compound after raising the barricade to the squeal of rusted metal on metal.

At first glance, COP Johnson's security was not impressive. The steel barricade and small guard force might have kept children and the occasional stray dog from entering the compound, but not much else. Any serious threat, be it a dismounted force or a Vehicle-Borne IED, or VBIED, would make short work of both the barricade and whatever it protected.

My assessment stood for exactly ten seconds. That was how long it took for Zain to edge our vehicle around a makeshift guard shack fashioned out of sandbags and concrete.

On the other side of the shack, we faced a narrow alleyway constructed of cinder blocks, at the end of which sat a sliding blast door. Twin turrets housing crew-served weapons sat above the door. The turret on the left had dual .50-caliber machine guns, while the one on the right sported an MK-19 automatic grenade launcher. Instead of crew members, an optics cluster featuring day TV and thermal cameras topped each weapon. As our car entered the alleyway, the turrets swiveled in our direction, tracking us until we reached the blast door, which silently slid open on well-greased treads.

Remote-weapons stations oriented on a perfectly constructed kill zone with a state-of-the-art blast shield. These folks had taken the idea of hiding in plain sight to the next level.

A squad of hard-looking men met us on the far side of the blast shield and directed Zain toward a series of interconnected industrial buildings. Though the men's unkempt hair, shaggy beards, and civilian clothes were meant to suggest otherwise, they were not natives. Neither were the HK416 rifles strapped to their chests. Unless I missed my guess, our parking attendants were Ray's fellow Rangers.

Zain followed their hand and arm signals and parked our battered sedan next to several vehicles in similar condition. Except that, judging by the way the Land Cruiser next to me rode low on its wheels, these vehicles had undergone some serious retrofitting.

"Do you think I could buy one of those?" Zain said, staring at the up-armored Land Cruiser.

"This is Syria, my friend," I said. "Anything is possible."

"Mr. Drake?"

One of the parking attendants had followed us over and was now outside my window.

"That's me."

"Great. We've been expecting you."

"That's what your indigenous guards said when we pulled up. But they forgot to introduce themselves."

"Yes, sir. If you'll follow me."

I might not be the most astute of observers, but I could recognize a brush-off when I saw one. Besides, it wasn't like I had anywhere to be. I climbed out of the car and motioned for Zain to join me.

"Sorry, sir," my escort said, "but your driver needs to stay with the vehicle."

"This isn't my driver," I said as Zain bristled. "His name is Zain, and he runs one of the largest intelligence networks in Syria. More important, he's my friend. Anywhere I go, he goes."

Arab pride is a notorious beast. The ancient Greeks might have started a nation-ending war because of Helen of Troy's beauty, but that battle would have been a mere footnote in this part of the world. Here, tribal blood feuds sparked by long-forgotten slights could span generations. The last thing I wanted to do was to inadvertently alienate Zain and his valuable network.

Besides, I'd already been hosed once by my own government. If nothing else, when the chips were down, I knew that Zain would keep people honest. At the same time, I didn't want to piss off our new hosts, whoever they might be. "Go ahead and call it in, Ranger," I said. "We'll wait."

Our escort hesitated and then gave a quick nod. Pulling a radio from his pocket, he stepped a few feet away for a brief conversation. After a series of hushed words, the Ranger motioned us forward. "This way, gentlemen."

Our guide walked at a brisk pace and didn't seem interested in conversation. We didn't exactly get a tour, but Zain and I did get to see some pretty interesting sights. In addition to the small fleet of vehicles, we walked past no fewer than three Russian cargo helicopters, a Hind gunship, and a small transport plane used for short-field takeoffs and landings. Each of these airships bore Syrian or Russian markings and seemed remarkably well maintained for its age.

Things were becoming more curious by the second.

After winding past an open bay filled with cots, chairs, and portable gym equipment, our silent guide led us to a door marked TOC in large block letters. He rapped on the door twice, and it was opened from the inside.

"That's it for me, gentlemen," our escort said, motioning us into the building. "Enjoy your stay."

I nodded my thanks and crossed the threshold from one world to another.

While everything thus far had fit the motif of an abandoned factory, this room was something else. Laptop workstations and radios were everywhere. A series of old-fashioned laminated maps covered two of the walls, with enemy positions outlined in red grease pencil. The final two walls held big-screen TVs—one tuned to Fox News while the other showed aerial footage from a loitering UAV.

Home sweet home.

"You Drake?"

The question came from a man standing in the center of the room, his hands on his hips like he was a captain manning a warship's bridge.

"Matt Drake, sir," I said, offering him a handshake. "This is Zain."

"Great to meet you both," the man said, pumping my hand with a viselike grip. "My name is Colonel Nolan Fitzpatrick, and I'm the commander of this task force. We're the theater quick reaction force, and right now, I'm feeling pretty underused. Sergeant Ray Unruh gave us a call and said you had a lead on the CIA's captured operator. That true?"

"Yes, sir," I said, my lips edging into a smile.

"Hot damn. That's the best news I've had in three days. We didn't fly all the way from Fort Bragg to sit on our asses while those CIA prima donnas sort themselves out. Son, if you've got the intel, I've got the brawn. Let's get to work."

"Yes, sir," I said again, this time feeling the smile all the way to my toes. After all the false starts, things were starting to move forward, and not a moment too soon. The DIA analysts thought that the jihadis intended to execute Shaw before the election. If they were right, the clock was not our friend.

S o, that's where we stand," I said, finishing my summary.

To provide Colonel Fitzpatrick with the full picture, I'd given him a total accounting of everything that had happened, starting with my aborted shoeshine in the Austin airport what seemed like ages ago. Though my retelling had burned through twenty minutes, the time had not been wasted.

Midway through my narrative, Colonel Fitzpatrick— or Fitz, as he insisted I call him—had beckoned his intelligence and operations officers, who in turn had begun issuing quiet instructions to their subordinates as we talked. Now the largest plasma TV showed satellite imagery of the park that Einstein had designated as our meet site. The second monitor showcased a topographical map of the same coordinates with known and suspected enemy locations highlighted.

The two Majors, who served as Fitz's planners, had already begun locating suitable helicopter landing zones close to the park. Now they were plotting aerial ingress and egress routes on their laptops. At the same time, Fitz's battle captain had issued a quickly prepared WARNO, or Warning Order, to the troop of assaulters currently on duty and had sent a runner to wake their commander.

The contrast between what was happening here and what was happening at Charles's command post couldn't have been clearer. I didn't know Sergeant Ray Unruh from anyone, but once this operation was over, I was going to rectify that shortcoming with a six-pack or two.

"What about the Syrian who tried to draw down on you?" Fitz said, leaning forward in his chair. "The one with the scar?"

I shrugged as I took a swallow of coffee from the cup that had magically appeared while I'd been talking. "The CIA Chief of Base intervened before I could get his biometrics, and my contact in the States hasn't gotten back to me. I don't know who the hell he is."

"I do."

Zain made the statement with such casual indifference that I almost choked on my second gulp of coffee. A part of me wanted to rip my asset's head off for not volunteering this information sooner, but I bit my tongue instead. In the mad scramble to leave the safe house, Zain and I hadn't had a chance to discuss the Syrian. In fact, this was probably the first time my asset had even heard my story in its entirety. So rather than vent my frustration, I took a breath and asked the obvious question.

"Who is he?"

"His name is Sayid. He's been on the American payroll for the last two years."

"Doing what?" Fitz said.

"The CIA was prepping his fighters for a covert mission. Sayid's men were given all sorts of specialized American equipment, including intelligence products."

"What kind of mission?"

Zain shrugged. "I'm not sure."

"Son of a bitch," I said as several pieces of information suddenly connected.

"What gives?" Fitz said. "You look like you've seen a ghost."

"When I walked into the TOC and saw Sayid standing with Charles, I could have sworn he recognized me."

"How?"

"That's just it—I'm not sure. But it doesn't bode well that Sayid's been on Charles's payroll the entire time. If he recognized a covert DIA case officer, what else does he know?"

"You think Charles is compromised?" Fitz said.

I shrugged. "I don't know. What I do know is that Sayid led the men who ambushed me. If anything, this places an even greater urgency on my meet with Einstein. The entire CIA rescue begins and ends with that traitorous fuck. Somehow, I don't think he has Shaw's best interests at heart."

Fitz nodded. "Ray's been on loan to the Agency folks since Charles and his paramilitary guys arrived back in-country. When Ray called to let me know you were coming, he was short on details but seemed less than thrilled at the pace at which the rescue operation was progressing."

"Fitz," I said, "don't take this the wrong way, but why aren't you colocated with the Agency folks?"

"Funny you should ask. Ceding operational control of the rescue to the CIA didn't sit well with my bosses at JSOC headquarters. Officially, we're here to augment the security for the aviators tasked with flying the CIA spooks in and out of country."

"And unofficially?" I said.

"Unofficially, we're standing by in case the CIA fucks this up. Like I said, if you've got the intel, I've got the brawn. But we've only got one shot. Once we cross into Assad's battle space, all hell is going to break loose. So my question to you is simple—does your asset have the intel?"

"There's only one way to find out," I said with a smile.

TWENTY-SEVEN

An hour later, I was alone in a closet-sized mission planning room, prebreathing oxygen from an oxygen console. An Air Force physiological tech, or fizz, sat in the metal chair across from me, monitoring my vitals. Right now the tech's job was fairly simple, but in another thirty minutes, his presence might make the difference between life and death.

The metal folding table in front of me was covered with maps, but at this point, they were more decorative than necessary. I'd verified the winds aloft, both current and predicted, every thousand feet from the surface up to twenty-five thousand. I'd planned my route, double-checked it, and then borrowed one of Fitz's jumpmasters for a second look. Everything checked out. I had the necessary landmarks, headings, and altitudes memorized and the azimuths and GPS coordinates programmed into my jump board. I'd helped one of the Unit riggers pack my chute, stacking the canvas cells on top of one another, ensuring there was no fold or roll in the canopy's nose or tail. In other words, the chute was rigged for a quick opening, which I would need.

Now there was nothing left to do but wait for the sun to set and hope that Syria's fickle winds didn't vary too much from the forecast. To say that this operation didn't have much of a margin for error would be kind of like saying that the bottom of Niagara Falls was a little wet.

At first blush, the unexpected Assad offensive had left me with one hell of a problem. I could no longer travel by road to meet Einstein, since the Russians were strafing anything that moved. Helicopter insertion was out as well. Colonel Fitz could risk transiting through Russian-controlled airspace only once—on the way to rescue Shaw. But the rescue could happen only *after* I'd met with Einstein, verified his bona fides, and obtained Shaw's location.

These constraints had left me back at the drawing board.

Okay, that wasn't true. They had actually left me hoping that the Air Force weather forecaster, who looked all of seven days out of high school, was better at predicting the winds aloft than he was at growing a beard. I needed a way to slip past the Russian air force patrolling the Assad-controlled sector where Einstein wanted to meet.

Since the Army aviators couldn't fly me, I'd have to fly myself.

If someone were to google the acronym *HAHO*, they would find dozens of cool pictures. These images would undoubtedly feature special operators wearing oxygen masks, and an assortment of impressive gear, as they glided across the sky beneath perfectly inflated parachutes. As I could attest, scores of otherwise intelligent young men had been seduced into becoming Rangers, SEALs, or Green Berets after seeing these recruiting-brochure-worthy HAHO pictures. In fact, the casual observer might come to the conclusion that the men depicted in these pictures were having the time of their lives.

And in this conclusion, the casual observer couldn't be more wrong.

A HAHO—High Altitude, High Opening—jump was an infiltration method used to transfer special operators from friendly to contested airspace without the enemy's knowledge. Put another way, the special operator jumped from a plane flying in friendly airspace, inflated his parachute, and glided to a landing zone in enemy territory up to twenty miles away. If everything went perfectly, the operator arrived at the landing zone undetected and no worse for wear.

But in the real world, HAHO jumps seldom went perfectly.

Conducting a HAHO was exceptionally risky. Special operators had to prebreathe oxygen before jumping in order to avoid hypoxia—a potentially fatal condition in which the jumper's oxygen-starved brain ceased to function. Even after prebreathing, jumpers were still at risk for the various afflictions associated with altitude sickness.

Then there were the environmental conditions to consider. Air temperatures at altitude ranged from a balmy negative twelve degrees Fahrenheit at twenty thousand feet all the way to a downright frigid negative forty-seven at thirty thousand. If a jumper's kit malfunctioned, he could literally freeze to death before arriving at the drop zone. And apart from the environmental and atmospheric concerns there was the inherent danger of dangling from a parachute, five miles above the earth, as the enemy did his best to find and kill you. A HAHO jump was a high-risk insertion used only when conventional methods weren't available.

It was also my only hope of getting to Einstein before the jihadis sawed Shaw's head off.

My phone buzzed. I fished the device from my pocket and stared at the screen. Another number I didn't recognize. If this kept up, I was going to have to add myself to the do-not-call list, assuming they had one of those for spies. I took an intercom dongle from my oxygen mask, plugged it into the phone, and answered.

"Drake."

"Matty?"

"Frodo! Where you been?"

"Shit's gone crazy here, brother. I've never seen anything like it. General Hartwright called James personally. He wanted you pulled out of Syria."

"Me specifically?"

"Yep. I was in James's office. He took the call on speakerphone, and I heard every word."

"And James just rolled over?"

"Come on, Matty. You know our boss. Does the Chief strike you as the roll-over type? He told the Director that if he wanted you out of Syria, he could goddamn well call you himself."

"He did."

"I had a feeling he might. That's why I tried to give you the abort code before they burned our phones."

"Say again?"

"You heard me. Right after James hung up, the burn notice came down. James held off the techs long enough for me to get the one call to you."

"Looks like the burn notice didn't stop you for long."

"What can I say? I'm resourceful. Where are you now? Istanbul?"

"Not exactly. I'm still in-country. I linked up with a bunch of your old mates."

"What's the plan?"

"Nothing's changed," I said. "I'm gonna meet Einstein and see what he knows."

"Are you kidding me? Everything has changed. You've been PNGed, brother. That means you have no official status. Do your new friends know that?"

"Not exactly."

"Meaning?"

"Meaning I may have forgotten to mention the whole PNGed part to the Unit commander."

Frodo sighed. "So the Unit guys are going to fly you to meet Einstein?"

"In a manner of speaking."

"Matty."

"Look, I've got one chance. Einstein is right smack in the middle of Assad-controlled territory. The roads are locked down due to the ongoing fighting. That means I've got to be damn sure that Einstein has a handle on Shaw before my new friends come busting through Assad's airspace. I've got to go in solo."

I could almost hear the wheels turning as Frodo considered what I'd said. It didn't take him long to divine the meaning behind my words.

"Matty, this is starting to sound like a suicide mission. You have no idea whether Einstein's on the level, and even if he is, you're operating without sanction. The DIA is going to disavow you. You could find yourself cut off in Assad's battle space with no way home. Don't do this—we'll find another way."

"There isn't time."

"Bullshit. This is me you're talking to. If you go in alone and get rolled up, what does that do for Shaw? Nothing. This isn't just reckless—it's stupid. You know I'm right."

Maybe I did, but it didn't matter. Not anymore. I'd finally come to that realization. Now it was time to help Frodo do the same.

"I see her," I said, the words coming out as a croak. I'd wanted to say them to so many people, so many times, but I couldn't. Not face-to-face, or maybe not while I was safe in the States while Fazil and his family were decomposing in the unforgiving Syrian sand. But this time, things were different.

Or maybe I was different.

"See who?" Frodo said.

"Abir. She waves at me from over her mama's shoulder. You remember how she'd pop up and flash us that grin? I see her doing that all the fucking time."

"Like a flashback or something?"

"No. Like she's in the room with me. She smiles and plays peekaboo. Real enough that I could reach out and pinch her chubby cheeks. But I can't. She's dead. They're all dead. I promised him, Frodo. I looked the man in the eye and promised him."

"Matt, you can't—"

"Listen to me, brother. I'm fucked up. I know it. Believe me, I do. And I also know that I'm not getting better. In fact, I think I'm getting worse. I get the shakes, I can't sleep, and when I look at Laila, I see Abir's mother. I've tried to make things right. I can't. No matter what I do, Abir will still be dead, and you'll still be a cripple. I understand that now, but I also understand that Shaw's life is on the line. Maybe the rescue will turn out right. Maybe it won't. Either way, I have to try. You understand, right?"

It surprised me how much emotion was wrapped up in my final question. How much I needed my best friend to say he understood, because if he didn't, then maybe I really had lost my mind. So I stood in that tiny room, waiting for Frodo to grant me absolution.

But absolution wasn't what he offered.

"I know you," Frodo said. "We've been through more shit than any two people have a right to ever see, and we aren't even married. I know you, and I know you're gonna do what you're gonna do regardless of what I say. So rather than try to talk some sense into your ignorant redneck ass, let me say this instead—how can I help?"

Instead of absolution, Frodo offered something better. Friendship.

"Here's the thing, brother," I said, trying to cover the hoarseness in my voice. "This is shaping up to be a shit storm of biblical proportions. I need to focus on Einstein and getting to Shaw before it's too late. I don't have the bandwidth to sort out Charles, Scarface, and the DIA Director making me persona non grata. Straight up—I need you watching my back, just like always. Can you dig it?"

"Hell yeah, I can dig it. I got you, Matty. Need anything now?"

"I do," I said, remembering my new friend from East Tennessee. "There's a DIA chemist back at the CIA safe house. Her name is Virginia Kenyon. Get in touch with her, bring her up to speed, and pass me her contact info. When Einstein starts talking about the chem weapon, I'll need Virginia to validate what he says."

"Got it. Anything else?"

"One more thing. I'm sorry."

"I've told you a thousand times, you thickheaded hick: What happened in Syria wasn't your fault."

"Maybe that's true," I said, "and maybe it's not. Either way, I'm not apologizing for Syria. I'm apologizing for not bringing you with me. You should be here. Now. This doesn't feel right without you riding shotgun. For that, I'm sorry."

A long pause and then, "Go take care of business.

We'll continue the Oprah shit over some beers once you're back."

"Thanks, brother."

"Good hunting, Matty."

The line went dead. I'd made peace with Frodo, but he was right. This was starting to look awfully like a suicide mission.

But maybe that was the point.

TWENTY-EIGHT

Spread your feet."

I widened my stance, moving through the familiar routine I'd endured a thousand times. But this wasn't like any of the countless prejump inspections I'd undergone before other operations.

Not even close.

The rucksack full of my equipment—radio, tactical harness, body armor, and rifle—was conspicuously absent. I was meeting Einstein as a spy, not as a soldier. That necessitated looking like a local, not a Ranger, so I'd traded my radio for a combination cell-satellite phone and a backup battery. A Glock pistol was secreted in a holster tucked deep in my waistband, and a suppressor, threaded for the Glock's stubby barrel, was hidden in a pocket, along with two spare magazines. Underneath my cold-weather gear and disposable flight suit, I was dressed in clothes that would blend with the populace's, including my long-sleeved shirt with its ever-present handcuff key sewn into the cuff.

I felt more than a little bit exposed, but that was the price of doing business.

"Turn to your right."

I complied, the words familiar even if the voice was not. Normally, it was Frodo's unmistakable baritone barking the jumpmaster's prejump inspection commands.

Not today.

Today, one of Colonel Fitz's Unit jumpmasters was pinch-hitting. While I was certain that he was more than qualified, he wasn't accompanying me on the jump. For this insertion, I was a lone ranger in every sense of the term.

"Turn to your left."

The jumpmaster's hands were sure and quick. His precise motions were the epitome of efficiency as he checked and double-checked my rig.

"Arms over your head."

I raised both hands in anticipation of the final checks, drawing a deep breath from my oxygen mask as I tried to settle my nerves and ignore the woman and toddler standing just to my left. They'd materialized while the jumpmaster was doing his checks, but for once, I refused to acknowledge their presence. Instead, I concentrated on what was real. I concentrated on Syria.

The sun was just now drifting below the horizon, and an orange half-light softened the jagged corners and hard edges of the slowly decaying metal buildings. A nearby hill boasted an ancient Roman fortification, the blocks of hand-cut cream stone still forming recognizable structures even after two thousand years of neglect. Vegetation sprouted from the fortress's nooks and crannies, looking impossibly green against the burgundy sky.

Viewed through the twilight's magical filter, the scene could have been torn from Ireland's emerald hills.

But this wasn't Ireland or Scotland, or anywhere else a person would choose to visit. This was Syria, and as Abir and her mother could attest, Syria was synonymous with just one thing—death. The deaths of my asset and his family. The thousands of innocents killed in the never-ending civil war. The dead men Frodo and I left in our wake after the ambush we nearly hadn't survived. So it was with more than a little surprise that now, as I prepared to finally confront Syria at her most ruthless, I thought about life.

At one time, Syria had been known as a place of culture and learning. According to the Bible, the apostle Paul encountered the risen Christ on the road to Damascus. After his conversion, Paul's writings became the bulk of the New Testament and inarguably altered history. Could it be that this war-torn husk of a country had within it the potential to experience its own road-to-Damascus conversion? A conversion away from the tyranny and death that currently held sway?

I didn't pretend to know the answer to this or the multitude of similar questions swimming through the debris inhabiting my mind. What I did know was that until someone confronted the evil men holding this country hostage, the sunset drenching the surrounding buildings in burnished gold would be nothing more than a sunset. I couldn't save Syria, but God willing, I might just be able to save Shaw.

That would have to be enough.

"All good," the jumpmaster said, completing his final check. "You're cleared to fly."

I nodded my thanks and ran gloved fingers down the series of innocuous-seeming buckles and straps, paying special attention to the red cutaway pillow next to my sternum. If something unexpected happened, this four-inch-by-three-inch handle would allow me to cut away the main chute and trigger my reserve. If that happened, my insertion would be a bust, but a busted insertion beat becoming a lawn dart any day.

After verifying that my rig was in order, I knew that I'd delayed the inevitable long enough. Turning to confront the two phantasms, I saw only empty space. Abir and her mother had vanished. I wasn't sure what their silent presence implied about my upcoming mission, but it couldn't be good.

"Ready?"

This time Colonel Fitz asked the question. Though my prejump checkout had started with just me and the Unit jumpmaster, we'd slowly gained an audience. Now the large bay that served as a hangar was filled with men who had begun to appear in twos and threes as the jumpmaster had gone about his work. The commandos had stood silently, the normal banter and ever-present gallows humor consciously absent. Instead, they'd watched and waited as the jumpmaster's commands interrupted the gathering stillness. Fitz had joined the throng moments ago, but he, too, had maintained the silent vigil right up until the point when the jumpmaster had issued his final command.

Now the time for silence was over.

"Ready," I said, surprised to find that this was true. Even with the ambiguity surrounding what might happen next, I was ready. Ready to permanently put everything behind me, one way or another.

"Good," Fitz said, resting a callused hand on my shoulder. "I'm not much for *Braveheart* speeches. Frankly, this organization doesn't expect them. We pride ourselves on being the epitome of the quiet professional. We go about our nation's business without fanfare or recognition. Our success is measured in hostages brought home and enemies removed from the battlefield. Even so, there is one ethos that we hold to above all else—'I will never leave a fallen comrade to fall into the hands of the enemy.'"

Fitz paused as if to allow his words the weight they deserved. "That phrase is part of the Ranger Creed, but it also embodies this organization. Almost three decades ago, two of our brothers laid down their lives to protect their fallen comrades in the streets of Mogadishu. In response, we secured the crash sites and didn't leave until we'd recovered every forensic piece of our fallen. This profession offers very little in terms of guarantees—we run toward the sound of gunfire knowing that each and every mission might be our last. But this we hold to as our holy writ—if you go into harm's way, you will not be forgotten. We will expend every ounce of blood and sweat, down to the last full measure, to bring you home."

Fitz paused once more, and the silence was now absolute. "Our entire task force is gathered for one reason—to bear witness as I make this same promise to you. You are going into harm's way because a brother-in-arms has fallen into the hands of the enemy. There is no higher calling. I can't promise you that you will survive this calling, but I will swear this—you will not be alone. When you call, we will answer. That is our vow. Questions?"

I shook my head, not trusting myself to talk past the lump in my throat.

"Good," Fitz said, handing me an electronic device about the size of a dime. "You know what to do with this?"

I nodded, squirreling the miniature piece of equipment into one of my flight suit's zippered pockets.

"All right," Fitz said, slapping me on the back. "Godspeed, Matt Drake. Find our fallen comrade, and we will come. And when we come, hellfire and brimstone will come with us. Good hunting, son."

With that, Fitz stepped aside, making room for the line of assaulters that had formed behind him. Each man gave me a handshake or a squeeze on the shoulder. Each stranger looked me in the eye for one reason only—so that I would know the faces of the men who would be running toward the sound of gunfire on my behalf.

After the final commando slapped me on the back, I turned and shuffled toward the Antonov An-2 Colt plane that would be my ride. Grabbing the canvas door, I pulled myself into the cargo hold and strapped into one of the webbed seats. The aircraft's retrofitted turboprop engine turned over, coughing a cloud of jet fuel exhaust, and just like that, I was on my way.

As the aircraft taxied from the hangar onto the strip of pitted concrete that served as a runway, I looked out the grime-encrusted window. Someone once said that people sleep peacefully in their beds at night only because rough men stand ready to do violence on their behalf. In the hangar behind me, some of the roughest men I'd ever had the pleasure of meeting stood at attention as Colonel Fitz rendered a parade-field-worthy salute with his bear paw of a hand.

The turboprop's roar turned into a full-fledged howl. The plane bumped down the concrete on its oversized rubber tires before taking to the sky in a liftoff that wasn't graceful as much as practical. As the nose pitched up to an almost-forty-five-degree angle, and the wood-and-canvas plane fought for altitude, I felt an inexplicable sense of peace. My mission was still just as suicidal, the conditions just as dangerous, the outcome just as uncertain. And yet for the first time in months, the world seemed right.

I was exactly where I was supposed to be.

"Okay," the pilot said, his voice crackling over the intercom. "We're a go. ETA to insertion point, two zero minutes."

Twenty minutes. Time enough for one last phone call.

TWENTY-NINE

The mismatch between the Colt's powerful turbine engine and its flimsy construction produced a constant vibration reminiscent of a jackhammer on speed. The web-belt seat beneath me quivered like a tuning fork, and I could feel the structural strain in my fillings as the plane climbed skyward.

Originally of Soviet design, the An-2 had been purchased and then manufactured in large numbers by North Korea specifically for ferrying their army of special operations forces into South Korea undetected. The aircraft's simple design and absence of structural metal made the craft extremely hard to detect by radar. This was what I was counting on as the pilot spiraled us ever upward into one of the planet's most contested sections of airspace.

Resisting the temptation to look outside and track our progress across the dimly lit Syrian countryside, I took my cell phone from a pocket and once again attached it to the intercom dongle that hung from my oxygen mask.

Ever since the first paratrooper had climbed combat-laden onto the first transport aircraft, the hellish flight to the drop zone had been a period of introspection. Now modern technology allowed me to pass this time in ways more creative than praying the rosary or exchanging dark jokes with my seatmates. Instead, I could place a call to someone half a world away. But as my quivering fingers punched the numbers on the phone's touch screen, I couldn't help but think that my paratrooper ancestors might have had the better of things.

I entered the final digit and before I could lose my nerve hit Send. Milliseconds later, the call went through, and I could hear the line ringing. A million valid reasons why this was a bad idea came and went as I hoped the call would go unanswered. But it wasn't a prerecorded message that broke the silence. It was a real live voice.

"Hello?"

"Hey," I said. "It's me."

The response popped from my mouth without thought, the familiarity of her voice provoking the familiar in me. But we were no longer quite as familiar as my subconscious wanted to pretend.

"Matt? Where are you? Are you home?"

"Not yet, baby, but soon."

The silence stretched as I lingered in the warmth of Laila's voice. *God, I missed her.*

"Are you okay?"

Laila would have made an excellent spy. Her appearance and aptitude for languages aside, she had a way of reading people that bordered on the mystical. By our third date, I'd confessed that I worked for the DIA. My admission hadn't been an attempt to impress her. Somehow, she'd already realized that parts of my life didn't add up. No, I'd told my future wife the truth because I was afraid of losing her. After six years of marriage, I was still afraid of losing her. Not because I ever worried that she'd betray her vows, but because I couldn't imagine what life would be like without her.

"It's been a rough couple of weeks," I said, hoping that she'd hear the veracity in my voice but not pry.

"Why is it so loud?" Laila said.

"Sorry. I'm at work."

"And you're calling me? Is everything all right?"

I paused, looking out the filthy piece of scratched Plexiglas that passed for a window. Inky blackness stared back. The endless civil war had taught Syria's people the folly of leaving lights on after dark. Lights attracted attention, and in this godforsaken place, attention equaled death.

"I'm thinking about taking a break when I get back," I said as the Unit jumpmaster waved to get my attention and held up two gloved fingers. *Two minutes.* "Maybe go to grad school or something. What do you think?"

This time, the silence stretched long enough that I thought I'd lost the connection. Then she spoke.

"Matt?"

"Yes?"

"Promise me something. Promise to come back to me. Okay?"

"I promise," I said.

The call ended before she could reply.

I told myself that I didn't have time to call her back, but that wasn't the reason I turned off the phone and sealed it in my cargo pocket. My wife would have made an excellent spy, and excellent spies can hear the lie in another person's voice.

Even if that voice belongs to their husband.

THIRTY

The blast of cold air hit me like a punch to the chest. Desert countries were funny like that—brutally hot in the daytime, with temperature swings in excess of forty degrees at sunset. But this was a different kind of cold. At twenty-five thousand feet, nothing could survive without help. At least I hoped we were at twenty-five thousand feet. To traverse the distance I had to cover once my chute opened, I was going to need every foot of altitude the rickety plane could provide.

"How we doing?" I asked through the intercom cord I'd plugged into my oxygen mask.

"One minute," the jumpmaster answered, his helmet visor already frosted over from the sudden temperature change. "We're at altitude, and the winds are holding. Take a look."

Ignoring the fluttering in my stomach, I shuffled toward the gaping door that, until two minutes ago, had been a solid part of the aircraft's fuselage. Now it offered an unobstructed view of the Syrian sky as well as my gateway to what would be, one way or another, the final chapter of my Syrian odyssey.

To say that I was scared of heights would be a bit inaccurate. I was terrified. Terrified in that soul-crushing, panic-inducing manner that small children reserved for the unseen monsters that lurked beneath their beds. Over the course of my time as a paramilitary operator, first as a Ranger and later as a DIA case officer, I'd lost count of the number of well-educated, and equally well-meaning, psychologists who'd told me that I would eventually conquer my fear of heights.

Twelve years after I'd raised my right hand and sworn to defend my nation against threats both foreign and domestic, many of life's absolutes had faded from black or white to shades of gray. But not my fear of heights. Despite the diagnoses of no fewer than six learned doctors, I was more convinced than ever that my fear of heights was incurable. Most days, I wasn't required to confront my phobia, but on days like today, I really wondered why I hadn't followed Mom's advice and gone to dental school. Sitting in a plastic chair and smelling stinky breath certainly had its drawbacks, but dentists didn't usually hyperventilate on their drive to work.

God, but I hated heights.

Shuffling across the bouncing floor, I edged past the jumpmaster, grabbed the handholds bolted into the aircraft's bulkhead, and leaned into the slipstream.

At first glance, things weren't too terrible. This high

up, the sky was populated with millions of stars spread across the blackest of canvases. The moon was in its last phase, and a sliver hung just off the plane's left wing, spilling ivory light across my dirty boots. In spite of the frigid temperature and the rushing torrent of wind, the scene was peaceful. Pastoral, even.

But I wasn't here to stargaze. In less than thirty seconds, I was going to jump into this maelstrom on a one-way trip. This meant that I needed to ensure that the pilot's calculations matched my own.

I needed to look down.

Drawing a shaky breath, I lowered the night-vision goggles mounted to my helmet and adjusted my line of sight from the heavens to the earth. The results were instantaneous. My stomach started turning cheetah flips, my palms grew slick with sweat, and my legs nearly buckled.

In the grand scheme of things, my jumping from a plane into darkness five miles above the earth made about as much sense as a blood-phobic doctor working in an emergency room. Then again, if the world made sense, members of a death cult masquerading as Islam wouldn't be strapping bombs to seven-year-old children.

Pushing both my morbid thoughts and terror aside, I searched the green-tinged landscape, looking for the landmarks that would mark my insertion point. After a second or two, I found what I sought—the intersection between 216, the north–south-running road that bisected the city of Manbij, and M4, a west–east-running highway. But the intersection wasn't just beneath our wing as I'd expected. Instead, the roads showed as a haze of black against the ambient green from the night-vision goggles. My landmark was at least five miles away.

We were off course.

"This isn't it," I said to the jumpmaster. "We're supposed to be on top of that intersection."

The jumpmaster looked where I was pointing, cross-referenced the tablet strapped to his kneeboard, and then leaned out the doorway.

"You're right," he said. "Stand by."

He flipped the toggle on his intercom cord, switching from the channel we shared to a direct link to the pilots. I saw his lips move but wasn't able to make out his words. A moment later he toggled back.

"Change of plans," the jumpmaster said. "We're getting pinged pretty hard by a pulse-Doppler radar. The pilots think it's coming from a pair of Russian Su-27 Flankers. If their radar locks us up, we're done. We can't get you any closer. If you wanna jump, it's got to be now."

Fucking Russians. "How far is the landing zone?"

The crew chief punched several buttons on his tablet. "Nineteen miles."

"Winds?" I said.

"Still holding steady at forty-five knots."

In theory, the MT-1 ram air parachute strapped to my back should have been able to fly twenty or so miles under these conditions.

In theory.

But theory was one thing on a practice jump and something else altogether on an operational insertion. Right about now, dental school was looking pretty good.

"Fuck it," I said. "Let's go."

In the Ranger Regiment, we had a saying that no plan ever survived first contact with the enemy. In other words, you could prepare, but the enemy always had a vote. Right now, the enemy was voting against my jumping at the planned insertion point. That was a pain in the ass but, in theory, surmountable. I just hoped that this would be the only time the enemy decided to vote.

"Green light," the jumpmaster said, and slapped me on the shoulder. "Go, go, go!"

I crossed myself and then launched from the relative safety of the aircraft into the great unknown. I wasn't Catholic, but I'd adopted the comforting gesture prior to my first jump ages ago. A theologian I was not, but distinctions in dogma tended to vanish once bullets started flying. Our chaplain liked to joke that there were no atheists in foxholes, and this was doubly true for paratroopers.

The one-hundred-knot slipstream buffeted my body like a breaking tsunami. For a heartbeat or two, the earth and sky spun as I somersaulted through the first part of my jump. This had always been my nightmare: that I would plummet in an uncontrolled fall, watching earth chase the sky until I hit the ground with the subtlety of a cinder block.

Fortunately, tonight was not the night for that.

My right hand held the rip cord's metal handle in a death grip, and I yanked with all my strength. The canopy shot upward, like a cork exploding from a champagne bottle, dragging the rest of my rig with it. The chute inflated with a glorious popping sound, like sheets crackling in the wind. In the space of three seconds, I decelerated from almost one hundred miles an hour to a leisurely eighteen.

Navy fighter pilots liked to bitch about the stress of a catapult launch from an aircraft carrier. Don't get me wrong—I'm sure getting hurled into space wasn't a lot of fun, but it was a matter of perspective. If given the choice, I'm sure the flyboys would take their ergonomically designed seats and climate-controlled cabins over a HAHO jump any day. Nothing says fun like getting yanked out of your britches as your parachute whiplashes you skyward with all the compassion of a hangman's noose. And that was before you spent the next twenty to thirty minutes dangling above the earth in subzero temperatures while riding cyclonic winds toward enemy-occupied territory.

I'd take a catapult shot in rough seas any day. At least a Navy fighter jet had heat.

Unbuckling the straps that held my jump board to my chest, I consulted the multiple displays and then made an adjustment to my course via the twin steering toggles connected to the chute's suspension lines.

Flying the chute was relatively simple: Pull the right toggle above your head to about ear level to turn right. Do the same with the left toggle to turn left. But like everything else in my world, the devil was in the details. Unlike a powered aircraft, my parachute was at the mercy of the winds and was constantly falling. A shift in wind direction or strength could be catastrophic to the mission or fatal to the jumper. Unlike a sailor caught in a storm, I had no way to lower my sails in order to ride out the gusts.

One way or another, I was in this until my feet hit the ground.

I ran through my jump board's displays, verifying the wind speed every thousand feet and maintaining my course via the digital compass. The first ten minutes or so of my flight had gone just as planned, even though it was bitterly cold, and my arms were getting a hell of a workout. Every pull on the toggle to adjust the chute's course was the physical equivalent of a pull-up. After fifteen minutes, my forearms were quivering.

That's when I realized I had a problem.

My gut had been trying to tell me something was wrong, but it was the GPS readout that finally gave me the bad news. While I was on course, I was not on glide path. In other words, I wasn't covering as much distance as I'd intended. The wind's speed had decreased, and my forward airspeed was plummeting.

I was going to miss my landing zone by several kilometers.

On a training drop, this would result in a longer hump back to the landing zone, or LZ, to link up with the rest of the team. Tonight, it meant that, instead of touching down in the isolated field I'd chosen for its proximity to my meet site with Einstein, I was going to land short.

Just how far short had yet to be determined.

My altimeter chimed, alerting me that I'd just crossed through ten thousand feet. I had about three minutes to find a new LZ.

Pulling up the imagery I'd downloaded onto the tablet, I entered the ground speed supplied by the GPS, my current altitude, my rate of descent, and the wind direction. A moment later, the computer rendered the data into a projected flight plan. It looked like a cone, stretching from a blue icon in the center of the map, representing me, outward in a pie slice of green lines.

The bad news was that the pie slice ended almost three kilometers short of my intended touchdown point. The good news was that I could easily land anywhere within the arc of ground enclosed by the green lines.

As I watched, the green wedge began to shrink. Time to make a decision.

Tracking along my flight path, I found a possible solution—a second farmer's field. If I landed there, I'd be almost four kilometers from my original intended touchdown point and another two from the meet site with Einstein. However, the privacy offered by the line of trees ringing the plot of land made the spot appealing.

Even in the dead of night, a man parachuting to earth tended to attract attention. Once I landed, I'd need several minutes to dispose of the parachute and residual equipment, and the field's anonymity, not to mention the possibility of soft, tillable earth, would offer just that. Sure, the extra distance to the remote LZ increased my risk of discovery, but risk was inherent in every part of this mission. The field might not be ideal, but its benefits outweighed its shortcomings.

At this point, that was about the best I could hope for.

Glancing at my watch, I did a final set of calculations.

Even if I had to travel on foot, I should be able to cover the extra distance in time for my rendezvous with Einstein. My decision made, I locked in the new LZ, updated my flight plan, and made the course corrections the computer recommended. I kept my head on a swivel as I flew, looking for power lines, cell towers, and errant trees. Any of those obstacles could snag my chute and turn what was now a suboptimal event into one that was catastrophic. There were many mission setbacks from which I could recover. Getting hung up in a three-hundred-foot utility tower wasn't one of them.

As I broke through fifteen hundred feet, I could smell the uniquely Syrian scents of wood fires, open sewers, and animal dung. While I was floating above the earth, it had been easy to forget what lay beneath me as I concentrated on flying my chute. But this close to the ground, the devastated nation's medieval nature was readily apparent.

Sweat trickled down the back of my neck as I turned my head left and right in slow pans, searching for landmarks. I detested this part of the jump. From here on in, I had to ignore the looming collision of flesh and earth in favor of flying my chute, even as the ground grew larger in an unstoppable rush.

After a panicked moment, I found the solitary structure I'd marked as my initial approach point. I doglegged into a turn and saw the field just beyond. Passing through five hundred feet, I sailed over the structure on silent wings and then pulled down on my left toggle, turning my chute into the wind.

For the first time in my nearly twenty-five-minute

flight, I felt the wind on my face. Fixing my attention on the centermost portion of the field, I fought the butterflies that ground rush always generated. A final scan showed the ground free of obstacles, and then I was committed, flying by instinct rather than by instruments. The point on the ground I'd designated as my landing spot swam toward me. I yanked downward on both toggles, flaring the canopy to cushion my landing, then sank the last twenty feet.

It was then that I noticed that one portion of the field was a little taller than the rest. A pile of stones stood about six inches tall and four feet wide. I had no idea why the stones were there. Perhaps they'd been a marker for an ancestral burial ground or were the remnant of an abandoned fence or a onetime livestock pen. In truth, their purpose didn't really matter.

What did matter was that the jumble of rocks was full of jagged edges, and I was heading straight for it.

THIRTY-ONE

I jerked hard on the toggles, trying to gain the bit of lift I'd need to skim over the top of the rock pile. But in that same instant, the brisk breeze that had been battering my face for the final portion of my approach dropped away.

In Syria, wind was a fickle thing.

I wasn't an aeronautical engineer or pilot, but I didn't have to be to understand what happened next. Just as with an airplane lining up for its final approach, the headwind had been providing me with lift. When the breeze vanished, my lift disappeared right along with it. Instead of sailing up and over the jumble of stones, I careened toward it like a child belly-flopping from the community pool's high dive. I shot out my left leg to keep from impaling myself.

Then flesh met stone at ten miles per hour.

The results were predictable, if not pleasant. My ankle

snapped with an audible crack. I saw stars and passed out. When I came to, I was lying facedown in the dirt. The wind had returned with a vengeance, and my inflated parachute was dragging me across the field like a makeshift plow.

Fortunately—or unfortunately, depending on how you looked at it—this was not a new scenario for me, or any paratrooper, for that matter. Ever since the first man had trusted his life to a backpack full of silk, jumpers have been knocking themselves unconscious in the drop zone. Normally, the fix for this predicament was fairly straightforward: Grab hold of your risers, pull yourself to your feet, and gather your parachute. But a simple fix for a simple problem becomes infinitely more complex when a shattered ankle is added to the equation. Ignoring the throbbing agony already radiating up my leg, I tried to get to my feet—or, rather, one foot.

I failed.

I managed to push myself somewhat upright, bearing the weight on my right leg while using my left as an awkward pivot point. I was in the process of reaching for my risers when the wind gusted. In an instant, my chute went from a mostly deflated, docile creature to a bucking bronco. Once again, I was facedown, plowing my way through the rocky soil.

At some point in every mission, an operator has a moment in which he wonders why exactly he bothered to climb out of bed that morning. My moment had just arrived.

Gritting my teeth, I grabbed the toggles with both

hands, rocked my weight backward, and tried to spin into the chute. I wanted to harness my parachute's forward momentum like a water-skier used the boat's motion to pull himself from the water.

It didn't work.

The wind gusted again, and I fell to the ground, wrenching my broken ankle as the parachute snapped merrily along, dragging me behind it like an enormous kite's misshapen tail.

My situation was rapidly deteriorating from comical to potentially deadly. My last scan of the LZ at altitude hadn't revealed a human presence, but neither had it revealed the collection of stones that had ruined my ankle. I couldn't afford to keep flopping around like a beached whale, hoping that one of the four factions of fighters who called this neck of the woods home didn't stumble across me.

Time for plan B.

I reached for the red cutaway pillow with my right hand, then pulled it across my body like I was throwing a jab toward someone on my left. The parachute released, sailing away in a crackle of fabric.

My forward motion stopped.

Spitting out a mouthful of dirt, I turned into a seated position and flipped down my night-vision goggles. The world swam back into view, rendered in comforting shades of green. After a moment of searching, I found what I was looking for and breathed a sigh of relief.

There was a reason why I hadn't just cut my parachute free earlier. Without me to hold it earthbound, the lightweight chute would have sailed through the air, wrapping itself across the first obstacle it encountered. That might have been okay if the chute came to rest somewhere nearby. But it was just as likely that the wind would carry the parachute far out of reach or, even worse, tangle it around a telephone pole or tree. If that happened, not only would I be unable to retrieve the parachute with my broken ankle, but the first person who saw a two-hundred-seventy-foot length of silk snapping in the breeze would raise an alarm.

There were many aspects of my presence I could disguise or explain away. An errant parachute wasn't one of them.

Fortunately, the parachute had come to rest against the man-made structure I'd used as the initial point for my flight plan. The squat one-story building was manufactured from stone and appeared to be a barn or some sort of storage shed. Even better, it looked unoccupied.

In a final stroke of good luck, my facedown voyage across the field hadn't been entirely in vain. The wind had carried me away from the stone wall that had been my nemesis and toward the structure where my parachute now rested, about fifty meters away. The distance would be no stroll in the park, but neither was it insurmountable. Things were starting to look up.

And that was when the dull bass thumping of rotor blades echoed from somewhere behind me.

The distinctive sound of helicopter blades churning through thin desert air can't be mistaken for anything else. For me, this sound had often been the herald of good news. Sometimes, the good news came in the form of a high-pitched whistle as an AH-6 Little Bird gunship nosed into a rocket run, obliterating a nest of Iraqi insurgents. Other times, it was the mature-sounding bass of a UH-60 Black Hawk flaring for a landing in preparation to take me home.

Either way, I was programmed to associate the *whump whump whump* of helicopter rotor blades with something positive.

But not today.

Today, all that was good had ended at the edge of Russian-controlled airspace some twenty miles behind me. For the first time in my life, the helicopter rapidly closing on me was not from Team America. Just that quickly, my night turned from bad to potentially fatal. Scanning the sky with my night-vision goggles, I whispered my second prayer of the night.

According to my premission briefing, there were almost as many helicopter variants in theater as there were factions of armed men trying to kill one another. While the *whump*ing of rotor blades wasn't exactly a happy sound, it wasn't necessarily my death knell, either.

The vast majority of helicopters were transports. These rotorcraft were either lightly armed with defensive machine guns or fitted with rudimentary munitions known as barrel bombs. Barrel bombs were fantastic for terrorizing urban centers, but much too valuable to waste on a single man standing in a farmer's field. The helicopter's door gunner might take a potshot or two, but otherwise I should be fine.

Unfortunately, the steel monster I spotted thrashing through the air wasn't a transport. It was a dual-rotor monstrosity of Russian make. Officially, it was known as the Ka-52 Alligator. Unofficially, we called it death personified, and it's caninelike snout was lined up on me.

I froze, watching the helicopter edge closer, praying its thermal optics were fixed somewhere else. Anywhere else. After all, I was still just one man standing in an uninteresting field. Surely the Syrian battlefield contained more lucrative targets. But apparently, the ex-commies piloting the killing machine were having a slow night. I'd no sooner located the helicopter than twin flashes of light split the darkness to the accompaniment of artificial thunder.

Rockets.

I dove headlong for the ground. Not only had the damn chute wrecked my ankle, but it had also left me perfectly equidistant between the two structures that might have provided me with protection—the ankle-breaking wall and the parachute-snagging barn. Facedown again, I had just enough time to register the fragrant smell of cow manure before the detonating warheads split my world in two.

The explosion tossed me in the air like a rag doll, my left foot flopping from side to side as white-hot lightning bolts pulsed through my leg. The shock wave hammered my body, driving the air from my lungs like a body blow from Smokin' Joe Frazier. When I came to my senses, my ears were ringing, the night-vision goggles were gone, and I was dry heaving.

Wiping the bile from my mouth, I poked my head up and tried to locate the helicopter. Big mistake. Dual images of everything but the gunship greeted me. I turned my head to the side, just in time to eject another burning stream of bile. A concussion and a broken ankle in less than twenty minutes. This operation was going to be one for the record books.

The thumping rotors returned. I looked up to see the inky outline of my nemesis almost directly overhead. The helicopter was sliding in and out of the thin cloud cover like a circling shark.

The first pair of rockets had gone long, both of them detonating against the barn's wall. The pilot wouldn't make the same mistake a second time. I'd seen enough gun camera footage to know that faking dead was more effort than it was worth. Modern gunships sported thermal optics. There was no way to confuse the heat signature of a man whose heart was still beating with that of a rapidly cooling corpse.

The helicopter pilot knew I was still alive, and he was coming back to finish the job, plain and simple.

I wish I could say that some brilliant bit of tactical insight floated into my mind or that I pulled my pistol and defiantly squeezed off my magazine at the looming angel of death, but neither of those things happened. My body was bruised and broken, and the gunship had me dead to rights. Escape was impossible, so I didn't try. Instead, I raised both hands and flipped my Russian executioner the bird. I might have also screamed, *Come and get me, motherfucker*, because, well, why not?

And that's how I know that God has a sense of humor. Even though He'd conveniently ignored my previous prayers, the dual-middle-finger salute apparently got the Almighty's attention. As the helicopter rolled its stubby wings level in what I knew was the pilot's final adjustment before unleashing another rocket volley, a stream of yellow tracers arced into the sky. The bullets came from somewhere to my right, reaching for the helicopter like a probing tentacle.

The gunship rolled right and nosed up, pirouetting toward the threat with a nimbleness that belied its seventeen-thousand-pound bulk. Firing rapidly, the helicopter unleashed four or five rocket pairs, each launch smashing through the sound barrier with an earsplitting roar. A second stream of ground-based tracers joined the first, but the Russians were undeterred. The gunship fired another salvo of rockets while adding its 30mm cannon to the mix even as one of its engines began belching flames where a crimson stream of tracers had hit home. The helicopter wobbled, righted itself, and then limped out of view, a cloud of greasy smoke trailing behind it.

At this point, I genuinely didn't know who to root for: the Russian pilots who'd just tried to kill me or the ISIS sympathizers who would surely do so if given the chance. Maybe both the Russians and ISIS would have to get in line, because once again, Abir and her mother were greeting me. The two were standing by the barn's entrance, draped in shadows. Abir gave an excited wave when she caught my eye, and she squirmed in her mother's embrace. The broad smile stretching across her chubby face certainly didn't feel malevolent, but before I could return her wave, she and her mother were gone.

The hallucinations were appearing with greater frequency, but I had no idea what they meant. Was my subconscious trying to tell me something? If so, what? That I was on the right track? Or that I was edging ever closer to a complete break with reality? I just didn't know. But what I did know was that I needed to get out of the field before the gunship crew decided to give up on the machine-gun nest in search of easier prey.

Gritting my teeth, I crawled toward the stone barn on my hands and knees, dragging my broken ankle.

THIRTY-TWO

Five agonizing minutes later, I made it to the barn's entrance. Or at least the barn's new entrance, courtesy of the pair of 80mm high-explosive rockets that had slammed into the wall. The soil in front of the opening was littered with stone fragments mixed with razor-sharp metal shards.

When a rocket detonated, the warhead's ten pounds of high explosives sent chunks of superheated steel from the rocket's casing scything through the air in every direction. I was impressed that the wall was still standing. And while crossing the minefield of metal and rock slivers on my hands and knees hadn't been a lot of fun, it beat the alternative. It could have been my body shredded instead of the stone.

As with many things, I've found that happiness was often a matter of perspective. As I crawled into the barn, my perspective changed for the better. A battered car was resting against the far side of the dimly lit structure. The car, a late-model Kia, looked so inviting that I almost hopped over to the front door and climbed inside. Almost. But as much as I wanted to slide into that undoubtedly plush interior and go for a spin, my ankle was demanding attention in no uncertain terms.

Easing onto an overturned bucket, I ran my hands down the length of my leg, searching for evidence of a compound fracture. Don't get me wrong. A broken ankle is no laughing matter, but if my hands found bone protruding from the skin, all bets would be off. That kind of injury was mission ending.

Fortunately, my fingers discovered nothing more serious than swelling.

This was a pleasant development, but it didn't negate the need for treatment. Escaping the murderous helicopter was all well and good, but the shock and accompanying adrenaline had begun to fade. My ankle hurt like a son of a bitch. If I didn't find a way to stabilize it soon, I would risk passing out from the pain or sustaining permanent injury from freely moving bone shards.

A workbench fashioned from rough wood ran the length of the far side of the barn. I hobbled toward it, using a shovel as a makeshift crutch. Even so, each step was agony as pieces of fractured bone ground together.

On the bench, I found the usual debris one would expect in a farmer's workshop—a vise, a grinder, a hammer, a few scattered wrenches, and a screwdriver or two. I grabbed a pair of wrenches and fit them lengthwise against my ankle, but abandoned the idea. The metal handles were much too thin to offer real immobilization. Besides, I was afraid they'd slip and slide across my pants, even if I found a way to bind them together.

Hobbling another few steps to my right, I ducked under the workbench and struck pay dirt—a pile of discarded wood. Quickly sorting through the rough-hewn scraps, I found a pair of suitable lengths. The wood was cracked with age, and the pieces weren't the same size, but they would do. Setting the wood aside, I removed my outer shirt, and then cut my T-shirt into strips. After fashioning the rags to a satisfactory length and thickness, I placed the wood along my boot and tied the makeshift splint together with the strips of fabric. Once I was sure the knots were secure, I took a hobbled step back toward the car, still using the shovel as a crutch.

The results were immediate. Pain still radiated up my leg, but my ankle no longer flopped from side to side as I moved. I'd immobilized the break, but done nothing about the underlying injury. The recipe for fixing a broken ankle once the bone was set was simple—stay off it and wait for the limb to heal.

Unfortunately, that wasn't an option.

Reaching down to my boot, I adjusted the laces and fiddled with the knots until it was as tight as I could make it without cutting off the circulation. The swelling had already ballooned the canvas fabric to its breaking point, but I didn't dare ease the pressure. At some point, a medic would have to cut away the boot, but for now, like my improvised splint, it was the best I could do.

My phone vibrated as a silent alarm was triggered.

Forty-five minutes to go until my meet with Einstein. Forty-five minutes to cover five kilometers. Under normal circumstances, traveling that distance in the allotted time would have been a walk in the park. But now those five kilometers might as well have stretched to the far side of the moon. On foot, I'd be lucky to get a kilometer before the broken ankle became too much to deal with.

Once more, my eyes returned to the battered Kia. With the Russians still flying close air-support missions in support of Assad's ongoing offensive and rocketing anything that moved, driving to the meet site would be risky. Then again, so was jumping out of a perfectly good aircraft loitering five miles above the earth. At this point, the mission's importance outweighed any potential risks, and my mission was to get to Einstein before the clock ran out on Shaw.

I hobbled over and opened the driver's door. The interior lights responded with a cheerful glow, and I felt a renewed sense of hope. Functioning interior lights meant the battery was still charged. Step one to starting the car was complete. Climbing inside, I closed the door and started step two—looking for the keys. They weren't in the ignition or under the dashboard.

My pulse accelerated.

A car with no keys was about as useful as a car with a dead battery. Suddenly, the dusty barn, with its hidey-holes and piles of assorted tools, didn't look so quaint as I imagined all the possible places a suspicious farmer could secrete away a set of keys. I felt along the steering column, but stopped before doing anything more. Like most special operators, I'd attended a crash course on how to escape from restraints and hot-wire cars. Unfortunately, rewiring a car's ignition took special tools and time, and I possessed neither.

Continuing the search, I ran my fingers along crevices and compartments, finding nothing until my fingertips discovered the latch for the glove box. I popped it open, and the plastic bin fell open with a promising jingle. Reaching inside, I probed around until I felt cold metal.

Keys.

I selected the correct one, inserted it into the ignition, and twisted.

The engine coughed to life, and my mission was once again viable.

I put the car in gear, gunned the engine, and made it exactly two feet before the unmistakable sound of metal on metal forced me to stop. Already knowing what I'd find, I put the vehicle in park, climbed out, and began to search for the culprit. I hopped along on my right foot while holding on to the car for balance. I didn't have to hop far. Both front tires were completely flat, the rubber shredded by rocket shrapnel.

I might have found a car, but I was still going nowhere fast.

THIRTY-THREE

The twin flat tires were a punch to the gut. I'd been in this business long enough to expect that an operation would not go entirely as planned. Even so, this mission was starting to border on the ridiculous. I'd jumped early, landed in the wrong LZ, broken my ankle, and survived a strafing run by a marauding Russian gunship.

Other than that, things were going swimmingly.

My phone vibrated. I dug it from my pocket and saw a single word dominating the otherwise black screen.

Status?

The message was from Colonel Fitz, and in that instant, I realized my oversight. According to our communication plan, I was supposed to text him a brevity code word, letting him know my situation once I landed. *Buckeye* if the insertion had gone as planned and my meet with Einstein was still a go. *Wolverine* if I needed extraction.

I thumbed the message, preparing to reply, but felt confounded by the flashing cursor. Sometimes, even the most highly planned operation went down the shitter. The trick lay in recognizing when an op was heading south in time to keep from getting sucked down the commode with it. With a broken ankle, I physically would not be able to make the meet with Einstein on the agreed-upon timeline, or, more realistically, at all. With a car, the rescue operation had still been feasible. Not easy, or even particularly tactically sound, but doable, especially with a captured man's life hanging in the balance. But without a way to get to Einstein, I was dead in the water.

Frustrated, I shoved the phone into a pocket and leaned against the Kia, surveying the inside of the barn.

The makeshift garage/storage facility held a great many things, but two spare tires weren't among them. Letting my eyes wander across the dimly lit interior, I saw what I'd expected to see—unused lumber, piles of rags, cans of gasoline, and assorted tools. One of the gasoline cans was a different size and shape than the other three it was clustered alongside. That gave me the beginnings of an idea. I crutched over to the unique can, unscrewed the cap, and took a cautious sniff.

Diesel.

Just like my father, this farmer had learned the value of distinguishing diesel fuel from regular gas by using a distinct container. This precaution prevented careless farm boys, like me, from accidentally adding diesel fuel to a conventional engine. However, the battered Kia ran on normal gas. This meant . . .

I began a more thorough search of the barn, my heart pounding. After making a circuit of the rubble-strewn interior, I found what I was looking for. In a back corner, partially obscured by a pile of scrap wood and a portion of the roof that had collapsed during the rocket attack, was an object covered with a large canvas tarp. Holding my breath, I peeled back the tarp to reveal a tractor's skinny front tire.

Hot damn.

Not wanting to declare victory just yet, I slowly worked the filthy tarp from the tractor's frame, sneezing at the combination of dust and grit. After several minutes, I was looking at the familiar chassis of an older-model Ford tractor. Though not a farm equipment expert, I'd spent much of my childhood atop one tractor or another. Our family ranch was barely profitable, so Dad had never been able to afford the newer John Deere models with their climate-controlled cabins. Instead, we'd subsisted on a fleet of vehicles that had rolled off the assembly line long before my father had been a sparkle in my grandfather's eyes.

At the time, I'd hated the underpowered equipment. Now the rusted metal frame and shoulder-high knobby tires felt like home. Somehow, in this desolate land that now more resembled the setting of Stephen King's *The Stand* than a country once considered the cradle of civilization, I'd found a touchstone. Something that grounded me and perhaps reminded me of the man I'd been before my world had come undone. As oracles went, an ancient tractor was hardly as inspiring as Paul's road-to-Damascus conversion or even Moses's burning bush.

Still, it was undeniably a sign in the desert, and right now, I'd take what I could get.

Setting my good foot on the pitted metal running board, I grabbed the thin steering wheel and pulled myself onto the worn seat. The tractor's simple cockpit consisted of a gearshift, a throttle, and two shattered gauges.

In other words, it was paradise.

Leaning forward onto the tractor's narrow hood, I unscrewed the gas cap and peered inside. Three-quarters full—more than enough for what I had in mind. Easing back onto the seat, I reached under the gauges, found the dangling ignition key, and turned on the electrical system. A single red light bloomed and then was extinguished as the engine's glow plugs finished preheating the viscous diesel fuel. I stomped on the clutch with my good foot, eased the gearshift into neutral, and pressed the stubby starter button. The engine turned over, sounding like a cranky old man unexpectedly woken from a deep slumber. I worked the throttle, coaxing the engine with more fuel until it caught. The tractor shuddered, belching a cloud of noxious diesel fumes.

I was in business.

Putting the tractor in gear, I eased off the clutch and was jolted in my seat as the massive rear tires engaged, pushing free of the rubble. It took both hands to turn the stubborn steering wheel as I aimed for the gaping hole that the detonating rockets had opened.

Then I was rolling across the field.

I pulled my phone from my pocket and consulted the set of stored maps, matching the terrain around me with the satellite imagery. Once I was sure of my orientation, I angled the tractor's nose toward a road on the other side of the field and cranked the throttle upward.

The engine responded, and the tractor shot forward.

Not exactly how I'd planned on traveling to the meet site, but it would do. Driving with one hand so that I could text with the other, I found Colonel Fitz's message and thumbed a one-word reply.

Buckeye.

THIRTY-FOUR

Spy-craft lore is littered with impossible and often-times unbelievable tales. Everything from ancient Greek warriors hiding in a wooden horse to a stunningly beautiful Russian agent plying her craft in New York City under the FBI's oblivious nose. Many of these stories have even found their way onto the big screen. I had to believe that if someday someone made a movie about this goat rope of an operation, the part about my riding to meet an asset atop a smoke-belching 1940s-era tractor wouldn't make the script.

Even Mark Wahlberg would have a hard time making this rattletrap look cool.

But cool or not, riding the tractor really wasn't such a bad plan. In some ways, it was a variant of hiding in plain sight. After all, what sane spy would go to the trouble of a covert insertion only to trumpet his existence by rolling into Manbij on a roaring piece of farm equipment? The idea was so ludicrous, it might just work. At least that's what I hoped, because, with less than twenty minutes until my meet with Einstein, I had no plan B.

My phone vibrated. Fitz.

Roger. Standing by.

Three little words that represented the collective might of a task force of assaulters waiting to go into harm's way. I thought through the plan once more as I guided the tractor by moonlight. My night-vision goggles, like my parachute and associated equipment, had been packed in an aviator kit bag and secured in the Kia's locked trunk. Hiding in plain sight was all well and good, but I still needed to be able to pass for someone who belonged here. This meant I needed to sanitize myself of anything that would mark me as out of place.

The pistol resting in my lap, and the corresponding suppressor and two spare magazines in my right pocket, was my sole breach of this policy. The stubby pistol had fifteen rounds in its magazine and one in the chamber. Not exactly a full combat load, but if I found myself in a situation where fifteen bullets weren't enough, another magazine probably wouldn't make much of a difference.

In theory, I shouldn't have to fire the pistol at all. The concept of the operation I'd hammered out with Colonel Fitz was relatively simple. I'd establish contact with Einstein and verify his identity. He'd take me to where Shaw was being held captive, and Colonel Fitz would track my every move via my phone's GPS and a loitering UAV. Once I was satisfied that Einstein was on the level, I'd send the final brevity code. Then the Unit assaulters, even now kitted up and sitting in their helicopters, would be on the way.

At ten minutes out, Fitz would break radio silence by calling my phone, and I would talk him onto target while providing real-time intelligence updates. He and his lethal band of brothers would hit the target, rescue Shaw, and destroy the chem weapons facility. Einstein and I would climb onto one of the helicopters, and we'd all fly off into the sunset.

Simple.

Except that, so far, this operation had been anything but. As if to confirm this thought, I wound around a bend in the road to find a collection of vehicles occupying the crossroads in front of me.

By the moon's weak light, it was difficult to see exactly how many men I was facing, but the spidery outlines of the crew-served weapons bolted to the beds of the two pickup trucks were plain as day. The vehicles were backed across the length of the road so that their rear bumpers were almost touching, allowing the DShK machine guns resting on improvised pintle mounts the freedom to traverse across all avenues of approach.

Wonderful.

Easing back on the throttle, I decreased speed while still maintaining my course toward the roadblock.

At this point, I had no other option. Though I could see the outline of the crumpled buildings that passed for Manbij's outskirts somewhere ahead, I was still a good two kilometers from the city proper. This meant that the terrain on either side of the road was primarily abandoned farmland, giving me nowhere to hide.

The driver's-side door of the truck on the right opened. A fighter climbed out and began walking toward me. After he covered ten or so steps, his red lens flashlight flared to life. The fighter played the beam over me first and then the tractor. Apparently satisfied with what he saw, the fighter directed me off the road with short, abrupt motions. His flashlight's red lens moved up and down like an iridescent bobber against a sea of black.

I followed his instructions, pulling to the side of the road and bringing the tractor to a slow stop even as my mind raced. Much of what would happen over the next few minutes depended on the identity of the men behind those vehicle-killing machine guns. Or, more specifically, the identity of the organization to which they'd pledged their allegiance.

I was well within Assad-controlled territory, but that didn't count for much. Battle lines here were about as permanent as footprints in the perpetual desert sand. With so many factions enclosed in such a small piece of real estate, the possibilities were almost endless.

Even so, mounting a roadblock along such a heavily traveled thoroughfare ruled out the possibility of bandits. If I had to guess, the people in front of me hailed from one of the big three: Assad's army, the remnants of ISIS, or the conglomerate of tribal leaders and freedom fighters who called themselves the Free Syrian Army. Now I just had to figure out who was who before the fighters manning the checkpoint decided that I played for an opposing team.

This mission was nothing if not interesting.

The fighter walked toward me with quick, measured strides, his AK-47 held at the ready. Stopping about five feet away, the man gestured toward the tractor and made a slashing motion across his throat.

Not a good sign. I'd hoped to use the tractor's laboring engine as an excuse to make the ensuing conversation brief, but this was not to be.

I eased back on the throttle, bringing the engine's rumble down to a more manageable chortle, but the distinction in noise levels was lost on my would-be interrogator. He made the slashing motion again, this time with more vigor.

I reached down, found the ignition key's cool metal, and turned counterclockwise.

With a final cough, the engine died, leaving only a metronome-like ticking as the metal frame cooled. The sentry stepped closer. His flashlight spilled across my face and then my body. The beam paused at the pieces of scrap wood and fabric holding my shattered ankle together before coming to rest on the tractor's battered front tire.

"Brother, are you hurt?" the sentry said.

I nodded.

"In the helicopter attack?"

I nodded again.

The sentry spat before letting loose a stream of Arabic too rapid for me to follow. I picked up enough bits and pieces to understand that he was cursing the Russians, a sentiment I could appreciate. Finally, his words sputtered to a stop. He was looking at me expectantly, and I realized I must have missed something. Leaning forward, I pointed toward my ear and shook my head.

"Do you need to go to the hospital?" the sentry asked, stepping closer and enunciating.

"Inshallah, I do," I said, not faking the roughness of my voice. Between the dirt and dust from the collapsed barn and the airborne grit that was Syria, my throat felt like I'd been gargling with shards of glass. Hopefully, my hoarseness would obscure my accent.

The sentry nodded. "We will take you. Welcome to the Caliphate, brother."

So the good news was that I no longer had to worry about the ancient tractor giving up the ghost and leaving me stranded with a broken ankle kilometers short of my meet site. The bad news was that my newfound chauffeurs appeared to be ISIS foot soldiers.

Right about now, going head-to-head with a Russian gunship didn't seem quite as daunting.

THIRTY-FIVE

The kilometers rolled by much faster now that I was in the front seat of a Toyota Hilux truck instead of the tractor's open cabin. Even so, my newfound mobility had its own set of challenges—namely, that we were driving in the wrong direction. Each minute took me farther from the meet site while bringing me closer to a choice I didn't want to make—whether to kill the teenage boy seated in the driver's seat next to me.

Once the decision had been made to take me to an ISIS-controlled hospital, the men at the checkpoint became the epitome of efficiency. At the sentry's shouted command, several more fighters had materialized from behind the modified technical trucks containing the crew-served weapons. One of the men offered me a drink of water from his canteen while two others helped me down from the tractor.

Their on-site medic performed a quick triage of my wounds, pronounced my ankle broken, and announced his admiration for the improvised job I'd done splinting the bone. After the medic had determined that I did indeed need further medical attention, a vehicle stashed in the ditch parallel to the main road rumbled to life.

I was helped into the front seat, given a handful of painkillers, and assured that doctors would be able to set my ankle and see to the contusions and cuts I'd sustained over the past two days. My driver was given explicit instructions in what seemed, even to my ears, to be rudimentary Arabic. Then we were off, heading down the road at fifty kilometers per hour.

In that moment, perhaps more than at any other time during the months I'd lived in this country, I understood the appeal of ISIS at a visceral level. Moments before, I'd been operating at the very ragged edge of civilization. My broken ankle had been splinted with scrap wood, and my transportation had been a rickety tractor. But all that changed once I'd entered ISIS-controlled territory.

Now my injury had been attended to and my thirst quenched, and I was on the way to an actual hospital. Far from shaking me down for money or executing me outright, these men projected a sense of competence mixed with order that I was certain hadn't been seen in this country for the better part of five years.

The legion of policy analysts and think-tank fellows who'd tried to understand Syria's religious fault lines and tribal intricacies had completely missed the point. At their core, people craved stability and safety, and ISIS offered both in spades. Provided, of course, that you subscribed to their malignant form of apocalyptic Islam.

Nobody's perfect.

A haunting whistle echoed through the truck's cabin as my driver filled the silence. Other than acknowledging the fighter's instructions, he'd said nothing so far. At first I'd assumed that he was just quiet, but the whistle made me think otherwise. As he transitioned from the first verse to the chorus, I recognized the tune—"Hotel California" by the Eagles.

Not exactly on the jihadi top ten list.

Shifting in my seat, I looked at the boy, considering.

The Glock tucked into my waistband dug into my skin as I moved, reminding me of the easiest way to resolve the situation. Now that I had a vehicle and was clear of the ISIS checkpoint, the choice of what to do with the oblivious teenager should have been obvious. Shaw's life was in greater jeopardy with each second, and the fanatical death cult that held him was in possession of a chemical weapon.

A weapon they intended to employ against a Western target.

Every minute I delayed brought the terrorists a minute closer to success. Yet somehow, I couldn't draw my pistol and bring this portion of the operation to a close. With his pitiful attempt at a beard, my driver didn't exactly resemble a hardened ISIS killer. Acne covered his cheeks in red splotches, and his hair hung low over his forehead in an unkempt mop. Every so often, he'd shake his head to force the thick curls from his eyes. The teenager more resembled a sheepdog than a terrorist.

In a sane world, he'd be arguing with his mom for ten

more minutes of Xbox time. But this wasn't a sane world, and the AK-47 lying on the seat between us wasn't an Xbox controller. At the end of the day, he'd made a choice, and choices have consequences.

I leaned forward, easing the pistol from its hiding place with my right hand while raising my left over my head in an exaggerated stretch to hide the motion. I needn't have bothered. Other than a quick glance at me, the boy kept his eyes on the road. As I steeled myself for what would happen next, he pursed his chapped lips together and began to whistle the same tune in a perfect note-for-note rendition.

Setting the Glock on the seat beside me, I looked at his profile and made my decision.

"You like the Eagles?" I asked, the words sounding incredibly loud in the harsh silence.

The boy jerked as if slapped. "Yes," he said, his Arabic coming in fits and starts. "Sorry. Wrong. Haram."

Haram—forbidden by the sharia law that governed the Caliphate. A haram violation could be punished by death, depending on the severity of the offense. People who listened to music might escape with just a beating, while someone caught smoking could be crucified for their sin. The law and order ISIS provided came at a steep price.

"It's okay," I said. "I like their music, too. Do you speak English?"

The boy snapped his eyes toward me, his stare finding mine in the dim light. A range of emotions flickered across his face as he tried to decide how to answer. Fear, confusion, and perhaps even hope made fleeting appearances. Finally, his features settled into a world-weary resignation that looked tragically out of place on a face so young.

"Yes."

Now that he was speaking his adopted language, the boy's accent was unmistakable—American, just like mine.

"What's your name?" I said.

"Ali."

"Where are you from, Ali?"

"Chicago."

Chicago—home to one of America's largest concentrations of Pakistani immigrants. In an instant, the boy's story unfolded in my mind as clearly as if I were reading it from an intelligence report. His Muslim parents had immigrated to escape the uncertainty of Pakistan, hoping for a better life. If I had to guess, Ali had been no more than four or five at the time—old enough to remember fleeing, but too young to understand why.

"Why are you here?" I said.

The openness I'd seen in Ali's features evaporated as he shot me a hard look. "To fight for the Caliphate. I want to be a good Muslim."

His answer had the staccato feel of rote memorization. Of something he'd said often in response to endless questioning. He thought that I was testing him.

"So, *are* you?" I said.

"What?"

"A good Muslim?"

Ali looked at me again; this time his expression was unreadable.

In that moment, I thought I'd lost him. Radical Islam targeted the vulnerable—boys who had not assimilated to their new cultures, who lived their faith with the fervency of the young, who were only too happy to answer a call to arms to defend that faith against infidels if it meant that they could belong to something greater than themselves.

But then he spoke.

"I don't know."

And with those three words, I knew I had an opportunity, no matter how slight. I'd come back to this land of nightmares and cruelty to save a life.

Perhaps I could save two.

"Ali, what's your mom's name?"

The driver who was not a boy but not yet a man swallowed, his too-large Adam's apple rising and falling in his slender throat. "Iffat."

"Did she know you were coming here?"

His shaggy curls bounced as he shook his head.

"Would she be proud of what you've done? Proud that you joined the Caliphate?"

Another long swallow and then, "I used to think so. Now . . . now I don't know."

I'd let go of the pistol's cold metal, but still my heart raced. Up until this point, we'd been just two people having a conversation. A haram conversation perhaps, but still, just a conversation. What I was going to say next would change that. Yet my lips formed the words anyway. When I left Syria this time, I intended to leave without regrets or not at all.

"Do you want to go home?"

He looked at me and then at the road. His face scrunched up as the hardened visage of a would-be terrorist returned to the unformed planes and angles of a teenage boy. A single tear wormed its way down his dirty face.

Ali wiped at the tear with the back of his hand and cleared his throat with an embarrassed cough. Turning to face me, he opened his mouth.

But before he could speak, the windshield shattered in an eruption of glass.

THIRTY-SIX

The screech of metal on metal filled the cabin as our truck thrashed from one side to another. My head smashed into the passenger's-side window despite my seat belt. For the second time in the same day, I saw stars. If I ever made it out of this godforsaken country alive, I would start wearing a crash helmet.

Permanently.

"What?" Ali said, the word coming out in a long croak. He hadn't been wearing his seat belt, and blood leaked from his mouth in ropy streams. Two of his teeth were missing.

I shook my head, trying to piece together what had just happened.

We'd been rammed—T-boned, to be exact. The impact had occurred on Ali's side of the truck, but I couldn't see the other car's headlights, which meant that the driver hadn't wanted to be seen. Which meant that the crash had been intentional. Which meant . . .

"Get down!" I screamed, reaching for Ali's bony shoulder. But now the seat belt that had kept me from harm only moments ago thwarted me. The locking mechanism snapped the belt across my chest, stopping my fingers inches away from the boy's shirt.

"What?" Ali said again, his brown eyes still glazed.

"Down!" I said, thumbing the seat belt release button with one hand as I grabbed his triceps with the other.

My fingers circled his warm flesh, and I was in the process of dragging him to the floorboard when more glass shattered. This time, I heard the accompanying bark of automatic-weapons fire rather than the shriek of metal on metal.

I jerked Ali to the filthy floor mat, forcing his thin frame into the narrow space beneath the dashboard, covering him with my own body. I was already too late. I'd felt him spasm and now a warm, sticky wetness spread across my hands.

"You're okay," I said as glass shards filled the cabin, catching the moonlight like desert snowflakes.

But Ali was not okay. His breath gurgled as he whimpered, blood pouring from multiple chest wounds. If I'd had a trauma kit and a medevac helicopter on standby, maybe he'd have stood a chance. But I didn't. I had my bare hands and a dying boy who was crying for his mother.

Ali shuddered twice and then expelled his final breath with a wet cough. One second he'd been alive; the next he was gone. Once again, I'd been spared. Once again, the person I'd hoped to protect was dead. As life left Ali's body, something inside me died. Despite my best efforts, Syria had won. Again. Maybe that's what came from trying to do good in a place infused with evil. Maybe death and destruction were all that Syria had left to offer.

But that was okay. Death and I were old friends.

Turning from Ali's body, I set the whole of my being toward finding a way to survive the next few minutes. This single-minded intensity wasn't driven by concern for my own life. Instead, I wanted to live long enough to do one thing—kill Ali's murderers. Every last one of them. I didn't know why we'd been ambushed or by who. I didn't care. I just knew that the men who had been foolish enough to take this boy's life would pay for their mistake with their own.

An eye for an eye and blood for blood. This was a sentiment even Syria could understand.

Keeping my body pressed against the truck's floor, I patted the floor mat until I found my Glock. As soon as my fingers touched the pistol's cool metal frame, I pulled it to my chest and wormed between the seats. Pushing myself into the back of the cabin, I gritted my teeth to keep from crying out when my shattered ankle banged against the truck's interior. Rounds continued to smash through the glass and punch into the truck's metal frame, but my new vantage point put me in the eye of the storm.

Shooting a vehicle's occupants was harder than it seemed. A truck was filled with glass, metal, and all manner of plastic and composite obstructions, and each material had the potential to alter a bullet's flight path in unpredictable ways. If I could duck out of the direct line of fire, I would stand a pretty good chance of surviving the initial ambush. This meant that if my attackers really wanted me dead, sooner or later they'd have to check their work in person, and since the ambushers had gone to the trouble of ramming us instead of just spraying our vehicle from a distance, I was fairly certain they intended to check their work.

The barrage of lead continued for several more deafening seconds. I used the time to orient myself so that I was lying flat on my back, head toward the driver's-side back door, feet facing the passenger's side. Holding the pistol in my right hand, I eased my left up along the door, finding the locking mechanism and ensuring it was released. Then I huddled on the floor, trying to make myself as small as possible while waiting for a break in the storm of flying lead.

I didn't have to wait long.

Just when I thought I'd gone deaf from the reports of multiple AK-47s firing on automatic, I realized the shooting had stopped. Propping my good leg underneath me, I reached up with my left hand to grab the door handle while I held the Glock in my right, pointed at the driver's-side window. I took short, even breaths, trying to calm my racing heart while waiting for the next act to begin.

My odds of surviving were not high, but to have any chance at all, I needed to exercise tactical patience. Not an easy proposition when I just wanted to lay waste to my unseen assailants, but necessary.

So instead of moving, I kept still and concentrated on my breathing. As I waited, I pointed the Glock toward the threat, bisecting the driver's window with the pistol's stubby front sight post.

A second barrage of bullets wracked the truck, this time splintering the windshield as at least one gunman adjusted his firing position. The two seats in front of me jerked under the onslaught, chunks of fabric filling the air as round after round snapped past my head. About the time I started to believe that wedging myself against the floor really was going to save my life, a line of fire burst into life across my right leg. The leg without the shattered ankle.

Of course.

Swallowing a curse, I wriggled my toes and found that they still functioned in spite of the wetness spreading across my pant leg. Either the wound was bad or it wasn't. At this point, maintaining my sweaty grip on the door handle was more important than stemming the stream of blood snaking down my leg. My assailants were coming, and I had one chance to get this right. If anything distracted me in that critical instant, a grazing wound to the leg would be the least of my worries.

As abruptly as it had begun, the second storm of bullets stopped. I took a breath. Let it out.

Did so again.

Waited.

Waited until the driver's-side back window was darkened by the silhouette of a head.

I squeezed the Glock's trigger twice in quick succession. The head jerked, and I was already moving. Flinging open the driver's-side back door, I kicked off with my semi-good leg. Gunshot wound or not, my adrenaline-saturated muscles launched me completely out of the truck. One moment I was in a vault of blood and death; the next I was lying flat on my back in the middle of the road.

Time to get to work.

Rolling onto my shoulder, I spotted a crumpled form. It wasn't moving, but as my old platoon sergeant used to say, anything worth shooting once was worth shooting twice. I squeezed the pistol's trigger, and the man's head disintegrated. The Glock's retort reflected against the roadway, bombarding my already stressed eardrums, but I still heard an AK-47 answering my shot.

My new target was to the left, standing in front of the Toyota's wrecked hood. If I'd bailed out of the cabin on my feet, his 7.62mm slugs would have torn through my chest and abdomen, killing me instantly. But I hadn't. Instead, I'd flopped onto my back like a dying fish, and his stream of bullets had passed over me, shattering glass and pummeling the open back door instead.

He missed.

I didn't.

I shot him twice in the abdomen, and once in the head as he fell.

Two down.

How many left?

Fragments of stone peppered my cheek as rounds hammered the road inches from my face. I kicked off the pavement, driving toward the underside of the car that had rammed my truck.

The newest gunman was using my lack of height to his advantage. I could see the muzzle flash from the AK-47 he was pressing over the top of the car, but I couldn't see him. Since I was still alive, I figured that he couldn't see me, either, but the situation favored him. If he kept sweeping his rifle back and forth, sooner or later, a burst would find me, ending our Mexican standoff. This was why I was sliding under the vehicle frame separating us as fast as my wounded leg could push.

Stone shards dug into my skin, opening furrows across my neck and back. I kept pushing. I saw a pair of shins. I kept pushing, pistoning my leg. The shooter's AK-47 was rocking on automatic. If I shot him in the leg, he'd fall to the ground with his finger still on the trigger, and that would be bad.

Instead, I wormed my way closer, straining until I'd reached the far side of the car. Then I took a breath, pressed the pistol into my chest with a two-handed grip, and kicked myself out from beneath the car.

My leg screamed as my compromised ankle flopped against the ground.

The pain didn't matter.

The bullet wound to my other leg burned as the pain-dulling shock wore off.

That didn't matter, either.

What mattered was the man standing spread-eagle above me.

I clipped his leg with my shoulder as I pushed out from beneath the car, and he looked down. His eyes widened.

My final thrust hadn't carried me as far as I'd intended, and the car's frame trapped my Glock against my chest. My assailant could have ended things then and there if he'd stomped on my head, but he didn't. Instead, he tried to bring his AK-47 to bear. An understandable reaction, but wrong all the same. His rifle had more than a foot to traverse.

My pistol required just inches.

Squeezing the trigger, I angled the pistol over the car frame's metal lip as hot brass cascaded onto my chest.

My first two shots missed.

The third didn't. The 9mm hollow point blew through his groin, exiting his back in a spray of gore. He screamed something in Arabic and dropped his rifle. The hot barrel slammed into my head, burning my face. I kept firing. With a gurgled scream, the man toppled to the ground. I pulled him toward me, even as I pressed the Glock against his chest and kept pulling the trigger.

He shuddered as the rounds tore through his chest cavity, turning his internal organs to mush. I kept firing until through my scrambled senses I realized two things: one, my pistol was empty; two, the man was dead.

I dropped the Glock, my fingers searching for and finding the wooden stock of his AK-47. I pulled the rifle under the car with me, keeping the corpse in front of me as a shield in case there was another gunman. I heard a muffled sound and prepared to resume the gunfight before my damaged ears and addled brain identified the noise as a car engine roaring to life.

Easing my head around the corpse's shoulder, I watched as the tires spun on a second truck. Thinking it was headed toward me, I seated the AK-47's stock against my shoulder. But before I could fire, the vehicle spun around in a narrow doughnut and raced off down the road. I considered loosing a burst after the fleeing vehicle, but didn't. Instead, I placed the rifle on the cold, pitted concrete, took a spare magazine from my pocket, and reloaded the Glock.

I tried not to think about the boy in the front seat who'd died crying for his mother. The boy who looked like the son that Laila and I would never have.

I tried not to think about him, but I still did.

His name was Ali, and he deserved to be remembered.

THIRTY-SEVEN

Fifteen minutes after extracting the battered but still drivable truck from the scene of the ambush, I was almost to the meet site. The road I'd been following was lined with a series of parks on the left and the customary stone walls denoting family residences on the right. While the rest of the nation was in the process of tearing itself apart at the seams, the war seemed to have bypassed this little section of Syria completely.

The orderly road continued for another half kilometer; I proceeded at a stately pace past a well-adorned mosque, the twin minarets illuminated by warm orange light. This place was the picture of suburbia. It was hard to imagine that, less than ten miles from here, the hulk of a bullet-ridden car contained the body of a boy named Ali. A boy who'd just wanted to go home, but now would never have the chance.

War rarely made sense, but this conflict was a doozy.

The fighting here was worse than the tribal strife of Afghanistan or the insurgent violence that had consumed Iraq. Here, a death cult competed for attention with a maniacal despot who used chemical weapons on his own people as proxies from half a dozen nations fought both for and against the dictator. In Syria, the battle lines weren't just confusing; they were nonexistent. Whatever idealistic outcome I'd once wanted for this nation was gone, scoured away by blood and tears. At this point, I cared about freeing Shaw and prying the new chemical weapon from the terrorists' hands.

Any aspirations I'd held beyond that had died with Ali.

Leaving the mosque behind, I passed an industrial complex on my right before coming to another intersection. I turned left and made my way down a side street on which stood a series of shops, their exteriors covered by collapsible metal shutters. Keeping one hand on the wheel, I used the other to scoop my smartphone from the seat next to me so that I could consult the moving map display.

According to the imagery I'd downloaded prior to leaving COP Johnson, this road dead-ended at a series of industrial buildings. I'd planned to leave the truck in one of the adjacent parking lots and continue to the meet site on foot. That, of course, had been before I'd shattered my ankle and taken a grazing round to the quadriceps of my other leg. Now I would have to call an audible and hope that Einstein could adjust on the fly.

Passing a soccer field, I slowed and killed the headlights. Then I searched for a clump of trees at the far corner of the field. In a first for this mission, the trees were exactly where I expected them to be. I turned the truck off the road, nudging the battered frame between two of the largest Turkish pines before switching off the ignition. Without the sound of the Toyota's wheezing engine, the night's stillness crashed through the open windows, bringing with it the smell of rotting trash.

In a typical clandestine encounter, the meet between asset and handler occurred within a four-minute window. Variations on either side of that window meant that something had gone wrong, and the meeting should be aborted. Though this meet had become anything but typical, tradecraft was still tradecraft. The digital clock on the truck's dashboard showed that I had exactly five minutes until my rendezvous with Einstein.

Time for the audible.

Keying the encrypted DIA app, I brought up my conversation thread with Einstein and began to type.

Change of plans. Look for a white Hilux truck at site Bravo. Climb in.

So much for tradecraft. My text had all the subtlety of a bullhorn, but I saw no other way. Normally, a handler trained his or her asset as their relationship progressed. Code words that denoted meeting sites, methods, and recognition signals were provided and memorized. In a normal scenario, I could have texted Einstein a series of benign-seeming phrases that would have alerted him to a crash meeting in the passenger seat of my truck.

But this wasn't a normal scenario. Einstein had turned

down my initial pitch flat. Business as a weapons scientist for hire was booming, and he had no reason to jeopardize his lucrative career by becoming my asset. I'd made him repeat the name of the DIA covert-communications app before he'd disappeared, but that was as far as our relationship had progressed. Instead of a new asset, I'd been left with nothing but a monstrous expense report spanning two continents.

But this had been before he'd taken a job with the Saudis working on a little side project that the U.S. didn't sanction but didn't actively oppose. A side project that had morphed into the role of lead scientist for a terrorist organization's WMD program.

In reality, Einstein was damn lucky he'd survived this long. I didn't agree with President Gonzales on most policy issues, but the man rained down Hellfire missiles like he owned stock in Boeing. That Einstein hadn't yet been the recipient of a U.S.-taxpayer-funded trip to paradise said something about the prevalence of targets in this part of the world.

This aside, something had changed with Einstein since our last meeting. I doubted that his sudden desire to side with the angels had anything to do with newly discovered morality. In all likelihood, his arrangement with his current customers had gone sour, and Einstein was looking for an escape hatch. At least that was the more charitable explanation. A pessimistic person might think that Einstein's willingness to help, and access to the exact information I needed, was too convenient by half.

Either way, because he wasn't my asset, Einstein had zero tradecraft training. This meant that the instructions I texted him were about as cryptic as a Betty Crocker recipe. Only the knowledge that Colonel Fitz and his Delta operators were thirty minutes away by helicopter gave me the slightest bit of hope that I could pull this off.

Then again, if Einstein was setting me up, thirty minutes might be twenty-nine minutes too long.

My phone vibrated with Einstein's reply.

Understood. Two minutes.

My palms tingled as sweat droplets formed on my neck and forehead. No matter how many times I'd done this, I never got over the nerves that accompanied a crash meeting. Normally, Frodo was watching my back, but tonight, my only companion was a UAV, slicing through the dark sky more than eight miles above my head.

Tonight, I was an army of one.

I eyed the rearview and side mirrors. Outside, the world slept while, inside the truck, the air was charged with nervous energy.

The number of operational rules I'd broken to force this meeting was enormous. My nonstandard communication strategy with Einstein aside, I hadn't been able to conduct a reconnaissance of the meet site ahead of time, I was in an unfamiliar vehicle, and I had no paramilitary team providing overwatch. Given the insular nature of this neighborhood, I'd kept my surveillance detection run to almost nothing. This meant that if a countersurveillance team was in place, they'd probably made me.

Yet as bad as the situation was, there was precious

little I could do to make it better. If I played things safe, I might live, but Shaw would most certainly die. Everything else paled in comparison to that one indisputable truth.

My phone vibrated.

Entering the park.

Setting the phone in my lap, I scanned across the open ground in front of me, wishing for the night-vision goggles I'd abandoned back at the farm with my parachute and jump gear. The terrain stretched for a good hundred yards, rolling through a series of small hills toward a lonely copse of trees where I expected Einstein to emerge. I let my eyes lose focus as I probed the darkness, searching for movement with my peripheral vision.

Nothing.

Rubbing my thumb across the phone, I considered sending the brevity word that would trigger Fitz, but didn't. Once Fitz and his men were airborne, I knew his cell reception, and by extension our communications, would be spotty. If I'd had a sat radio, I'd have given the command to go as soon as I'd received Einstein's confirmation text. The sat radio would have provided uninterrupted coms with Fitz, allowing me to wave him off if things went south. But with just a phone at my disposal, I wasn't willing to put the lives of another dozen men at risk.

No Einstein, no launch of Fitz and his men. For me, this part of the equation was simple.

A gangly figure limped into view at the far side of the field.

Einstein.

A childhood accident had left him with a leg that had never correctly healed, so even from this distance, his gait was impossible to miss.

As were the two men exiting the woods behind him.

THIRTY-EIGHT

For a long second, I watched the two men glide through the shadows, keeping pace with the seemingly oblivious Einstein. The pair made no attempt to close the seventy-five or so yards separating them from the lanky scientist, but neither did they deviate from the path Einstein chose across the otherwise vacant park. In a traditional scenario, this would have been cause to abort the meet and push to the alternate linkup location, but there wasn't time.

I had to have Einstein's information.

This meant that the scientist's shadows were dead men walking. Now I just needed a plan that would allow me to eliminate two trained killers when I could barely walk. I wasted precious seconds trying to come up with a way to deal with Einstein's minders from my current location before abandoning the idea. An unaware Einstein, a wide-open section of ground with great fields of fire, and my injured body all added up to just one possible outcome—disaster. If I had any hope of snatching Einstein from his tail, I needed to pick more advantageous terrain.

I needed to move.

I started the engine and, keeping the headlights off, backed down the same side street I'd followed to the park's entrance. I'd smashed the truck's reverse lights before driving to the meet site, but I still didn't want to risk turning the vehicle around. The human eye was naturally attuned to motion, and I wanted as little of it as possible. Backing down the street, while difficult in the dark, provided me with the greatest chance of remaining undetected.

Arriving at a T intersection, I swung the wheel to the right, then positioned the truck's nose toward the street to the left.

The narrow alley ran perpendicular to the field Einstein was traversing, presenting a natural choke point. A series of shuttered storefronts stretched down the street, interrupted by a single freestanding kiosk about fifteen yards in front of me. At first glance, the wooden structure didn't look like much. It was a simple vendor's stand assembled out of scrap lumber, but its placement was about as close to perfect as I would get—directly in the center of the pedestrian pathway leading from the park.

I grabbed my phone and thumbed Einstein a text.

Head to the end of the field and turn left. My truck is parked at the end of the alley.

The screen stayed blank for what seemed like an eternity, and then Einstein responded.

Why the change?

I debated telling him the truth, but decided against it. I didn't know how he would react to learning he was under surveillance. Besides, his surprise might just work to my advantage.

Will explain later. Text when you reach the end of the field.

Okay.

Stowing the phone, I scooped up my Glock, but left the AK-47 on the front seat. As much as I'd welcome the additional firepower, I needed to do my next bit of killing quietly. I needed the suppressor-equipped pistol.

I reached for the console and activated the truck's hazard lights. Then I eased myself out, balancing on my right leg and attempting to breathe through the jolt of pain the movement caused. The eight hundred milligrams of ibuprofen the ISIS fighters manning the checkpoint had given me took the edge off, but nothing short of morphine would dull the pain completely. Focusing on the task at hand, I tossed a rag over the driver's-side hazard light to muffle the sound and shattered the bulb with two quick strikes with the Glock's polymer handgrip. The orange strobe effect from both lights would be too bright, but one should be just about right.

My phone vibrated.

Showtime.

When this was over, I would tell Laila everything, security clearance be damned. Then I'd spend a week or two lying on a beach, inspecting her tan lines. If I felt really motivated, I might try to master the riff from "What Would You Say," just in case Dave Matthews needed another guitarist for his next tour. Or maybe I'd make Mom happy and apply to dental school. After all, as long as there were guys like me around, I had a feeling there'd be no shortage of people with grills that needed to be straightened.

Either way, once this fiasco was over, so was my career as a spy.

Ignoring my throbbing leg, I hopped over to the edge of the kiosk and lowered myself to the ground. Propping my back against the structure's wooden frame, I fought the spasms rippling across my quadriceps and calf muscles. The sheen of sweat coating my forehead had nothing to do with the temperature.

My ankle hurt like a son of a bitch.

I removed the trusty suppressor from my pocket and threaded it onto the pistol's barrel by feel. At the far end of the alley, the truck's one remaining hazard light winked at me, throwing orange-tinged shadows across the broken pavement. I heard the first set of footsteps just as I locked the suppressor into place with a final turn. Setting the pistol on my lap, I looked at my phone.

At the end of the alley.

I slipped the phone back into a pocket and pushed myself into a squatting position, holding the pistol in a two-handed grip, suppressor pointing upward. I'd done everything I could think of to turn a shitty situation to my advantage. Now either the plan would work or it wouldn't. From here on out, I could do nothing but wait and pray.

Strangely enough, neither of those options seemed very appealing.

A heavy footfall, followed by a rasping sound as shoe leather dragged against concrete, announced Einstein's presence.

His DIA-created targeting file had many holes, including the details about the accident that had caused his limp. What I did know was that Einstein had been a rising star within the Pakistani WMD community. As such, the infamous Pakistani intelligence service, the ISI, had jealously guarded his personal details, precisely to prevent people like me from pitching their brilliant pupil. Still, I didn't need the targeting file to know that a man with a debilitating limp wouldn't be happy about walking the better part of a kilometer to reach his linkup point.

But that was okay. Einstein could yell at me all he wanted once both his guards were dead. As I mentioned before, sometimes happiness was all about perspective.

The off-tempo walk grew louder, and Einstein's dark form materialized to my right. He passed within inches of me, but as I'd hoped, the truck's pulsing orange hazard light distracted him. He actually stopped after passing my hide site, his back to me as he thumbed a message into his phone. He was close enough that I could smell the plethora of spices accompanying his Indian and Pakistani food, but I was more focused on what was behind him—namely, his two minders.

Einstein finished typing, and my own phone vibrated. For a long moment, I was terrified that he would pause in place until I replied. But just when I thought I'd have to alter my already tenuous plan, he shrugged his narrow shoulders and started walking. I wanted to scream with relief, but settled for a shakily exhaled breath.

So far, so good.

Einstein lurched toward the flashing orange light while I waited to ambush his pursuers.

I didn't have to wait long.

Fortunately, the street's twisting confines had forced Einstein's minders to tighten their surveillance. As such, my would-be asset was only twenty meters from me, about half the distance to the parked truck, when I heard the next sets of footfalls. I rolled my shoulders, working loose the kinks, adjusted my grip on the Glock, and pushed myself onto the ball of one foot.

Then they were on me.

In an ideal situation, the two sentinels would have crossed my hide site on the same side, making my difficult task a bit easier.

But not tonight.

Tonight, they passed on either side of the wooden kiosk, staggering their passage by three or four meters. The first man moved by my right shoulder, his eyes fixed on Einstein's back. His pace quickened as he surged forward, narrowing the gap before Einstein reached the bend in the alleyway and disappeared. A pulse of orange light revealed a bearded face and an AK-47 in a tactical harness before the night swallowed him.

The second man flowed by to my left, and I knew I was in trouble. He moved like a panther. His pace was measured and even, and rather than fixating on his target or his partner, his eyes swept to either side of the alley, probing the darkness with deadly intent. Though I didn't so much as breathe when he slipped past, something triggered his predatory instincts. One second, he was peering at the shuttered storefronts. The next, his eyes met mine. I saw his expression change as a flash of orange light washed across his face.

It was time.

To his credit, my target didn't even try to bring his rifle to bear. He was right-handed, which meant the barrel was pointed to his left, angled away from me and therefore out of the fight. A less experienced man would have died while attempting to bring his rifle on target.

But not him.

Instead, he snapped a vicious kick that caught me under the ribs as I was squeezing the Glock's trigger. The blow knocked my pistol off azimuth, sending the first round into his shoulder instead of his head. My second shot passed harmlessly behind him, sparking off a shuttered storefront. He grunted but didn't cry out. Instead, he hammered my head with his rifle's wooden stock, even as he stomped downward, pinning my gun hand to the ground.

I craned my head out of the way of the killing stroke

from his rifle, but the blow still caught me in the upper shoulder, rendering my left arm a tingling length of useless flesh. If my attacker had continued forward, further closing the distance between us and allowing his body weight to drag me to the pavement, the fight would have been over. Instead, another strobe of orange light showed the rifle stock rising upward as he reversed the stroke, preparing to hammer a fatal blow across the bridge of my nose.

This time, I closed the distance.

I pounded his kneecap with my forehead. The blow left me woozy, but his knee gave way and, with it, the foot clamping my pistol to the ground. My wrist shrieked, and my trigger finger was slow, but it still moved the requisite three-quarters of an inch. The suppressor spit three times, and three holes blossomed in my opponent's groin, stomach, and chest.

He collapsed, the AK-47's barrel clattering against the concrete. I pushed the suppressor against his forehead and squeezed the trigger a final time. Without pausing, I switched gun hands as my left arm flickered back to life, and I sighted down the barrel at the remaining fighter. Something had caught his attention, and he was now facing me, rifle lifted, stock welded against his cheek in a shooter's stance.

But he didn't fire.

Maybe the flashing hazard light had robbed him of his night vision, or maybe he couldn't make out who was who in the dark huddle of bodies. Or maybe, for the first time in this goat rope of a mission, luck favored me rather than my enemy.

Whatever the reason, I took advantage of it.

Like I'd practiced thousands of times on the firing range, I shot with my off hand, squeezing until the man trying to kill me was nothing but a sack of flesh and blood crumpled against the concrete. Only once I was certain that my two attackers were good and truly dead did I allow myself the luxury of taking stock of my wounds. Judging by the swelling and pain, I knew my wrist was probably broken. Besides that, my head hurt like a son of a bitch, and my shoulder throbbed.

But I was alive.

I released the Glock's empty magazine with my thumb, reloaded one-handed, and then began a rudimentary frisk of the body closest to me, searching for information on my two attackers. While my probing fingers didn't find a wallet or passport, they did discover something much more interesting. Handcuffs. The jihadi was carrying handcuffs.

Why?

I removed the metal shackles and slid them into my pocket just as my cell phone began to vibrate.

Einstein.

Placing the device against my ear, I croaked a barely audible hello.

"I'm at the truck, and you're not," Einstein said, his Oxford-educated English more precise than my own. "I trust you have a good reason."

For the first time in a long time, I began to laugh.

THIRTY-NINE

"Now what?" Einstein said, glaring at me across the truck's darkened interior.

His voice had lost some of its haughtiness, but I suppose finding your rescuer sprawled on the ground next to two dead bodies tends to induce humility. Even so, he still sounded a bit too entitled for my taste.

"Now you start the engine and drive," I said, glaring right back at him.

"Where?"

"Anywhere but here. Chances are, your two dead friends were supposed to report in. When they don't, someone's going to come looking."

Einstein's face wrinkled with distaste at the mention of the two dead men. Since I now boasted a shattered ankle, a bullet graze to my leg, and a badly sprained, if not outright broken, wrist, I'd been in no condition to load the bodies into the kiosk I'd used as an ambush site. Truth be told, I hadn't really wanted to. It was about time Einstein got some blood on his hands—metaphorically speaking or otherwise.

Einstein started the engine, put the Toyota in gear, and began to drive. Coming to the first intersection, he turned left—away from the ambush site and the wave of reinforcements that would soon be coming.

"Shouldn't you be giving me directions to the exfil spot?" Einstein said.

"Exfil spot—how cute. You've brushed up on your espionage lexicon. No, I'm not taking you to the exfil spot."

"Why the hell not?"

"Because I'm not sure you're worth saving."

Einstein's head snapped toward me, his confusion evident.

"What do you mean?"

"Take a left here," I said as we wound our way out of the neighborhood and back onto the main thoroughfare. "Let's cut to the chase. I gave you a chance to join my team, and you turned me down in favor of shopping your expertise to the highest bidder. So be it. I'm a capitalist, too. But now you've experienced a change of heart. Call me cynical, but I don't think that's because you've suddenly found religion. I'm more inclined to believe that, somehow, I'm the only thing standing between you and an unmarked grave. That's fine, too, but before I rescue your sorry ass, you need to convince me that your skin's worth saving. Get it?"

"I bloody well get it," Einstein said, biting off each word.

"Good. So tell me what you know and how you know it. Start at the beginning, but talk fast. Our extraction window is closing."

Einstein shot me a look of pure malevolence, but he began to talk. They always do.

"My original job was for Assad. He wanted a novel chem weapon—something not detectable by conventional methods. Something that used nontraditional precursors."

"Because he needed to bypass the sanctions," I said.

Another look from Einstein, this one with more surprise than anger.

Yes, motherfucker, I'm smarter than I look. I might not be a scientist, but I'm not just a knuckle dragger, either. The DIA had done a respectable job preparing me for my initial Syrian assignment, including a refresher course on weapons of mass destruction. I couldn't synthesize a nerve agent, but I understood the process enough to know that the existing sanctions made obtaining the necessary precursors a bitch. What I didn't know was how Einstein had managed to engineer a work-around.

"Why doesn't the weapon trigger our chem detectors?"

"Because it's not a chemical weapon," Einstein said with a smile. "At least not in the traditional sense."

"Please enlighten me, Doctor Doom."

"I found a way to weaponize dimethylmercury."

"Come again?"

"It's not a poison, but it is toxic. Extremely. The mercury collects in the brain and the symptoms of exposure are very similar to mad cow disease. The effects are irreversible once the compound enters the bloodstream."

"How is the weapon introduced?"

Einstein actually smiled when he answered. "After experimenting, I learned how to aerosolize it."

Experimenting.

As Einstein said the word, I saw images captured by the CIA paramilitary team's body cameras. Images of the execution chamber. Frodo had forwarded the pictures to me during the flight to Syria, and I'd paged through them until I couldn't anymore. Even now, I could still see the dead men, women, and children sprawled across the floor in heaps.

Children.

"I had no choice," Einstein said. "By then Assad had passed me off."

"To who?"

"The terrorists."

"Wait a minute. You're saying that Assad knowingly gave your weapon to the ISIS splinter cell?"

"Yes."

"Why?"

Einstein shrugged. "I'm not certain, but I can guess. The war is good for Assad. The longer it drags out, the more time he has to annihilate the dissidents protesting against his regime under the guise of fighting terrorism. I think that he wanted the splinter cell to have the weapon because he knew they would use it."

"Thereby turning world sentiment in Assad's favor," I

said. "If terrorists used a weapon of mass destruction in Europe or the U.S., Westerners would demand retribution in the form of dead terrorists."

Einstein nodded. "Exactly. And if some of those *terrorists* happened to be dissidents or Syrian rebels, do you think your countrymen would care? A dead Arab is a dead Arab."

"Pull in here," I said, pointing to a darkened side street.

While I didn't share Einstein's dismissive view of my fellow Americans, what he'd said made sense in a strange sort of way. For some time, intelligence community members had theorized that Assad, and the various splinter cells that had once been ISIS, might be in a symbiotic relationship for the exact reasons Einstein had just outlined.

Still, right now, whether Einstein was telling the whole truth didn't matter. We would cover all this again in agonizing detail during his post-operational debrief. What I needed now was to verify that he'd lived up to his part of the deal. I needed Shaw's proof of life, his location, and the weapon's chemical formula.

Everything else was gravy.

"Did you bring the weapon's formulation?" I said.

Einstein nodded. "The details are on my phone."

"Send the file here," I said, giving him Virginia's e-mail address. "A chemist will review the data. Once she gives me the thumbs-up, you're clear in that regard. What about proof of life for the captured American?"

Einstein looked away. "I couldn't get it."

"That was our deal."

"To hell with your deal. The jihadis have been watching me. I suspected it for some time, and the men you killed proved that I was right. I'm a scientist, not a soldier. I couldn't get to your friend, but I know he's being held in the building housing my lab. I can even tell you which room, but I can't access it myself. You'll have to trust me."

On the surface, the explanation seemed plausible. For some reason, Einstein had obviously fallen out of favor with his benefactors. Still, I had a feeling that the truth wasn't as convenient as he'd like me to believe. In his heart, Einstein was a cold, ruthless bastard who'd made his living inventing new ways to kill innocents. He'd had a chance at redemption when I'd pitched him, and he'd thrown it away. I was way past extending him the benefit of the doubt.

"Okay," I said, "we'll wait."

"For what? By now the jihadis will have realized I'm gone. You said so yourself. Why are we waiting?"

"Because I don't trust you. My scientist is looking at the information you provided." I held up my phone. "Once she's reviewed it, she'll let me know. If she likes what you sent, I'll trigger our exfil. If she doesn't, you and I will have a problem."

Einstein's eyes widened, but for once, he said nothing. Instead, we sat in silence, waiting in the darkness as Shaw's time ticked away.

Then my phone vibrated.

I keyed in the password to find a single-word text from Virginia.

Avalon.

She'd reviewed the data and thought the chemical formula was credible. We were in business.

"Start the engine," I said, switching to Colonel Fitz's chat feed and keying in the brevity code word instructing him to launch. "We're getting the hell out of here."

FORTY

P ark here," I said, staring out the window at our target. For a weapons laboratory and execution chamber, the building situated one hundred meters away was surprisingly mundane. The structure was two stories high and encircled by a chain-link fence. The building's facade was weather-beaten and worn, the paint long since scoured away by wind-borne grit. If anything, the building looked a bit dilapidated, but otherwise ordinary.

Which was precisely the look I'd be going for if I were a member of a terrorist splinter cell living under the protection of a homicidal dictator while dodging the West's prying eyes and ever-present Hellfire missiles. Like much of Syria, this building was holding secrets just below its benign exterior, assuming of course that my new chauffeur was telling the truth.

"What now?" Einstein said, his voice giving the question a hard edge.

He'd not been in favor of returning to his lab, and he was clearly edgy. His fingers tapped out a nervous beat on the steering wheel as he slouched low in his seat, desperate to keep his recognizable profile from sight.

I took this as a sign that he was telling the truth, but at the same time, there was no way I was sending Colonel Fitz and his boys in blind. Einstein and I weren't a squad of Rangers, but we were the closest thing Fitz's operators had to a sniper team providing overwatch. We weren't going anywhere.

At least that was the plan.

"Now we're going to have what we infidels affectionately call a come-to-Jesus moment," I said, turning from the building to Einstein's dark form. "Based on your information, a team of killers is heading this way. At my say-so, they will fall upon this building and make what Moses's angel of death did to the ancient Egyptians look like a schoolyard brawl in comparison. But first, I need to know that you're telling the truth."

Einstein opened his mouth, but I waved him to silence. "Before you speak, I want you to understand what's riding on your answer. With me?"

Einstein nodded.

"No, you're not," I said, picking up my phone. "But you will be."

I scrolled through the stored photos until I found the set I wanted. The set I'd asked Frodo to get for me when I'd outlined my intentions during our VTC on the Gulfstream. As usual, Frodo had found a way to come through, even though my request had necessitated the activation of surveillance teams in two different countries for a half dozen targets. Gaining approval for, not to mention executing, such a complicated tasking on such abysmally short notice should have been impossible for anyone short of the DIA's director.

But for Frodo, this was just another day at the office.

Clicking on the first image in the series, I held up my phone so that Einstein could see.

"If you're lying, you'll die. That's a given," I said, thumbing through the pictures one by one. "But so will your mother, your father, your three brothers, and your baby sister, who is right this minute taking notes in her economics class at Oxford. Pretty girl, by the way."

"You're threatening my family?" Einstein said, anger contorting his face.

"I don't threaten. I inform. For instance, I just informed you that the veracity of your words holds considerable power over your family's well-being. But I think that's only fair, don't you? After all, if you're lying and this is a trap, the men who are heading this way will probably die, and me with them. Then again, so will every human being who has the misfortune of sharing your DNA. Do we understand each other?"

"I understand you're a bloody barbarian."

I grabbed Einstein by the front of his shirt and jerked him toward me.

"A barbarian is the person who did this to innocent women and children," I said, trading the image of Einstein's sister for the pictures from the CIA paramilitary team's body cameras. Einstein paled and tried to look away, but I was having none of it. Switching my grip to his thick black hair, I forced his head back to my phone.

"Look at this, you motherfucker. Women and children. Babies. You did this. You. A barbarian would have brought you your mother's head in a box and a video of your pretty little sister getting gang-raped. A barbarian would have put a bullet in your skull as soon as you gave him the information he needed. But I'm not a barbarian. I'm a man of my word. And my word is that I will extract you from this mess alive, and leave your family untouched, if you're telling the truth. But that's a big if. If just one syllable turns out to be a lie, my vengeance will be biblical. So, now that you're properly informed, I'm going to ask again—are you telling the truth?"

"Yes," Einstein said, the answer coming out in a hiss.

"Good," I said, releasing his hair. "I'm glad we had this talk."

FORTY-ONE

Peter followed the faded navy carpet leading to the Situation Room with a bounce in his step. So far, the deception plan he'd leaked was still holding. The talking heads at MSNBC, CNN, and the rest had lamented the loss of American life, but were also using the deaths as evidence that America could not afford to get further entangled in the Syria mess.

As a result, Senator Price was once again on the defensive. His surrogates were sparring with TV commentators over the Senator's increasingly unpopular proposal to commit a significant U.S. boots-on-the-ground contingent to Syria. From Peter's perspective, the longer the conversation centered on the Republican's ill-conceived strategy, the less time between now and Tuesday the President's campaign staff would have to spend addressing the economy's anemic growth.

On the operational front, General Hartwright, the

DIA Director, had removed Drake from Syria, leaving Charles firmly in command. In a final piece of good news, Shaw's capture was still a closely guarded secret. Even the paramilitary operator's next of kin didn't know the truth.

Taken in sum, the carefully engineered pieces of Peter's plan had begun to yield results. The latest poll numbers showed the President edging back into safe territory. Peter was fairly brimming with joy, and it was all he could do not to whistle as he deposited his phone on the appropriate storage shelf, keyed his personal security code into the cipher pad, and entered the Situation Room.

Unfortunately, his newfound euphoria was short-lived. The length of table he'd expected to find empty boasted four people in addition to the President.

That was three people too many.

This meeting was supposed to be a notional update on the status of the CIA's attempt to rescue Shaw. Notional because the update Beverly would be providing to the President had been written by Charles and approved by Peter.

According to the future CIA Director's latest report, the network of Syrian rebels once dedicated to assassinating Assad was now closing in on Shaw's location. The would-be assassins had uncovered a number of promising leads, and Charles was confident that the men would have Shaw in hand within the next hour or two.

In reality, Peter couldn't have cared less. By his reckoning, the CIA paramilitary officer was already dead. The man's fate had been sealed the moment Beverly had authorized her poorly conceived raid. That Shaw was currently still alive was nothing more than semantics.

No, what mattered now was keeping the situation under wraps long enough for the American people to usher Jorge Gonzales back into the Oval Office. For this to happen, the next forty-eight hours needed to be uneventful. This in turn meant that, for the next two days, Peter needed to make sure that actionable intelligence detailing Shaw's location never made it to the President's desk.

Peter believed that the President was a good man, perhaps even a great one. But more than that, Peter knew in his heart that Jorge Gonzales was the right man to sit behind the *Resolute* desk's weathered oaken timbers. Still, Peter wasn't naive when it came to his friend's limitations. For all his admirable qualities, President Jorge Gonzales simply did not have the steel core necessary to let one man die so that thousands could live.

Kristen's death had turned Peter, however unwillingly, into just such a man. To shield his friend from the pain he himself had experienced, Peter would do what was needed even if President Gonzales could not. This was Peter's sacrifice, and he bore it willingly, but all would be for naught if the President was somehow persuaded to authorize a half-cocked rescue mission.

And judging by the expressions on the three unexpected faces around the President, half-cocked missions were exactly what they had in mind.

"Sorry, Mr. President," Peter said, pouring himself a cup of coffee from the carafe in the center of the table. "I was under the impression that our update didn't begin for another fifteen minutes."

Peter shifted his gaze from the President to Beverly as he spoke, promising retribution if the ice princess had made a play behind his back. For once, Beverly didn't return his unspoken threat with a haughty look. Instead, she stared down at the legal pad in front of her, allowing a curtain of blond hair to shield her face.

Interesting.

Perhaps Beverly wasn't the guilty party.

"No need to apologize, Peter," the President said, the strain of the past forty-eight hours evident in his voice. "Generals Etzel and Beighley you know. This third gentleman is James Glass. He's a Branch Chief with the DIA's Directorate for Operations. There's been a development in the search for Shaw, and these gentlemen asked to speak with me prior to Beverly's formal update. It would be good for you to hear this as well. Please, sit."

Peter glared at the men as he took the indicated seat.

General Jeff Beighley was the JSOC commander, and he and General Etzel had been West Point classmates. Physically, the two men couldn't have been more different. Beighley had short red hair and a commando's compact, muscular build, while Etzel looked more the academic, with his Buddy Holly–style black reading glasses and lankier physique.

Still, appearances aside, the two men were cut from the same cloth. If they agreed on a proposal, Peter was almost certain that he wouldn't like it. With a confidence he didn't feel, Peter pulled a small notebook from his suit jacket pocket, opened it to a clean sheet, and uncapped the attached pen.

"Thank you, Mr. President," Peter said, keeping his growing sense of alarm from his perfectly modulated voice. "Gentlemen, please continue."

General Etzel exchanged glances with Beighley while the DIA liaison, an eye-patch-wearing mountain of a man whose massive hands looked as if they should have been wielding a sledgehammer rather than a pen, stared back at Peter.

These men had been about to attempt a coup by circumventing Peter's influence, no two ways about it. President Gonzales might be too trusting to realize what was happening, but Peter had no doubt that Beverly knew. He would have words with the soon-to-be-retiring Director after this little meeting, but first he needed to defuse this plot before it gained legs.

"As we were saying, Mr. President," Etzel said in a not-so-subtle reminder to Peter who was actually calling the shots, "the Syrian JSOC detachment commander, Colonel Fitz, now has actionable intelligence detailing Shaw's location. He's requesting permission to conduct a raid to rescue Shaw. I believe we should grant it."

"My, my," Peter said, deliberately interrupting before the President could answer. "I seem to have missed quite a bit. Forgive me for playing catch-up, General Etzel, but where did this actionable intelligence originate?"

"We have a case officer on the ground in Assad-controlled territory. He's linked up with an asset that was part of the splinter cell holding Shaw. We've verified the asset's bona fides through previous reporting, and the asset has provided us with Shaw's location."

"That's strange," Peter said, looking past the General to his nemesis. "Beverly, I hadn't realized the CIA possessed a case officer with this level of access in Syria. My understanding was that we were relying on a network of indigenous agents for precisely this reason. Why haven't we heard about this mysterious case officer and his magical asset before now?"

General Beighley leaned forward, physically imposing his bulk between Peter and the CIA Director. "The case officer in question belongs to JSOC, not the CIA. Director Castle was informed of his existence only moments before you were."

"Hmm," Peter said, feigning his best puzzled expression as he looked from Beverly to General Beighley. "That's perplexing. The President specifically gave the CIA operational control of Syria, and if Beverly didn't know about your case officer, she couldn't have authorized his insertion into Assad-controlled battle space. I guess I'm still a bit confused. Who exactly approved this operation?"

"Excuse me, Mr. President," General Etzel said, swiveling in his chair. "I don't see why any of this is relevant. I—"

"It's relevant," Peter said, talking over the former aviator, "because yesterday there was only one case officer in the entire Syrian theater who didn't belong to Director Castle—a DIA case officer named Matt Drake. A man who announced his presence to the CIA Chief of

Base by walking into the TOC and pointing his pistol at one of the Chief's trusted commanders. The same commander who right now is risking his life, and those of his men, attempting to locate Shaw. The Director of the DIA—who is strangely absent, I'd like to note—responded to this near catastrophe by ordering Drake to leave Syria. Immediately. So please, for all our sakes, put my worries to rest. Tell me that the name of your case officer is not Matt Drake."

"Mr. President," General Beighley said, "sir, you need to understand—"

"It's a simple question, General," Peter said. "Is it Drake or not?"

"I'm not going to—"

"It's Drake."

Peter turned his head in surprise. The answer hadn't come from Generals Beighley or Etzel but from the DIA Branch Chief, James Glass.

"Mr. President," Glass said, his voice rumbling like a rock slide, "the case officer in question is absolutely Matt Drake. And before Mr. Redman asks, everything he just said is true. Yes, Mr. Drake took the leader of the Chief of Base's asset network into custody. Yes, the DIA Director ordered Mr. Drake to leave the country in response, and, yes, Mr. Drake ignored that order. Instead, he chose to risk his life by meeting his asset deep within Assad-controlled territory. All of that is true. What is also true is that I've known Matt Drake for the better part of five years. He was a decorated Ranger before he came to the DIA's Directorate for Operations. In those five years, he's had more successful recruitments than anyone else in my organization. I know him personally, and, Mr. President, if Matt says he has the goods, we need to believe him."

"Sir," Peter began, but the President silenced him with an uplifted hand.

"I know what you're going to say, Peter, but I also know that Shaw's life is my responsibility, and I don't take that responsibility lightly. General Beighley, what do you recommend?"

"Sir, the JSOC QRF is ready to launch. Give them the go-ahead. Let's bring this boy home."

"What about the Russians?" Peter said. "How are you going to carry out an operation in their battle space without their knowledge? We at least need to coordinate the operation with them."

"Mr. President, I think that's a bad idea," General Etzel said. "We don't have time to sort through the international implications of this mess. Shaw is running out of time. We can inform the Russians as we're executing."

"You want to ask for Russian approval as we're transiting their airspace?" Peter said.

"That's exactly what I'm recommending. Mr. President, there's a good chance the Russians won't even detect our helicopters. The birds flying the Delta assault team to the objective are second-generation improvements on the MH-60s used during the bin Laden raid. They are extremely stealthy. If the Russians don't know what to look for, I doubt they'll even notice our presence. That aside, I would recommend advising the Russians of our intentions once we're airborne. Time is of the essence, and in this case, begging for forgiveness is better than asking for permission."

"I concur," General Beighley said. "The Russians don't own Syria. We need to get our man back. We can sort out the political repercussions later."

"Sir," Peter said, not able to mask the desperation in his voice, "please just take ten minutes to consider the ramifications before you authorize this. If you would let me—"

"Director Castle," the President said, talking over Peter, "what do you think?"

From the other side of the table, Beverly lifted her gaze from the legal pad on which she'd been furiously scribbling. For an instant, her blue eyes slipped from the President's face to Peter's before centering back on the President. Even so, Peter had seen enough. He recognized what he saw in that glance.

Himself.

Beverly was a political animal, and thanks to the e-mail Charles had supplied, Peter held her political future in the palm of his hand. This had been too close for comfort, but the mutiny was over, and Peter would be victorious. If she wanted to be the President's successor, Beverly would side with Peter. She had no other choice. Charles had seen to that.

"Mr. President," Beverly said after clearing her throat, "I think you need to send in the QRF. Bring Shaw home."

And just that suddenly, Peter's victory turned to ash.

FORTY-TWO

Peter ascended the stairs leading from the subbasement at a run, ignoring the curious glances from the Secret Service Agents standing post. His stomach churned, threatening to send bile rocketing up his esophagus, but this wasn't why he hurried. The President had just made a disastrous choice, one that might bring an end to a career twenty years in the making, but Peter still had one card left to play.

Assuming he reached his desk in time.

Peter tore through the hall, passing paintings of Lincoln and Franklin Delano Roosevelt. On many occasions, these men had brought him hope as he'd strolled by the portraits at all hours of the day and night, carefully laying the path that would ensure Jorge Gonzales's second term.

Even Inauguration Day almost four years before had been a cause for only muted celebration on Peter's part.

Any political hand worth his salt knew that a President's major policy achievements had to wait until his second term. Press too hard in the first, and the voters would take out their wrath during the midterms, destroying the Congressional majority Peter desperately needed to pass the sweeping domestic-focused agenda he envisioned.

Even here, Peter had left nothing to chance. Passing game-changing legislation that survived more than one administration took the participation of both political parties. Laws that were passed along party lines were often repealed in the same manner once the majorities in Congress shifted.

With this in mind, Peter had spent the last four years quietly cultivating relationships with Republican Senators and Congressmen, particularly those who represented districts or states that Jorge had carried. These vulnerable legislators needed to be seen as bipartisan, standing above the typical Washington morass, and Peter was only too willing to help.

For a price.

Senator Sandford Kime was typical in this regard. The two-term Republican hailed from Pennsylvania, and Jorge had carried the state by five percentage points. Sandy was up for reelection next year, and he desperately needed a legislative win or two, particularly ones that showed he could reach across the aisle when the cause was worthy.

Enter Peter's Veterans Administration initiative. Exactly one week after President Gonzales's reelection, Sandy Kime would announce that he was fed up with the abysmal state of veterans' health care and offer up a bill that would privatize much of the VA. The newly re-elected President, under Peter's guidance, would embrace the initiative lock, stock, and barrel, calling on the Senate and the House to follow suit. Just like that, Senator Sandy Kime would have a legislative notch in his belt, and Peter would have a Republican cosponsor for his free-college-for-all initiative.

Except that Peter's years of painstaking strategy and patience had just been upended by a well-planned ambush coupled with an unexpected treachery.

Et tu, Beverly?

Once he'd understood that the President's decision was final, Peter had excused himself from the Situation Room in a hurry. Fortunately, his unexpected departure from meetings was a common occurrence.

Peter worked at a pace that dwarfed that of even the most committed Washington acolyte, and he kept a grueling schedule that had broken many a staffer ten years his junior. Even so, his productivity came at a price. Peter consumed coffee in quantities that would have humbled the most caffeinated Seattle hipster.

As such, trips to relieve his troubled bladder were frequent.

After standing up from the table, Peter had told the President he would return shortly. But rather than head for the bathroom, Peter ran to his office and the one thing that might yet help him snatch victory from the jaws of defeat—a phone.

But not just any phone.

Once he'd skidded across the final turn into his office, Peter slammed the door behind him, rattling the framed Harvard diploma hanging precariously on his wall. The diploma and a single picture were the only personal touches Peter permitted in the tiny office. His work was too important to allow himself to be distracted by anything other than the changes he'd vowed to bring about to the country he loved.

The Harvard diploma was there to remind Peter that, while he'd come from nothing, equal parts hard work, perseverance, and suffering had allowed him to achieve greatness. The photo embodied both the reason for sacrifices he'd endured and the source of his suffering.

Kristen grinned back at him from her high school senior picture. His sister looked beautiful, more than a girl, but not yet fully a woman. Her blond hair fell in soft waves to her shoulders and her blue eyes sparkled with thoughts of her future.

A future cut much too short.

Even twenty years later, the photo still cut his heart in two. But today, the image of his carefree sister fortified him. What he was about to do could not be undone, but Peter knew that his sacrifice would not be in vain. More than twenty years ago, he'd stood in front of his sister's flag-draped coffin and made a promise.

Today, he would honor that vow no matter the consequences.

Dropping to his knees, Peter reached under his desk, grabbed his messenger bag, and dug through the pockets until he found the secure phone that Charles had given him. With the seconds until disaster ticking away, Peter didn't have time to reflect on the potential consequences of his actions. He didn't even bother to climb into his comfortable leather chair. Instead, he knelt on the floor in a position of supplication and began to dial.

As the ringing filled his ear, Peter looked at the photo perched on his desk and had just one thought.

No more Kristens.

FORTY-THREE

Hello?"

In a rush Peter exhaled the breath he'd been holding. The phone had rung a half dozen times before it was answered. In that time, a score of scenarios flashed through Peter's mind, each one worse than the one before. For the span of ten agonizing seconds, Peter had wondered whether the person on the other end of the line would even answer, since the number was unfamiliar and the contact unexpected.

Then the ringing had ceased.

"Hello," the voice said again in slightly accented English.

"It's me," Peter said, the words coming out in a rush.

"Peter? This is a surprise. Why are you calling me on this number?"

"I'm sorry, my friend," Peter said, each passing second

registering with the subtlety of a pealing church bell. "I don't have time to explain. I need your help."

A moment of silence and then, "Okay. What can I do?"

"We are about to make a mistake. A terrible one."

"'We'?"

"My country," Peter said. "If you can help prevent that mistake, you'll have my unconditional gratitude. The unconditional gratitude of the newly elected President's senior adviser. Do you understand?"

Another beat of silence. Then, "I understand. How do I help?"

"Stop us."

FORTY-FOUR

RUSSIAN-CONTROLLED AIRSPACE, SYRIA

Lieutenant Dmitri Androvinoch stared at the radio in the cockpit of his Su-27 Flanker, wondering if he'd just imagined the last transmission. His eyes flicked across the multiple instrument panels with a fighter pilot's precision. He verified his heading, his altitude, his navigational display, and the turbine gas temperatures of the twin Saturn AL-31F turbofan engines that transformed sixty-seven thousand pounds of steel into the nimblest of dancers.

Everything was exactly as expected. Everything but the last set of instructions from ground control.

"Say again last transmission for Badger Three Four," Dmitri said, keying the radio-transmit button on his control stick.

For a minute, he'd assumed that he'd been dreaming, but a second check of the instruments put that notion to rest. Everything showed within normal ranges, which

proved that the last transmission had not been a product
of too many late nights coupled with too much vodka. In
Dmitri's dreams, his aircraft was always one malfunction
away from killing him. If the digital readouts were in the
green, he must actually be awake.

"Badger Three Four, this is Outrigger Base. You have
a mission change. Intercept a pair of rotary-wing bogeys,
heading zero seven five, range two hundred miles. Do
not allow them to enter Russian-controlled airspace.
Over."

He hadn't imagined the radio transmission, but that
didn't mean it made any more sense the second time he
heard it.

Since arriving in theater four months ago, Dmitri had
spent untold hours flying CAP, or Combat Air Patrol,
against a nonexistent enemy. Neither ISIS nor the Syrian
rebels possessed an air force, so after weeks of inactivity,
Dmitri had started conducting his lonely patrols without
a wingman. No reason to waste the jet fuel of two Flankers when one was more than enough.

But tonight, something had changed.

On occasion, ground control had him check on a
Turkish aircraft buzzing along their border to the north,
but the heading Dmitri had been provided took him in
the opposite direction—toward American-controlled airspace.

"Outrigger Base, Badger Three Four. Confirm weapons status. Over."

"Badger Three Four, Outrigger Base. You are weapons free. I say again, weapons free. Try to intercept the

helicopters before they enter our airspace. If they refuse to turn back, bring them down."

"Badger Three Four copies all," Dmitri said, slewing his Zhuk-ME multimode radar toward the heading Outrigger Base had specified. He transmitted a quick energy burst and watched as a pair of icons representing helicopters flickered into and out of existence on his targeting screen.

Dmitri frowned as he tuned the radar, steering more energy down a narrower azimuth in an attempt to gain better resolution on what had to be the American helicopters. If Dmitri had to guess, he'd bet that the helicopters were outfitted with some sort of stealthy modifications to hide their radar return.

Even so, the algorithms that processed and deciphered his targeting radar had been upgraded just before Dmitri's Syrian deployment, and the work seemed to be bearing fruit. He didn't have a perfect lock, but he didn't need one. He could always use the radar information to slew his electro-optical targeting system and then find the helicopters via their distinctive infrared signatures.

Either way, the approaching aircraft were still in American airspace, but wouldn't be much longer. Once they crossed the imaginary line dividing Russian- and American-controlled airspace, Dmitri's orders were clear.

Dmitri wrenched his fighter into a steep bank, slamming the throttle forward. In the space of a single heartbeat, the engine noise went from a comforting rumble to an all-out battle cry as afterburners ignited, turning the Flanker from a simple plane into a ballistic missile.

Confusing as the order had been, Dmitri was sure of one thing—his nights of boredom had just ended.

Chief Warrant Officer Three Joel Glendening inched the collective upward with his left hand as he nosed the cyclic forward with his right. The MH-60 Black Hawk responded as he'd intended, the composite rotors biting into the air in larger chunks even as the jagged line representing the temperature of his helicopter's turbo-shaft engines edged further into the red.

The MH-60's all-digital display was a far cry from the simple analog instruments that Joel had cut his teeth on, but even today's remarkable technology was no match for the laws of physics. The thin desert air couldn't sufficiently cool the eight-hundred-degree engines. If Joel held this airspeed for any longer than the nine minutes and thirty-three seconds ticking downward on his engine display, he would risk causing permanent damage to the helicopter.

But that was okay. According to the moving map on his second multipurpose display, he needed to maintain his blistering pace for just seven minutes and twenty-three seconds. Then he'd slow from his almost one hundred fifty knots to a full hover in the time it took a Ferrari to accelerate from zero to sixty.

After that, the real fun would begin.

"How we doing, Chief?"

The voice asking the question sounded slightly distorted as it crackled over the helicopter's intercom system, but Joel would have recognized the distinctive tone anywhere.

As a member of the Army's vaunted 160th Special Operations Regiment, Joel had flown countless missions in support of an untold number of bearded shadow warriors. Still, Colonel Fitz was in a class all his own. Utterly fearless, the Unit commando embodied the warrior ethos, and Joel found himself purposely aligning his flight schedule to match the Colonel's missions. Colonel Fitz's operations were executed with an audacity and precision that made Joel remember why he'd volunteered for the Night Stalkers' grueling selection process in the first place—to fly men like Colonel Fitz on missions deemed too risky for anyone else.

This operation was shaping up to be no exception.

"So far, so good, sir," Joel said, eyeing the moving map display as he answered. "In six minutes, I'll hit the release point. Exactly one minute and twenty seconds later, you'll be standing on the target building's roof."

"That's what I'm talking about, Chief," Fitz said, reaching from his jump seat located between and slightly behind the pilot and copilot seats to slap Joel on the back of the helmet. "You know why I like flying with you guys? I can set my watch by you fuckers."

"Plus or minus thirty seconds, sir. Night Stalkers don't quit."

At that moment, a bright red icon on Joel's threat display flared to life, accompanied by a warbling tone in his headset. A rush of emotions tumbled through Joel's mind—fear, disbelief, and anger chief among them. But it was a sense of disappointment that he felt most strongly. Disappointment because, for the first time in the ten-plus years since he'd joined the Regiment, Joel had a feeling that he might just miss his hit time.

Twenty-five thousand feet above the pair of Night Stalker helicopters and approximately one hundred miles away, Lieutenant Androvinoch looked at the symbols on his heads-up display with a sense of unbridled satisfaction. He'd never actually locked up a hostile airborne target before. Within a week of arriving in theater, he'd realized the odds of his doing so on this combat tour were almost nonexistent.

And yet here he was, streaking through the sky like the bird of prey his fighter was meant to be, his R-27 Alamo A air-to-air missiles targeting the pair of helicopters that were even now unsuccessfully attempting to mask their approach into Russian-controlled Syrian airspace.

His airspace.

According to his tactical computer, the helos were within thirty seconds of crossing the invisible line denoting the border between Russian- and American-controlled territories. If he went by the letter of his instructions, Dmitri would be well within his rights to engage the Americans now, since, by the time the eighty-six-pound warheads swatted the helicopters from the sky, both aircraft would be solidly within Russian airspace.

Still, although Dmitri might be young, he was no

fool. Laying waste to the jihadis and the rebels was one thing. Starting a shooting war with the Americans was something else entirely. Instructions from Outrigger Main or not, Dmitri wanted his actions firmly on record before he turned the two aircraft skimming along the desert floor into smoking piles of metal and twisted flesh. Taking his gloved left hand off the throttle, he keyed the international distress frequency, known as Guard, into his UHF radio and began to transmit.

American helicopters, you are entering restricted airspace. Turn around or you will be fired upon. I say again, turn around or you will be fired upon."

Joel's eyes snapped from his aircraft-survivability screen—on which a triangular red shape symbolizing a missile lock bounded his helicopter's blue icon—to his radio, as he tried to make sense of what he was seeing and hearing.

"What the hell's that?" Colonel Fitz said, shouting over the warbling siren that accompanied the missile lock's visual indication.

"Stand by, sir," Joel said, his voice still crisp and professional even as his sphincter tightened. Toggling his radio-selection switch to UHF, Joel thumbed the transmit button on the cyclic stick between his legs.

"Last calling station," Joel said, his voice calm despite the fact that his stomach was twisted in knots. "This is a U.S. Army helicopter proceeding on an approved mission through sector Charlie. I say again, this is a U.S. Army helicopter proceeding on an approved mission through sector Charlie. Stand down. Over."

Stand down? The American's arrogance was breathtaking. The blustering helicopter pilot had just acknowledged to the assorted nations undoubtedly eavesdropping on the unsecure frequency that he had knowingly violated Russian airspace. Dmitri had been more than accommodating, and the Americans had returned his kindness by spitting in his face. Verifying the information from his targeting radar, Dmitri made a decision. The intercept course he'd been following at just over Mach 1 had closed the distance to the American helicopters considerably. Perhaps it was time to demonstrate his intentions in a manner that left no room for interpretation.

Activating the aircraft's master arm switch, Dmitri edged the Flanker's nose downward, lifted the trigger guard on his stick, and squeezed the trigger.

The stream of red tracers split the night sky like a lightning bolt. In turn, Joel was forced to execute the one battle drill he'd never thought he'd actually use: react to air attack.

"Taking fire!" Joel shouted on his wingman's frequency even as he bottomed the collective and cranked the cyclic to the left, banking to the aircraft's limits in a desperate attempt to maneuver inside the attacking plane's dive angle. In the world of air-to-air combat, a helicopter's single advantage was its nimble turning radius. By turning into the attack, Joel hoped to cause his attacker to overshoot.

Short of praying, he had no other option.

"What the hell?" Colonel Fitz said, his voice colored with equal parts surprise and anger.

"The Russian jet fired on us," Joel said, arresting the MH-60's precipitous descent with a jerk of the collective. Any lower and his landing gear would be kissing sand.

"Turbine Six Three, this is Six Four. Did the Russian shoot at us?"

"Affirm, Six Four," Joel said, echoing his wingman's bewildered tone. "You hit?"

"Negative, Six Three. But that burst of cannon fire looked like it almost took off your nose."

"American helicopters, American helicopters." The Russian voice echoed across Guard before Joel could reply. "There will be no more warning shots. Turn back now or you will be fired upon. Acknowledge. Over."

Joel paused for a moment, his thumb over the radio-transmit toggle. He was furious, but he was also damn lucky and knew it. The Russian bastard could have loosed an air-to-air missile. In that scenario, Joel and his wingman would have been knocked from the air without ever even seeing their killer. But the Russian had fired a warning shot instead. Joel couldn't claim to understand the geopolitical ramifications of what had just transpired, but he did know that the Russian pilot was offering him a way out.

He intended to take it.

"Russian aircraft," Joel said, "we acknowledge and are proceeding back to American airspace."

The words tasted sour on his lips, but he said them all the same. Enduring a bit of humiliation was better than ending his career as a pile of burning wreckage strewn across the desolate Syrian desert.

"What the fuck, Chief?"

"Sorry, sir," Joel said, the anger in his voice mirroring Colonel Fitz's. "He's got us. No way in hell we can cross into Assad-controlled territory with that fast mover up there circling like a vulture."

"You're aborting?"

"No choice, sir. You know me—I've flown into hell and back for you guys, and I'll do it again. This is different. If we turn inbound, he'll smoke us. Sorry, sir. Your operative is on his own."

FORTY-FIVE

placed my phone back in my lap, my mind still reeling as I tried to digest Fitz's words.

Mission aborted.

That part had been pretty unambiguous, but the rest was still a bit hazy. Something about the Russians locking down the airspace and firing on Fitz's helicopters. My first tour in Syria had convinced me that the norms I associated with Western civilization didn't apply here, but what had just happened was outrageous even by Syria's standards. A Russian fighter had fired on two American helicopters.

This was dangerous territory.

"What's going on?" Einstein said. The edginess to his voice was growing more pronounced with every minute we remained within sight of his former laboratory and Shaw's current prison.

I'd never met Shaw, and probably wouldn't have even

if everything had gone according to plan. But once again, the enemy had decided to exercise his vote. Now my plan looked about as solid as a cloud of dust scattered by the fickle Syrian wind.

"Keep an eye on the building," I said.

I was more concerned with giving Einstein something to focus on than worried about the need for additional security. Somewhere above us, a Sentinel was watching with its unblinking eye. The stealthy UAV was relaying my phone calls and documenting the mission for posterity. The semiautonomous aircraft represented the pinnacle of aerospace engineering—a wingman who never tired, who could see in the dark, and who was immune to enemy radar.

In short, the hundred-million-dollar drone was the perfect machine to watch my back, and yet I would have traded the technological marvel for a crippled Frodo in a heartbeat.

Frodo.

"I'm going to make a call," I said, getting out of the truck in search of privacy. I dialed Frodo's number from memory as I hobbled to the rear of the vehicle and put the phone to my ear. If prisoners on death row were granted a last meal, maybe a spy on a hopeless mission could pray for a final miracle.

Any way I looked at it, Shaw was in trouble. Even if I was up for a one-man rescue worthy of a cut-rate Jason Bourne flick, that ship had sailed about the time I received my fourth mission-ending injury. A shattered ankle, a gunshot wound to the leg, a broken wrist, and more concussions than the Bengals' offensive line suffered meant that, in my current condition, I'd have trouble rescuing Shaw from a class of unruly kindergartners. The smart thing to do—the only thing to do—was to turn the truck around and start driving for American-controlled territory. With more luck than I was entitled to, perhaps Einstein and I could make it back to friendly lines before dawn.

But even as the idea took form, I discarded it. Last time I'd left this country, my best friend had been in a medically induced coma, and my asset and his family were dead. The next three months had been no better. I'd shut Laila out, abandoned Frodo, and exiled myself to Austin on the premise that distance somehow equated to healing.

But premise had been all it really was. Instead of friends and family, I'd kept company with a dead toddler's ghost and shared my most meaningful conversations with Jeremiah the shoeshine man. Far from providing any semblance of healing, the months of separation had made my situation worse. The shakes came more frequently and with greater intensity. Each day, Abir seemed less a phantasm and more a flesh-and-blood little girl.

How long before I started practicing Arabic with her?

How long before I decided to join her?

I stared at the unassuming building a football field away, fingers stretching into the chords for "Tequila Sunrise" as Frodo's phone rang unanswered. The mournful E minor in the song's bridge seemed oddly appropriate right now. In another bit of songwriting brilliance, Messieurs Henley and Frey had perfectly captured the battle between darkness and light through alternating E minor and C major chords. In the bridge's final verse, a melancholy A minor transitions to a bright D seven, sonically rendering a hopeful sunrise after a night filled with despair. I didn't know if a tequila sunrise was in the cards, but I did know that, one way or another, this was where my journey had to end—exactly where it had begun.

I'd once seen an interview with a surviving member from Easy Company of *Band of Brothers* fame. When pressed to explain how he'd maintained his sanity during his unit's continent-spanning fight against the Nazis, the grizzled veteran had summed up his mental state with a surprisingly straightforward statement. "Once I accepted that I was already dead, everything else was easy." Leaving might be the rational choice, but for me, it wasn't an option. To paraphrase that unassuming veteran, I was already dead. And dead men didn't run.

"Matty? Is that you?"

"It's me, brother," I said, relief washing over me as Frodo's voice filled my ear. "I'm in a bit of a jam."

"Hang tight, buddy. I've got eyes on you. The UAV's got another thirty minutes of loiter time, and I'm working to retask a replacement as we speak. Start heading east and I'll vector you past the roadblocks. I'll get you home."

"Any chance of the QRF getting through?"

"No. I'm sorry. The fucking administration rolled over. Other than the Sentinel, there will be no more incursions into Russian-controlled airspace. Your hitters aren't coming."

"The President's fine with leaving Shaw to the jihadis?"

"He doesn't see it that way. James is in the Situation Room, and he ducks out to give me SITREPs when he can. The President's staff was split about sending Colonel Fitz in the first place. The JSOC commander and James were all for it. The President's limp-dick Chief of Staff was against it. Director Castle cast the deciding vote."

"The CIA Director?"

"Yep. Apparently she's got more balls than the Chief of Staff. Anyway, now that the mission almost went south, she's got egg on her face, and he's calling the shots."

"What about Shaw?"

"According to Charles, his indigenous Syrian network has eyes on Shaw's location and is about to attempt a rescue."

I shifted the phone from one ear to the other as I looked across the still night. Other than a flickering mercury light casting pale shadows across the chain-link fence in front of the building, nothing moved.

Absolutely nothing.

"If the CIA has assets here, they're really good at hiding," I said. "Other than Einstein, there isn't another living soul around."

"I hear you, brother, but according to James, the President's gun-shy after nearly starting a shooting war with the Russians. The cavalry isn't coming. If you don't want to abandon Shaw, at least pull back and find somewhere to lie low. Maybe you can help the CIA's Syrian assets once they show."

"Come on, Frodo. You can't bullshit a bullshitter. With that Sentinel orbiting at fifty thousand feet, you've got the best seat in the house. Does your eye in the sky see a convoy of technical vehicles heading this way?"

For a moment, I thought my friend was going to lie to me. I should have known better. Friends are brave enough to tell each other the truth, even when the truth is catastrophic.

"No, Matty," Frodo said, the words coming out with a sigh. "I retasked the Sentinel as soon as I realized it was you on the phone. Nothing's moving."

"That's because Charles's guys aren't coming. You know it, and I know it."

To Frodo's credit, he didn't argue. He simply asked the next logical question. The one I didn't have an answer for, or at least not an answer he was going to like.

"What now?"

I looked at the building in front of me, praying for some sort of omen. I had no idea what form this omen might take, but right about now, I wasn't all that choosy. I'd accept anything from a phantom toddler to a burning bush, but what I got instead was a whole lot of nothing. The truck creaked on tired shocks as Einstein shifted behind the steering wheel, but other than that, nothing changed.

Nothing at all.

Maybe the Almighty wasn't in a talkative mood, or

maybe He was otherwise occupied. Either way, I was on my own.

"Here's how this is gonna go down," I said, my semblance of a plan coming together even as the words left my mouth. "I'm gonna use Einstein to get into the building. Then I'm gonna find Shaw."

"I don't want to hear that bullshit," Frodo said. "You and I have both been around the block enough times to know that isn't gonna work. This is what I think—you feel like you can't come home without Shaw, so you're going to make sure you don't. This is a suicide mission."

"You're wrong, brother," I said, feeling clarity for the first time in months. "I know you can't see it, but you're wrong. I'm scared out of my mind. I do want to bring Shaw home, more than anything I've ever wanted. But I'm not suicidal. If I was suicidal, I'd be going this alone. But I'm not alone. I've got you."

"I'm a broken-ass cripple, Matty. How can I help you from here?"

So I told him in five short sentences. It was a plan of sorts, but one so desperate that even if it succeeded, Frodo and I would both be considered persona non grata by our respective organizations. If it failed, I'd be dead, and Frodo would spend the better part of his adult life in prison.

Like I said, it wasn't pretty, but it was all I had.

When I finished speaking, I had a thought—a fleeting one, but it shamed me nonetheless. For the briefest of instants, I wondered if what I was asking was too much. If my best friend would turn me down.

But that wasn't Frodo.

"Okay, brother," Frodo said without a second's hesitation. "I'm on it, but I'm gonna need room to maneuver. The chatter on the jihadi websites has spiked. We think they're going to execute Shaw in the next thirty minutes. I won't even be able to get where I need to go that fast. You've got to buy me time."

"I'll buy you time," I said, staring at the building's shadowy form, "but not much. You've got to hurry."

"I'm already gone," Frodo said, and ended the call.

It occurred to me that, for the first time in my friendship with Frodo, I was glad that he wasn't standing beside me. Even if he'd been in his pre-ambush prime, the two of us trying to rescue Shaw would have been a fool's errand. But now, with a broken body that had kept him six thousand miles away, Frodo might just stand a chance of saving my life one last time. But first, I had to do my part.

Putting the phone in my pocket, I got back into the car.

Einstein hadn't liked my plan before. When he heard what was in store for us now, he might just decide that death by Hellfire was a better option.

FORTY-SIX

W e aren't leaving, are we?"

Einstein asked the question with a finality to his voice. It was the type of question a pestering child might ask, one to which he already knew the answer.

"Rest assured, we're leaving, but not without the American who's sitting in that building. Got it?"

Einstein shook his head and looked away. I watched the muscles of his jaw clench and unclench as he fought against the inevitable. Say something and risk the rough side of my tongue, or sit there and sulk in silence.

His internal monologue lasted for all of two seconds.

"Look," he said, turning back to me, "I don't bloody well pretend to understand what you do any more than I suspect you'd be able to help an analytical chemist select the correct sorbents for a class one nerve agent. But it doesn't take a tactical genius to know that you can't shoot your way into that building. Your friends aren't coming. There's no one left."

"You're wrong," I said. "Someone's working on our behalf. He's not here. But you are."

"Me? There's no bloody way in hell I'm going into that building. None."

"Yes, you are."

"Or what? You'll kill my family? Fuck off."

"No," I said, expelling a breath, "I won't do that. I misjudged you earlier. I don't often do that, but I did with you."

"What does that mean?"

"It means that you're even more of a narcissistic, self-centered piece of shit than I thought. And that's saying something. If you possessed even a hint of something redeeming inside that shriveled thing you call a soul, you'd have asked about your family by now. A good man would have even tried to bargain for them, perhaps offering himself in their place. But you're not a good man, are you?"

Einstein didn't speak, but the snarl on his lips was answer enough.

"No, you don't really give two shits about your family, at least not when your own life hangs in the balance. So I'm gonna have to persuade you with the only thing you truly value—your own life."

"If I don't help you, you'll kill me? Is that it?"

"Not me," I said, shaking my head. "I won't have to. Seven miles above us, a Sentinel drone is loitering. It has lots of cool bells and whistles, but you know what it doesn't have? A Hellfire. Because Hellfires are old-school. Too much collateral damage. Instead, that bird has a belly full of laser-guided small-diameter bombs. The kind of ordnance you put through a window to kill the guy sitting on the couch when you don't want to hurt the guy eating at a table five feet away. Really is a marvel of modern technology, but that's not important. What's important is that in about five seconds, I'm going to open this door and start walking toward that building. If you're not with me, step for step, one of those small-diameter bombs is going to come winging its way earth-ward and bury itself in your skull up to its stubby little fins. Is that a good enough reason?"

"I hate you."

"Glad we understand each other. Women and children—that's who you killed, motherfucker. Trust me, the only reason you're still drawing breath is that I need your help. Otherwise, you'd already be a grease spot in the sand. Now, as much fun as this conversation's been, time is running out. You have a decision to make. Follow my instructions or try your chances with my eye in the sky and her belly full of bombs. What's it gonna be?"

Einstein looked at me for several long seconds, his jaw clenched as his massive brain ran through about a thousand different scenarios at the speed of light. Undoubt-edly, he was searching for the one scenario that would allow him to fuck over yours truly and walk away scot-free. But I wasn't worried, for the exact reason Einstein himself gave. He might be Doctor Doom, but we were in my world now. I was his lifeline. If he wanted to maintain his ever-so-tenuous hold on that lifeline, he would have to follow me into deeper water.

"Okay," Einstein said, biting off the word. "What do I do?"

"For starters, you take my pistol," I said, handing him the Glock. "Then you punch me in the face. Hard."

For the first time since I'd made his acquaintance, Einstein did exactly what I asked.

In hindsight, I probably should have added a bit more clarity to my instructions, like by substituting the word *chin* or even *cheek* for *face*. But I hadn't. Einstein responded to my oversight by blasting me squarely in the nose with an intensity that belied his small stature. One second, I was staring at him across the car's darkened interior, preparing for a shot that would ring my bell. The next, I was choking on the blood pouring down my throat.

Say what you want about my little chemist, but he had a right hand that would have done Tyson proud. Which was good, because, before we were done tonight, my little scrapper might just need to bite through an ear or two.

FORTY-SEVEN

The shaking started sooner than I'd expected. The twitching began as Einstein started the vehicle, and the tremors progressed from my fingertips to my major muscle groups with frightening speed. By the time Einstein had parked the truck, and we'd begun to walk up the gravel pathway to the chain-link fence surrounding the former ball bearing plant turned lab-prison, I could no longer disguise the shudders. Einstein responded with the compassion I'd come to expect from a scientist who sold death to the highest bidder.

"What's bloody wrong with you?"

"I'm hobbling on a broken fucking ankle," I said with a whisper. "Cut me some goddamn slack."

My answer came out with more venom than I'd intended, but it still did the trick. Einstein grabbed my arm, helping to support my weight.

I needed to remember that Einstein was scared shit-less, too. That was mostly good, because for our little scenario to have a snowball's chance in hell of working, he needed to be terrified. But it was also bad, because frightened people make mistakes, and we couldn't afford any. Not one. I'd run operations on tight margins before, but nothing like this.

This boondoggle was in a class all its own.

Headlights from a passing car played over the steel gate, and the tremors intensified, my teeth rattling in sympathy. Just beyond the gate was a building that held a chemical lab and a contingent of jihadis intent on saw-ing off an American's head in exactly fifteen minutes and thirty-three seconds. "Tight margins" didn't even begin to describe what we were up against.

As if on cue, Abir manifested just on the other side of the fence. For once, she wasn't smiling at me from over her dead mother's shoulder. Instead, she stood on the gravel, just staring, her dark eyes boring holes through me. Was her appearance a good sign, or had I finally lost my mind? I didn't know and didn't care.

Like the Easy Company veteran, I was already dead.

"Ready?" I asked, shifting my attention from the tod-dler to Einstein.

The question was more rhetorical than literal. At this point, we were committed. The security cameras that Einstein had assured me were present would have already captured our shambling approach. Unless one of the small-diameter bombs that the Sentinel didn't actually carry fell on our heads in the next five seconds, we were going into that building. Then again, a dead toddler was watching me from the other side of the fence.

At this point, anything was possible.

"I'm bloody well ready, you son of a bitch."

"Easy on the foul language, Doctor Doom. I'm the one with the broken fucking nose, remember?"

My face felt like someone had surgically removed my nose and transplanted a cantaloupe in its place. A fucking pulsating, fucking throbbing cantaloupe full of fucking burning needles burrowing into my fucking face. Einstein had broken the shit out of my nose, and if my other injuries hadn't also been demanding my attention, I might have given Einstein a shot or two in the face to help sell our story. Fortunately for him, that was easier said than done. With my hands secured behind my back with the dead jihadi's handcuffs, my swollen nose now occupying half my face's real estate, a splinted ankle, and a bloodstained bandage covering my leg, I was in a pretty sorry state.

But that was the point.

"Tell me what you're going to do," I said, trying to take my mind off our destination.

"I know what to do."

"Tell. Me."

Einstein gave an exasperated snort through his nose, which didn't win him any points from me. I was going to be a mouth breather for at least the next four weeks. In any case, Einstein began to talk.

"You tried to kidnap me. My minders died protecting me. They shot you as you drove away, and you crashed your car. I captured you. Now I'm bringing you here."

"Why?"

"Because killing two Americans is always better than killing one."

"Exactly. And when the guards are close enough?"

"I shoot them and give you the gun."

"Then you lead me to where the American is hidden. I kill his guards, and we barricade ourselves in his cell and wait for the cavalry."

"And then we go home."

"And then we go home."

Einstein's voice had seemed less than certain. It was almost as if he didn't quite believe we had a prayer of pulling this off. To be honest, I didn't, either. If I was really left to my own talents, I wouldn't have felt too sporty about our odds of survival. But I wasn't in this by myself.

I had Frodo.

I didn't tell this to Einstein for a couple of reasons. One, I wanted him to be on his best behavior, and desperation paired with pending death tended to do that to people. Two, as we'd been talking, we passed through the gap in the rusted fence and now stood at the reinforced steel door that marked the building's entrance. I tried to pause for a moment, if nothing else to gird myself with a final breath before I fully committed to this path of madness, but I didn't get the chance. As Einstein stretched out his fingers, the door swung open on silent hinges revealing a black-clad jihadi.

Showtime.

FORTY-EIGHT

What is this?" said the jihadi who opened the door. "Where are Hassan and Muhammad?"

"Dead," Einstein said, shoving me into the room with a bit more force than was necessary. "He killed them."

I sprawled at the guard's feet, my handcuffed hands unable to break my fall. I turned my head aside at the last moment, narrowly avoiding banging my busted nose against the mud-encrusted concrete, but a moan escaped my lips all the same. Clearing my throat, I hawked a glob of equal parts snot and blood next to the guard's black-sneakered foot.

He responded with the wholehearted compassion I'd come to expect from a homicidal jihadi. Letting loose a stream of curses that would have made the Prophet blush, the jihadi delivered a series of kicks to my shoulders and back. I curled around my abdomen as much as my restricted hands would allow, trying to absorb the blows with the uninjured portions of my body. I wanted to stay conscious long enough to make sense of what was happening.

Okay, so the shoving-me-through-the-door part wasn't exactly in the script we'd rehearsed, but Einstein's ad lib seemed to be working. I was inside the building housing both the chemical weapons lab and Shaw. Step one of our plan was complete. From here on in, everything would be gravy.

Sure, it would.

"Ishmael, let the brothers know we have company. I'll see to our guest."

This was a new voice.

I looked up to see the guard Ishmael joined by another man. Unlike Ishmael, who was dressed in jihadi casual—black cargo pants and top, with greasy hair and a thick, bushy beard—the new arrival looked suave. He could have been the Arabic equivalent of the guy who played the world's most interesting man in those Dos Equis commercials. He wore simple yet expensive clothes—Italian shoes, dress slacks, and a button-down shirt. His thick black hair was neatly styled, and his obligatory beard was trimmed almost down to the skin. When he spoke, his Arabic had an Iraqi tinge.

Ishmael, still breathing hard from the half-hearted beating he'd administered, made his way toward a narrow corridor on the right side of the room, leaving Einstein and me alone with Mr. Suave. The newcomer waited until the door closed behind Ishmael before turning to Einstein.

"How is it that Hassan and Muhammad are dead while you are still very much alive?"

"I'll tell you how," Einstein said, his face twisting with anger. "You didn't listen to me."

"Which time did I not listen to you?" Mr. Suave said, eyeing me. "When you were trying to sell us to Mr. Drake, or once you decided to sell Mr. Drake to us? Conversations with you can be confusing."

Well, son of a bitch. This was definitely not part of the script. Seems like my Pakistani weapons scientist was playing both sides. Who would have thought?

"I brought him here," Einstein said, "just like you asked."

"So you did," Mr. Suave said. "Is this his weapon?"

Einstein nodded and handed my pistol to the newcomer, who took the offered weapon and turned it in his hands. "A Glock 19 with a custom-fit suppressor. Very nice hardware, but I was expecting something a bit more exotic from an American intelligence operative. Pity."

Along about now, the warning bells that had begun to ring when Mr. Suave first strolled into the room turned into screaming police sirens. Whoever this guy was, I knew that his very presence somehow changed the equation. Edging to my side, I grasped the frayed stitching on my left shirt cuff with my right index finger and thumb. I pinched the elusive bit of fabric between my fingers and began to worry the thread, using my body to shield my hands from my audience.

"Look," Einstein said, his impatience obvious, "I've done what you asked. My part in this is over."

"On this we agree," Mr. Suave said with a smile.

I could see what was about to happen next, but Einstein, so experienced in facilitating death from the safety of a sterile laboratory, was woefully unprepared for the way the world actually worked in the back alleys and gutters his clients called home. In one fluid motion, Mr. Suave extended his arm and shot Einstein through the forehead. The scientist's head snapped backward like he'd been hit with a right cross instead of a hundred-forty-seven-grain subsonic projectile traveling at nine hundred eighty feet per second. A mixture of crimson blood and gray brain matter splattered across the wall with a wet-sounding slap.

Just that quickly, Einstein's tremendous intellect was reduced to organic sludge. The whole episode was a not-so-gentle reminder that all living things, no matter how great or how small, existed within the confines of Adam's original curse. At the end of the day, none of us was greater than the dust from which we'd been formed.

"Excellent suppressor," Mr. Suave said, ignoring my would-be asset's crumpled form. "But I assume you already know that."

Mr. Suave didn't point the pistol at me. He didn't have to. Unlike Einstein with his tenuous grip on the weapon, the Iraqi held the Glock with obvious familiarity.

"I've been looking forward to this," Mr. Suave said, switching to nearly flawless English as he squatted down to my level. "I know you speak Arabic, but learning a foreign language's nuances takes a lifetime. I don't want there to be any misunderstandings between us."

Now that he'd moved closer, the Glock was pointing at my head. The pistol was far enough away that I couldn't grab it, even if my hands were free. But the weapon was close enough to deliver a killing shot long before I could cross the twelve inches separating us.

Dangerous didn't even begin to describe my new friend.

"Who are you?" I said, attempting to buy time as much as gain information. The first row of stitches came away, and I could feel the handcuff key embedded in the seam. Another five seconds—ten tops—and I'd have it. That wouldn't exactly put Mr. Suave and me on equal footing, but it would be a hell of a lot better than my current situation.

"Come now, Mr. Drake. All will be revealed in good time, or as these barbarians like to say, inshallah—as God wills it."

Mr. Suave laughed at my shocked look, clearly enjoying himself. "No, Mr. Drake, I am not a jihadi. I am a businessman, and you, sir, will be exceptionally good for business. I must say that I misjudged you. Your scientist friend staked his life on the probability that you would come for your captured companion. He was right, and yet he's still quite dead. Isn't it ironic—don't you think?"

"Did you just quote an Alanis Morissette song?" I said, partly out of astonishment and partly because my forefinger had just touched the ceramic key's tip.

Five more seconds.

"Indeed, Mr. Drake. As you might imagine, references to pop culture are lost on the *abu ayouras* who call this facility home. Working with them, while necessary, has been most trying. Under different circumstances, I would welcome a chance to engage in a more extensive dialogue with you. Unfortunately, our time together is at an end."

"Why?" I said, wiggling the key's first centimeter from the ragged cuff. "I'm not going anywhere."

Mr. Suave laughed again. "That is true, but I hear footsteps in the hall, which means you are about to become indisposed. You see, while I accept the deaths of Hassan and Muhammad as part of the cost of doing business, their jihadi brothers aren't quite so enlightened."

As if on cue, a scrum of black-clad terrorists spilled into the room, swarming past Mr. Suave without even acknowledging his presence. The fighters fell on me en masse, fists pounding my head, feet stomping my broken ankle, kicks battering my bruised body. The pain was agonizing, and this time, I willingly sank into a foggy oblivion. As the blackness overtook me, a single chilling sound followed me under.

Mr. Suave's laughter.

FORTY-NINE

Hello? Can you hear me?"

The words came from an unimaginable distance, reaching me across a sea of darkness. I opened my eyes. Blinked. Then fell back into the blackness like a drowning victim sinking into the water's embrace.

"Wake the fuck up!"

The voice had a harder edge now—the tone of one who gave orders and expected to be obeyed.

A command voice.

I opened my eyes, thinking perhaps that I'd been a victim of a particularly bad hangover. Unfortunately, it took only two full breaths to disabuse me of this notion. I'd experienced a hangover or two in my life, but I'd never hurt this bad. No, what I was feeling now definitely went beyond mere alcohol.

"Who are you?" I said, trying to gather my wits. The room was dim, and through my blood-encrusted eyes, I could discern only shadows. It was as if my surroundings were abstract art, rendered in shades of black and gray.

I closed my eyes. Drew another breath. Tried not to retch.

The stench in the enclosed space was overwhelming—the sour odor of unwashed bodies, the sharp ammonia smell of piss, and the metallic scent of blood. Overtop of everything rode the moldy scent of confinement.

"You first," the voice demanded. "You'll have to forgive my shyness, but it's been a rough couple of days."

I tried to push myself into a seated position and failed, sliding back on my side. At the moment, I was hard-pressed to find any extremity that was working as advertised. My hands were still handcuffed behind my back, but now a chain ran from my legs to a ring drilled into the cold concrete floor.

Shuffling on my side as far as the chain allowed, I found a pitted cinder block wall with my forearm, and inched my way upright, my body screaming in protest. The somewhat erect position made breathing a bit easier, and I coughed up a mouthful of blood and took a deep breath. The influx of oxygen helped to clear the mental fog, but my surroundings still didn't make any sense.

"Where are we?" I said, aiming my words at the dark form huddled at the opposite side of the cell.

"I was hoping you could tell me. Somewhere in Syria, I think, but I'm not sure. I woke up here two days ago."

At the word *Syria*, what I was seeing finally made sense. I was in a cell with another American, which meant . . .

"You Shaw?" I said, and spit out another blood clot along with a tooth or two. The boys who had administered my second beatdown knew a few things about throwing punches.

"Who's asking?" the voice said, caution infusing its tone.

"My name's Matt Drake. I'm here to rescue you."

I don't know what response I was expecting, but it wasn't laughter.

Then again, I suppose laughter was preferable to tears.

FIFTY

P ardon my reaction," Shaw said once his chuckles had
subsided, "but when I was picturing my rescue, this
wasn't it."

"No worries," I said, clearing the raspy feeling from
my throat. "I'm often underestimated."

I couldn't quite see the other operator's face, but I
had a feeling he was smiling. And that was good. People
often discount the tremendous difference a positive attitude can make during captivity. Right about now, Shaw
and I could use all the positivity we could muster.

"Sorry if this seems rude, but what's the plan?"

"Good question," I said, squeezing my fingers into
fists and then opening them wide in an effort to get my
blood flowing.

The good news was that, since the fingers on my right
hand still moved, my wrist injury was probably not a complete break. The bad news was that the increased blood

flow brought my nerve endings back to life, and they weren't happy. "Right now, the plan is still evolving."

"Evolving? That seems like a politically correct way of saying we're fucked."

"Not at all," I said as my probing fingers found the frayed cuff on my left sleeve. The cuff concealing a handcuff key. For a terrifying second, I'd felt nothing but empty fabric, but then I touched a bulge glued to my shirtsleeve with what had to be congealed blood.

The key.

"If we were fucked," I said, trying to keep the rush of emotion from my voice, "I'd have the decency to tell you. Call it professional courtesy."

Shaw laughed again, but he wasn't about to let the topic die. "If this was a football game, how would we be faring?"

With the tip of my fingernail, I began to slowly scrape away the clumps of dried blood. Now that I'd laid eyes on Shaw, I felt a renewed sense of urgency to get my hands free. Alleviating the sense of helplessness that came with being shackled was one of my motivators, but not the primary one. Hidden in the crotch of my underwear was our ticket out of here.

The jihadis are certifiable, but they're also prudes about some things, such as a man's undergarments. From debriefing other prisoners, we'd learned that, even if they dress you in one of their orange jumpsuits, the jihadis tend to let you keep your underwear.

Other than a compulsory pat down, they don't touch your junk.

This was why after landing in the farmer's field, I'd moved the dime-sized piece of electronic equipment Colonel Fitz had given me when he'd bid good-bye on the flight line from my zippered flight suit pocket to my boxer briefs.

The device was a beacon. It featured a powerful multiband transmitter paired with a coiled omnidirectional antenna. Because it was so small, the beacon had only enough juice for one coms shot, but with the Sentinel orbiting overhead, one shot was all I'd need.

This was a critical component of the plan that Frodo and I had discussed. To accomplish what I'd asked him to do, Frodo would need irrefutable proof that I'd located Shaw and that I was still alive, and the beacon offered both. I would activate the beacon if, and only if, I found Shaw.

That was our deal.

Now I just needed to get my hands free of the cuffs so I could reach into my drawers and give my saving grace a hard squeeze.

Unfortunately, I couldn't bring Shaw into the plan. At least not yet. If my years as a case officer had taught me anything, it was that the stupid jihadis had long since been sent to paradise. Maybe, just maybe, our captors had wired our cell for sound. Telling Shaw what I was doing was not a risk I could take.

Instead, I talked about football.

"Remember Super Bowl Fifty-one?" I said.

"Brady's fifth win?"

"That's it."

I could feel the key with my fingertip, but it wouldn't come loose from my sleeve.

"Sure," Shaw said, "but just so that I have the proper perspective, are we the Falcons or the Patriots?"

"The Patriots. Definitely. They won, right?"

Wedging my fingernail between the fabric and the piece of ceramic, I picked at the final glob of blood, and like manna from heaven, the key fell into my cupped palm.

Thank you, sweet Jesus. If I lived through this, I might just get a handcuff key surgically implanted.

"Yep, but the game was a little too close for my liking. I'd prefer something more along the lines of the Bears versus the Pats back in 'eighty-six. That was a blowout. If it's all the same to you, I'd rather our rescue didn't turn into a nail-biter."

"I hear you," I said, closing my eyes as I worked the key into the handcuff lock. Doing this with my hands behind my back was a bitch, especially when the fingers on one hand weren't cooperating. "But my coach always said you had to play the game you were in, not the game you wished you could play. Or something like that. When he said it, it sounded much wiser. Besides, without Ditka, the Bears have been shit for the last thirty years. Or maybe it was the Bulls? I get my Chicago teams mixed up."

"Did you actually play football?"

The key slipped into the lock, and I began to wiggle it ever so slowly. The locking mechanism seemed to be gummed up with something—blood, if the rest of me was any indication.

"Not so much played as sat the bench. I peaked early.

Like, in eighth grade. Still, my junior high coach was a regular Yoda. Full of life lessons, he was."

"Is everything you say bullshit?"

I gave the key a hard twist and felt the bodily fluids that had congealed inside the keyhole give way.

"Not everything. But I do have a propensity for bullshit. At least that's what my wife says."

"You're married?"

"Mostly."

"That's usually a binary question."

"It's complicated."

"What about the rescue? Is that complicated?"

"Afraid so."

The metal teeth in the handcuff clicked as the lock began to open.

"Are you bullshitting me about the rescue?" Shaw said.

"Of course not. Lying to a captured man is just bad form."

I'd intended to punctuate my smart-ass remark by lifting my hands up to show the set of handcuffs dangling impotently from my wrist. But before I could get to my theatrical finish, the door to our cell slammed open. Light flooded the cell, and I squinted against the onslaught, keeping my nearly freed hands behind my back.

Shaw and I weren't in a position to fight—not yet, anyway. If I had to endure another beating, so be it. The handcuffs were nearly unlocked, and the tiny ceramic key was resting in my palm.

Things couldn't have been better.

I stared at the dark figure standing in the doorway, willing him to get it over with. *Take your shots now, motherfucker. Next time I won't be wearing handcuffs. Then we'll see what's what.*

Then again, hopefully the next time the door opened, one of Colonel Fitz's Unit boys would be standing in the doorway. But even if Fitz was running a bit behind schedule, Shaw and I would be unshackled and able to fight. We were unarmed, but with a little luck, that might not matter.

My concealed beacon aside, I knew never to underestimate the ferocity a condemned man could muster, especially in close quarters. We'd learned that lesson the hard way during the Qala-i-Jangi prison uprising after the initial invasion of Afghanistan.

Unarmed Taliban prisoners had overrun their Northern Alliance guards and taken control of the prison. After six days of fighting, Afghan, British, and American forces put down the revolt, but by then, CIA paramilitary officer Mike Spann had already paid the ultimate price.

Now, almost two decades later, maybe Shaw and I could teach that same lesson to our jihadi captors.

I stared at the dark figure, waiting.

And that was my mistake. If I'd known what was about to happen next, I would have sprung at the individual, chained ankles or not. But I didn't know. So instead, I curled my legs into my chest, confident I could ride out a bit more punishment. At this stage of the game, beatings tended to be impersonal. A little something to remind the captive who was boss. Nothing more.

But as the jihadi stepped into our cell, his face was illuminated. In that moment, everything changed. The person in the doorway wasn't the jihadi guard who'd welcomed me into the compound, or even Mr. Suave.

Those faces I hadn't recognized.

This one I did.

Black hair graying at the temples, broad shoulders, a swollen nose, and a scar that stretched from his mouth to his ear.

A scar that I'd given him.

Sayid. He didn't look happy.

I twisted the key, hearing the familiar metal-on-metal rasping as the ratcheting locking mechanism released, but it was too late. The Syrian crossed the distance between us in a single giant step. Without breaking his stride, he drop-kicked me in the chin like he was punting a football.

My head snapped back, vertebrae compressing with a series of sickening pops. Pain exploded along the length of my jaw, and the handcuff key flew from my fingers.

For the second time in as many hours, the lights went out in Georgia.

FIFTY-ONE

Peter put his hand to his mouth, ostensibly to smother a cough. In reality, the gesture was to hide the smile that appeared, despite his best efforts to look somber. Only half an hour had elapsed, but what a difference thirty short minutes could make.

"How the hell did this happen?" the President said, looking from one face to another. "Can someone please explain that to me?"

Though the meeting was once again held in the Situation Room, the atmosphere couldn't have been more different. This time, Beverly, Etzel, and Beighley were huddled together like naughty schoolchildren on one side of the table while the DIA representative, Glass, was conspicuously absent. Peter, however, sat at the President's right hand.

Exactly where he belonged.

That President Jorge Gonzales had uttered a curse

word, no matter how mild, spoke volumes about his mind-set. In a way, Peter actually sympathized with the man. From the President's perspective, events in Syria were spiraling rapidly out of control.

But that was only because the President lacked a behind-the-scenes view of what Peter had orchestrated.

As promised, the Russians had delivered. The ill-conceived rescue attempt had been turned back, no fresh blood had been wasted on a dead man, and the entire debacle wasn't even a blip on the media's radar.

In a word, things were progressing perfectly.

It genuinely upset Peter to see the President beside himself, but he also understood that there was in front of him an opportunity for the taking. Peter just needed to keep up his impeccable acting skills until the moment presented itself. It was one thing to save the President from himself, and the election in the process, but it took a master manipulator to settle a score or two at the same time.

Peter had more than one grudge he intended to put to rest before the night was over.

"I don't know what to say, sir," General Etzel began, his cocksure attitude gone as he fielded the President's question. "It's extraordinary that the Russians were able to find our helicopters. It's almost as if someone told them exactly where to look."

Peter's feeling of mirth vanished as the significance of Etzel's words registered. Peter shot a glance at the General, trying to judge whether the Chairman of the Joint Chiefs was insinuating anything with his comment. Unfortunately, the former aviator kept his gaze focused on the President, revealing nothing.

The man must be one hell of a poker player.

Peter needed to nip the dangerous conversation in the bud. While the President understood in a general sense that Peter had been working to establish a back-channel relationship with his equivalent in the Russian government, President Gonzales certainly did not know that Peter had the Russian consulate's number memorized.

Or that he had been actively trading information with his counterpart for the last six months.

The arrangement had proven to be mutually beneficial, but Peter was not naive enough to think that his last phone call hadn't dramatically altered the relationship's balance. Once Jorge was reelected, Peter would come clean with the President.

After all, a successful Election Day tended to smooth over a multitude of sins.

Still, he was under no illusion that President Gonzales would be accommodating should the relationship come to light now. Especially given the fact that Peter had used his Russian counterpart to influence American foreign policy. That little tidbit needed to remain a secret regardless of the election's outcome. With this in mind, Peter was just preparing to address General Etzel's comment when Beverly of all people came to his rescue.

"I'm sorry, Mr. President," Beverly said, worry lines marring her normally flawless face, "but we don't have answers for you. Somehow, the Russians found and fired upon our helicopters. No one was hurt, but the Russians have announced in no uncertain terms that the airspace over Assad-controlled territory is closed. I'm sure we'll be able to smooth things over diplomatically, but I'm equally certain that this détente will not occur in time to save Shaw's life. For that, I offer both my deepest apologies . . . and my resignation."

Peter jerked. He'd war-gamed this meeting no less than three times and was prepared for a half dozen potential outcomes.

Beverly's resignation hadn't been one of them.

On the surface, her offer signaled his final and total victory. She'd gambled big on the rescue attempt, undercutting Peter in the process. When the operation had gone up in flames, so had her chances of redeeming herself with the President. She was done—it was just that simple.

Or was it?

Beverly had made a career out of trampling on the political skulls of those who had underestimated her. Could this be just another ploy? Was there an angle here that Peter wasn't seeing?

Peter prided himself on his ability to understand politics at an intrinsic level, but this was a scenario he hadn't envisioned. Perhaps now was the time to heed the old Roman adage about keeping your friends close and your enemies closer—at least until Tuesday night.

"Mr. President," Peter said, preparing to save Beverly Castle's career, "I think—"

The ominous sound of the security door's electronic locks disengaging interrupted him. Looking over his shoulder, Peter watched as the door swung open, admitting two men: the DIA knuckle dragger, Glass, and someone else. An African American man walking with a cane.

On its surface, the addition of the two newcomers should have been inconsequential. The clock had run out on Shaw's rescue, Beverly was on the ropes, and Peter had the President exactly where he wanted him.

And yet the African American man, who Peter noticed was missing part of his left arm, looked Peter's way when he shuffled into the room. Their eyes met for a moment, and Peter didn't care for what he saw.

Somehow, the game had changed once again.

FIFTY-TWO

Excuse me, Mr. President," Glass said, ignoring the rest of the room, "but you need to hear what this man has to say."

"And your friend is who?" the President said, a hint of Latino pronunciation flavoring the question.

Peter took this as a good sign. First, Jorge had uttered a curse word. Now his accent was starting to creep in. The President was pissed. Chances were that this joker Glass and his handicapped friend would be out on their asses in seconds. Then Peter could get back to the truly important business at hand—securing the President's second term.

"My name is Frederick Cates," the black man said, "but everyone calls me Frodo. I'd offer to shake your hand, sir, but I'm one short." He lifted up his left arm to punctuate the statement, revealing an empty sleeve.

"Excuse me for jumping in, Mr. President," General

Beighley said, "but Frodo is a former member of a JSOC special mission unit. He's spent the last five years on loan to the DIA Directorate for Operations—specifically, Mr. Glass here. You may remember that, several months ago, we had some trouble in Syria. Frodo was right in the thick of it. He sustained his injuries saving a DIA case officer's life."

At the words *DIA case officer*, Peter heard warning bells. The case officer in question had to be Matt Drake. The same Matt Drake who was conveniently in Syria once again and on whose supposed actionable intelligence the first potentially disastrous rescue attempt had been launched. A rescue attempt Peter was able to quash only by enlisting the Russians. It didn't take a genius to realize that whatever Frodo was going to say, it wouldn't be helpful to Peter's cause.

This meeting needed to come to an end.

Now.

"Mr. President, I'm sorry for interrupting," Peter said, feeling nothing of the sort, "but while I'm sure that Mr. Cates served with distinction, respectfully, his presence has no bearing on what we're about to discuss. I—"

"Actually, Mr. President," Frodo said, talking over Peter, "I'd be willing to bet that my presence has every bearing on what you're about to discuss. I don't mean to be presumptuous, but I'm here for only one reason—to keep you from making a tragic mistake."

"That's pretty arrogant," Peter began, but the President interjected.

"It's okay, Peter," the President said, squeezing Peter's

shoulder. "At this point, I think I know what everyone is going to say. Everyone but Mr. Frodo here. Do you go by Mr. Frodo or Frodo?"

"Just Frodo, sir."

"Okay, Frodo. Let me start by thanking you for your service. Too often decisions get made in this room without an adequate perspective on the potential consequences. Now, tell me what mistake I'm about to make, but do it quickly. Time and tide wait for no man, Frodo. Not even the President."

"Yes, sir," Frodo said, somehow forcing his broken frame to stand straighter as he addressed the most powerful man in the world. "Two men are about to die unless you save them."

FIFTY-THREE

Peter opened his mouth, but once again, the President beat him to the punch.

"I'm aware of Shaw," the President said with a frown, "but who is the second man?"

"Matt Drake, sir," Frodo said.

"Jesus," Peter said, not bothering to mask his exasperation. "That loose cannon got captured, too?"

"Not at all, sir," Frodo said, still the picture of calm. "Chief, if you would?"

The DIA mouth breather picked up a remote and with a stab of his meaty finger activated one of the flat screens mounted on the wall.

"Excuse me for assuming, Mr. President," Glass said as a frozen image filled the screen, "but I thought you'd want to see this, so I asked the tech team to have it preloaded." He pressed a second button, and the frozen image began to move.

Peter wasn't an operative, but he recognized UAV footage when he saw it.

"This was shot by a Sentinel approximately twenty minutes ago," Frodo said, narrating as the UAV's thermal camera zoomed in on a parked vehicle. Two bone white figures exited the vehicle and trudged toward a two-story building at the top of the picture. "The UAV is orbiting in Assad-controlled airspace. The two men you see are Matt Drake and his asset, Einstein."

"What's in that building?" the President said.

On the screen, the two figures passed the chain-link fence ringing the structure's perimeter.

"Shaw," Frodo said as the two figures disappeared inside. "Shaw, the terrorists holding him, and the laboratory where Einstein designed the chemical weapon the jihadis intend to employ."

"Drake just walked into the building," Peter said, shaking his head in disbelief. "Why would he do that?"

"To buy time," Frodo said, "or, more specifically, to buy me time. Time to convince you that you should launch the JSOC QRF again."

"Sir, this is ridiculous," Peter said, slapping the table. "I'll grant you that this insane man entered the compound, but so what? Other than increase the hostage count by one, he's done nothing of value. We still have no indication that he actually found Shaw."

"Actually, we have the best indication we could hope for," Frodo said, still focusing exclusively on the President.

"Which is?" President Gonzales said.

"The terrorists were supposed to livestream Shaw's execution five minutes ago," Frodo said, pointing to the digital clock whose red digits showed Damascus local time. "So far, we've seen nothing on the usual jihadi social media platforms. Their silence can only mean one thing—Matt Drake has bought us additional time. Don't waste it."

FIFTY-FOUR

don't agree," Peter said, turning to the President. "Sir, we can't afford to start a war with the Russians over two men who for all intents and purposes are already dead. I'm not trying to be callous. I understand a thing or two about sacrifice. I buried my little sister, for Christ's sake. We could claim ignorance or a misunderstanding the first time we violated Russian airspace. That won't fly a second time. Sir, if we go after these men, it will be an act of war. I can't allow that."

"And I can't allow you to leave them," Frodo said, his baritone rumbling through the room.

"What did you say?" Peter said.

"Mr. President," Frodo said, again ignoring Peter, "I hoped to be able to persuade you to do the right thing based on my eloquence, but maybe I'm not such a great speaker. Truth is, I was a damn good sniper, but my career as an operator is over. I don't know what my future holds, but I do know this—Matt Drake is the single bravest man I know. He's my brother, and if he's willing to risk everything by walking into the lion's den on the off chance he can somehow bring one lost sheep home, I have to be willing to do the same."

The former commando glanced down for a second as if gathering himself for what would come next. When he looked up again, his remaining hand shook against his cane's wooden handle, but his voice rang through the silence without so much as a quaver.

"Before I left my office, Mr. President, I wrote an e-mail with a time delay. A very detailed e-mail. It lays out exactly what happened over the last forty-eight hours up to and including your administration's decision to let two men die rather than risk an international incident. If I don't stop it, the e-mail will go out to Fox News, CNN, MSNBC, the *New York Times*, and the *Wall Street Journal*."

"You're blackmailing the President of the United States?" Peter said.

"I'm sorry, sir," Frodo said, his eyes never leaving the President's. "I've already submitted my resignation and will voluntarily surrender myself into custody. I'm ashamed of what I've done, but I'd do it again in a heartbeat. Men like Matt and me took a vow. We don't leave fallen comrades behind, no matter the cost."

"What about the Russians?" Peter said, feeling as if he were having an out-of-body experience. "Did you forget about them?"

"Fuck the Russians," Frodo said, directing a contemptuous look at Peter before turning back to the President. "Sir, we are the United States of America. The Russians pushed us out of Assad's airspace because we let them. It's time we started pushing back."

"You're insane!" Peter screamed, getting to his feet. "You're going to start World War Three. I—"

"Peter, stop. Now."

Once again, the President took charge of the room with a barely audible command. Even so, there was an edge to the President's voice, a sense of authority that broke through Peter's anger and silenced the words on the tip of his tongue. This was no longer his old friend Jorge Gonzales, the mild-mannered politician Peter had known for almost two decades. This was the President of the United States, and the President had spoken.

"Mr. Frodo," the President said, looking up at the cripple, "I want to establish something. I don't respond to threats. Not now, not ever. In truth, I can't decide what I detest more: the notion that you thought you could blackmail me into acting or that you believed such extraordinary measures would be necessary. Those men went into harm's way on my say-so. Mine. I may not have served in the military, but after four years in this office, I understand the burden of command. I will do whatever it takes to bring my boys home, Russians be damned. But Peter has a very good point. If I'm going to risk World War Three, I have to at least know that your friend and the captured CIA paramilitary officer are still alive. I need confirmation."

"You'll have it, sir," Frodo said. "Matt has a beacon

concealed on his person. As soon as he locates Shaw, he'll trigger it. We just need to be ready when he does."

Peter tried to speak, but the President turned toward the Generals instead.

"Gentlemen," the President said, looking from one man to another, "can we make this happen?"

General Etzel slowly nodded. "I have the conventional forces in theater to set the conditions, but the JSOC operators will still have to do the heavy lifting." General Etzel turned to General Beighley. "It's your call, Jeff. What do you think?"

The squat commando didn't even hesitate before directing his answer to the President instead of to his superior. "Sir, let's do it."

Beighley's words brought an accompanying nod from the President, and suddenly, everyone was all smiles.

Everyone but Peter.

He was too busy thinking about the rows of flag-draped coffins that would soon be joining Kristen's in the cold November soil.

FIFTY-FIVE

The floodlights felt like ice picks stabbing into my eye sockets. I blinked against the ungodly glare, tears streaming down my blood-crusted cheeks. Instinctively, I tried to wipe the grime from my face, but my hands refused to cooperate. My wrists were bound, but not with handcuffs. Plastic zip ties bit into my flesh, and that changed everything.

Regardless of what I'd told Shaw, this time, the game really was over.

Unlike handcuffs or duct tape, zip ties had no locks to pick and no tensile fractal points that could be reached with a good downward thrust. Without a knife, my hands weren't getting free. Shaw and I were at the jihadis' mercy, and judging by the giant rack of floodlights, whatever they had planned for us wasn't going to be pleasant.

"Ready?"

"Almost."

The Arabic conversation was taking place out of view. I could hear the voices, but couldn't see anything beyond the migraine-inducing lights.

Dipping my head so that my forehead took the brunt of the optical assault, I looked around the room. I tried to minimize my head movements so that I could get my bearings without drawing the jihadis' attention.

Earlier, I'd turned with Sayid's kick, and while the blow had rung my bell, I hadn't lost consciousness for long. Instead, I'd slipped into more of a hazy twilight, aware enough to feel my clothes being torn from my body and then the gritty sandpaper feel of concrete rasping against my skin as someone dragged me from one room to another.

When I'd finally come to my senses, I'd thought for an instant that the blinding white light signaled my arrival in the afterlife. But then my nervous system started providing a running tally of my numerous injuries, putting that idea to rest. Even if my earthly performance had landed me a bit shy of heaven's pearly gates, I thought the devil would do better than to welcome new souls with a piss-soaked slab of concrete. Syria might be hell on earth, but for better or worse, I was still in the land of the living.

For now, anyway.

A low moan and the rustle of cloth against stone drew my attention to the left. Shaw, barely conscious, lay beside me. The man-made suns in front of us directed the full brunt of their power on his hapless form.

What I saw made me suck in my breath.

I wasn't the only one who'd caught a beating. Shaw's face, already marred where the savages had cut away his ear, was nearly unrecognizable. His eyes were swollen shut, his face a mass of puffy tissue, giving him a sumo wrestler's chubby features. His lips were split in multiple places, and the jagged remains of teeth protruded from his mouth like a vampire's canines.

I could hear him breathe, but the sound was far from comforting. The air he struggled to draw past his ruined mouth gurgled in his chest, which made me think that his lung had collapsed or that he was drowning in his own blood.

Or both.

Either way, Shaw didn't have long. As I looked away from the CIA paramilitary officer's crumpled form, I realized that this prediction probably applied to both of us.

Now that my eyes could focus, the signs of what was about to happen were unmistakable. The blinding array of stage lights, the black jihadi flag hanging across the back wall, the orange jumpsuits we both now wore, even the thin, blood-soaked rug stretched across the concrete, all added up to only one conclusion—Shaw and I were about to play starring roles in a jihadi snuff film.

My heart thundered as I groped for something, anything, that could turn this situation to my advantage.

The beacon.

Freeing my hands was out of the question, but perhaps there was a way to trigger the transmitter with my weight. Even if it didn't work, seeing a zip-tied man dry humping the concrete might just make the jihadis reconsider their decision to kill us. After all, if I was already batshit crazy, why go to the trouble of putting me out of my misery?

I rolled onto my stomach, clenching my teeth against the pain, and that's when I realized my goose was cooked. I could feel the cold from the concrete leaching into my nether regions for one simple reason—my underwear had been removed.

Maybe these splinter cell jihadis who'd survived the destruction of ISIS were even smarter than I gave them credit for. Or maybe they had an underwear fetish. I didn't know. Either way, the result was the same. Until I triggered the beacon, the cavalry wasn't coming, and I no longer had the beacon.

Frodo was one hell of a persuader, but without proof that I was alive and had Shaw, I had no illusions about how this story would end. Two days before a Presidential election, an administration that had been willing to let an American captured on their watch face ritual execution rather than risk offending the Russians was not suddenly going to grow a pair.

Shaw and I were going to die, and there was nothing I could do about it.

The sobering thought brought with it memories of the last time I'd faced death. Then, Frodo had been by my side, one arm gone, a leg mangled, and nearly delirious with pain.

Like most in my chosen profession, I didn't dwell on death, but it was never far from my thoughts. I'd been to too many funerals, seen the folded flag handed to too many grieving spouses, to think I was invincible. Scores of men who were better operators than I'd ever be now slept within Arlington National Cemetery's eternal embrace. I didn't live a charmed life, but I had imagined that, when death finally came for me, I'd be facing it with Frodo at my side.

For the briefest of moments, I thought of Laila. How seeing her across the room still made my heart skip. How her skin smelled like lilacs. The snorting noise she made when she laughed, and the way her nose wrinkled and her green eyes flashed when she was angry. She deserved better than this.

Better than me.

She deserved someone to grow old with. Someone to rock her babies to sleep at night. Someone to coach their Little League teams. She needed someone safe—maybe a high school teacher or an engineer or a lawyer.

Someone who wasn't me.

I wasn't safe, normal, or even completely whole. I wasn't the man she'd grow old with, and I'd never hold her hand tightly in mine as she brought our children into the world. No, I'd never be or do any of those things, but I was still a Ranger. Even now, in my darkest hour, I was bound by something bigger than myself.

The Ranger Creed.

Recognizing that I volunteered as a Ranger . . .

Shifting my weight, I got my leg under me and strained against the floor until I'd managed to leverage myself into a sitting position.

. . . fully knowing the hazards of my chosen profession . . .

Lightning bolts of agony ripped through my torso as I struggled to my knees, bringing tears to my eyes. The pain went way beyond that of broken bones to something deeper—internal injuries, possibly a ruptured spleen.

. . . I will always endeavor to uphold the prestige, honor, and high esprit de corps of my Ranger Regiment.

I was going to die. Maybe not today, but someday the grim reaper would come for me, just like he came for everyone else. But I was not like everyone else. I was an Airborne Ranger. I had a legacy to uphold. Airborne Rangers don't die easy, and if today was my last day on this earth, I hoped only that the Almighty would grant me the leeway to demonstrate this distinction to as many jihadis as possible before my time was up.

"Ready. The feed goes live in thirty seconds."

Again one of the disembodied voices from the other side of the light, but this time, the words made perfect sense.

There was an art to sawing off a man's head, a method for ensuring that he didn't struggle as the serrated knife bit into his throat. After all, too much struggling tended to ruin the video. Unlike Hollywood-produced gore fests, this film could have no second takes.

As such, jihadi executioners had learned to ply their prey with a subtle bit of psychology to ensure their victims' docility. They did this by subjecting captives to mock executions. In this form of mental conditioning, victims were forced to endure repeated dry runs in which they were trussed up, dragged in front of a camera, and told they were going to die. Here, they fought and were beaten senseless, only to have the masked jihadi abort the execution at the last second.

This sequence was repeated sometimes dozens of times before the executioners actually carried out the gruesome acts. By this time, the psychologically battered victims had grown numb to the process. When the moment finally came, they rarely struggled, thinking it was just another rehearsal. Or perhaps, by then, the victims just wanted the madness to end, even if that end came in the form of cold steel biting into their necks.

In either case, the results were the same. The black-clad executioner decapitated a docile prisoner while the brutality was captured in high definition and later distributed to the legions of jihadi websites and chat forums.

But not this time.

Sayid and his friends were on a schedule. A schedule I'd disrupted with my untimely arrival, but a schedule all the same. They'd promised to livestream Shaw's execution on social media, which meant that, even now, violence-lusting jihadis were calling for blood. If my new hosts delayed, they'd lose face with millions of potential recruits. They didn't have time to engage in the usual array of mock executions.

This restriction put my captors in a bit of a quandary—how did they ensure a meek prisoner so that the beheading could be filmed in all its glory while still making their timeline?

By beating the victim senseless, of course.

It wasn't the optimal solution, since an unconscious hostage didn't convey the same amount of soul-numbing terror when the knife's serrated edge begin to saw through his flesh, but it would do the job in a pinch.

"Prepare him."

The casual command sent a chill down my spine. I tried to muster something that approached the righteous fury that had allowed me to rise to my knees, but all I could manage was a sense of terror as a figure from my nightmares walked in front of the lights.

Sayid.

And he was coming straight for me.

FIFTY-SIX

Major Vinnie "Boxer" McGrath shoved the throttles of his F-22 Raptor forward, sending the fighter's twin Pratt & Whitney turbofan engines into afterburner. The combined seventy thousand pounds of thrust compressed Boxer into his g-force-absorbing seat as the aircraft screamed down the runway. At less than half the distance required for a conventional plane, the Raptor's nose tilted up. A second later, the aircraft's wheels left earth in favor of the sky. With a flip of a toggle, Boxer adjusted the variable-thrust nozzles attached to the engines, and the stealth fighter's angle of attack changed from steep to nearly vertical.

Growing up, Vinnie had been desperate to be an astronaut. He'd spent many a night as he drifted off to sleep wondering what it might feel like to be strapped to the tip of a solid rocket booster. After becoming a Raptor driver, Vinnie wondered no longer. He lived his boyhood dream every time he firewalled the jet engines, turning his fighter into one of the fastest air-breathing projectiles ever created.

But as the runway of Al Asad Air Base in Iraq fell away beneath him, Vinnie reminded himself that this was no boyhood flight of fancy. Today, for the first time since he'd first strapped himself into a Raptor's cockpit twelve years ago, Vinnie was going to stretch his jet to its breaking point and beyond.

This thought brought with it equal parts apprehension and excitement. Vinnie pushed the emotions aside, dividing his attention between his heads-up display and the multipurpose screens that formed the heart of his aircraft's glass cockpit. Passing through first thirty, then forty, and then fifty thousand feet, Vinnie put the jet into a slight bank, turning into a circular holding pattern as he performed his flight-lead tasks and waited for his wingmen to arrive. Communications frequencies, navigation points, and weapons presets had all successfully transferred from the data cartridge he'd hurriedly loaded during the unusually quick premission brief. But in truth, none of these mundane checklist items occupied Vinnie's thoughts.

Instead, Vinnie's attention was almost exclusively captured by a single unassuming line on his moving map display. A line that represented the edge of Syrian airspace, or, more specifically, the section of airspace claimed by Assad's air force and their backers, the Russians.

"Boxer, this is Ringmaster. Flight is a go. I say again: Flight is a go."

The transmission originated from a Boeing E-3 Sentry AWACS early-warning aircraft orbiting squarely in Iraqi airspace. It came to Vinnie's ears via an encrypted radio, and he didn't reply.

At least not with his radio.

Instead, Vinnie touched a toggle on his side-mounted control stick. His touch sent a one-word acknowledgment, in an encoded stream of laser light, to an array dish mounted on the AWACS's dorsal.

For this mission, stealth was paramount. The Raptor was the world's first fifth-generation fighter. It had been designed specifically to slink into enemy-controlled airspace undetected and then wreak havoc on an unsuspecting air force. But all of the fighter's radar-absorbing properties would be for naught if something as inconspicuous as a radio transmission gave away the jet's presence.

To mitigate this risk, Vinnie would not break radio silence until absolutely necessary. Instead, communication between Vinnie, the AWACS controller, and his three wingmen would occur via the optical transmission system first birthed for the F-35 Joint Strike Fighter and then distributed to the Air Force's other premier aircraft—the F-22 Raptor.

Within seconds of his sending his response to the AWACS mission controller, a series of two-toned beeps in Boxer's earpiece heralded the arrival of optically transmitted text messages from the three other Raptors in his strike package. Craning his head over both shoulders, Boxer visually verified the presence of his wingmen via his helmet-mounted night-vision goggles. Once he was certain that everyone was in position, he edged the throttle up to the agreed-upon setting, configuring his jet for super cruise.

In yet another marvel for an aircraft whose capabilities often seemed more science fiction than science fact, the Pratt & Whitney engines were now powering the jet to supersonic speeds without the use of the fuel-guzzling afterburners.

But this amazing feat of engineering—much like the Raptor's radar-evading skin, adaptive radar, and computer-assisted flight controls—was lost on Boxer. Not because he didn't appreciate his jet's groundbreaking capabilities, but because as of thirty seconds ago, he and his silent flight of hunters had crossed to the other side of the green line on his moving map display.

They were now in Russian-controlled airspace.

Boxer and his flight of four Raptors were going to war.

FIFTY-SEVEN

Here we go," Chief Warrant Officer Joel Glendening said, more to give voice to the tension he felt infecting his crew than to announce a new phase in the mission.

"Let's do it, Chief," Colonel Fitz said, slapping Joel on the back.

Joel didn't bother to reply or explain what was happening on the glass display located prominently between his console and his copilot's. This time around, the Delta Force Commander was intimately aware of what the scarlet line on the moving map display represented.

After the aborted rescue attempt thirty minutes ago, everyone knew what they'd face once the helicopters crossed into Russian-controlled airspace. To a man, every aircrew member had volunteered for the second rescue attempt as soon as their JSOC liaison had provided them with the White House–endorsed plan. In fact, Joel had needed to turn aside potential crew members when he hand selected the men to accompany him on this second, and final, rescue attempt.

Judging by the press of bodies in the Black Hawk behind him, the Unit commandos had reacted in the same manner. Except unlike Joel, Colonel Fitz hadn't even tried to restrict the number of operators who'd insisted on climbing aboard to rescue Drake and the captured CIA officer.

For a moment, Joel almost pitied the terrorists holding the two Americans hostage. Almost. But then he remembered what was at stake. Joel had been in high school during the infamous *Black Hawk Down* mission, but the legacy of that day still burned bright among the 160th Night Stalkers. Two American special operators were in harm's way, and Joel and his comrades were flying to the rescue. As far as Joel was concerned, there was no better embodiment of the Regiment's motto: *Night Stalkers don't quit.*

Still, the righteousness of their mission aside, Joel had no illusions about what was waiting for his band of brothers on the other side of that thin red line. Last time, it had been warning shots.

This time, both sides would be playing for keeps.

Almost on cue, a transmission from the AWACS plane orbiting at the edge of Iraqi airspace slammed across the airwaves. Joel didn't know the wattage that the airborne command-and-control plane was capable of transmitting, but the signal seemed almost strong enough to rattle the fillings in his teeth. He hoped it would be enough to get the Russians' attention.

Or maybe he didn't.

FIFTY-EIGHT

Russian aircraft patrolling in sector Charlie at flight level three zero, this is American air traffic control. Two American helicopters will be transitioning across your airspace from east to west in three minutes. Do not deviate from your current heading and altitude. I say again, any changes to your current heading and altitude will be considered demonstration of hostile intent. Acknowledge. Over."

Dmitri Androvinoch could not believe the audacity of the Americans' radio transmission. He knew the Yankees had a reputation for stubbornness, but this turn of events almost defied belief. Less than an hour after he'd shown restraint by not turning the American helicopters violating his airspace into burning hunks of debris, the Yankees thanked him for his kindness by issuing directives as if they owned the sky.

Their arrogance was breathtaking.

Activating his targeting radar, Dmitri saw the same inconsistent return designating the stealth-equipped American helicopters as well as an early-warning AWACS plane, which he assumed was the source of the radio transmission.

Other than that, his screen was clear.

Surely the Americans didn't think to threaten him from an unarmed radar plane?

A quick glance at his aircraft-survivability equipment showed no active radars of the type attributed to either ground- or air-based antiaircraft-missile systems.

Were the American's bluffing?

"Outrigger Main, this is Badger Three Four," Dmitri said after thumbing the radio-transmit button on his stick. "Are you monitoring the American transmission?"

"Affirmative, Badger Three Four. Your instructions remain the same. Do not allow the Americans to enter our airspace."

"Badger Three Four confirms," Dmitri said. With a push of a button, Dmitri took the aircraft's master arm switch from safe to weapons hot. Then he yanked his Flanker into a tight spiral, aiming the aircraft's nose toward the encroaching helicopters.

It was time to finish the job.

FIFTY-NINE

Russian aircraft, heading one four zero, flight level three zero, this is American air traffic control. Return to your previous heading and altitude, or you will be fired upon. This is your final warning. Over."

Boxer watched the drama play out in real time as the red diamond-shaped icon representing the Russian Flanker continued its turn toward the two blue square-shaped symbols denoting the pair of Army MH-60 helicopters.

As instructed, he had yet to activate his onboard targeting radar, but he didn't need to. The AIM-120 AMRAAM air-to-air missiles housed in his internal weapons bay were already receiving targeting information directly into their navigational computers from the orbiting AWACS.

Boxer looked at the tactical display for a split second longer, verifying that the Russian pilot had not complied with the radioed instructions. Then he raised the trigger guard on his stick and squeezed twice.

He heard the weapons bay doors open and felt the jet shudder as first one, then a second missile dropped into the slipstream. Exactly two seconds later, the rocket motors erupted into tails of flame, and the two fire-and-forget missiles streaked along the intercept courses their internal computers had calculated after accessing the AWACS's radar feed.

D mitri rolled his Flanker level and was lining up his shot on the helicopters when he received the first indication that something was wrong. His acquisition radar beeped for the briefest of moments, indicating a new target. But when Dmitri dropped his gaze from his heads-up display to the multipurpose screen showing the radar return, no corresponding icon was present. It was almost as if something had been visible for a split second and then disappeared back into thin air.

That unsettling thought triggered something in his already nervous mind. In a flash, he was back in a pilots' class in which the instructor showed radar footage of American stealth bombers over targets in Iraq. The screen remained impressively blank except for the brief moment when the bombers' internal doors opened to release their hidden ordnance.

But why would the Americans have a B-2 orbiting over Syria?

In his next heartbeat, Dmitri realized that he'd correctly identified the cause but not the source of the glitch in his radar. An ungainly B-2 wouldn't be sharing airspace with him.

He was being hunted by a different type of predator altogether.

With a scream, Dmitri slammed the throttles forward and cranked his aircraft away from the American helicopters. He rocketed back to his initial altitude, all the while hoping against hope that the invisible American bird of prey had not yet loosed its ordnance.

His hope was in vain.

SIXTY

The icon on Boxer's display representing the Russian Flanker joined with the pixels signifying his missiles with anticlimactic precision. One moment, the symbols were separate. The next, they merged and then disappeared from his display entirely. One Russian interceptor was splashed, the airspace was cleared, and Boxer had yet to make a single radio transmission.

Such was the state of modern air-to-air combat.

After confirming that no airborne threats remained, Boxer optically delivered a brevity code word to the rest of his flight, and then he changed course for the second and final portion of his mission. As the answering chimes from his wingmen echoed in his headset, the AWACS mission controller again transmitted over Guard.

"Russian aircraft in sector Charlie, this is American air traffic control. Effective time now, all Syrian airspace is under American jurisdiction. Any Syrian or Russian aircraft that attempts to take off from now until the airspace is reopened will be considered hostile and fired upon. I say again, any Russian or Syrian aircraft that enters the airspace from now until it reopens will be considered hostile and treated accordingly. American air traffic control out."

Three minutes later, Boxer and his flight of four Raptors reached their loitering altitude and began to patrol, locking down Khmeimim Air Base, home of the remaining contingent of Russian aircraft in Syria. For the next twenty minutes, Boxer had orders to splash anything that tried to depart from the air base, preferably before the aircraft left the runway.

A new series of blips on Boxer's radar designated a flight of B-1 Lancer bombers forming up just inside of Iraq, adding muscle to the Raptor's stealth. If the Russians somehow didn't get the message, and Boxer was forced to fire on another wayward Russian aircraft, the Lancers would roar in at supersonic speeds and render the air base's two runways unusable with their payload of cluster bombs. But after what had just transpired, Boxer was fairly certain the Russians had received the message in the most unequivocal of fashions. What happened next would be entirely up to them.

Either way, Boxer and his band of invisible killers would be ready.

R ussian threat neutralized," Joel said, trying to keep the emotionless voice that pilots so carefully cultivated. He succeeded. Barely. But Colonel Fitz was under no such constraints.

"Hot damn!" Fitz said, screaming loudly enough that Joel didn't need the intercom to hear the Colonel over the helicopter's ambient noise.

"We cleared to the objective, sir?" Joel asked.

"Almost," Fitz said, sliding forward in the jump seat. "The DIA case officer has a beacon. As soon as he triggers it, we're in hot. Until then, we need to give him time to locate Shaw."

"Roger that," Joel said, "but our window closes in fifteen mikes. That's when the Raptors run out of fuel and have to pull off station. When they go, we have to go, or else we'll end up like that Russian bastard they splashed."

"I got it, Chief," Fitz said. "As soon as the beacon lights up, I want to be on the building's roof. Get as close as you can, but we can't hit the objective without the beacon."

Joel acknowledged Fitz's order with as much enthusiasm as he could muster, but he couldn't help feeling a sense of dread as the mission timer on his multipurpose display ticked ever closer to zero. He didn't know the DIA case officer in question, but Joel breathed a prayer for him all the same.

SIXTY-ONE

ow are you feeling?" Sayid said, taking a knee in
front of me.

The question was probably rhetorical, but I decided to
answer anyway. Beacon or no beacon, Frodo was my
friend, and more than that, he was my brother. He, like
me, was part of the special operations fraternity, and I
knew that he would never quit. When all else failed, I
had faith in my brother. Faith that he would move heaven
and earth to find me. But in order for him to work a
miracle, Frodo needed time. Time that only I could give
him. To give it to him, I needed to keep the shithead in
front of me talking instead of sawing. With my hands
bound and my body nearly broken, I had just one thing
left to use to distract the homicidal jihadi—my wit.

"Better than you must have felt when I smashed your
nose," I said. The new gaps in my teeth gave me a lisp
that was somewhat at odds with my tough-guy persona,

so I doubled down. "Were you a good-looking dude before? Can't really tell with your face like that."

I saw the blow coming and tried to turn my head with the punch, but didn't quite manage it. My reflexes were a bit on the slow side, and the Syrian seemed quite practiced at beating unarmed men. His fist caught me on the corner of the chin, snapping my head to the side. I managed to keep all my remaining teeth, but blood poured into my mouth as another clot or two came loose.

Perfect.

"Do you know who I am?" Sayid said, grabbing me by the hair so that we were eye to eye.

"Not really," I said, blood and saliva drooling from my mouth. "But don't take it personally. You inbred shitheads all look the same to me."

Another blow, this one landing just behind my right ear. The room spun, and I would have toppled over if not for the jihadi bearing my weight.

"My name is Sayid. I am here to kill you."

"Maybe I do remember you," I said, my words starting to slur. "Is your sister the one with the tight ass and curly hair?"

Sayid stomped on my broken ankle, and the pain made me vomit. I didn't know how much more of this I could take.

Then again, maybe this wasn't the worst way to go. If he stayed the course, sooner or later Sayid would beat me unconscious, and death would surely follow. It wouldn't be pretty, but it would probably be better than the alternative.

"Come, come, Sayid," Mr. Suave said. "I can't have you beating Mr. Drake beyond recognition or killing him outright, which is what I suspect he's trying to goad you into doing."

Like I said, the dumb jihadis had died a long time ago. Though, to be fair, I wasn't convinced the speaker actually was a jihadi. I didn't know what Mr. Suave's play was, but he didn't seem to be cut from the same cloth as Sayid and his ilk.

"Got to keep my face recognizable so you can zoom in when you saw my head off?" I said, directing the question at Mr. Suave.

"Mr. Drake," Mr. Suave said in English, "I'm afraid you underestimate me. Yes, your friend will soon feel the bite of the barbarians' knives. But that is not to be your fate. As I told you before, you are much too important to business."

"What kind of business?" I said.

"The business of chaos."

"Chaos brought on by your new chemical weapon?"

"Very good, Mr. Drake," Mr. Suave said with a smile. "But not in the manner in which you think. We've learned our lessons from Iraq and Afghanistan. The key is to keep your government interested in Syria while not provoking them into a protracted military response."

"Do you think this shit up yourself," I said, trying to process what Mr. Suave was saying, "or does your cabal get together for weekly strategy sessions?"

"I'll admit, my strategy requires a delicate balance," Mr. Suave said. "But it is certainly worth the trouble.

When your government focuses its collective attention on a country like Syria, American dollars follow. Billons of them. And those dollars inevitably find a home in the pockets of men who offer to bring about the stability your politicians so desperately crave."

"Men like you?"

"Among others."

"You never intended to use the chemical weapon?"

"Oh, it will be used, Mr. Drake, just not against America. Remember, we need balance. We want to keep your attention and treasure fixated on Syria, but we have no desire to become another front in your never-ending war on terror. The ISIS Neanderthals learned this lesson the hard way."

"You aren't a jihadi?"

The Iraqi's smile turned into a disapproving frown. "Mr. Drake, you disappoint me. I told you, I'm a businessman. The jihadis, you, your compatriot, and even the chemical weapon—these things are just means to an end.

"Now," Mr. Suave said, brushing nonexistent dust from his slacks, "I'd love to continue our conversation, but I have somewhere else to be."

"Maybe we can talk later?" I said.

With a smile of regret, Mr. Suave shook his head.

"I'm afraid not, Mr. Drake. Your scientist wasn't much of a double agent, but he did understand chemical weapons. Though it took him a time or two to get the formulation correct—am I right?"

Mr. Suave winked as if he'd just made an inside joke. I looked back at him, waiting for the punch line. My confusion must have been evident, because his smile slowly turned to a frown. "Come, come, Mr. Drake—I truly thought you were better than this. Do I really have to spell it out for you?"

"I guess so," I said, still not understanding. "Getting the shit kicked out of me tends to fuck with my world-renowned powers of deduction."

Mr. Suave sighed as if I were a particularly dim-witted student. "Your symptoms, Mr. Drake. They were long in coming, but surely you've noticed them by now?"

At the word *symptoms*, the logjam preventing my battered synapses from firing finally cleared. I flashed back to the video I'd watched while sitting with Frodo and James in DIA headquarters what seemed like a lifetime ago. A well-dressed couple eating dinner together at an expensive restaurant. The epitome of happiness, right before the man's hand had begun to tremble.

Just like mine.

Now it wasn't confusion that Mr. Suave saw on my face. He clapped his hands as his smile returned. "Yes, yes! You understand now, don't you?"

"Einstein," I said, remembering the scientist's distracted fidgeting during our initial face-to-face meeting months ago. At the time, I'd chalked his behavior up to nerves, and while I'd been right in my diagnosis, I'd been completely wrong about its source. Einstein hadn't been nervous about being seen with me; he'd been worried about the effectiveness of his newly developed chemical weapon.

The weapon he was testing on me.

For the first time, everything made sense. Einstein's unexplained sudden desire to defect. His refusal to work with anyone but me. It wasn't because we'd bonded during my failed attempt to pitch him. It was because I was his patient zero, and his new weapon hadn't worked as advertised.

A weapon that Einstein's benefactors had undoubtedly paid him handsomely to develop.

Einstein had been playing both sides from the start, hence the terrorist minders who'd tailed him to our meet site. If I'd been able to extract him, he would have gone willingly and used his jihadi blood money to start a new life. But as soon as he learned that Colonel Fitz and his boys weren't riding to the rescue, Einstein had hedged his bets and sold me to the jihadis to save his own skin.

I'm sure his financiers wanted to know why the first version of the weapon hadn't worked as promised. To answer that question, Einstein would have needed unrestricted access to his lab rat.

Me.

"Einstein?" Mr. Suave said. "Is that the name you gave our scientist? You thought too highly of him. I think Rosenberg might have been more appropriate. That was the last name of the husband-and-wife team who provided your nuclear secrets to the Soviets, yes?"

"You know your history," I said, trying to buy time as my thoughts cartwheeled. "I bet you'd kick ass on *Jeopardy!*"

"Joke while you can," Mr. Suave said. "The new version of our weapon works quite well, but it doesn't kill its victims outright. Instead, it slowly attacks the brain, much like mad cow disease. Unlike your CIA friend, you will still be alive after the cameras finish rolling today, but your lively wit will be a thing of the past."

"Why design a weapon to maim instead of kill?" I said.

"Balance and focus, Mr. Drake. Once we expose you to the new version, your prolonged demise will be televised for the world to see. Your suffering will ensure that your countrymen, and their pocketbooks, remain focused on Syria. Your government may even attempt another rescue, and they might succeed. But for you, the end result will still be the same. There is no way to extract the mercury compound from the victim's brain once the weapon is employed. Whether you die here or at home in your bed, you will spend your last days as a slobbering vegetable unable to control your own bowel movements. Good-bye, Mr. Drake."

Mr. Suave spun on his heel and walked away without waiting for a reply.

Which was just as well, because for the first time in my life I was all out of snappy comebacks.

SIXTY-TWO

We are live," the voice behind the lights said.

Next to me, a pair of black-clad jihadis grabbed Shaw, hoisting his limp body to his knees.

"How does it feel," Sayid said, grabbing hold of my hair and pulling my ear next to his lips, "to know you've failed? You came back to rescue that man, and now you'll watch him die. Just like your foolish *akhu al manukeh* asset and his family."

Because I was still processing the fact that Einstein had exposed me to a chemical weapon, it took a moment or two for Sayid's words to register. But once they did, the breath left my lungs in a rush. I turned to look at the Syrian, unsure if I'd imagined what he'd just said.

"Oh yes," Sayid said, his scar-induced sneer deepening. "It was no accident that your asset and his family perished. Just like it was no accident that you and your now crippled companion drove through our kill zone. I knew all about your asset, Mr. Drake. I always knew. Just as I now know with one hundred percent certainty that the rescue you still hope for is nothing but a fantasy. No one is coming for you, Mr. Drake. Absolutely no one."

The implications of what Sayid was saying were too staggering for my muddled brain to comprehend. Fazil's death was somehow connected to the ambush that had maimed Frodo? How? Sayid was Charles's asset. Had Charles tipped him off? Had Charles been feeding Sayid information the entire time? Did Sayid know about the beacon? Is that why they'd taken my underwear?

A flood of despair washed over me, crushing my spirit against the damp-smelling concrete.

Sayid was right, maybe more than he knew. I had faith in Frodo, but I also had to accept reality. Without a signal from the beacon, Frodo would never be able to persuade the President that I was still alive, much less that I'd found Shaw.

No one was coming.

Next to me, the jihadis holding Shaw began to chant, working up to a killing frenzy.

My fingers started to tremble.

The irony of the situation was not lost on me. The first iteration of Einstein's weapon had failed, so I'd done his work for him and returned to this place of death just so the jihadis could hit me with a more potent version once they finished with Shaw. Worse still, the agony of the last three months had been for nothing. I'd come back to Syria to save a life. To make up for the broken promise that had killed Fazil and his family. I'd come to offer penance somehow, to atone for my sins.

But I was doing nothing of the sort.

The Bible says that the wages of sin is death. But not my death. Instead, my transgressions were borne by the people foolish enough to depend on me. People like Fazil, his family, Laila, Frodo, and now Shaw.

Everyone around me was forced to suffer.

Everyone but me.

The tremors progressed with lightning speed, moving from my fingers to my arms, to my back, to my legs. My entire body was seizing. Maybe this time Einstein's weapon would finally accomplish its goal. Maybe my time in this soulless purgatory would finally end here, right where it began.

I sagged forward like a sack of bones, unable to hold myself upright.

The unexpected weight surprised Sayid. With a curse, he shifted his grip from my hair to my shoulders, trying to keep my deadweight from bowling him over.

He succeeded.

Mostly.

My torso didn't crash into him, but my newly freed head thudded against his chest.

For a moment, I let him bear the weight of my despair. He cursed again as my body convulsed, shifting my weight so that my head lolled to one side.

That's when I saw them.

They were standing together, hand in hand, just behind Sayid. A chubby-cheeked toddler with sparkling eyes and someone else.

The toddler smiled, her tiny fingers waving.

But for the first time, it wasn't Abir's face that drew my attention.

It was her mother's.

Yana didn't speak. She didn't have to. Her look spoke volumes. The man who'd raped and brutally killed her was inches from my seizing body.

Maybe God, or Allah, really did work in mysterious ways. Maybe old Jeremiah the shoeshine man had been right when he'd said that I couldn't go back, because maybe I'd been chasing the wrong thing all along.

In that second, I finally understood something that had eluded me since the day I'd left this country a broken man. Nothing could bring back the moment in which Fazil and his family had been murdered. That instant in time was gone for all eternity. No matter how many evil men I killed or good men I saved, Abir, with her chubby cheeks and gummy smile, would still be just as dead.

But I was alive. And if I had any hope of remaining that way, I needed to do something infinitely harder than rescuing Shaw from the jihadis.

I needed to forgive someone.

Myself.

The tremors stopped.

I gathered my leg beneath me and exploded upward with every bit of my remaining strength. My head speared into Sayid's chin, snapping his jaw with a satisfying *pop* as we both toppled to the floor, he on his back, me on his chest.

My hands were bound, my body broken, but my heart was still beating. I was alive, and as long as the Almighty saw fit to let me remain that way, I had work to do.

Surrender *is not a Ranger word*. . . .

I snapped a vicious headbutt into Sayid's nose, feeling the cartilage splinter against my forehead. Hot blood splattered across my face, but I wasn't done.

Not even close.

. . . *I will never leave a fallen comrade to fall into the hands of the enemy* . . .

Sayid screamed and tried to turn away, brushing his ear against my mouth.

That was a mistake.

I bit down and ripped the rubbery flesh from his head.

And then I went for his throat.

. . . *and under no circumstances will I ever embarrass my country.*

I bit and chewed and tore and hammered. I didn't stop. Not when the jihadis holding Shaw tried to pull me from Sayid's squirming body. Not when the building shook as a breaching charge detonated and concussions from exploding flash bangs scrambled my senses. Not even when the barks of suppressed rifles and the cries of dying men filled the air.

I kept biting and headbutting and smashing my broken body against Sayid's, screaming my battle cry, until gloved hands ripped me from my enemy, and a voice I recognized broke through my berserker's rage.

"It's over, Ranger," Colonel Fitz screamed in my ear. "Stand down. It's over."

Then, and only then, did I stop.

Sayid's corpse lay on the blood-soaked concrete beneath me, looking as though he'd been set upon by a pack of feral dogs. The sight was horrific, and the fact that I was the feral dog made it doubly so. I should have felt ashamed or at the very least disgusted, but I didn't. He was dead, and I was alive.

Nothing else mattered.

"The beacon," I said, turning from Sayid to Colonel Fitz. "I didn't activate the beacon."

"Fuck the beacon," Fitz said, helping me to my feet. "We have the Creed."

SIXTY-THREE

Peter took another swallow and tried not to grimace as the amber liquid fumigated his nasal passages while scorching its way down his already raw throat. Though he was only halfway through his second tumbler, Peter could already feel the whiskey's potency. The bar's once gloomy lighting now seemed soft and inviting, and the brunette in the corner booth, who'd been moderately attractive when he'd first arrived, was looking better with each painful swallow.

"Another?" the bartender said.

"Not just yet," Peter said, placing his glass gently on the offered coaster. He hated whiskey with a passion, and the bottle of twenty-fifth-anniversary Knob Creek wasn't doing much to alter his opinion. Still, he'd have one more round before his evening came to a close. Three tumblers of fine whiskey—no more, no less.

Just like that night more than twenty years ago.

"Whaddya think about the election?" the bartender said, gesturing to the silent TV mounted behind the bar.

"I think Gonzales is gonna win," Peter said, swirling the contents of his glass before taking another sip.

In fact, Peter knew he would. Even his most conservative pollster was predicting a Gonzales victory by better than seven points. Not exactly Reagan territory, but not too shabby all the same.

"Want something else?" the bartender said. "Excuse me for saying so, but whiskey doesn't seem to be your drink."

"It's not. I hate it. But my kid sister developed a taste for it in college. She didn't go for fruity shots like normal coeds; she loved the expensive stuff. We toasted together before she left with her National Guard unit on her first deployment. She never came back."

That wasn't exactly true. Kristen had come back, but her once athletic body had been burned beyond recognition by the IED that had taken her life. Thankfully, Peter hadn't been the one to identify her remains. That task had fallen to his father. The once joyful man hadn't uttered so much as a chuckle since.

"Sorry for your loss," the bartender said, reaching across the scarred oak bar to squeeze Peter's forearm. "Next one's on the house."

"No, thanks," Peter said. "I've got to pay. It was our tradition. I always paid."

"All right, bud," the bartender said. "Let me know if you need anything else."

The man retreated to the cash register, leaving Peter

alone with his thoughts, which were rather benign, all things considered. The President had authorized the rescue attempt against Peter's advice, but for once, the JSOC knuckle draggers had pulled off the operation as advertised. Matt Drake and John Shaw had been rescued, and no American lives had been lost in the process.

In fact, part of the reason President Gonzales was up seven points was a couple of artfully framed tidbits Peter had leaked about the raid to the usual suspects at the *Times* and the *Post*. President Gonzales now looked like a man who went to the mat for his men and women in uniform, consequences be damned.

The Russians were pissed, but so far, Putin had been content to publicly shout his indignation while quietly advocating for a return to the Syrian status quo. During their single terse phone call, President Gonzales had threatened to release footage of the Flanker firing on the two American helicopters in response to Putin's bullying.

For once, the Russian strongman had blinked.

No, things might not have gone the way Peter had wanted, but all in all, he wasn't in a bad position. Beverly was still on her way out, and she would exit on Peter's terms, thanks to the e-mail Charles had provided. Peter had scores to settle with Generals Beighley and Etzel, along with several misfits from the DIA, but the national security team would be infinitely easier to manage once Charles was sworn in as the new CIA Director. As Peter had always said, if Jorge Gonzales won a second term, anything was possible, and that *if* was becoming more of a *when* with each tick of the clock.

"Buy you a drink?"

Peter looked up from his whiskey to see the brunette from the corner booth standing by his shoulder. He rotated his glass on its coaster as he pondered her offer before slowly shaking his head.

The next day was the Tuesday following the first Monday in November. In other words, Election Day. Jorge might have this one in the bag, but Peter wasn't ready to let down his guard. Not yet, anyway. But in twenty-four hours, Peter would be in a much different frame of mind.

"Rain check?" Peter said, his eyes drifting from the brunette's face to the hint of cleavage offered by her lacy scoop-neck blouse.

"Sure," the woman said, leaning in so that her warm breath caressed Peter's ear. "Give me a call."

She slid a folded cocktail napkin into his hand and then left without another word.

Peter took another sip while watching the brunette slip out the door, alcohol-induced warmth spreading through his body as he thought about what the next twenty-four hours might bring.

Things were definitely looking up.

Peter lingered in a blissful state of equal parts intoxication and arousal for the next three seconds, which was exactly how long it took for him to unfold the note the woman had slipped him. Expecting to find a cell phone number written in a woman's distinct hand, Peter saw something else instead. Two words. Two words that had the power to change his life.

Unconditional Gratitude.

Peter coughed as the whiskey came racing back up his throat. As he sat at the bar, trying not to choke, he had just one thought.

Russian strongmen never blink.

EPILOGUE

You sure you don't want me to come with you?"

"Yes," I said, looking from the two-story brick house at the end of the cul-de-sac to the woman sitting in the passenger seat next to me. I'd never realized how much I'd taken for granted the simple luxury of looking at my wife's beautiful face. Now that her features didn't spontaneously morph into those of a dead Syrian woman, I found myself staring at Laila every time she caught my eye.

Okay, so the staring usually progressed to something else fairly quickly, but the simple act of meeting her gaze without flinching made me smile. In fact, the happiness I felt just from knowing that she was here brought with it a sense of lingering guilt. All might be well in my world, but the woman who lived in the house at the end of this street was in quite a different place.

Her world had shattered.

"You don't need to do this," Laila said, reaching across the car to take my hand. "You've done enough already."

I squeezed my wife's hand, but I didn't answer.

Though I knew she hadn't meant it, Laila's words were an indictment all the same. If I'd truly done enough, the two of us wouldn't be sitting in a rented car parked on a quiet residential street in suburban Chicago. After eight weeks, I now understood most of what had happened in Syria, but not everything.

I did know that Colonel Fitz and his men had made good on their promise. They'd rescued Shaw and me, and shortly after our evac, a pair of well-placed thousand-pound Joint Direct Attack Munitions, dropped from a B-2 stealth bomber, had razed the chemical weapons laboratory to its foundation. Einstein's creation had been destroyed, and the ISIS splinter cell was no more.

But not everything had been wrapped up with such a tidy bow. Mr. Suave had been nowhere to be found when Fitz's assaulters stormed the building, and I still didn't understand the linkage between Sayid, the ISIS splinter cell, Mr. Suave, and Charles. Even so, at this point, I no longer cared.

Once again, I'd returned from Syria with a broken body, but this time, something in my spirit had mended. After I'd landed at Andrews Air Force Base, James, Frodo, and Laila had met me planeside. I'd hugged Frodo, kissed Laila, and told James that my employment with the Defense Intelligence Agency was over.

For once, James Glass, night terror to Islamic jihadis

everywhere, had accepted my proclamation without argument. Or at least he hadn't bothered to contest my decision at that particular moment. Knowing James, this war was far from over, even if the first skirmish had ended in my favor.

Over the next eight weeks, I'd played a lot of guitar as my body had slowly healed, but I'd also spent quite a bit of time doing Internet research. I might have even asked Frodo for help a time or two when my conventional search methods ran into the proverbial brick wall. Coincidentally, or perhaps not, Frodo had hit pay dirt right about the time I'd felt well enough to undertake this pilgrimage to Chicago. After two long months, I was here, putting my detective work to use.

Now I needed to finish what I'd started that Friday morning in Austin.

"I'll just be a minute," I said to Laila, opening the car door and shuffling to my feet.

The worst of my injuries had subsided. A series of CAT scans and MRIs had confirmed what Mr. Suave had told me moments before he'd vanished. I had been exposed to an early variant of the chemical weapon, but the damage to my brain was not incapacitating and might not even be permanent. It was still too early to tell, but the military doctor likened my symptoms to those of an autoimmune disease like multiple sclerosis. I was currently in remission but was still susceptible to flare-ups. He advised me to avoid situations that could generate extreme emotional or physical stress.

I advised him to mind his own damn business.

My external injuries were faring better. My nose finally looked normal, my sprained wrist was functional, and the gunshot wound to my leg no longer leaked blood. Most of the bruising across my body had faded, but my lower back still ached like a son of a bitch from when an assortment of jihadis had tried to kick the living shit out of me. At least my ankle had healed. Sort of. I could walk without crutches, but it wasn't much of a walk. More a drunken shuffle than a self-assured stride, but I felt confident that my recovery had progressed enough that I should be able to traverse the relatively flat driveway and single porch step separating me from my goal.

My reluctance to come earlier had had nothing to do with embarrassment over my injuries. It was more of a sense of what I should look like when I brought the final Syrian chapter to a close. For the same reason a military casualty officer wears his dress uniform to make a death notification to a fallen service member's next of kin, I felt that my appearance needed to be such that it didn't detract from the message. The woman I was coming to see deserved my sympathy.

I didn't merit hers.

"Baby?" Laila said, leaning across the car seat.

"I'll be right back," I said, and gently closed the door.

I turned to the house and made it halfway up the driveway before realizing that I might have bitten off more than I could chew. The overcast sky signaled a gathering storm, and the Windy City was living up to its name. White-hot jolts of pain shot from my still-healing ankle as icy gusts buffeted me.

I gritted my teeth and made it through the first stanza of the Ranger Creed before I finally arrived at the porch. Just short of my goal, I paused to catch my breath and swayed on my feet as sweat poured down my face despite the frigid temperature. I'd had ample time to imagine how this encounter might go as I'd waited for my ankle to knit. This definitely wasn't how I'd pictured things.

Then again, no plan ever survives first contact with the enemy.

Grabbing hold of the sturdy wooden railing at the edge of the porch, I pulled myself up and summited the single step. With a shaking finger, I rang the doorbell.

A minute passed, maybe two, just long enough for me to consider how stupid I was going to feel if I had to waddle all the way back to the car, when the door opened. A pretty Pakistani woman looked back at me.

She was about ten years older than I, and her black hair fell past her shoulders in shimmering waves. Her dark eyes were arresting, and I had a feeling that when she smiled, she still stopped men half her age in their tracks.

But I also knew that her smile would never be the same again.

"Yes?" she said, her accent slight but present.

"Ms. Farooqi?" I said.

"Who are you?"

"My name is Matt," I said. "I'm here because of your son."

Her smooth face transformed into hard, angry lines as her eyes flashed. "I've told you people everything I know.

Still you come back. Are you a reporter? From the State Department? FBI? Leave us alone."

She tried to slam the door, but a gust of wind smashed into the doorframe. She staggered under the unexpected onslaught, and the door stayed open for a moment longer.

But a moment was all I needed.

"Wait. I'm sorry," I said, reaching across the void separating us to touch her arm. "I'm not one of them. I was with your son. When he died."

The words tumbled off my tongue with none of the eloquence I'd rehearsed, but they had an effect just the same. She stood, hunched against the wind, looking at me as anger warred with hope.

"Truly?"

"Yes," I said, stepping a bit closer. "I tried to save him, but I couldn't. I'm sorry."

With my admission, anger won.

"Are you looking for forgiveness?" she said. "Is that why you're here? To ease your conscience? So that you can go back to your life even though mine has ended?"

"No," I said, for the first time truly understanding why I was standing on this porch, talking to the mother of a boy I'd known for less than an hour. "I don't want any of that, even if you could grant it. I'm here to tell you just two things: First, your son was a good boy. He might have made bad choices, but he was a good boy. Before he was killed, he asked me to help him escape. To come home. Second, he loved you. He was coming home for you."

Her dark eyes swam with tears as she searched my face for the truth. I met her gaze without flinching.

After a long moment, she gave a little nod.

"I believe you," she said, her voice thick with emotion. "I believe you."

She reached out and touched my face, her fingers tracing the still-fading blue and green bruises, and then, without another word, she ducked back into the house.

The door slammed shut.

Wiping the tears from my eyes, I took a deep breath of the crisp winter air and turned from the house to my car, preparing to once again do battle with the gusts of air hammering my head and shoulders. As I started down the driveway, the car door opened, Laila got out, and the untamed breeze stilled.

The sudden calm surprised me, but I guess it shouldn't have.

After all, wind was a fickle thing.

ACKNOWLEDGMENTS

Some writers are extraordinary craftsmen whose first words put to paper launch them into the publishing stratosphere. I am not one of these people. Instead, I'm a guy who needed seventeen years, an MFA in writing popular fiction, and three failed manuscripts to produce the novel you just read. With this in mind, I have quite a few people to thank.

My growth as a writer, slow as it may seem, can largely be attributed to the amazing beta readers who were willing to read my work and provide their feedback. Many of these folks read and critiqued more than one of my novels and I would not be here without them. They include Kevin Unruh, Tommy Ledbetter, Joel and Michelle Kime, Kelsey and Natalie Smith, and Erica Nichols. Of these amazing people, Erica has read every single manuscript and was kind enough to provide my protagonist's last name. Thank you, Erica.

As part of my journey, I graduated from the MFA program at Seton Hill University. Everyone there was nothing short of spectacular, but permanent and adjunct faculty members Nicole Peeler, Michael Arnzen, Albert

Wendland, David Shifren, Patrick Picciarelli, Vicki Thompson, Maria V. Snyder, and Shelley Bates all helped to make me a better writer. Thank you for your time and collective wisdom.

A number of my fellow Seton Hill students also lent me their expertise as critique partners and confidants. In particular, Randee Paraskevopoulos, Nancy Parra, Stephanie Dunn, Jayme Brown, Laurie Sterbens, Bill Fay, and Dawn Gartlehner were of immense help as I fleshed out the character that would ultimately become Matt Drake. Thank you all.

Second only to my Seton Hill family is the collection of friends and fellow thriller writers I've been lucky enough to find, many of whom I first met at the annual ThrillerFest writing conference. K.J. Howe, Josh Hood, Sean Parnell, Ryan Steck, and Brad Taylor were all kind enough to read an early version of *Without Sanction*. Bill Schweigart and Nick Petrie were also incredibly generous with their time, providing detailed feedback that was both timely and critical. Thank you all.

Someone once said that flying a helicopter consists of hours of boredom interspersed with moments of pure terror. If you substitute *despair* for *boredom*, writing a novel is a similar experience. While learning to navigate the despair and terror, I was fortunate to have novelist and Bram Stoker Award winner John Dixon as my copilot. John, I don't have the words to relay how much I value your friendship and insight. Thank you.

Over the years, I've benefited from the collective experience of a number of publishing industry professionals. Matt Schwartz provided hours of insight for the reasonable cost of a beer or three, while my amazing editor, Tom Colgan; his assistant, Grace House; and the entire Berkley team transformed *Without Sanction* from a rough manuscript into an incredible novel. Also key to this transformation was my fabulous agent, Barbara Poelle, of the Irene Goodman Literary Agency. Barbara is equal parts friend, book whisperer, and force to be reckoned with. This book is better because of her.

Writing *Without Sanction* would not have been possible without the technical expertise of a number of kind souls. Doctors Kirby Kendall, Myles Gardner, and Danielle Dickinson did their best to explain chemistry to a hapless writer, while Nate Self, Jeff Mishler, Greg Glass, and Brandon Cates helped me understand what it means to live the Ranger Creed. Retired Sergeant Major Jason Beighley took me through a HAHO jump and read an early version of that scene, while Colonel Kelsey Smith reined in the worst of my aerial excesses. Any technical inaccuracies are my responsibility, while anything that rang true is a testament to this superb cadre of subject matter experts.

As a writer of military and espionage thrillers, I'm keenly aware that I stand on the shoulders of giants. This genre is full of stellar authors, and Tom Clancy, Daniel Silva, Vince Flynn, Brad Thor, Nelson DeMille, Brad Taylor, and Mark Greaney have been huge influences on my writing. Thank you all for setting the bar so very high while making the impossible look easy in the process.

Finally, I'd like to thank my family. My three children, Will, Faith, and Kelia, had front-row seats as this dream painstakingly became a reality. Thanks for your patience and for letting your dad disappear into make-believe worlds for hours at a time. I love you guys.

Last but certainly not least, I'd like to thank my wife, Angela. She's been on this journey with me since the beginning and her faith has never wavered. She's my first reader, constant source of encouragement, and, most important, the one who never stopped believing. Thank you, baby. Without you, this book, and everything else good in my life, simply wouldn't be. I love you.

—DON

Read on for an excerpt from the next
Matt Drake Thriller,

THE OUTSIDE MAN

Available from Berkley in March 2021

ONE

Austin in February is paradise. While the rest of the country is gripped with snow, biting cold, or both, the self-professed home of the weird is in full flower. Endless blue Texas skies stretch from horizon to horizon, temperatures hover in the low sixties, and woodsmoke and slow-cooking brisket flavor the air. In February, it's hard to have a bad day in Austin.

But I was giving it a helluva try.

I stomped on the gas pedal as the traffic light changed from yellow to amber. The eight-cylinder Hemi replied with a chest-rumbling growl, sending my truck hurtling through the intersection. A split second later, I slammed on the brakes, bringing the five-thousand-pound Dodge Ram to a screeching stop. A comfortable six inches now separated my pickup and the bumper-sticker-adorned electric blue Prius ahead of me.

On the bench seat to my right, a packet of papers slid

toward the floorboard. I made a grab for them and missed, snagging the thin green tissue wrapping a bouquet of crimson roses instead.

All things considered, I'd take the flowers over the papers any day. Even with the papers scattered across the truck's floorboard, I could still read the words RADIOLOGY DEPARTMENT stamped across the tops of the pages in sterile block letters. At this distance, the spidery blue handwriting filling the margins wasn't legible, but I knew what the doctor had scribbled all the same.

The Prius driver glared in his rearview mirror, and I chuckled. Apparently the COEXIST sticker plastered to his bumper didn't extend to fellow Austinites. At least not during lunch-hour traffic anyway. Though to be fair, I wasn't in much of a *coexist* mood myself. But this had nothing to do with the angry Prius driver. No, my ire was focused on the man in the late-model Honda one intersection to my rear.

The man who wanted to kill me.

My name is Matt Drake, and I do not have a normal vocation. For the last year, I haven't had much of a vocation at all. However, before my self-imposed leave of absence began, I worked in a unique field. A field in which the ability to tell the difference between a distracted driver and a trained operative transitioning from surveillance to interdiction was a matter of life and death.

This is why I knew that the dark-complected man driving the Honda was focused on more than just traffic. At the previous stoplight, he'd cut off a white Tesla

Roadster to edge in behind me, abandoning any pretense of remaining covert. He hadn't followed me through the red light, which bought me a bit of time, but not much.

As I waited for the signal in front of me to change, the Honda's driver reached above his head, adjusting the sun visor. This innocuous-seeming motion provided final confirmation. The driver was wearing gloves. Gloves in sixty-degree weather. And not just any gloves. The thin Nomex variety that stretched from his hand to midway up his forearm. The type of gloves favored by just two groups of people—pilots and shooters.

My leave of absence was officially over.

Shifting in my seat, I drew the Glock 23 tucked into my Don Hume in-the-waistband holster and press-checked the pistol. A shiny .40-caliber hollow point winked back at me. Easing the slide forward, I set the pistol on the seat between my legs and considered what to do next.

The signal turned green, and traffic heaved forward. Or at least most of it. Mr. Coexist did not. Instead, he rolled toward the intersection at a snail's pace, burning time until the light cycled yellow. Then he accelerated, surging through the juncture at the last moment. As his tiny car barreled beneath the now-red traffic signal, he bade me farewell with a one-fingered salute.

Behind me, the shooter eased through the intersection, nudging up to my bumper.

The key to defeating an ambush is actually pretty simple—don't get caught in the kill zone. I didn't know where the shooter intended to initiate, but since lead had yet to start flying, the kill zone had to be somewhere in front of me.

Which meant I needed to act. Now.

Smashing the brake with my left foot, I shifted the truck into neutral and revved the engine with my right. As the RPM crept past six thousand, I tightened my seat belt, locked the Glock under my right leg, and prepared to throw the transmission into reverse.

And that was when a woman pushing a stroller stepped into the road.

TWO

The woman was dressed in black yoga pants and a hot pink tank top that showed off toned brown arms. White earbuds accessorized her outfit—the wireless kind because Austinites are nothing if not hip. She rolled the stroller right in front of my truck's vibrating hood as if she didn't have a care in the world—again, Austin in February. Though even if she'd been the most vigilant of mommas, a gunfight on South Congress probably wouldn't have been on her radar. That just wasn't her life.

But it was mine.

Behind me, the shooter was talking on his phone. Which meant he wasn't alone. Which meant that my window was closing.

Slamming the gearshift into reverse, I wrenched the wheel to the left. The Hemi didn't disappoint, much to the chagrin of the driver of the compact Hyundai to my right. One moment, the Hyundai's driver was contemplating the perfect Austin sky. The next, the black brush guard covering my front bumper scraped along his emerald green quarter panel as I turned my truck perpendicular to the threat behind me.

Not a perfect solution, but it would do.

Grabbing the Glock, I exploded out of my truck, coming face-to-face with the woman pushing the stroller. To her credit, she went into immediate momma-bear mode. Though her eyes were as wide as saucers, she put herself between me and her precious cargo. Then she screamed out a question.

"Are you crazy?"

Books could be written in response. Still, I understood why she might ask. My current appearance was what my wife playfully called *rustic*. At least I hoped it was playfully. My hair was a bit on the shaggy side, and my face hadn't seen a razor for the better part of three days. My pearly snap shirt was ironed, my jeans clean, and my Ariat cowboy boots freshly polished. But there was still something about me that didn't sit right with the woman. Maybe it was that my broad shoulders and scarred knuckles were somehow at odds with my carefully cultivated ragamuffin appearance. Or maybe it was something else.

Something more primal.

Either way, I didn't have time for niceties. Grabbing the woman by her toned arm, I jerked her and her stroller toward the relative safety of my truck's front wheel well.

"FBI," I said, pulling her forward. "Get down!"

Now, before you get the wrong idea, I am not a law

enforcement officer of any kind. The men and women of that career field must stand before juries while swearing to tell the truth, the whole truth, and nothing but the truth, so help them God. My own relationship with the truth was a bit more problematic. For example, I have found it beneficial to impersonate an FBI agent from time to time. This is because most Americans seem preconditioned to trust FBI agents and obey their commands.

Unfortunately, my new friend was not like most Americans.

"Get your hands off me," she said, pulling away with surprising ease.

This girl worked out. Maybe Pilates or kickboxing.

I grabbed her left arm, fingers encircling her biceps, and tried to drag her back toward safety. She expressed her displeasure with a rather respectable right cross. Her knuckles connected squarely with my cheekbone, and I felt the jarring impact all the way to the base of my neck.

Definitely kickboxing.

"The man behind me has a gun," I said, sliding beneath a jab as I wrestled her and the stroller behind the truck's front tire.

"So do you," she said, attempting to stomp one of her pristinely white cross-trainers through my instep.

God bless Texas girls.

I got my foot out of the way. Barely. When this was over, I might have to pay her kickboxing instructor a congratulatory visit. I'd snatched Muslim Brotherhood members off the streets of Cairo with less fuss.

A police siren cut through the air, once again proving Dad's adage that when it rains, a bear craps in the woods. I have no idea what that means, but Dad sure seemed certain when he said it.

The she-lion posing as a suburban mom aimed an elbow at my groin. I turned with the blow, catching it on the outside of my thigh. Ignoring the pins-and-needles sensation running the length of my leg, I edged over the truck's hood. What I saw on the other side wasn't pretty. One of Austin's finest was out of his patrol car, pistol in hand. His thick shoulders and narrow waist contrasted with his baby face and rosy cheeks. He didn't look a day over twenty, but young or not, he was running in my direction, ready to take care of business. As our eyes met, he skidded to a halt, dropping into a shooter's stance.

Right next to the Honda.

I tried to shout a warning, but wasn't fast enough. The policeman jerked like a marionette, spasms racking his body. The accompanying series of *pop*s was surprisingly soft. The shooter had a suppressed submachine gun—a Heckler & Koch variant if I had to guess. The 9mm pistol rounds didn't pack the stopping power of an assault rifle's, but the weapon was accurate, compact, and easy to suppress.

In short, the perfect tool for an assassin.

The cop collapsed to the ground in a tangle of limbs. The blood-soaked right side of his uniform meant that at least one of the slugs had found its way either through or under his vest. That distinction was important. *Through the vest* meant that the assassin was firing rounds designed to defeat body armor. This, combined with the suppressed HK, would point to a shooter who was both well financed and well trained.

As my SEAL friends liked to say, the only easy day was yesterday.

"Stay here," I said to the she-devil. For the first time in our short but turbulent relationship, she listened. Maybe it was something she saw in my face or heard in my voice. Or maybe with her mother's intuition she somehow interpreted the meaning behind the suppressed gunfire and breaking glass. Either way, she nodded, blond ponytail bobbing, as she scooped her squirming baby out of the stroller.

"Where are you going?" she said, pressing against the truck's tire.

"To end this."